FAUSTUS RESURRECTUS

FAUSTUS RESURRECTUS

A DONOVAN GRAHAM NOVEL

THOMAS MORRISSEY

NIGHT SHADE BOOKS
SAN FRANCISCO

First Edition

ISBN: 978-1-59780-405-9

Night Shade Books
http://www.nightshadebooks.com

For everyone who has a pipe dream

PROLOGUE

AFTER THE CEREMONY

The sharpest tool we had was a bottle opener.

The big man blinked, uncomprehending.

How did this *happen?*

The full moon added to the light of the bonfire, illuminating bodies scattered where they tried to escape. None was in one piece.

The big man took one aimless step then another, refusing to absorb the meaning of his surroundings.

We were supposed to be giving thanks...

Business at the commune had been killer these past few months: personal care items were up, the microbrew had gained some popularity and, best of all, the summer's crop of White Widow had topped out at twenty-three and a half percent THC. It was while he and Greta were smoking some of the fruits of that first harvest, lying naked in bed on a beautiful summer morning, that she'd come up with the idea.

Mother Gaia has shown us such bounty. We should offer our *energy to* Her, *to give thanks and praise to Her glory.*

Best energy I know, he'd replied, *is sex.*

When they'd set up that morning for the orgy, the sweet summer grass had tickled their ankles. Oak trees spread green-leafed shade over them, and even the moss coating the stone hollow where they'd set up the bonfire had been bright chartreuse. Greta had said the vitality was a good sign.

Someone expressed reservations about messing with weird religions.

1

This isn't "weird," Greta had said. *We're all about positive energy.*

Now the green was gone, withered, freezer burned to death on the first of August. The foliage had shrunk to husks, trees twisted and gnarled. He tried to understand how this could be.

Coletun.

What happened to him?

He couldn't stop shaking.

"I'm gonna come back for you. Mister Fizz made me bigger and stronger than you."

Beneath the bloody horror he saw Greta's face. "Baby…" he whispered, extending a trembling hand.

Her head rolled to the side, exposing the jagged edge that nearly severed it from her body…

The next thing he knew he was fumbling through the pockets of the jeans he'd stripped off hours—years—ago. Drying blood made his grip sticky, but he managed to untangle his cell phone.

"9-1-1 Operator. What is the emergency?"

"You have to come! They're all dead!"

"Calm down, sir. Who is dead? Where are you?"

"Blue Moon Bay. In a field, about a half mile northwest from the commune. The Churner's Commune. You have to come *now!*"

The thing had burst from the heart of the black bonfire, an icy white lance that blinded him when it struck. His stomach had gone numb; he didn't remember, didn't want *to remember, anything beyond that.*

"The Churner's Commune?"

"Hurry! I think…I think *I* killed them all."

ONE

THE FIRST DAY OF THE BEGINNING...

"**...a**ll those receiving your Bachelor's Degree in the arts, please rise."

There was dutiful applause. Donovan Graham rubbed his eyes and let his sunglasses drop back on his nose. The tassels hanging from his mortarboard brushed his face like strands of purple spider web. He waved half-heartedly at them, then stopped as the back of his head started to pound. He took a swig from a bottle of water but it only partially alleviated his cotton mouth.

"All those receiving a Master's Degree in the arts, please rise."

More dutiful applause. He heaved himself upright and looked around. At twenty-seven, he was younger than many of the other grad school students; at two inches over six feet, he was bigger than most.

And I drank more French martinis than any of them last night.

"All those receiving doctorates, please rise."

A final round of clapping.

Give me another couple of years.

Overhead, clouds still threatened rain. He would have welcomed it; it might have cooled him off. Right now a hot, damp beach towel wrapped his entire body, or at least that's what it felt like.

They announced a new speaker and everyone sat. Donovan scanned the dais and saw the Philosophy Department standard, a cobalt blue banner decorated by white, silver and gold letters and insignias. Next to it sat

3

Father Maurice Carroll, distinct among the crowd of professors—sitting couldn't completely hide his 6' 9" frame. He'd been a basketball player in his college days at Georgetown and would have gone pro if he hadn't blown out both knees in a pickup game with some local kids. In his late sixties, with a full head of gray-white hair and matching beard and moustache, he looked content and mildly amused.

The speeches finally ended and Doctor Keel, the president of the university, stepped to the microphone. "Today really is the first day of the beginning of your lives. I know it's cliché, but that doesn't mean it's not true. From here on out, you are college graduates, a status that confers privilege and demands responsibility. Enjoy the moment, but use it."

The graduates were herded like cattle into the chutes of individual department commencements. Donovan saw Joann next to the fence separating graduates from guests. One corner of her mouth curled into the wry grin he'd fallen in love with three years earlier on the other side of the world, in Hawaii. He waved and smiled as she snapped a few digital pictures. Students surged around him in a tide of black robes and colored sashes. He pushed his way across the current to her.

"Hey graduate." She leaned across the fence to kiss him. "Congratulations."

"I owe it all to clean living and the love of a good woman."

"Clean living? How's your hangover?"

"Better now." Above the heads of the masses, he saw the cobalt banner moving towards its building. He looked for a gap in the fence but saw none. "I'll see you over at the Philosophy Department."

"Okay."

She kissed him again and he got a whiff of her hair as she turned back into the crowd. Somewhere he'd read that the most sensual position from which to watch a woman was three-quarters behind. His view of Joann confirmed it. Her dark gray business skirt stretched tight over her well-toned thighs and behind, while her shoulder-length blonde hair was up loosely, allowing a few strands to curl down to her neck just above the collar of her suit coat.

Lucky man, he thought.

~

When the Philosophy Department ceremony was over, Donovan made his way over to Joann. "Phi Beta Kappa?" She slid her arms around his neck. "I had no idea I was sleeping with such a brilliant scholar."

He grinned. "Took me by surprise, too. I remember getting things in the mail, but I kind of just blew them off. It was Father Carroll who made all this happen."

"No." She looked into his eyes with total seriousness. "*You* did. You put in the time, you did the work. You earned it."

"He certainly did," Father Carroll said, joining them. "I know what you're capable of, Donovan, even if you sometimes forget." He glanced around. "Your parents aren't here?"

"The Colonel was unable to attend. My mother sends regrets. They've promised to be here for the PhD ceremony, whenever that is." Donovan hid his emotions with a shrug and looked past Joann. "On the other hand, babe, I see *your* father."

Short and wiry, Conrad Clery cut through the sea of people towards them. Light off his glasses gave him the white eyes of a shark when it rolls in for a bite. "Darling! I'm glad I found you. There's someone I'd like you to meet." Golf-strengthened hands gripped Joann's shoulders as he bussed her cheeks. "Father." Almost as an afterthought, he said, "Oh, congratulations, Donovan. The first Master's is always the hardest."

"What are you doing here?" Joann asked.

"I was one of the speakers over at the Law School commencement. Didn't I tell you?"

Her wry smile returned, with slightly less warmth than she'd shown Donovan. "It must have slipped your mind." Her cell phone rang. She checked the number and frowned. "I'm sorry, gentlemen. Work." She took a few steps away.

Father Carroll turned to Donovan. "I have to get some things from my office for my trip to England. Could you give me a hand?"

"Sure."

Conrad put a hand on Donovan's arm. "If I could have a word with him first?"

Father Carroll raised a bemused eyebrow. "Of course. It was nice to see you again, Conrad. Good luck and God bless."

"To you, as well." Conrad started to steer Donovan away. "Oh, Father—if you get to London while you're over there, there's a terrific restaurant in Knightsbridge, Marcus Wareing at The Berkeley. Ask for Simon; tell him I sent you. He'll take care of you."

"I appreciate that, Conrad. I'll keep it in mind."

Donovan casually moved out of Conrad's grasp. "What's up?"

"Phi Beta Kappa *and* honors; impressive. I'm also Phi Beta Kappa." Joann's father took out a cigar, snipped off the end and carefully placed it in his mouth. Holding a gold lighter—*solid gold, I'm sure,* Donovan thought—he puffed until the tip glowed branding-iron orange. "Your Master's is 'Philosophical Hermeneutics'; what is that, exactly?"

"The study of interpretation technically, but really it's the search for truth." Donovan knew Conrad already knew the answer, but he played along. "Traditional hermeneutics studies interpretations of written works; religion, law, literature. Modern hermeneutics studies everything. That would be me, specializing in mythology and religion."

"Why those particular fields, if you don't mind my asking?"

"I like them. They interest me."

"Driving a truck used to interest me, when I was in school. I even did, as a way of paying for my books. Then I grew up." Conrad remained casual. Fragrant smoke hung in the air between them. "What sort of career does one pursue with a degree in Philosophical Hermeneutics?"

"One pursues a doctorate and teaches. That process begins this fall." Donovan showed him a bland smile. "Something on your mind, Conrad?"

"What would you interpret my manner to mean?"

Donovan let that one go.

Conrad examined the crowd as it thinned before turning his gaze to Joann. She hung up and came back towards them. "Is everything all right?" he asked.

She wiggled one hand. "Cautious optimism."

"New lead on Dinkins?" Donovan asked.

"Dinkins" was the Dinkins Shelter case, an investigation that was becoming a hairball for the Brooklyn District Attorney's office. Back in March, Joann had been the Assistant DA riding when the David N. Dinkins Memorial Shelter exploded into a riot that had gutted the shelter and left three guards and nine homeless men dead. So far, her attempt to build the case against the riot's instigator wasn't coming together, because there was some question who started it. Against the counsel of some colleagues, Joann was insisting they had yet to find the ringleader, a man she referred to as "Charming Man" because witnesses referred to him as "smooth" and "speaking well."

She nodded. "I was going over the list of the shelter wreckage and saw they had fourteen broken cameras. The shelter's inventory listed fifteen supposed to be installed. I sent DeFelice to search the site. He found it." She took a breath. "Now we have to see if anything on it survived."

"Not bad, Counselor."

Pride glowed in Conrad's eyes. "Honey, do you have a moment? There's someone I'd like you to meet over at the Law School."

She looked at Donovan. He nodded. "Father Carroll wanted me to give him a hand in his office. Do you know where it is?"

"I do." She pulled away from her father and ran her hands over Donovan's chest, giving him a solid hug. "I'm so proud of you. Congratulations again, baby. I'll see you there in a few minutes."

❦

"Still among the living, I see," the priest observed, deliberating before a shelf.

Donovan paused in the doorway. Books and objects covered every inch of Father Carroll's office and were stacked on every flat surface. Papyrus scrolls, ceremonial daggers, swords, candles, books, crosses, and talismans; each had a story attached to it. Every time he went there, Donovan got a little thrill. The stuff was so...cool.

"The Wrath of Khan-rad is old news. He was reassuring himself that despite my degree, I'm still not good enough for his daughter."

"Pity he only recognizes quality in cigars."

Donovan inspected some open books on the desk. "Scorpions?"

"Some light reading for the trip." The priest busied himself finding more volumes. "What are you and Joann up to this holiday weekend?"

"Tomorrow we're taking my motorcycle upstate to a bed and breakfast." Donovan moved a coffee table book and saw something underneath it. "What's this?"

The priest picked it up and brushed the frame off with his palm. He smiled. "This is actually why I wanted you to meet me here. It's for you." He handed it Donovan. Under the glass was a copy of his master's thesis. "It's one of the best I've ever read."

"Where did you—?"

"I made copies to submit to the university for your degree. This is the original."

The title page faced him. Donovan remembered the night he'd printed it on his computer, the culmination of countless hours of reading, research and writing:

DESIRE OR DESTINY?
Free Will Versus Predestination In
The Faustus Legend

"Yeah, it came out pretty well, I guess." He was so touched he was embarrassed. "Thank you. For everything."

"This is quite an achievement." The priest embraced him in a bear hug. "Enjoy yourself this weekend, and this summer. This fall you're in for a whole new experience. A doctorate requires a tremendous amount of energy."

"I'll be ready." Donovan didn't want to think about going for his PhD. Instead, he gestured at the books. "Scorpion mythology is pretty heavy reading for a plane ride."

"It's for something pretty heavy."

"Really?"

"I would presume so." Father Carroll returned to the bookcase and selected another book. "I was asked to research this by the police."

"I remember something about scorpions in the news about a week ago. The guy killed in the hotel. Is this connected to that?"

"It seems logical, but I couldn't say for sure. All I was asked for was some background on scorpions and their meaning in mythology."

"Need any help?"

The priest glanced up at his tone. He read Donovan's face and said, "Donovan, you are the best student I've ever had, and I welcome your input, as always. I believe, however, God has for you a destiny in life greater than 'research assistant.'"

"It'll lighten your carry-on bag."

"This field is rarely about personal comfort." He continued to gaze at the bookshelf, but Donovan recognized him weighing options. He'd seen Father Carroll do this in class, but this time he seemed more...intense? "I suppose I could make a few calls before my flight leaves, to make certain it's acceptable. If you really want to...?"

"Research scorpions? No problem."

"You're certain this won't interfere with your plans?"

"Not in the slightest," Donovan assured him. "I'll take care of it."

"All right, then." Father Carroll began to gather some of the books into a stack. He glanced up. "Why are you smiling?"

"Are you kidding? I tend bar for a living. Helping a police investigation beats the hell out of pouring mojitos in midtown."

~

Later that night, with Joann stretched out across her king-sized bed fast asleep, Donovan went out to the living room of her Brooklyn Heights loft. All the excitement of finishing his Master's, the overwhelming relief, left him both euphoric and drained.

And now…what?

He stood naked and inspected his body in the mirror of a night-black window. He'd never achieved the chiseled, zero-percent body fat look of a gym rat, but he never worried when he rode the subway either. He knew he could take care of himself. That, however, wasn't the issue, at least not in a physical sense.

"What would you interpret my manner to mean?" Your meaning has been clear to me for a long time, Conrad.

He considered Joann's father's words in a more charitable light.

Of course he's skeptical. He and The Colonel were practically separated at birth. Talking to one is like talking to the other. They're men of action. An academic job doesn't impress either of them.

The final words of the commencement came to him:

"Enjoy this moment, but use it." His lips curled up. *Okay, I will; professionally, I'm helping a police investigation. Personally…*

When he considered what he really wanted, the answer was actually a question:

I wonder if she'll marry me?

The thought made him smile all the way back to bed. Quietly he lifted the thousand count sheet and spooned behind Joann, but before sleep came, one final question occurred to him:

Why would the police need to know about scorpions?

TWO

WHERE DEATH DELIGHTS TO HELP THE LIVING

When Joann went work the next morning, Donovan returned to his apartment on West 48th Street to do Father Carroll's research. It was difficult to maintain his focus; the idea of proposing marriage was so big he found himself daydreaming about their life together. He liked what he saw. The books remained untouched until, with some reluctance, he put the idyllic images away and got to work.

The priest had offered no guidelines regarding pantheon or creed, asking only for information on the religious and mythological significance of scorpions. Donovan worked through the morning into mid-afternoon, and around three he paused to run out to a local cheesesteak place. He was satisfied with the amount of information he'd accumulated—scorpions and their images exist in nearly every major culture in history—but troubled he had no idea how to present his data to the police.

As he ate, he debated how to approach the problem. Should he focus on Egypt, on Isis and Selket? The Scorpion Man of the Gilgamesh epic? Maybe he ought to explore the alchemical process of evolution, lowest to highest, scorpion to eagle via the *serpens mercurialis*? Or examine Sadrafa, the half-scorpion, half-serpent god who predated Mithras in ancient Iran? Dorje Drollo of Tibetan Buddhism? The way scorpions represented the treachery of Jews to medieval Christians? All of it? Unlike any paper he'd written for school, this "assignment" had no context that might help draw conclusions. He wanted to do Father Carroll proud, which meant figuring out what the police wanted and giving it to them.

But how?

Wadding up his cheesesteak wrapper, he went to the loft kitchen above his living room. A bundle of *NY Post*s sat next to the garbage can, and he went through them until he found:

BUGGED!
MAN STUNG TO DEATH

A close-up of a scorpion, alien and threatening, dominated the page. He skimmed the story and saw it was pretty much as he'd remembered: a man had been found dead in a midtown hotel bathroom, victim of scorpion stings. In an incredible sequence of events, the woman in the room next to him had just flown in from Nevada, and the scorpions had apparently come along in her luggage, gotten free, and caught him unaware.

Or not.

If this was just a bizarre accident, the cops probably wouldn't be asking about religious and magical significance of scorpions.

In the story was a quote from an NYPD detective sergeant named Fullam. If this *was* the case that needed the research, he would have been the one who contacted Father Carroll.

I wonder if his name will open any doors?

❧

"Mister Denschler was extremely unlucky to have been in such the wrong place at the wrong time," said Doctor Pommeru. "Of the thirty species of scorpions native to the United States, only the Arizona bark scorpion is capable of causing a lethal reaction in humans. Those are what killed him."

Fullam's name had opened the door to an appointment with Doctor Shad Pommeru, the medical examiner who performed the autopsy. He was a thin, frail man with a habit of nodding his head, birdlike, every few seconds. He and Donovan were on a small elevator, descending from the main floor of the medical examiner's building to the morgue in the basement.

The doors opened, and they stepped out into a small, well-lit area with offices opposite and to their left. A faint odor of spoiled meat permeated everything. Double doors to their left led to the street-access ramp. A water-stained wedge of wood propped one open to let in a spring breeze.

It didn't help. A pair of men in security guard uniforms nodded to them. Silence cocooned the scene.

"The freezer is around this way," Pommeru said, taking the lead. "I prepared the body after I spoke to Sergeant Fullam. He asked me to give you my complete cooperation, and so I shall."

"Thank you." *He did?* "I don't think this will take too long."

Pommeru nodded and pulled the stainless steel door open. A fresh gust of spoiled meat wafted out. Donovan stepped to one side, trying not to think about the cheesesteak he'd eaten as the doctor wheeled out a sheet-covered gurney.

"Arizona bark scorpions do not deliver all of their venom in one sting," Pommeru said, "The envenomation creates pain and swelling, like a bee sting, but would not normally be fatal. An amount of poison this large, however, left him no chance of survival." He paused before lifting the sheet. "Did Sergeant Fullam explain entirely the condition of the body?" Donovan shook his head. "Ah. Well. Be prepared."

Donovan hadn't given much thought to whether he'd be able to deal; in truth, he'd never seen a body that hadn't been embalmed and lovingly prepared for a funeral. "Okay."

Pommeru pulled the sheet aside.

The corpse looked lumpy, misshapen, like a human-shaped bag filled with water balloons. Tiny stab wounds pocked Denschler's skin, each a dark entry point atop a bump. The bumps had swollen to different sizes, turning his body into a topographical map on which the scorpions had climbed. Lines in his face suggested an expression of abject terror even two weeks after the event. "Oh." Donovan breathed slowly. "I see." Most startling was a gaping burgundy gash between his legs. His genitals were missing, and the wound had crusted over like dry aged meat. Donovan looked away.

"What happened to his—?"

"The Arizona bark scorpion is carnivorous." The doctor consulted some papers on a clipboard. "Official cause of death is a combination of cardiac arrest and respiratory failure, induced by the introduction of thirty-four separate doses of scorpion venom. Tissue analysis indicates he was still alive while the genitals were, ah, consumed." He offered the clipboard. "Is there anything else in particular you need to know?"

Jesus. Donovan stared at the body, trying to store the image even as his natural revulsion resisted. With a sense of relief, he accepted and scanned the clipboard. There was a lot of jargon he didn't quite understand. "I can't think of anything right off. Could I have a copy of this?"

"Take that; I have the original."

"Thank you." He watched Pommeru cover the body, and suddenly felt a coward for his squeamishness. "Let me give you a hand."

Pommeru nodded, hauled open the door and grabbed the gurney's front. He led Donovan to the freezer's left rear wall. The smell of spoilage in here was much stronger. He bumped another gurney as he adjusted his end, and a movement startled him. The body on that gurney was covered by a sheet up to its chin, with a wooden shaft sticking out of one eye socket. When Donovan jostled the gurney, the shaft had wiggled. He continued to not think about the cheesesteak as he stepped back out and suppressed a shudder.

"If you have any other questions," the doctor handed Donovan a business card. "If I am not here, you may call my cell phone." He gestured back towards the way they'd come. "Please excuse me if I don't see you out, but I have some work to do."

"No problem. Thank you again for your time."

Donovan rode the elevator back up to the building lobby and collected his motorcycle helmet from the security guard at the lobby front desk. On the wall behind the desk was the motto of the Office of the Medical Examiner:

Taceant Colloquia Effugiat Risus Hic Locus Est Ubi
Mors Gaudet Succurrere Vitae

The guard had already provided him with the translation:

"Let conversation cease. Let laughter flee. This is the place where
death delights to help the living."

Donovan pushed the lobby doors open and went out to First Avenue, eager to clear the smell of the morgue from his nostrils.

Ate his balls; Jesus!

His mind churned as he walked slowly towards the Vulcan.

If this all happened the way the paper said, involving Father Carroll doesn't make sense. So the cops must think the scorpions were used as a weapon to murder this guy Denschler. By whom? And why? And did the scorpions really eat his balls—gah!—or did something else happen? Did someone take them for some reason? Maybe that's what Fullam wants to find out. Maybe a sexual angle is where I should approach from. Scorpions? Gelding the victim? There can't not be a connection.

He swung his leg over the motorcycle and sat. Donovan's current bike was a Kawasaki 900 Vulcan, midnight-metallic blue with gray and white trim around the gas tank and side panels. Chopper-style without any exaggerated features, it had a curved black leather seat, slightly elevated handlebars and a profile lean enough to allow him to ride between traffic.

The image of the wound, dried out and blood-crusted, made him cringe. *Pommeru said he was alive when it happened. And he could see it, too, unlike that guy with the arrow in his eye—*

He sat upright on the bike.

Arrow. Scorpion. Genitals…

A pattern started to appear. He frowned, considering it for a moment, then slipped his helmet on and started the Vulcan. Rather than head back uptown, though, he circled the block and parked at the top of the morgue's street ramp.

He left his helmet on the bike and went back down the ramp and through the swinging doors. The guard office was empty. "Doctor Pommeru? It's Donovan Graham." He jogged down the hall and around to the freezer door. "I wanted to take a look—"

The freezer door slammed open. Donovan saw a flash of white—the doctor's coat—as the little man flew out at him. They collided and bounced into the opposite wall. Donovan's head cracked into the tile. He saw stars. Pommeru looked past Donovan's shoulder, eyes widening. Donovan started to turn. A gurney shot like a cannonball from the freezer, crashing into the wall. The body on it flopped off, landing on top of Donovan. Donovan gasped and thrust it away. Someone big—someone *huge*—stormed out. Dressed in a ragged black suit, he was roaring and violent and Donovan only caught a glimpse of his face before the giant snatched two handfuls of his leather jacket. With no effort he raised Donovan's body off the ground. Donovan kicked his steel-toed boot at the giant's kneecap. The giant grunted and dropped him. Donovan launched himself at the enormous midsection. He plowed his shoulder into the giant's stomach, drawing a "whoosh" of breath fouler than the smell of corpses, and followed it with two hard punches. The giant stumbled, then swung clumsily. Donovan ducked under the blow and charged again, bulling the giant back towards the open freezer. The giant pounded an arm down on his back. It felt like a telephone pole hitting him, and Donovan dropped like he'd been shot. He rolled over and shoved the gurney. The metal table clanged into the giant. Donovan seized Pommeru's coat and dragged him away.

"Come on! Come on!"

The giant loomed behind them, eclipsing the fluorescent light with impossibly broad shoulders. Donovan scrambled to his feet and shoved Pommeru up the corridor. "Run!"

They made it out the swinging doors, and Pommeru kept going. Just outside the door was a fire axe. Donovan smashed the glass and snatched it free. He gripped the axe in both hands, waiting to defend himself.

The giant didn't follow them out.

Donovan remained standing guard, but as seconds ticked by, he felt less and less threatened. After two minutes he crept to the swinging door. What he could see through the tiny window looked normal. A few blocks away, a siren approached. Feeling a bit more confident, he nudged the door open with his shoulder and slipped inside. Still nothing. He worked his way back. The freezer door stood wide open, but no one living was inside. The gurney remained where the giant had knocked it aside, dented and crimped. The body lay in a heap, the arrow in the eye socket propping the head up at an odd angle.

The giant was gone.

∾

Donovan sat alone at the table in the medical examiner observation room, where grieving relatives can view remains behind glass. He was drinking a can of soda, thinking about mutilated bodies, when a sharply dressed man a few years older than him entered. The man was clean-shaven with razor-cut hair. His intensity projected a force field ahead of him.

"Maurice said you have a 'unique approach to problem solving.'" He looked Donovan over. When he spoke it was neither accusatory nor challenging, but leaving no doubt who had to prove himself to whom. "I hear you can take care of yourself, too. Nice to know you're working for me."

"You're Sergeant Fullam?"

"You're Donovan Graham." Fullam sat at the table with Donovan. "Maurice called me yesterday, said you could give me the information I needed. I didn't expect *this*, but okay. I understand following your gut. In the future, though, save that 'better to ask forgiveness than permission' bullshit for your professors, okay? You want to do something like this, you call me first."

"No problem."

"What have you got?"

"I don't think this was a one-in-a-million accident, and I don't think you think so either."

Fullam took out a notepad and pen. "Whatever I think, I won't open my mouth until I have facts. I asked about scorpions. Tell me about scorpions."

"That's my point—it's not just scorpions or a guy missing his balls. The body with the arrow in its eye was missing its legs, or, more accurately, its thighs. In Western astrology, each sign of the zodiac has a corresponding body part: Scorpio is the genitals, Sagittarius is the thighs."

"You think people are being murdered according to the zodiac?"

"I think that describes the two bodies you have."

Fullam looked at him for a moment. "You came up with this after seeing the bodies for five minutes?"

Donovan didn't back down. "Not saying I'm right, but it fits."

"And the missing body parts?"

"Sounds like a ritual."

"What do you mean?"

"Sacrifice and ritual killing are like murder and serial killing; one is an end to itself, one has a larger purpose. Anton LaVey said, 'A sacrifice is used to *sustain*, a ritual to *attain*.' You track a sacrifice by figuring out to whom it's made. Ritual killings, you figure out what the ritual is designed to do."

Fullam made some notes. "Any thoughts on that?"

Donovan shrugged. "Sorry. No idea."

"Doctor Pommeru says that when the body with the arrow was brought in a few days ago, it had all its parts. After you left, he went to work in the freezer and saw the giant in there, cutting the thighs off. Says it wasn't for you, he'd be dead."

Donovan considered this. "I've never saved anybody's life before."

"Welcome to the club." Fullam snapped his notepad closed and stood. "'Ritualistic zodiac murders'; it's an interesting theory. I'll give it some thought. Quick question, though—how did you figure out his balls were taken and not eaten? I specifically asked Doctor Pommeru not to give you that information."

"If the scorpions had really eaten them, the wound probably would have been more ragged. The knife strokes in the wound could have been from the autopsy, but the scorpion-genital connection is basic astrology." Donovan stood. "Can I go?"

The sergeant nodded. "Unless you want to help clean up downstairs."

ↂ

"Frank Fullam?" Joann asked.

"Do you know him?"

She sipped some orange juice. "Only by reputation."

Even with the delay at the morgue they'd made it to the bed and break-fast outside of New Paltz the previous evening. After an energetic celebra-tion of Donovan's graduation, they'd awoken to a private breakfast in their room.

"Is that a good thing or a bad thing?"

"He's got a little history. A bit of a reputation as a loose cannon."

"Really? He came across as the opposite to me. Very buttoned-down."

"Not always, from what I've heard." She held her juice glass between her palms. "He used to work Vice in Brooklyn. He had trouble with the old boys' network and got transferred to Manhattan because of it. He got a promotion, but he has to be *very* careful now. There are people who wouldn't mind seeing him gone. In fact, that's probably why he asked Fa-ther Carroll for help instead of NYPD Intelligence. Outside the politics."

"I *thought* that was a little odd. The NYPD has at least a half-dozen 'cult cops' versed in the paranormal. I met one in class one time. Fullam could have gone to them."

"But he didn't. He asked you." She toasted him. "And now he has a lead."

"And I have a sore back." He winced, then smiled. "Giants and zodiac murders; pretty weird start to a career."

"A career?"

"I don't want to tend bar my whole life. Helping the cops could open some doors."

"Those doors are a little more dangerous than teaching." She shook her head. "You're lucky you didn't get hurt badly enough to miss any shifts at the restaurant."

Donovan only half-heard her as he tried to remember every detail. "He wasn't a really skilled fighter, but I guess with his size he doesn't need to be. He was *huge*. I don't know how he got away, but the cops figure he escaped into the sewer outside the autopsy room. I'm sure the alligators will give him a wide berth." She laughed, and he felt absurdly pleased with himself. "By the way; speaking of weird things, I'm sorry I didn't ask. Was there anything on the camera DeFelice found at the Dinkins Shelter?"

Her eyes lit. "There was, actually. Each of the cameras had a back-up disc, digital images that stayed for forty-eight hours before they were recorded over. We're still cleaning up what we found, but we may have a picture of Charming Man."

"'Charming Man'; hah. Charming up until the point he got everyone to start killing each other. What a waste of talent," Donovan said. "I try to use mine only in the service of good."

"It's worked on me so far."

He gazed into her face. His heart pounded. *Propose now!* Instead, he took her hand and stood. "Want to test it again?"

THREE

SOMETHING FAR MORE SINISTER

O n Tuesday Donovan returned to work at Polaris. Polaris was on the east side of midtown Manhattan, an upper-end restaurant with a clientele of cougars and people used to getting what they wanted. He liked tending bar there, but over the next few days he found himself distracted from mixing North Star cocktails and cosmos by thoughts of his future.

A ring, a site, a way to propose...

He took care of the first concern with a visit to Lars, a jeweler friend of Father Carroll's who also read runestones. They designed a ring that Lars promised to get to work on right away. As for a site, he figured he and Joann would pick one together. One thing he *did* know was who he'd ask to officiate the ceremony. On his next afternoon off, Donovan rode the Vulcan to East 4th Street, off Avenue C., to ask him.

ଏ

Cinnamon-scented steam wafted from the imported coffee shop next to the building. Donovan pressed the door buzzer for Father Carroll's apartment. The answer came after several moments.

"*Yes?*"

"Welcome back, Father. Have you got a minute?"

"*Donovan? Of course, come up.*"

Donovan took the stairs two at a time and found the priest waiting for him on the third floor. He offered a hearty handshake and a clap on the shoulder. "*Dia duit*!"

"'*Djiah gwich*'?"

"'Good day.' I picked up a bit of Gaelic while I was visiting Father Driscoll."

"Really?" Donovan followed him inside. "What should I say in response?"

"'*Dia is Muire duit*.'"

"'*Dijahs murrah gwich*.' How was England? How does Stonehenge look?"

"It's interesting, what's visible to the public, anyway." Father Carroll led him to his study. Although his apartment had high ceilings, he had to duck through the doorways. "Can I get you something to drink?"

"Soda or water is fine, thanks."

He motioned Donovan to another room. "I'll be right in."

Father Carroll's study was similar to his office, but with relics and books that were much more significant. On one wall he'd mounted his Crest of Thagaste, denoting his status as one of a dozen clergymen in Christianity holding an Augustine Dictate. The Augustine Dictate authorized him to investigate the paranormal in ways not normally condoned by church bodies. Around the study, Donovan noted books open as they had been at the office. This time, however, the priest wasn't researching scorpions.

"Apparently," Father Carroll entered carrying two bottles of water, "the English Heritage group wasted a lot of time trying to 'naturalize' Salisbury Plain, making Stonehenge look as it did thousands of years ago. It was dying a slow bureaucratic death until this man, Lord Teesdale, took it over. Whatever his plans are, the only thing anyone knows is what they see, which is the entire plain draped in gray material. The site looks like something by Christo." He sat behind the desk, and Donovan took the opposite armchair. "But I'm told you had an interesting holiday as well. Francis called me." He offered Donovan one bottle and opened the other. "How are you?"

"I'm fine. A little bruised is all." He waved off the concern. "We can talk about that in a minute, if you want, but that's not why I'm here. I wanted to tell you—well, I'm going to ask Joann to marry me."

"You are?" A broad smile split the priest's gray beard. "Donovan, that's *wonderful*. Congratulations. She's a lovely young woman."

"Thanks. If—*when*—she accepts, I was hoping you'd officiate at the ceremony?"

Father Carroll's eyes crinkled behind his glasses. "I would be honored, sir."

"Thank you." Donovan smiled, relieved to check off another item on the list. "I haven't figured out how to ask yet, but I'll keep you updated."

"What do your parents think? Have you told them?"

"No, I figured Joann and I could take the trip down to D.C. and tell them together. I thought about asking Conrad for her hand, but I have a pretty good idea what his answer would be." Donovan paused. "Actually, *you're* the first person I've told."

"Well." Now the priest beamed. "I will certainly do my best to make the most of this happy event. Cheers and blessings." He raised his bottle, and they drank a toast.

"Lars is making the ring even as we speak. I can't wait to see the look on her face."

"I'm sure it will sparkle like the stars."

Having shared his news, Donovan felt an idiot grin rise on his face. He looked at the books around them. Images of constellations and zodiac symbols faced up from most pages. "I guess I hit on something with the 'zodiac murders' thing. Did Sergeant Fullam ask for more help?"

"He did."

"You've helped him out before." Donovan raised his eyebrows. "That's kind of interesting."

"He told me you uncovered this astrological connection between the two bodies at the morgue." The priest sipped his water. "My best pupil."

"I made it when I thought about scorpions and arrows. The missing organs clinched it." Donovan gestured at the books. "Have you been building on my guess?"

"For the moment, I'm at a loss. Astrological rituals are primarily concerned with fortunetelling. Some make reference to animal sacrifice, but human mutilation? Particular to zodiac signs? I have no idea."

"Joann and I are having dinner tonight, but I can give you a hand for a bit." Donovan surveyed the room. "Where should I start?"

"You had success the way you handled researching scorpions. Perhaps we ought follow that blueprint."

Donovan chuckled. "Blueprint? Not exactly. I studied stuff for hours before I got the bright idea to check out the body."

"The Lord works in mysterious ways," the priest said. "Your consciousness had to become preoccupied for your subconscious to be inspired."

"So...God wants us to study fine print until our eyes cross before He'll help?"

"The time you feel was wasted enabled the Universe to unfold as it did, allowing you not only to save a man's life, but to gain valuable information for our cause."

"I was lucky. I know how to throw a punch. Nothing supernatural about that."

"Perhaps." Father Carroll sounded amused. "But you were faced with choices and you made the ones that produced those results. Either your instincts—free will—are the best I've ever seen, or there was a guiding hand behind your actions."

"Predestination."

"I believe it was a combination of the two. Free will allows us to make those choices, and if we choose as you did, we allow God to shape the world through our actions."

"And if we don't?"

"Then the world, as the unfortunate Mister Denschler and others discovered," the priest gestured at the books, "can be shaped by something far more sinister."

☙

The bar on Pearl Street was crowded with brokers and traders who hadn't yet gone to catch their trains. Cornelius Valdes looked up from the vodka he'd been nursing and into the mirror behind the multicolored bottles. Joe Lopter was still there, against the wall, glad-handing other well-dressed men as he'd probably been doing for the last fifteen years.

Not that I would know.

Valdes wiped some condensation from his glass, eyes shifting to his own reflection. Dressed in suit and tie, he looked like many of the men in the bar. The double chin and paunch many of them possessed, and he'd been developing before everything had happened, were long gone however, carved away by a fifteen-year diet of government-dictated subsistence.

At least I still have my hair.

Dark and thick, it had recently begun to show salt in the pepper. Crow's feet deepened the corners of his eyes. Their presence reminded Valdes of the good humor he'd possessed once, then lost, and now recently redis-covered.

Fifteen years, eight months and four days later. Give or take.

He watched Lopter swill the last of his drink, set the glass down and begin a round of good-bye handshakes. When he walked out the door to

Pearl Street, Valdes drifted to the window to watch.

Enjoy your freedom for now, Joe. It's not your time.

Yet.

છ

The following Wednesday evening, Donovan sat on his motorcycle out-side of Joann's building. He'd picked up the ring from Lars that afternoon, and although he didn't plan to propose yet, he liked the feel of it against his thigh.

Joann came out of the building, changed out of her work suit into jeans and a leather jacket that were more appropriate for motorcycle riding. Her hair was tied loosely up, and she swung her own helmet in one hand. He took a folded piece of cloth from his pocket and proffered it.

"What's this?" she asked

"A blindfold."

"Mystery tour?" Her mouth curled in a half-smile filled with curiosity as she accepted it. "Am I dressed for it?"

He kissed her. "You are dressed properly." She wrapped her arms around his neck and went back for more. He matched her, then pulled back with a grin. "But I'm not telling you where we're going. That's why it's called a 'mystery tour.'"

છ

They rode into Manhattan across the Brooklyn Bridge. The lane was clear ahead of him, Joann held him tightly, and the weather was perfect.

Lucky man.

On Christopher Street he turned the Vulcan off the West Side Highway towards the center of Manhattan. They parked, and he helped her with her helmet.

"Are we almost there?"

"Almost."

They stepped into a building's tiny lobby. A group of twentysomethings crowded in behind them. A baby-faced man in business casual business clothing saw the blindfold first. He smiled and whispered to his friends, who all turned to stare. Donovan winked and put his finger to his lips. When the elevator came, they urged him to bring her on alone. The door slid shut on their giggles.

"I choose to believe that we are not being observed at the moment, and that we were not just the subject of scrutiny by person or persons unknown."

"Because that would be embarrassing."

"Because that would be embarrassing." She touched and drew herself to him. "And, if we're going to play games, I'd prefer to do it without an audience."

His lips had just touched hers when the elevator groaned to a stop and the doors shuddered open. Immediately she turned her head to the side. "It feels cool." She sniffed. "It smells like wood, and air conditioning, and…people?"

Donovan undid her blindfold. Joann blinked a few times to adjust her eyes, and when she saw where they were she turned to him with a big smile. "Dance House?"

"Dance House."

Dance House was a studio that offered dance lessons of all kinds, from Latin to swing to ballroom and hustle. They'd been talking about taking lessons for months, and now she eagerly made her way into the studio's lobby.

"Since I've done some swing already," he said, "I thought it might be a good idea to start there. If you want, we can do the salsa class afterwards, too."

She stepped into a studio filled with couples. The air inside was dusty and a little warm with excess body heat. Along a side concrete wall, a boom box was set up on a table. CDs lay scattered around it, in and out of jewel boxes. Mirrors lined the wall perpendicular to the windows. The hardwood floor was dull but still shiny in the corners where feet hadn't scuffed it learning "one-two-cha-cha-cha."

She turned to him, gold flecks shining in her eyes.

"Swing, salsa; let's do it all."

෴

"Excuse me, sir, are you Stuart Brandeis?"

Brandeis paused at the bottom of the steps to his Cobble Hill brownstone. The man asking was well dressed, with a kind smile and a bit of a twinkle in his eye. He clutched a messenger bag to his side as though afraid it might be snatched from him at any moment.

Process server? Brandeis wondered. The Brooklyn court house wasn't too far from where they stood, and he *had* been having problems with his ex-wife…

"Did Victoria send you? Is this about an alimony payment?" Brandeis asked, his lip curling into a sneer. "Because I told her I was restructuring my mortgage to give her her pound of flesh."

"No, no, quite the opposite. I'm a representative for Mrs. Brandeis." He proffered a business card. "She has asked me to approach you and see if you might be interested in reconciliation."

Brandeis took it and read:

CORNELIUS VALDES
Attorney

"What do you mean, 'reconciliation'?"

Valdes heard the shift in his voice, saw the anger in his eyes melt to hope. *Perfect.* "If you'd like to come with me, we can discuss the terms she has suggested I offer you." He gestured for the man to precede him up the street.

Brandeis paused. "What is this, some kind of game? She trying to get more money out of me?"

"I assure you, Mister Brandeis," Valdes smiled, "this is no game."

ᏽ

Joann had to be at work early the next day, so after dance class and dinner in Tribeca they made their way back to Brooklyn on the Vulcan. Instead of going to her loft, though, Donovan parked outside her building and they strolled to the end of Montague Street, to the Brooklyn Promenade. They held hands as they walked. Below them, cars sped by on the Brooklyn-Queens Expressway. Across the bay, the skyline of lower Manhattan sparkled with a thousand jewels of unextinguished fluorescent tubes, traffic signals and vehicle headlights. Scant clouds allowed most of the city's ambient light to escape, casting the outlines of the buildings black against a dark, deep purple sky.

"Great night, hunh?" She stopped, leaning back on the iron railing as she turned. "Sorry I have to bring it to an end. Now that we have a partial profile of Charming Man off that camera, I've got to interview a lot of the shelter workers again."

"Somebody has to get the bad guys." He rested a hand on either side of her. "So Dance House is a date, for at least the next three Wednesdays?"

"At least? At *last*. It's about time we're doing this. But why now?"

"School's over. Now that I've got more free time, I'd like to spend it doing something besides writing papers."

"You don't want to pick up more bar shifts, make some more money?"

"I may have to," he felt the ring's box in his pocket, "but not yet. Besides, that's not what I mean by 'wisely.'"

"I hate that you only make good money when you work at night. I miss you."

"I wish things were different, but..."

"I know, baby, I know." She touched his face, letting her hand linger on his cheek. "We're building something, and it takes time. I get that. Sometimes, though, the lack of together time thing just sucks."

"A lot," he agreed.

"Which is why I'm glad we're doing Dance House."

"Yep." He did a standing push-up, slowly drawing himself closer to her. Her breath trickled out like venting steam. His lips touched hers. "Actually, I have a confession to make. As much as I enjoyed tonight, and look forward to the next few weeks, the free time thing isn't the only reason I wanted to take dance lessons now."

"Okay." She kissed him back, softly at first. "Then why else?"

"I want to be able to dance well." He kissed her harder as he reached into his pocket. "At our wedding."

Her eyes flew open.

The ring attracted every bit of the Manhattan skyline, intensified it, and released it back to the stars. A round, 1.25 carat diamond sat in a platinum cathedral mount, accented by tiny diamonds. The band, also platinum, was squared at the edges, adorned by intricate, unobtrusive engraving.

"Magical" barely does it justice, he thought.

Nothing had prepared him for the emotions surging through his body. Now that the moment was here, it was different, infinitely different and better than any scenario he had imagined. He caught his breath, and when he spoke he was surprised at how even his voice was. He got down on one knee.

"Joann Clery, will you marry me?"

She blinked in surprise. Heat spread over her skin, flushing it pink. Her eyes became very serious and she examined every inch of his features.

"Oh my God."

She pulled him to his feet. Her entire body shivered and she leaned into his embrace. He held her, feeling her offer herself to him heart and soul, before finally raising her head to meet his eyes.

"Yes."

She wiped away tears, smiled and kissed him fiercely.

"Let's go celebrate," she purred.

So they did.

FOUR

PRESSURE MAKES DIAMONDS

Now that the engagement was official, Donovan felt free to enjoy it. Unfortunately, he was scheduled for back-to-back doubles the following two days, and he barely saw Joann, who was herself busy with the Dinkins Shelter case. After working almost thirty-three hours in those two days, he finally made it to Black King, the Irish pub around the corner from Polaris, for drinks with the other bartenders.

"Shots," Guzman announced. He was a tall, thin Mexican with a big square head and thick black hair. He passed around shot glasses full of something brown. "Maybe we can drink some sense into you."

Corey, the youngish manager Donovan liked best of his bosses, snorted. "Have you *seen* his fiancée?" He raised his glass. "*Salud*, Donovan. If she has a sister…"

"Only child," Donovan said. "Sorry."

Four shots (so far) of Jack Daniel's had been a good start, and when Guzman had pulled out a blunt of White Widow, Donovan lit it up with no hesitation. He enjoyed getting high, especially after working crazy shifts. Joann rarely partook anymore—as a member of the NY Bar, drug testing was always a possibility for her—and since Donovan really didn't like to get high alone, an opportunity like this was an engagement gift from above.

Jools, the petite blonde who had come by Polaris for her check and decided to join them, cocked her head. "Are you getting married tonight?"

28

Donovan took a second to process the question. "Tonight? No."

"Then how come a priest just came in?" She giggled and pointed. "And he's coming over here."

Donovan turned in his seat. "Father Carroll? Father Carroll! We're drinking a toast to the engagement. Want a shot?"

The priest declined with a polite smile. "No, thank you. Do you have a moment, Donovan?"

Jools and Guzman both made faces. "Donovan's in trouble!" she giggled.

"Feel free to employ capital punishment, Father," Guzman said. "This young man has strayed from the path of righteousness, and must be corrected."

"I'll bear it in mind," the priest said dryly.

Donovan got up and followed him outside. "What's up?"

"A situation has arisen." Father Carroll looked him over. "Are you capable of functioning?"

"Hey, I just worked four shifts in a row *and* I'm celebrating my engagement. I'm allowed to partake."

"I'm not judging, I'm asking you to assess whether you're able to participate in something very important and probably quite disturbing." He gestured at the cab that waited curbside. "Are you able?"

The four shots attacked his stomach lining. "What are you talking about? What happened?" Fear wrenched him. "Is it Joann?"

The priest blinked. "Oh. Good heavens, no. No, Francis has asked for you."

"Sergeant Fullam?"

"Are you able?"

"Being high doesn't mean I'm a giggling moron. I'm just not as…focused." Donovan took a couple of deep breaths. The weed's THC made his skin buzz. "Sorry. Give me a few seconds." He ran to the twenty-four hour deli down the block and bought himself a pack of cupcakes and a bottle of water. "Sweet things kill my high," he explained, climbing into the back seat of the cab. "It's why I try not to eat when I smoke. And drinking gives me dry-mouth."

Father Carroll watched him with a tolerant expression. "If you say so."

The cab headed south on Lexington. "What happened?" Donovan asked. "Where are we going?"

"Brooklyn. Red Hook. Francis believes he's located the Capricorn victim."

"He has?"

"Hanging in a burned out building, missing its knees."

"Capricorn the Goat is death by hanging? How do you think that works?"

"I've no idea. He would like us to see the site, to perhaps find something traditional police eyes might not see or understand."

Donovan took a bite of cupcake. The cab made the left turn from Lexington onto 42nd Street, heading east towards the FDR. "He asked for me?"

"He was impressed with what you did at the morgue, and how you figured things out."

"Wow. Better not screw this up." Donovan chewed and shrugged. "Sorry. I'm not being flip. I guess I'm a little…surprised. I mean, we did those field trips for parapsychology class to 'haunted' sites, but this is beyond that. *Way* beyond."

"It is. Can you handle it?"

"Hell yes." He grinned. "This is usually Joann's thing, going to crime scenes and working with cops. I always thought it might be kind of cool, but—"

"'Cool'?" Father Carroll raised an eyebrow. He paused. "It reads differently than it lives, I'll grant you that."

"Guess I'm about to find out." Donovan took the second cupcake from the package. "As long as I can help without being part of the actual system. I mean, I see the crap Joann is taking for this whole Dinkins thing and it kills me. I don't know that I have the political savvy to handle it as well as she does."

"I'm sorry, what is the 'Dinkins thing'?"

"Last February there was a riot at a homeless shelter in Brooklyn. A few guards and some of the residents were killed. You might have seen things in the paper?"

"I remember it, of course. She's involved?"

"She was the ADA riding when the call came in. After they picked up the pieces, she was responsible for building the case against whoever instigated it, because she's the DA's Golden Girl and it's a high-profile case. Problem is, the one guy really responsible for everything—she's calling him Charming Man—seems to have gotten away. She's been holding off going after the smaller fish until she can find out who he is, but every day the press is climbing all over them to do something."

"Pressure often comes from those who can neither control nor understand reality."

"My father says pressure creates diamonds." Donovan let down the window on his side. Fresh air battered his face. "He used to tell me that when I played Little League."

"Perhaps, but pressure tends to destroy more than it creates."

"It hasn't destroyed Joann yet."

"I'll pray for her nonetheless, although we may be able to do more than that for her tonight. The burned-out building where we're meeting Francis, where the body was found, is the David N. Dinkins Memorial Shelter."

"Really?" Donovan looked strangely at him. "Odd coincidence."

The cab turned down Verona Street. Donovan saw the ruins of the shelter in the middle of the block, cordoned off by a hastily erected chain-link fence. The shelter was a large building that resembled a high school gymnasium, with a smaller building for the intake/processing offices in front of it. Both buildings seemed lifeless, but a light illuminated a scorched window frame on the top floor of the larger one.

Here we go.

Although the nearest streetlight was half a block away, he could make out the sergeant leaning against a nondescript Crown Victoria. He straightened as the cab pulled up. "Maurice." He extended a hand. "Thanks for coming by. You too, Mister Graham."

"Call me Donovan."

The sergeant's nostrils twitched, and his face grew stony. "You functional?"

A red flush crept up Donovan's neck. "Ah, I was celebrating—"

"I didn't ask you *why*. I'm asking if, in spite of your state, you'll be any use to me?"

His abruptness was startling. Donovan nodded. "Yes."

Fullam gave him another few seconds of examination before turning to Father Carroll. "I've been looking at mutilated bodies ever since Mister Graham made his observations at the morgue. I'm tired of it. This one seems to fit best for Capricorn. Let's take a look and see what you can come up with."

He gave Donovan another stony glance and started towards the shelter. Donovan motioned for Father Carroll to go first. *Well, at least I wasn't banished.*

Inside, the sergeant led them up a stairwell pocked by mildew spots, graffiti and peels of paint. "Whoever did this was smart enough to put him upstairs, top floor. Less likely to be found right away. Also, a lot of garbage is spread around, pretty much polluting any chance Crime Scene had to get anything. We bagged and tagged a lot of it, but whoever these people are, they don't leave much to chance."

"'These people'?" Father Carroll asked.

"There are at least two: the giant who took the thighs off Father Roehling's body—that was the name of the archery victim, by the way, Father Arthur Roehling—and Mister X, who did the actual killing." They rounded a landing that stank of urine. "One good thing that came out of that fiasco at the morgue was we were able to compare the cuts made on Mister Denschler with those the giant did on Father Roehling. Even allowing for the hurried circumstance, Doctor Pommeru showed me the cuts were made by different people. The giant took Father Roehling's thighs, Mister X took Denschler's genitals as well as…" He gestured ahead of them.

The large loft he brought them to might once have been a storeroom. All that remained now was garbage, strewn about to an average depth of four inches. The despair ran deeper. A couple of filthy, stained mattresses occupied one corner. Band and gang graffiti fought for space on the walls; scorch marks obscured some of both. Shadows loomed over and above everything, preventing Donovan from seeing anything clearly enough to decipher.

"After the riot, the city was supposed to knock these buildings down. The citizens of Red Hook are still waiting. Meanwhile, squatters get in here sometimes, leave their mark. That's where the victim, Stuart Brandeis, was found."

Fullam indicated around a brick corner, to a cul-de-sac that must have been a janitor's walk-in closet. Donovan looked around the corner and faltered as, for an instant, he saw exactly what he knew couldn't be there: a partially dismembered, purple-faced corpse.

Psychic flashes? I didn't think the weed was that *strong…*

"Are you all right?" Father Carroll asked.

"Yeah." He saw Fullam shake his head in disgust. "Tripped on something."

In reality, a smashed sink was in one corner of the closet, while a square drain occupied the center of a filthy ceramic square near the outside wall. A pipe extended above the top of the walls, about eight feet off the ground, with a clear spot on its rusty surface. Donovan got a slight shiver as he realized the spot had been polished by the rope during Brandeis' struggles. A large metal hook jutted from one wall, incongruous in its newness.

"After incapacitating Brandeis by duct-taping his arms to his sides, the killer strung him up using a chain and a noose he made from a sleeve of a sweater we found."

"A sweater?" Father Carroll was gazing about the room. "Not a rope?"

Fullam shook his head. "The chain had links big enough to loop over that hook, so the killer could adjust the height from which Brandeis hung. Maybe it was a game to see how long he could keep the man alive. After he got tired of it, he took out a chain saw and cut through Brandeis' legs just above the knee. He took them over there," he waved, "and cut the lower part off, keeping only the knees. Odd thing—before he did that, he put tourniquets on each of Brandeis' legs. Hung, but not bled out."

Donovan peered closer into the janitor's closet. A burst of red had sprayed against the wall, and a rust-colored stain scabbed over the drain in the floor. A couple of dark blobs dotted the floor nearby. Tiny bumps mixed in with the red mess on the wall, and he felt nauseated as he wondered whether it was skin or fragments of bone the chain saw had thrown.

"The killer apparently took his time doing this, because cigarette ashes were all over the floor." The sergeant indicated at some gray smears. "Unfortunately, he's seen *CSI: New York*, and knew enough not to leave the butts—with his DNA—behind."

"Why here?" Donovan asked. Fullam glanced at him with cop eyes. "I mean, it's obviously out of the way, but there must be tons of places that are out of the way to do something like this. Is there a connection between here and Mister Brandeis?"

"Brandeis was a teacher. He lived not too far away, over in Cobble Hill."

"Proximity," Father Carroll asked, "or something more?"

"Good question. Can you see anything around that might answer it?"

The priest put a hand on one of the lights. "May I?" He adjusted the light stand, turning the illumination around the walls. Now they could see the graffiti more clearly, but there was so much, drawn over and around itself, that it quickly became evident to all of them it was only mindless scribble.

"Nothing appears ritualistic." Father Carroll began to walk around the room, inspecting the markings. "However, a question: it seems they've taken the body parts they needed at the time of each murder, correct? Then why didn't they take Father Roehling's thighs when they killed him?"

"I talked to the detectives on the Roehling case. Mister X was interrupted in the middle of the murder. He escaped without mutilating the body."

Something scurried out of a pile of fast food garbage, making Father Carroll start. He adjusted his glasses. "There's a witness? Did he provide any information?"

"So far, *she* hasn't. Mabel Muglia is the caretaker at the rectory where Father Roehling was murdered. She's been in shock since she interrupted the attack."

"Perhaps I could speak to her."

"Yeah, I thought about that. Probably not a bad idea; you're a little more sympathetic than a lot of cops." Fullam took a deep breath in through his nose and turned to Donovan. "Not you. I don't want you talking to her. I appreciate what you've done so far, Mister Graham, but Maurice is an official police consultant. You're not. I'm not going to put myself or this investigation at risk by involving a pothead. No offense."

Donovan felt an irrational urge to light up the blunt Guzman had given him. *That would be childish.* "Just because I get high doesn't mean I can't help you. In philosophical hermeneutics, achieving an altered state of consciousness is a *positive* thing."

Fullam's face and voice were flat. "In a police investigation, it's not."

ↄ

He gave them a ride back to Father Carroll's building in the Crown Victoria. Donovan sat in the back seat, quiet the whole way. The sergeant's attitude stung, but he didn't want to antagonize the situation further.

"I'll messenger you over a copy of the case file and the witness' address," Fullam said as they got out. "Tomorrow morning I'll call and let her know you're coming."

"Have a good night, Francis."

"You too." Fullam gave Donovan one last look-over. "Mister Graham."

Donovan watched the Crown Victoria drove away. "'In a police investigation, it's not.'" He turned to Father Carroll. "I *can* help."

"If that's what you believe," the priest regarded him with a combination of empathy and professorial challenge, "how will you prove it?"

"I don't know—yet. But I'll figure something out." He raised his arm as a cab drove down East 4th Street. "He said I couldn't talk to the witness, but he didn't say I couldn't see the place where the Sagittarius murder was committed." The cab pulled up, and he opened the door. "I might find something there."

"After over a week? Something the police haven't already discovered?"

"They don't see things the way we do. Will you help me?"

Father Carroll examined him. Donovan recognized his "weighing of options" face. "Is that really what you want to do?"

"Haven't I proven it yet?"

"As a student, without question. But Donovan—this isn't the classroom."

"I understand that. And I understand I'm not an 'official' police consultant. This is something I never considered doing, but I like it. I *want* to do it. I *can* do it."

"All right, then." Father Carroll sighed, but he was smiling. "I'll call you tomorrow."

ᘓᘔ

The Reverend Arthur Roehling had been an associate Episcopal priest attached to the Church of the Transfiguration, on East 29th Street. At 10:15 the next morning Donovan, slightly hung over, leaned against the wrought-iron fence bordering the church garden, next to the lych gate. The lych gate was modeled after those in English churchyards, a place where coffins would be held while a brief service was performed before entering the church. It was decorated with images of scallop shells in homage to the Santiago de Compostela pilgrims. He thought about Paolo Coehlo's book and again resolved to take that walk himself someday.

Father Carroll arrived shortly after he got there, and they were greeted by an elderly Hispanic woman who brought Father Carroll up to see Mabel Muglia. While they talked, Donovan went to the room where Father Roehling had been murdered. As soon as he opened the door, a headache began to throb in a band from temple to temple. He'd studied cases of psychometry—getting impressions off scenes or objects—but immediately dismissed the possibility in himself.

Psychic sensitivity? Try shots of Jack coming back to haunt you.

It was a small room furnished simply with dresser, bed, night table and desk. Everything bore signs of wear but was clean. Whatever damage had been done during the murder had been repaired, and Donovan guessed no one had entered the room since. He glanced around, making a slow, 360 degree turn to take everything in. Freshly plastered spots scarred one wall. He leaned on the dresser to examine them but saw nothing unusual. His hand brushed something and he glanced down. A fine layer of waxy red droplets sprinkled the dresser top.

Red wax?

He stared for a moment, then took a step back and looked at the scene. An image from the previous night appeared before him, startling him with a revelation. He left the room and went downstairs. The housekeeper was at the kitchen table with a cup of tea, gazing at nothing. Donovan sensed in her a desire for closure to this horrific incident, and he was surprised at how much he wanted to provide it.

"Could you please ask Father Carroll to give me a call when he finishes with Miss Muglia?" he asked. "I have to go."

Hope lit her face. "Did you learn anything?"

But he was already out the door, jogging back to his motorcycle.

ꙮ

The ruins of the Dinkins Shelter looked worse in the daylight. The gate in the chain-link fence, which Fullam had locked, was now open and swinging. Donovan took off his helmet and ran inside. Racing past the crime scene tape, he took the steps two at a time to the top floor.

Red wax.

He leapt up the final three stairs and stopped dead.

Two men in dark blue windbreakers stood near the janitor's closet, packing up the crime scene spotlights from last night. They looked at him.

"Who the hell are you?"

FIVE

AN ELEMENT OF SATANISM

"This is the second time you've used my name to justify yourself," Fullam said. "There won't be a third."

The two of them were standing outside the janitor's closet where Stuart Brandeis had been found hanging. The crime scene cops, who had contacted Fullam after a few tense moments, maintained a discrete distance as they finished packing up their equipment, casting an occasional suspicious eye at Donovan. The sergeant's attitude did not soften them any.

Donovan sidestepped the issue. "I have results," he said simply.

Fullam started to speak but stopped. He took a deep breath through his nose and walked Donovan out of earshot of the crime scene men. "Let me be clear: this is not your show. You don't get to pick times and places, you don't get to do whatever you want and leave *me* to pick up the pieces. You are not an official part of the system, and I will not be fucked by the system because of that fact. Do you understand me? The only reason I have even tolerated this much is that you put your own life at risk to save another man."

"And I showed you the astrology link was the starting point here."

"'Starting point' isn't 'finish line.'" Fullam's face hardened. "Explain to me why the Capricorn victim was hung with a stainless steel chain and a noose made from a vicuna sweater instead of a rope."

"Is that what the sweater was? Vicuna?"

37

"Got the lab results an hour ago."

Donovan considered this and nodded. "Vicuna is a type of goat. It's goat's hair."

The tightness around Fullam's mouth lessened just a little, and Donovan could see he'd already figured it out. "Sherlock Pothead Holmes. All right. We're on the same page, and you've got a pretty good handle on *how* Mister X is doing it. Give me something so I can find out *who* he is, or this will be the last time we see each other without bars between us."

"I can't promise this will do that." Donovan turned towards the closet, pointing towards the line of blood splatter and letting his finger move down towards the floor. "But you see that stuff that's mixed in? Last night I saw it and thought it was bone or muscle or skin or something the chain saw had thrown when the legs were cut off. Some of it might be, but some of it, and that," he indicated at a couple of blobs near the scabbed-over drain, "is red wax. I saw what I think is the same stuff in Father Roehling's room."

Fullam bristled. "You went after I told you—"

"I didn't speak to the witness. While I was waiting for Father Carroll, I saw it on the top of Father Roehling's dresser."

"Father Roehling was a priest. Priests burn candles. And I told you—squatters get in here. Candle wax has been dripped all over the place."

"This isn't drippings. Look at the spots and dots; it was blown by someone onto the wall and, I'm guessing, onto Father Roehling's dresser. In the Episcopal church, red candles are pretty much for holidays—in an advent wreath, for instance. On the other hand, red candles have meaning outside the Episcopal Church, and blowing wax or powder or herbs is a step in all kinds of rituals. Blowing could mean traces of saliva in the wax. Saliva means DNA; an ID." Donovan shrugged. "Maybe."

"Maybe." Fullam settled cop eyes on him for a long moment. Finally he said, "Thanks for your input. I might be in touch." The tension in his voice was gone, replaced by more businesslike determination. He angled his head towards the stairs. "Get out of here."

ↄ

Donovan didn't check his cell phone until he got back to his apartment. He had one message: *"Hey, baby, it's me. Just wanted to remind you, dinner at seven, with Dad, at Daniel. I'll meet you at the bar at six-thirty."* Tonight they were going to tell Conrad about the engagement. He looked at his watch. It was almost one o'clock.

Plenty of time to find some body armor.

The buzzer for the downstairs door sounded. Donovan pushed the intercom. "Yeah?"

"*Ah, you're home.*"

"Father? Come on up." Donovan buzzed him in, then opened the apartment door. Takeout menus that had been left outside his door fluttered around his feet like leaves. As he stooped to gather them up, he heard the priest's footsteps pounding on the stairs. When they reached the fourth floor landing, Donovan glanced up. Father Carroll's face was slightly flushed and a thin, dark line of perspiration bisected the Georgetown logo on his sweatshirt.

"Hey, Father. You didn't run here from the Church of the Transfiguration, did you?"

"Oh, no." The priest shook his head and mopped his brow with his sleeve. "I'm coming from home. I had to substitute for Father Montoya at the 11:30 mass after I left Miss Muglia."

"Busy day."

"But informative."

"Mine, too." They went into Donovan's apartment. "Sorry to have left you so suddenly, but I found something in Father Roehling's room I had to check out."

"You did?"

"Droplets of red wax on the dresser where he was killed. When I saw them I remembered something like them in the janitor's closet at the Dinkins Shelter. I went back to see. Fullam was not pleased with me—not at first, anyway—but he's going to take samples of both. He's looking for saliva and DNA; I'm hoping he can tell us what's in the wax. Maybe there's something to help us figure out what religious or philosophical school this ritual comes from."

"It's Satanic."

Donovan's head jerked over. "What?"

"Miss Muglia told me the killer wore a charm, an amulet, around his neck. From her description—inverted five-pointed star, goat's head—I surmised it was a Sigil of Baphomet. I sketched one out and she confirmed it." He glanced over and noted a faint smile on Donovan's face. "Is there something amusing about an element of Satanism?"

"Oh, uh, no." His expression turned sheepish. "I'm sorry, it's just...a satanic killer in Manhattan? And I'm helping to stop him? Not exactly a typical summer job."

"No, it isn't." Father Carroll examined him before showing a small smile. "Given the satanic element, and the involvement of the giant you bested at the morgue, our path becomes clearer. Our priority must be to prepare ourselves in every way, mentally, spiritually, and physically."

Donovan felt a charge in his stomach. "Want to take a run to my gym?"

ↁ

They left his building to run west, to the promenade along the Hudson River. A steady breeze dotted the surface of the water with whitecaps and kept the June sun from growing too warm. As he dodged a tourist who was lining up a picture of the *Intrepid*, Donovan felt Father Carroll's eyes on him. "Is everything okay?"

"I might ask you the same question. This is more than sport, Donovan. I hope you do understand that."

"I'm taking it seriously, Father. It's just that it's one thing to study mythology and weird religions, and another thing to have to deal with them in reality."

"If there was anything I wanted you to take away from my classes, it's that 'reality' is an extremely flexible concept."

"I get that—in theory. But you learn more in one performance than in a hundred rehearsals. This is my first performance, and I am definitely learning. Come on, don't you get any sense of excitement or adventure out of what we're doing?"

"More at some times than others," Father Carroll admitted. "Regardless, it is imperative to prepare fully. That's something you *must* take seriously."

"I do. Mentally, I've been studying this stuff forever. Physically, I've been working out at gyms since I was ten and The Colonel taught me how to box."

"And spiritually?"

"Spiritually...okay, so philosophical hermeneutics has made me pretty skeptical. A lot of devils quote Scripture." He sidestepped as a bicycle rode past. The rider didn't even look up. "When it comes to organized religion, it isn't 'religion' I have a problem with, it's 'organized.'"

"Clever words."

"Best I can do is believe in myself. Occasionally wrong, never uncertain."

"Belief in oneself is a way of expressing belief in the glory that God has manifested within you. It's not for us to know or understand God's plan, but to trust that His guidance of our actions will keep us walking the righteous path. We need only the courage to follow His lead. Such is faith, and I see it within you. It's why I've involved you in this situation."

Donovan couldn't have explained why, but the priest's words reassured him. Still, he felt uncomfortable expressing it. "Well, I won't let you down. Whatever reason I'm involved, I can do good here. I already figured out the astrological connection, and now I found this red wax. If it's not just some cheap candle drippings, it might help us understand what's going on."

As they approached Canal Street, Donovan spied a homeless man rummaging through a cardboard box. Father Carroll reached into his sweatpants pocket and took out a dollar, which he dropped at the man's feet as they passed. The man glanced down and gratefully snatched it.

"As long as they have souls they deserve help," the priest said.

Donovan's gym was downtown by City Hall, one of the old-time boxing ones that had existed before "fitness centers" with chrome barbells and juice bars in the lobby. Every so often a local paper would do a feature on its "colorfulness" and "authenticity" and the membership rolls would swell, but when people found out you had to work hard on the heavy bags and in the professional-sized ring, things would die back down.

"Austere," Father Carroll commented. "But powerful."

The gym was deserted this time of day but heat and dried sweat filled the air up to the thirty-foot ceiling. If the attendant thought they made a strange pair—Donovan thought it sounded like the beginning of a joke: "A priest and a bartender walk into a gym…"—he made no comment.

When he was warmed up he moved to one of the heavy bags. He tugged his boxing gloves on, allowing the priest to tie the laces, and started right in, pummeling the bag with combinations and occasional kicks. While he did, Father Carroll jumped rope. Three rounds elapsed. When the clock buzzed the third time Donovan stopped and put his hands on his hips, gasping for air. Sweat rolled down his face and back.

"Man, people have no idea how hard it is to just stand and hit something."

The priest was barely winded. "I recognize the boxing, but never in conjunction with kicks and some of those other moves. What were you doing?"

"*Krav maga*. An Israeli system of street fighting. I studied it for a couple of years. Basically, it's controlled brawling; you fight as hard as you can with whatever you have at hand, and try to do as much damage as quickly as possible to your opponent. The way my instructor described it, it trains you how to fight in a situation where if you lose, you die. It's helped when I've been a bouncer."

"I see."

"I started going to classes after I got my head opened up in a bar fight by a long-necked bottle of beer—never did see what kind. Wouldn't drink it anymore if I knew what it was."

"A prudent attitude."

"But not our focus just now."

"No." Father Carroll turned professorial. "We are facing a man without limit on his thoughts and deeds, a man intent on traveling the darkest of paths to obtain what he wants. What does such a man want?"

"What does any man want? Money? Power? A hot girlfriend? Maybe the wax will tell us something."

"Perhaps." Father Carroll set the jump rope aside and went to an elliptical machine. He set the timer and climbed on backwards. "A pity the Sigil of Baphomet is so generic a symbol of Satanism. If only we had something more specific to reference, we might identify the ritual. I can't imagine there's a great number of satanic astrological rituals of this sort."

Donovan sucked in air and held up one boxing glove. "Let's grant it's satanic; what if it isn't an *astrological* ritual?"

"What do you mean?"

"I think astrology might just be a theme for the murders." He went to a wall-mounted bag and began to work hooks and uppercuts. The bag jerked and popped. "Each zodiac sign has specific colors, right? But the wax at both murder sites was the *same* color."

"In candle magic, every zodiac sign has its own hue," Father Carroll agreed. "Sagittarius is purple or royal blue, Capricorn black. Red is wrong for both." He paused, intrigued. "Go on."

"You pointed out that most astrological rituals are geared towards fortunetelling. We've been looking at everything that way and getting nowhere. What if Mister X isn't interested in fortunetelling? What if he's looking for something entirely different?"

"Such as?"

"Don't know. Yet." Donovan slammed a right hook into the side of the bag and smiled. "But we're trained for this. We'll figure it out."

⁂

When Charles C. Haight designed the New York Cancer Hospital for the west side of Central Park in 1884, he borrowed heavily from the great Renaissance chateaux of the Loire Valley. Two- and three-story buildings, all connected above and below ground by corridors and tunnels, surround a courtyard speared by a skyscraping smokestack. Five massive round towers, each four stories high, guarded the building corners. The shape of the towers was conducive to fresh air and sunlight, while the accoutrements of French design were hoped to have a beneficial effect on the psyches of terminally ill patients. In its era, it was one of the most impressive constructions on Central Park West.

Time and advancements in medical science eventually outdated the facility's capabilities. The plan to convert it to residential space has long been bogged down, leaving it to the mercy of nature and vandals. Bordering plants have grown amuck, obscuring the detail work. The courtyard is choked with garbage and the structure fortified by bricked-up windows and a wooden fence topped with barbed wire. Its more modern neighbors on West 105th and 106th Streets heighten its incongruity. A castle whose vampires have left in search of more sanguine feeding grounds, it stands desolate, isolated…

…but not abandoned.

On the last block of 106th Street before Central Park West, Valdes sidestepped into an alley between a rundown three-story building and that wooden fence. He carried four large shopping bags. Although the sun had gone down and the streetlights didn't penetrate here, he knew where to push. A section of slats swung noiselessly inwards.

"No entry!" Immediately, a hulking shadow loomed over him. "I make the rules! The rule is: no entry!"

"It's all right, Officer Burt. It's me."

Officer Burt, a bear of a man who reeked of old tension sweat, gazed blankly as he processed this information. When he did he stumbled back, nodding deferentially. "Oh, uh, sorry, Mister Valdes. The rule is: no one comes in but you or who you say."

"That's right." Valdes passed over the shopping bags. "Have someone relieve you, and take these down to Bridget in the dining hall, all right?"

"Yes, sir."

"And Officer Burt? Keeping us secure is important. You do a fine job of it."

Officer Burt stood a little straighter as he shambled off. Valdes nodded, satisfied. In the past few months he'd been sorting through homeless men and women, selecting some to perform tasks mundane but necessary. By providing them with a marginally better existence than they'd known and a sense of belonging, Valdes had fostered fierce loyalty within them.

Loyalty I *don't betray.*

He entered the shell of the hospital and descended three flights of stairs, guided by a string of bulbs that George—the mousy former high school shop/English teacher with a penchant for molesting his students—had rigged. At the bottom he made his way along a stained, dripping corridor to a shadowy doorway. He gave a cursory glance around as he unlocked the door but was confident he was alone—everyone knew not to come to this part of the hospital's labyrinthine sub-basements.

Inside, the room was paneled with grimy, chipped tiles and a three-by-three section of metal squares that had once held rolling morgue drawers. There were a few items of furniture: a table and valet chair reclaimed from the junk heap by Melvin, the carpenter on the run from Jamaican authorities for his enthusiastic use of a machete, a standing mirror fogged around the edges by time and moisture, and a battered meat freezer powered by cables coiled, snakelike, around the floor.

Stripping with unconscious efficiency, he walked naked to the valet chair. Gooseflesh rose on his skin but he knew it wasn't from the cool damp. Draped over the chair back was the suit he wore whenever he went to make a sacrifice (murder was so judgmental a word). The dark cloth had a bit of a funk to it but he had come to accept it. According to the book the integrity of the ritual would be spoiled if he washed away any bodily fluids his efforts generated, either his own or those of his sacrifices. He dressed quickly, eager to go out and take another step closer to his ultimate goal.

Before he left the room, he did two things: flipping open the seat of the chair, he removed one of the two remaining black velvet sacks from inside. A blue design—two zigzagging lines resembling waves—was sewn onto it. He traced it with a finger, the material slick under his touch.

"The Water-Bearer," he murmured.

He unhooked a professional's messenger bag from the back of the chair and slipped the sack inside, next to the bone saws and two red candles. He touched everything in the bag, making certain nothing was missing, then turned to the table. On top of it sat the book. The title, *Vade Mecum Flagellum Dei*, had been embossed once but now was nearly invisible from wear. Its midnight purple cover had the texture and warmth of freshly flayed skin—the first time he'd touched it, Valdes had thought it was a living thing. Flipping a bulk of pages over, he revealed a cut-out section; inside was the Sigil of Baphomet he'd worn during each sacrifice. He removed it and looped its chain around his neck. A smile crept across his face.

He closed the cover and left.

SIX

GRASPING AT STRAWS

"Odd." Donovan glanced at his watch. "Conrad's late."

He and Joann sat on a plush orange couch at one of the tables in the lounge of *Daniel*, the epitome of French restaurants in Manhattan. Donovan preferred the bar but had chosen a table in the lounge because he knew Conrad didn't like barstools—they made his feet dangle like a child's.

"That's not like him, but traffic is ridiculous today, with the UN conference."

"He needs a motorcycle." Donovan sipped from his neat Bushmill's. A mental picture of Conrad Clery on a bike made him smile. "I always imagined he'd wear a leather helmet and those really big goggles if he ever got one." She smiled, distracted. He put his hand on hers. "Nervous?"

"About this? No."

"What's wrong?"

"Something is coming down soon at work." She sipped her Chopin martini and shook her head. "Sorry. I promise I won't let it drag us down tonight."

"What kind of thing? With Fullam?"

"Fullam?"

"The zodiac murders thing. He found Capricorn hanging in the Dinkins Shelter." She stared, confused. "You didn't—? I figured because it was in the Dinkins Shelter you would have heard."

"No, I didn't. How do you know about it?"

"Last night, he called Father Carroll to see it and asked him to bring me. Since I had been, ah, celebrating our engagement with some people from work I was not in the best shape, but I went." He explained about the body, the vicuna noose, and the wax at both murder sites. "Fullam thinks he might be able to get DNA samples from it. I'm thinking if the wax isn't from cheap card store candles, it might be mixed with something that will tell Father Carroll and me its ritual use." He cocked his head. "What?"

"I'm trying to grasp that you went to a crime scene high."

"Sort of. But, in fairness, I had no way of knowing I was going to end up there. And it didn't stop me from helping, anyway."

"No, I suppose not." Joann regarded him with a mixture of amusement and disbelief. "If he calls you back with something…you know this is serious, right? I mean, you get that, don't you?"

"What makes you think I don't?"

"You went to a crime scene *high*. It suggests a certain lack of perspective."

He conceded her point. "I'll try to limit doing that to my off hours."

"This man," she persisted, "whoever he is, has murdered people with scorpions, arrows and a noose made of goat hair, in addition to whatever else he came up with for other zodiac signs. That's pretty sick. He also has a giant assistant who tried to kill you once already. You might be working with the police, but they have training and weapons. You don't. I don't want you to get hurt, Donovan."

"I can take care of myself."

"In a bar fight, yes. But this is barely the same *reality* as a bar fight."

"Then it's a good thing I've studied alternate realities."

"Clever." She squeezed his hand. "Don't make me a widow before we're married."

"I promise I won't." He held her eyes and felt the bond between them. She did, too, and they said nothing for a moment.

The waiter brought another round of drinks, breaking the spell. "Anyway," she went on when he'd gone, "whatever the big thing coming on my case, it can't be that. I've been getting signals something's coming for a few days now." She sipped fresh vodka. "Which is why I don't want to think about it tonight. Telling Dad about us is as dramatic as I want to get."

Since Conrad was the most accessible of their parents they'd decided to break the engagement to him in person. *Daniel* was not cheap; Joann knew her father appreciated the luxury of the restaurant, and since it was a little out of Donovan's price range she'd already made arrangements with the maitre d' to pay the check. The gesture touched Donovan even though it made him feel a little odd. He glanced about the lounge, at the people and wealth he knew primarily from the outside looking in.

"Joann, sweetie! Sorry I'm late." Conrad's voice returned him to the present. He rose to meet his father-in-law to be.

"Hi, Dad." Joann also got to her feet. "Don't worry, we just got here ourselves."

"Ah." He embraced her warmly while Donovan stood by. Donovan had learned to extend a hand only at the exact moment Conrad would have no choice but to follow social niceties and shake it. He waited until Joann broke from her father. "Well, it's wonderful to see you. And hello, Donovan." He shook Donovan's hand briefly. His face grew serious as he turned back to her. "I'm glad you asked me to dinner. I've heard one or two things lately, and maybe I can give you a head's-up."

"About Dinkins?" Joann asked as they sat.

"As a matter of fact—" Conrad raised his arm for the waiter. "I have a friend at the *Times*. He was told the mayor is going to offer his perspective on the issue. He told me the mayor's perspective will be that the Brooklyn DA ought to press forward with the prosecutions of the homeless people you've got now. He feels time is being wasted by searching for this 'Charming Man,' if he even exists."

Donovan felt Joann tense at his side. "How does Raphael feel about that?" she asked.

Raphael, Donovan knew, was Raphael Suarez, the Brooklyn District Attorney, Joann's boss.

"He won't have a choice—this is the mayor of New York City making the call."

"This is what happens when rich people get into political office," Donovan said. "They think they can play king and rule by decree."

Conrad gave him a sideways glance. "As I understand it, he's planning to mention it in his press conference about the new crime bill, next Thursday or Friday."

"How am I supposed to find Charming Man before then?"

"I'm sorry, sweetie, I don't know." Conrad looked past them and nodded. A waiter approached, carrying a silver ice bucket with a bottle of Veuve Cliquot Grand Dame inside. "But let's set all that aside for tonight. I think a little celebration is in order, no?"

Donovan's eyebrows rose. "You know?"

"I've been an attorney for longer than you've been alive, Donovan." Genuine happiness—an emotion Donovan had rarely seen from the man—lit his face. "I know how to read signs."

With an effort Donovan noted, Joann put the Dinkins Shelter away, smiled and held out her ring for inspection. "Isn't it beautiful? Donovan designed it himself."

Conrad glanced at him with mild surprise before leaning in and raising his glasses to see it up close. "Very nice."

"I have a friend in the jewelry business."

The hostess approached and told them their table was ready. "Have the champagne brought over," Conrad directed Donovan, putting an arm around Joann to guide her away. With a smile, she stood her ground until Donovan took care of it. Conrad's smile never left his face as he went a few steps ahead, waving to a crony. Donovan would have hated to play poker against him.

"He seems to be taking it well," he murmured in Joann's ear as they wove through the dinner crowd to their table. "Is there another shoe to drop?"

She kissed his cheek. "You can handle him."

And, at least for dinner, he did.

ↀ

The mayor's impending involvement in the Dinkins Shelter case had Joann spooked, and over the next few days she put in long hours at the DA's office. Donovan saw little of her. Although he was also working, he felt her absence acutely when he had to settle for brief, longing phone calls stolen from her job. He hated the helplessness he felt for her situation and wished he could offer some kind of assistance. The only way he could think that would allow him to help, though, would have to involve Fullam. He'd heard nothing from the sergeant since they'd parted, leaving him at a dead end. It was a frustrating situation, but at least he was consoled by the prospect of their weekly date.

ↀ

"But it's Wednesday," Donovan said into his cell. "Dance House, remember? Practice for the wedding? You still have time to get home and change."

"*I know, baby, but I have to work. I'm sorry.*"

Damn. "Don't worry about it. I can reschedule the class." Disappointed, he dropped down onto his couch. *Wonder what time the Mets are on?* "You sound exhausted."

"*You have no idea.*"

"Maybe you could take a break? I could come by the office with some takeout." He looked at the pile of menus near his door, menus he knew he'd better clean up soon if he didn't want to see cockroaches. "I mean, you must get time for dinner, right?"

"*No, I…*" She sighed. "*I'm not at the office.*"

"Where are you?"

"*I can't really talk about it. I'm sorry about Dance House. Whenever you reschedule will be fine. I'll make sure I'm not working.*"

"All right." He idly reached for the remote. "Call me if you can. I'll get some takeout and be here."

"*Okay, baby. I love you. I'm sorry. Have a good night.*"

"I love you, too. Bye." He closed his cell. "Damn. That *sucks.*"

He put the phone on the table and went to see what takeout menus had been jammed under his door that day. On the coffee table, his phone buzzed. He took a pile of menus and went to get it, saw it was Joann's cell and paused. *She changed her mind, I hope…?*

"*Mister Graham?*" Fullam's voice surprised him. "*I understand you're free tonight?*"

☙

The setting sun washed the sky red and purple, pollution from the rush-hour exodus making the colors extra vibrant. Donovan's favorite thing about summer in New York was the sunsets. The gorgeous colors almost made up for the humidity that turned the city to soup until October.

Beneath this picturesque canopy he guided his Vulcan down the West Side Highway, through the Brooklyn Battery Tunnel and along the edge of Bay Ridge on the Belt Parkway. He was headed out to Coney Island, to the New York Aquarium, to join the lieutenant and Joann. As he rode, he thought about what Fullam had told him.

A man found drowned out in the swamps near JFK missing his lower legs—definitely Aquarius. Makes sense to look for Pisces out at the aquarium.

A tiny thrill tightened his stomach.

He called me to get involved. He must think I can do more. Or, he's desperate. But why is Joann there? What does she know?

To avoid tipping their presence, Fullam asked that he not bring his bike near the aquarium. Instead, Donovan took the Stillwell exit to Neptune Avenue and parked on West 8th Street opposite the 60th Precinct. In the near-distance KeySpan Park, stadium of the Brooklyn Cyclones, shone as a beacon of minor league baseball. Down the block and across Surf Avenue, crowds had shifted from the beach to the rides and eclectic attractions of Coney Island's boardwalk. Donovan watched them and again felt the thrill, the secret thrill of having knowledge others didn't. Tonight at the aquarium, he was looking for a murderer.

Beats the hell out of pouring mojitos in midtown.

Joann met him at the rear service gate, near the Seaside Pavilion. She was dressed in dark jeans and a long-sleeved t-shirt, with a rough plastic pistol on her belt. Donovan recognized it as a taser. "Hey, babe," he said, embracing her. "Are you okay? You look really fried."

"Gee, thanks."

"You know what I mean."

She nodded. "Dad was right—the mayor is going to make his opinion about Dinkins known tomorrow. It'll force Raphael to take me off the case and give it to Jessie Parker."

Jessie Parker, Donovan knew, was another rising attorney at the DA's office. "Ow."

"Yeah. So this is, I think, my last shot at Charming Man."

"Charming Man here? How? Why?"

"After you told me about the Capricorn victim being found in the Dinkins Shelter, I started thinking. I talked to Frank, and we agreed it was possible the location was chosen because the killer was familiar with it, which meant Charming Man and Mister X *could* be the same person. He agreed to let me speak with Mabel Muglia at the Church of the Transfiguration. I showed her the pictures we got of Charming Man off the shelter camera, and she said it *could* be him."

"That's a lot of 'could.'"

"It's all I have. Frank is still scrambling around trying to get help for this, so he has no problem with me being here. He found the Aquarius victim two days ago, and we've been staking out this place since. We've had his partner, Josh Braithwaite, with us up to now, but he couldn't make it tonight."

"So he asked me."

"You *and* Father Carroll."

Donovan blinked. "Father Carroll is here?"

"They're both in the security office. Are you ready for this?"

"What do you mean?"

"I mean, this isn't a crime scene that you go to even though you're high. This is serious. Are you ready?"

Donovan examined her face and body language. The stress he saw made him more determined to help. "Absolutely."

∽

Not as big or elaborate as a Sea World, the New York Aquarium is part of a chain of parks run by the New York Zoological Society. Although Donovan hadn't been here in years—the Aquatheater and the *Alien Stingers* buildings were both new to him—he had fond memories from when he was younger. The first motorcycle ride he'd taken on the back of his uncle's Harley-Davidson had been to Coney Island; they'd come here to see the sharks.

Joann led him through the aquarium to the entrance hall. Inside, the lighting was low and the air cool. Tanks set into the walls glowed with artificial illumination and natural colors. To their left, a series of large windows revealed a lively collection of reef fish darting about the coral. Ahead was the security office door and the public entrance to the grounds.

The security office was a videogamer's dream—small, with everything reachable while sitting at the monitor console. The console monitored a half-dozen television screens that showed the park's attractions and various sites. Gray carpet lined the walls as it had in the entry hall.

Fullam turned from the monitors and extended his hand as they entered. "Mister Graham. Glad you could make it."

"Sergeant. Call me Donovan." Donovan noted that, instead of his black priest attire, Father Carroll wore a dark blue chamois shirt and dark blue slacks, but no collar. "Working undercover, I see." The priest smiled tightly and also shook his hand. Donovan looked at Fullam. "We're it?"

"My partner couldn't make it tonight so, yeah, just us four. You've been capable so far. Can you handle it?"

Donovan glanced at Joann. "Yeah, I can."

"Good." Fullam gestured to a map of the aquarium on one wall. "Without manpower we can't watch every access point into the aquarium, so you, Maurice and I will be staked out at various points inside the grounds, the most likely sites for the murder. Joann will be Big Sister in here, keeping an overview. We, the curator and the cleaning crew are the only ones who are on the grounds right now. Once they're gone, we wait."

Donovan looked at the office wall, at a list of hazardous fish and the immediate medical treatment for each. "He's got a hell of a choice, but why here? Why tonight?"

"We don't have many options." Fullam eyed him. "I mean, you could be right. He could just stab someone with a plastic fish in the toy department of Macy's, or in a back alley somewhere."

"Suffering seems to be a key in these murders, as does a certain sense of the theatrical," the priest added. "Stabbing someone with a toy lacks the dramatic flair of, say, attacking piranha."

"Not perfect circumstances," Joann said, her eyes going hopefully to the monitor screens, "but at least straws to grasp."

༨

The curator, Dick Katz, left first, and the cleaning crew finished at nine o'clock. Donovan and Father Carroll stayed out of sight in the aquarium entrance hall while Fullam escorted everyone out.

"You seem pretty calm," Donovan observed, idly tapping on the glass of a tank. "Don't you think anything's going to happen?"

"It may or may not. The Lord has a plan which we don't always understand."

"So if a murder happens tonight, it's God's will?" Donovan frowned. "God sanctions murder? That sounds kind of harsh."

"Allow me to re-phrase: I think people act in ways that don't honor God, but may be necessary to His plan. Since we can't know all the designs of that plan, all we can do is follow our faith and believe we are doing right."

"Hmm. Sounds like a bit of a cop-out."

"Cop-out assumes there is a knowable answer. There is not, not in this lifetime." Father Carroll smiled. "We do the best we can. The rest is in God's hands. Once you accept that, life loses much of its anxiety."

"If you say so. I'd rather keep things in *my* hands, and not bother Him."

Fullam appeared and motioned them to follow him. "There are pretty much three places to commit the Pisces murder in here," he said. "The Shark Tank, *Alien Stingers*, and the blue-ringed octopus. If we focus our efforts there, maybe we can let him in, but not out."

He led them through the plaza, past the penguins and the sea otters, and descended stone steps that led into the "underwater viewing" section of the Sea Cliffs. Inside, the exhibit wound beneath and behind the outside cliffs in a high, wide tunnel. To their right the walls were dominated by thick slabs of glass that served as viewing windows into enclosures of the penguins, sea otters, fur seals, sea lions and walruses.

Cute, Donovan thought, watching small furry animals swim and frolic.

The left side had dozens of pictures of animals, fish and seabirds as well as maps and a few interactive exhibits. A life-size replica of a walrus sat in the middle of one section—Donovan was surprised how big it was—while another section had a model of a killer whale's head rising from the floor.

"The octopus tanks are over here," Fullam said, leading them past glass tanks filled with colorful sea horses. Donovan paused to look at them and felt an odd sensation. He shook it off and followed the others to stand in front of two windows that revealed a large rock wall. Plaques in front of the tanks identified the species of octopi, but the one that interested them was *hapalochlaena maculosa,* the lesser blue-ringed octopus.

"This may be our murder weapon," the sergeant said.

The creature was small, its body about three inches long with an arm span twice that. Donovan skimmed the information and learned that the blue-ringed octopus is reported to be the most poisonous of the cephalopods. Normally grayish-beige, the octopus has light brown patches that darken and show bright blue rings when it's irritated or threatened. It secretes two poisons, the more dangerous being a neuromuscular venom that paralyzes all the muscles of the body, including the lungs and heart.

"Maurice, why don't you stay here?" Fullam asked. "If our man is going to use this thing, he'll have to get inside the staff area, which is only accessible over there." He nodded at a door marked "Authorized Personnel Only." "Are you okay with that?"

"Of course." A seal torpedoed at one of the glass walls, only to turn away at the last instant with a blink of his huge black eyes and a flick of his flippers. "At least I have interesting company."

"Can I make a suggestion?" The sergeant indicated at a recessed corner. "Pick a spot where no one can see you on first entrance. We have no real certainty how, when or if this will happen, so…"

"Best to be cautious. I understand. God watch over you, gentlemen."

"You, too."

Donovan followed Fullam out.

☙

"You ever been on stakeout before?"

Donovan shook his head.

"You want *Alien Stingers* or the Shark Tank?"

"Makes no difference to me. Wherever I'll do the most good."

"Take *Alien Stingers*," Fullam suggested. "It might keep you awake. Could be a long night."

"You don't think anything is going to happen?"

"It could happen here, it could happen tonight, it could happen tomorrow or somewhere else. This is a pretty good guess for *my* case. Your fiancée probably has the right expression for hers: 'grasping at straws.'"

"She told you we're engaged?"

"I'm a detective. I figured it out when I saw the ring." Fullam looked at him, cop eyes tempered with amusement. "Congratulations."

"Thanks. You don't think Mister X and Charming Man are the same person?"

"I don't know enough to make a guess, so I won't." Fullam scratched his neck. "It seems like a long shot to me."

Donovan gestured around them. "What do you think the odds are of something happening tonight?"

"No idea. Frankly—and no offense to your fiancée, I understand she's got a lot riding on the Dinkins Shelter case—I hope nothing does happen tonight. Tomorrow I'll have Josh and maybe one or two other detectives to help. I'll feel a lot better with them having my back rather than two civilians and an ADA. Again, no offense."

"If it's any consolation, I'm not high tonight."

Fullam grunted.

"Seriously," Donovan went on, "I had no idea I was going to go to a crime scene that night. Believe me, I never would have smoked or had anything to drink if I'd known."

"Well, that's why you have to be ready all the time in this work: you never know when you're in for a surprise."

Before Donovan could answer him, Fullam's radio beeped.

"*Frank, I've got Mister Katz on the line,*" Joann said. "*Apparently one of the cleaning crew left some keys here. Mister Alcantarilla was able to get Katz before he got too far and asked if they could come back.*"

"Case in point." Fullam shook his head and lifted the radio to his mouth. "All right, I'll go let him in. Tell him to meet me at the back gate."

"*Check. Also, before we get started, I want to hit the ladies' room.*"

"Fine. Let me know when you're back." He clipped the radio to his belt and turned to Donovan. "Anything else?"

"Do you want me to come with?"

Fullam shook his head. "This will go faster if I do it alone—I'll get them in and out. Take the *Alien Stingers* building—the Sea Wasp set-up is a lot like the octopus one. After I let Katz and Alcantarilla out I'll take a spot by the Aquatheater and watch the Shark Tank."

"Got it."

"If you see anything, let me or Joann know immediately. I appreciate your help, but this is something for professionals to handle."

"I understand."

"Okay. Stay in touch. Like I said, this could be a long night."

SEVEN

PISCES

"You won't have any trouble getting into the aquarium now," Dick Katz said. "You can let us go."

He and Ben Alcantarilla sat tied together in the back of the Alcantarilla Cleaning Experts truck. Valdes crouched beside them, holding the cell phone for the curator to speak into. A single overhead bulb illuminated the truck's cargo area. The giant lurked on the edge of the light, a nightmare emerged from under the bed.

Valdes snapped the cell phone closed. "We may need help with other things."

"Don't you animal rights people have some fur coats to throw paint on? We at the Zoological Society give our animals the finest care! There's no need to set them free!"

The giant snorted. "Animals? That's not why—"

"Coeus." Valdes shot him a warning look. "Animal Freedom Fighters believes *any* imprisonment of animals is wrong. As one of the animal oppressors, you *have* to help us liberate them."

"And then you'll kill us!"

"The police lied to make you more afraid, more easily manipulated according to their whims." Valdes showed him a gentle smile. "I'm no murderer. In fact, I'm…a judge."

"A judge? Please, Your Honor," Alcantarilla pleaded. "Don't hurt me. I just clean the aquarium. Sometimes I even sneak food to the penguins

57

when no one's looking." His eyes darted to Coeus, whose bowed head scraped the truck's ceiling. "I love animals," he sobbed. "Really, I do. Don't kill me. Please."

"Do what I tell you," Valdes said, "and I won't." He slid open the little door between the truck's back and its cab. "Let's head out, Lude. To the back gate." He handed the security pass card he'd taken from Katz's pocket through the slot. "This will raise the security gate in the parking lot."

"Yes, sir, Mister Valdes, sir!" The chubby girl handled the card like the sole valentine she'd gotten in third grade. "I'll get us there right away." She tugged the "Alcantarilla Cleaning Experts" baseball cap over her greasy blonde hair and seized the steering wheel in a death grip. "You can count on me!"

e/o

Donovan crossed the little wooden bridge above the pond outside the *Alien Stingers* building and stepped inside. The lighting in here was as low as it had been at the Sea Cliffs; enough illumination to see but not enough to startle the fish. *Alien Stingers* was all about jellyfish, anemones and corals, set in a hall with an unworldly, almost psychedelic feel. Bright, fluorescent backdrops highlighted towers of water while translucent creatures drifted among glistening silver bubbles. The floor, walls and ceiling of the room were black, intensifying the colors and making Donovan feel like he ought to smoke a joint before going any further.

Not while I'm working. But there's always tomorrow.

The colony of sea wasps, white against a bright red backdrop, was in its own tank, as though its deadliness required solitary confinement. The tank itself was a column of water that extended from floor to ceiling, with black rocks at the base and tendrils of green plant grasping skyward. He stared for a moment before reading the small, adjacent placard. The sea wasp, also known as a box jellyfish or boxfish, species *chironex fleckeri*, has a poison that attacks nerves, skin and the heart, causing excruciating pain before finally killing. Any attempt to remove the stinging tentacles makes them stickier and drives the poison deeper. He remembered the scorpions that had killed Mark Denschler and frowned.

Nasty, brutal stuff.

Here in the muffled, psychedelic room, he allowed himself free rein to think.

You wanted to help, here you are. He thought about Father Carroll's words, and about plans he might never understand. *Now what?*

 es

"Watch your mirror," Valdes instructed Lude. "Let me know when the gate opens."

She grunted, all her concentration focused on backing the truck up to the gate. The pink tip of her tongue wormed free.

"Now once we go, drive around to the front and wait there," Valdes directed her. "Also, at the risk of sounding like a comic-book bank robber, keep the engine running. I'll be back before you know it."

"Gotcha! I'll be ready to go!"

Her enthusiasm kept Valdes's smile alive for another second before he turned to Coeus. "You know what to do when the gate opens," he said.

"I'm not *stupid*," the giant growled.

Valdes hauled Katz to his feet. "You're coming with us."

"It's opening!" Lude called. "The gate's opening!"

This is it.

Valdes savored the moment before nodding to Coeus. The giant slammed both of the back doors open. Valdes caught a glimpse of a sharply-dressed man standing outside. Coeus stormed from the truck, snatched the man by the shoulders and lifted him off the ground. The man shouted in surprise. Coeus slammed him to the cement and stomped a boot down. The man managed to roll away, rising to his knees as he drew a gun. Coeus growled and lashed a backhand out, sending the man and the gun flying in different directions. The gun hit the ground, bounced once and fired. The bullet ricocheted off a metal pole that supported a huge picnic area tent.

"Donovan!" the man yelled, staggering upright.

"Coeus, shut him up." Valdes climbed down from the truck, pushing Katz ahead of him. "We have work to do."

Coeus leapt forward, snatched the man's lapels and flung him like a pillow. The man flew into the picnic area, slid over a table, and crashed to the ground in a motionless heap.

es

The more he wandered, the more heightened Donovan's sense of unreality became.

Staking out a satanic murderer in the New York Aquarium? Yes, Father, reality is an extremely *flexible concept.*

Rather than scaring him, the adrenaline rush had him ready, eager, to see what came next. He shook his head and smiled to himself.

Stay cool. Coming across like a hyperactive five-year-old won't just screw your reputation, but Joann's too. And if you ever want Fullam to ask for help again…

He stood still, eyes closed, breathing deeply, allowing his mind to calm. The nerves and anxiety quieted, but in the place where he should have been relaxed he still felt restless. He consciously loosened his muscles, but they tightened as soon as he opened his eyes. It was a sensation he'd experienced before, one whose meaning he'd never quite grasped. In this context he understood and, for an instant, the clarity of it startled him.

I'm restless because I'm in the wrong place.

He left *Alien Stingers* by the southern door. A picnic area sat adjacent to the building, filled with one-piece table/benches, shaded by an enormous tent. Next to it, the back gate stood open and deserted. The air was still and thick. Donovan peered around the corner. No one was there, no vehicle stood in the narrow alley leading to it. A faint waft of diesel floated within. His heart began to beat faster.

If they came and went, Fullam wouldn't have left the gate open. If they came and are still here, where's the truck?

He turned from the gate and scanned the area. No one was in sight, no shadows moved, but something lay on the concrete: Fullam's gun.

Oh no.

A groan and movement in his peripheral vision made Donovan jump. He whipped the taser from his back pocket. About thirty feet away he saw a figure struggling to stand.

"Sergeant?"

"Don't—worry about me, goddammit!" The arm Fullam used to brace himself to stand folded. He collapsed, banging against the table before he hit the ground. "Mister X! Him and the giant have got Katz!" He flung an arm outward. "Stop them!"

Donovan clutched the taser's black pistol grip, eyes raking the area as he pulled out his radio. "Joann! Call 9-1-1! They're here, and they've got Katz!"

"*What?*" Panic in her voice was a cattle prod in his stomach. "*Who? I see the truck in front on one monitor, but—*"

"Frank's hurt! They have Katz!"

His urgency cut through to her, and he heard her prosecutor voice when she spoke. "*I'm on it! 9-1-1! Be careful!*"

"*What's happening?*" Father Carroll's voice chimed in. "*I don't see anything! Donovan, where are you?*"

"Father, there's nobody there? You don't see them?"

He heard the priest scuffling around the exhibit. "*No, nothing! I don't see them!*"

Dread swelled his lungs as he fought to breathe. *That means*— "Go help Fullam! He's in the picnic area next to *Alien Stingers*!"

"*What about you?*"

"They're not at the octopus or jellyfish!" He started to run. "They've got to be at the Shark Tank!"

⁊

Coeus carried Katz slung over one shoulder like a side of beef, using both hands to keep the curator's struggles under control. Valdes let the giant precede him up the stairs inside the building, then closed and locked the door.

"Keep him quiet until I set everything up," he instructed.

⁊

The Shark Tank itself is enclosed within a larger building whose front is lined with oversized picture windows. A wooden tunnel encloses these windows, darkening the space to allow better viewing of the sharks, rays and sea turtles within. On the walls inside this tunnel are a series of large illustrations describing how sharks are "our friends." Donovan ran across the plaza, past the photo booth, followed the outside of the tunnel to one end and slammed into the fence on the far side of the building. He searched for the "Authorized Personnel Only" door but he was on the wrong end of the tunnel.

Damn!

To his left the tunnel beckoned, pitch dark and mysterious. He stuffed the radio into his pocket, shifted the taser to his right hand and put his left hand on the tunnel wall. He'd just started in when lights flickered from inside the building and illuminated the tank. He went to the window, his face illuminated a ghostly greenish-white. Startled stingrays skimmed the tank floor, kicking up clouds of silt. Sea turtles and the sawfish darted about.

The sharks circled.

Eight swam in the tank: a small but aggressive female lemon shark, a lazy sandbar shark, and the largest ones, six sand tigers. Five were females, all from eight to ten feet, with a nine-foot male to court them. Long-healed gashes and scars in the sandpaper hides evidenced his efforts. Tails propelled the sharks along their preprogrammed ovular tracks, eyes never moving, jaws never entirely closing. He pressed his face to the glass and searched for the surface beyond the water, where Katz might be. He could only make out shapes. Something glinted and slashed down. Fluid spurted over the tank, and viscous red drops trailed to the sandy floor.

Blood in the water.

The sharks broke their circle. Donovan saw a struggle on the platform. A huge shadow—the giant, Donovan realized—threw something that hit the water with a cannonball splash: Katz. His feet had been cut off.

A cold wind blew through the tunnel. Donovan's muscles hardened. Every nerve ending screamed about the presence, the evil, now in the air. It was everything he'd studied in books and never believed could be real. Suddenly he wanted to be back in midtown pouring drinks, doing anything but standing in front of the shark tank seeing this. He beat a fist on the glass.

"*No!*"

Katz struggled to escape, kicking feebly. His movement swirled the blood around, casting the scent wider. The lemon shark plunged through the widening cloud of red. Two of the sand tigers dove in, one driving her snout into his stomach before twisting to bite his ribs. The other seized a leg and dragged him under. Donovan had a complete, hellish view of the frenzy. The rest of the sand tigers attacked, eyes rolling backwards as they bit. Teeth shredded cloth and flesh, turning the water murky with gory debris. Incredibly the curator still lived, thrashing his way towards the side. One of the ten-foot sand tigers sped up behind him and slammed him into the glass in front of Donovan. Donovan jumped but he didn't— he *couldn't*—tear his gaze away. Katz's face contorted, pleading for help, and his eyes rolled back in a ghastly parody of the attacking fish. Another shark came, and another. They seized his remaining limbs in their jaws and pulled. The last bubbles burst from the curator's lungs as they tore him to pieces.

"Donovan!"

Father Carroll half-carried, half-dragged Fullam along the tunnel. The sergeant's hair and clothing were mussed but he clutched his Glock with determination. The priest stared at the scene in the tank and groaned.

"They got him." Donovan pushed off the window. The cruelty he'd seen ignited an anger he'd never experienced, one that burned away his fear. "But they're still inside."

He led them to the tunnel's other end, where a wooden fence with a door prevented them from going further. Donovan couldn't get the vision of Katz's hell out of his head, and he let it feed his anger. He took a step back and threw his weight against the wooden slats. They splintered and slammed inwards. The "Authorized Personnel Only" door was five feet beyond it, leading into the tank's building. This door, however, was heavier, and it took the combined effort of Donovan and Father Carroll to break it down. Fullam took the lead, limping up the flight of stairs they found. Donovan noticed his arm hung oddly from his shoulder but he managed to keep his gun ready.

The stairs led up to a platform that ringed about sixty percent of the tank. A narrow walkway bordered the rest. Fish-stink overpowered them, permeating the white walls and staining the rubber-matted floor. Buckets of food were stacked neatly along the platform rear, in a glass-fronted refrigerator next to steel shelves of SCUBA, cleaning and maintenance equipment. Above the water, ropes and pulleys led to a skylight that, presumably, allowed new sharks to be lowered directly into the tank. The skylight stood partway open in deference to the night's warmth. Near the edge of the platform, in the middle of a fresh pool of blood, red wax shimmered while it cooled to solid. At the platform's far end, a door stood open, revealing more stairs that led to the roof.

Fullam let out a yell of warning. Donovan dove forward, skidding through a puddle of splashed water as the giant swung an arm the size of a construction crane. He ducked and hammered punches into the giant's side and exposed kidney. It was like hitting a cinder block, and about as effective at moving one. The giant swept his arm back. His elbow caught Donovan on the side of the head and spun him around. Blackness swirled at the edge of his vision. Behind him he heard Father Carroll suck back his fright. Blue sparks arced and the giant bellowed. He grabbed the priest's arm and swung him around so hard Father Carroll's feet left the ground and sailed above the tank's churning surface. The taser went flying across the platform as the giant let go, sending Father Carroll crashing into an equipment rack.

"Nice try, *priest*," the giant sneered

"Coeus!" A new voice came from the doorway, commanding the giant.

"Let's go!"

Donovan shook his head clear in time to see Coeus stomp towards the far door; the lights seemed to get brighter as he got further away. Fullam got to his knees and tried to aim with his awkward arm. The giant stopped, seized a rack that must have weighed over six hundred pounds, and lifted it above his head. Equipment, valves and flippers bounced everywhere. Donovan dove at Fullam and knocked him flat as the steel rack flew above them. With a deafening screech of metal against concrete it clattered down the stairs they'd just come up.

Father Carroll scrambled to his feet and lunged at the giant. Coeus laughed, an odd, staccato sound, and seized the priest's shirtfront. Father Carroll beat at the enormous hands ineffectively. The giant marched towards the edge of the tank, eyes wide with anticipation. The priest tottered back, hands waving wildly. One foot slipped off the platform—

Donovan crab-scuttled across the slick floor, through blood and fish guts and the cooling wax, and slammed an uppercut between Coeus' legs. The giant howled and staggered back. Father Carroll wrestled free from his grip but staggered above the blood-frothed water. Coeus retreated with a grunt. Father Carroll yelled as he lost his balance.

"Father!"

Donovan grabbed him by the belt buckle. Father Carroll grabbed his wrist. His momentum almost carried them both into the tank before Donovan heaved backwards, dragging them onto the platform.

"Come on!" Fullam barked, already back on his feet.

Coeus saw him coming and shot his arms out, hauling two more racks down across the doorway. Fullam pulled up short and reached to pull one aside.

"Don't touch it!" Donovan shouted.

From around the corner of the doorway, the killer's hand pressed Father Carroll's taser against the steel. Fullam saw and jerked his hand back. The killer jammed the taser, still on, between the doorframe and one of the racks.

Fullam bounced around the doorway looking for a way through, but the sizzling of the wet, electrified metal stopped him. Father Carroll sat dazed by a pool of Dick Katz's blood. Donovan eyed the ropes over the tank. Several led directly to the skylight, including the closest. His last thought before moving was, *that can't be more than six feet away.*

Fullam saw him at the last second. "What are you—?"

Donovan took a running start and launched himself over the water. He caught a line with his whole body.

"Are you fucking *nuts?!*"

Donovan didn't hear. His momentum spun him as sweat greased his hands and he slipped a foot. Below, the feeding sharks turned the water to chum. He clutched the line tighter and stopped dropping. Light years away he heard shouts. They were nothing; his existence had narrowed to the rope, the white walls, and his strength. He looked down. Out of the water came a ten foot sand tiger, Katz's torso in her jaws. The curator was dead—

He has *to be!*

—but the sight froze Donovan's heart. The shark jackknifed back into the tank. A mushroom of water and vapor marked the spot. Somebody screamed, maybe it was him, but he shut his ears to it. The skylight was so close…

He flopped onto the rooftop, trembling and winded. An unintelligible grunt came above him. Donovan scrambled to one side. A gigantic boot slammed down where his head had been. Before he could move the boot skipped across the gravel and kicked him hard in the ribs. Donovan gasped and fought the stars from his vision. He kept moving, knowing to stop was death. He pulled himself around the corner of the window. Coeus loomed on the other side, light from below casting satanic shadows across his face. Donovan saw the dark-haired man climb down over the edge of the building. The giant barred pursuit, clenching and unclenching his fists.

"Coeus!" The killer's voice drifted up from the ground. "Forget him! Go!"

Donovan crawled to his feet, keeping the opening between them. Coeus feinted and stepped back. Donovan blinked. In that instant he lost sight of the giant. It was as though Coeus had merged with the night.

❦

Lock the door behind you and keep the taser handy.

Donovan's words echoed in Joann's mind as she searched the screens fruitlessly for several minutes. A flash here, a glimmer there taunted her until she couldn't stand it anymore. She picked up the taser, wondering if this was how the guards had felt when all hell broke loose at the Dinkins Shelter.

Down the short hall was the door leading to the aquarium entrance, to the lobby where the ticket booth sat bracketed by glass doors. She swallowed and gently turned the knob. Scarlet "exit" signs reflected off the glass of the lobby's reef exhibit. Outside, the white running lights of the Coney Island Cyclone strobed. Within the reef tank, fish darted among colorful, jagged coral. The kaleidoscope effect made her pause, adjusting her eyes before she got dizzy. She looked down and, horrified, saw her shadow extend across the floor—the light from the short hall framed her perfectly in the doorway.

"Target…" She spun to yank the door closed. It was on a hydraulic arm, and after an eternity she felt the latch click. She leaned against it, panting like she'd run a wind sprint. "Jesus, be careful!"

"Sound advice."

The voice startled her. A dark-haired man in a black suit stood a few feet away. In one hand he held a gym bag, in the other a hand axe whose edge glistened wetly. "Good evening, my dear." It was the voice she'd heard described by so many participants in the Dinkins Shelter riot, as soothing as chamomile tea and honey.

Charming Man!

The words spurred her to action. Joann drove the taser at him in an uppercut but the man was obviously expecting something. He dropped the bag and the axe and clamped his hands on her wrists. Surprised, Joann barely managed to stop him from breaking her arm. He pulled her to him, his face a pleasant mask covering something more sinister than murder.

"Sweet dreams."

He wrenched her arm about and jabbed the taser into her stomach. Voltage shot through her nervous system. Joann's muscles stuttered and trembled, and she collapsed to the carpet. Her eyes twitched, unable to focus on anything but the bloody axe inches from her face…

Nothingness swallowed her.

❧

A slim steel pipe propped open one of the skylight windows. Donovan grabbed it for a weapon and scanned the rooftop. Empty. He ran to the edge of the roof. The darkness below was absolute, as empty as the ocean at night.

Movement at his eye level snapped his head up. Running across the top the Sea Cliffs building, silhouetted against the Coney Island nimbus, was Coeus. Donovan scrambled to follow, taking a long running start before jumping across the gap between the Shark Tank building and the Sea Cliffs. He didn't quite make it. His stomach crashed into the edge of the Cliffs building, and he almost lost his weapon scrambling to gain a foothold. He swung a knee over and pulled himself up in time to see Coeus climb over the aquarium fence and drop to the Boardwalk below. Clutching the pipe, Donovan bolted after him. He climbed the fence, dropped to the Boardwalk—

Coeus towered above him. Donovan dove as the giant snatched at his head. He came to his feet swinging the pipe at Coeus's knees. The giant howled, staggering but remaining upright. Donovan pivoted in for another swing. Coeus seized him by the scruff of the neck. Donovan tried to curl his body. The monstrous fist pounded him, lifting him off the ground. He gagged but refused to throw up all over the giant's shoes. Coeus stepped back and dropped him. Donovan lurched upright and jabbed two quick lefts into the giant's nose. They were good, solid punches that made the giant reel. He snatched the steel pipe and swiped it viciously. Coeus stumbled to his knees. Donovan stepped up for a home-run swing at the enormous, misshapen head. The giant caught Donovan's arm, grabbed his belt and hoisted him up. Donovan twisted and writhed in his grip. Coeus growled and started to bend Donovan's body backwards. Just then, finally, sirens began to wail along Surf Avenue. The giant hesitated. With a frustrated snort he hurled Donovan across the Boardwalk. Donovan belly-flopped on the beach and rolled against an overflowing garbage can. Grains of sand skid-burned into his skin. By the time he'd untangled himself, Coeus had pounded almost to the West 8th Street subway station.

He grabbed the pipe and followed.

The giant crossed above Surf Avenue. Below, oblivious, units from the 60th Precinct, ambulances, even a pair of fire trucks raced through the streets and blasted through the security gate barring the aquarium parking lot. Sirens screamed above the music and laughter of Coney Island. Flashing lights tinted everything as red as the water of the shark tank. Donovan held the pipe and sprinted up the walkway.

The token clerk sat in her crime-proof booth, eyes shocked wide. "The giant!" Donovan shouted. "Which way?"

A train screeched along the tracks above their heads, slowing to a stop. The clerk's mouth worked but no sound came out. She brought one arm up and pointed.

"Go down and get some of those cops up here! Now!"

He vaulted the turnstile. Breath hissed from his throat as he pounded up the stairs. He stuck his head out and scanned the bottom one for the giant. No sign. He ran to the top and braced himself in the entranceway. The waiting train had cheerful yellow and orange seats, and all of its lights worked. Red bulbs were next to every door, lit to show the doors were still open. Donovan began to run down the platform, scanning—

A black-sleeved I-beam shot out from one door, swiping at his head. Donovan jerked out of the way and stumbled to the ground. Coeus lunged from the train. The doors slid shut, and the train moved forward. Its interior lights highlighted the massive silhouette. Donovan swallowed. He scrambled to his feet and backed to an open section on the platform, where he could fully swing the pipe.

Where the hell are the cops?

The giant sprang forward. Donovan smacked the steel across his cheek. Coeus snarled and swung crazily. Donovan danced back. He risked a glance behind him—he was running out of platform, and the only escape was across of both sets of tracks and two electrified third rails. He leapt down onto the tracks, quickly spun and clubbed the giant's tree-trunk ankles. His wrists flinched at the shock of hitting bone.

A few hundred yards away, on the opposite tracks, came a Manhattan-bound train.

The giant crouched low, grabbing for him. Donovan ducked and swung again, this time striking elbow.

"Ow! You hit my funny bone!" His words, spoken in the rasping growl, shocked Donovan. He stared, puzzled, at this childish reaction. The moment passed, and fresh rage coursed through the giant. "I'm gonna kill you!"

He jumped down. The train drew nearer. Donovan made sure to keep its lights at his back. The giant faltered; even in his psychotic state he resisted the bright light. Donovan picked his way over the humming third rails. The train rumbled closer, air-horn blaring. Donovan blocked out the sonic blast and waved the pipe, taunting. The giant took the bait and came for him. Donovan saw the train lights reflecting nearer in the frighteningly pale face. He swung the pipe at the giant's ribs. The giant snatched it. They played a brief tug-of-war before Donovan relinquished his grip. He plunged at the monstrous midsection and hammered body blows with both fists. The giant kneed Donovan in the chest. Donovan tottered backwards.

The conductor stomped his emergency brake. Sparks showered.

Coeus was mindless of everything but Donovan's death. The pipe was a toothpick in his ham-fist. "You can't beat me! I'm bigger and stronger!"

Donovan felt the ground shake. "But I'm smarter."

Squealing train wheels drowned the giant's response. He swept the pipe at Donovan's head. Donovan feinted and leapt back to the empty tracks. The pipe struck the third rail. The giant screamed as the electricity shot up his nervous system. Every sinew crackled, bending even his might. Roast pork smoked the air. His feet shuffled and his hair began to smolder. Donovan covered his head with his arms. The train rattled and groaned. Its headlights blinked as the power level fluctuated but the momentum was not to be denied. The giant just managed to release the pipe as the front of the train smashed into him.

Or did it?

As Donovan watched, incredulously, the train picked up speed. In a few moments it had disappeared into the night, leaving only the faintest echo of the staccato laugh:

Ha-Ha-Ha-Ha...

EIGHT

FALLOUT

After the aquarium, working the bar at Polaris was a surreal experience.

Donovan stayed on autopilot throughout the next night. Mindlessly he poured cocktails while navigating memories of the horror he'd seen, the anger it had inspired at the perpetrator, and the semi-guilty thrill of his actions in response to both. What he'd seen, what he'd done, stirred something within him that made both school and bartending unbearably boring and unutterably reassuring. *Reality is flexible.*

He wasn't closing that night, so it was a pleasant surprise to see Joann enter as his shift was ending.

"I have had a bad day and I wish to get drunk," she said. "Would you care to join me?"

Images of Katz being torn apart on the other side of the shark tank glass filled his mind's eye. "Absolutely."

❧

The night was warm with a breeze chasing humidity from the narrow streets of Greenwich Village. Donovan parked on Seventh Avenue South, and they went into Sushi Samba. The bright tropical colors of the rooftop bar, the greens and oranges and reds, lightened the room but not the mood. They grabbed the last two seats at the end of the bar and settled

70

in with a round of cocktails; Chopin martini, up, for her, a concoction with strawberry vodka called a *nina fresa* for him. He sipped it. *Good thing I'm secure enough in my masculinity to order paper umbrella drinks.* "I'm assuming the mayor's press conference went the way you expected this afternoon?"

"Did you get to see any of it?"

"We had the news on at the bar at one point, but no sound."

"It was quite a show." She took a long swallow. "As expected, he singled out Raphael by name as one of the main causes why the Dinkins case was going nowhere. His poll numbers have been slipping, and Raphael is a probable opponent next election. Raphael had no choice but to pull me this afternoon and give it to Jesse."

"He gave no credence to what happened at the aquarium?"

"Privately, yes. When we talked, I got the impression he would have been willing to give me more slack. But publicly..." She raised her glass. "Here's to the mayor being the recipient of a nice, long taser shock."

"Ow." He rested a hand on her leg. "I'm sorry, Jo."

"The thing is," she said, putting her hand on his and holding it in place, "I'm *sure* that was Charming Man who tasered me. He sort of looked like the partial picture we have of him, but it's more than that. His voice, the way he approached me, his manner—I know it was him. I *know* it."

"That's a pretty big 'sort of'."

She nodded and sipped more vodka.

"But if it's true, it means Charming Man and Mister X *are* the same person, and the Dinkins Shelter case *is* part of the zodiac murders case."

She shook her head. "I can't do anything about it now."

"You can't do a little investigating on your own? I'll help you. I've done pretty well with Sergeant Fullam so far."

She regarded him with a worldly smile. "It doesn't work like that. I appreciate the sentiment, but I have to follow orders. Raphael will find another high profile case for me, I'm sure. And speaking of Frank Fullam..." She dug into her purse and produced a folded envelope. "I had to go see him earlier. He gave me this to give to you."

"What is it?"

"Consulting fee. After everything last night, he figured you had it coming."

Donovan opened the envelope and saw it was a folded sheaf of papers with a check paper-clipped to it. The amount was not huge, but it was a nice, unexpected bonus.

"I looked the paperwork over," she went on. "It's all standard for police consultants. You have to sign them and get them back to him before you can cash the check."

"Really?" Donovan looked dubious. "I was thinking I could do more good outside the system. You know, to avoid having the mayor kick me off the case."

She grimaced. "Doesn't work that way, either. Hugh Yarborough, the Chief of Detectives and Frank's boss, was not amused that he brought civilians along on the stakeout. Father Carroll is already registered with the NYPD as an official consultant; you aren't. You sort of have to sign these to keep him off the hook."

"He works at Midtown North, right?" Donovan disliked being constrained but didn't want to see Fullam get in trouble. "I'll drop these off tomorrow." He stuck the envelope in his pocket. "Why did you have to go see him?"

"Sketch artist. I got a pretty good look at Charming Man, or Mister X, or whoever he is. Hopefully Frank can make something out of it." She finished her martini and waved for another round. When it came, she took another big swallow. "He told me what you did at the shark tank last night."

"Not much. They got away."

"He said you swung out on a rope over the tank while the sharks were still feeding." Donovan could feel the weight of her disapproval. "What is wrong with you? What were you *thinking*?"

"That I could catch them." He downplayed it even as his heart raced at the memory. "They were getting away, the other exits were blocked. It was the only way."

"*Sharks*, Donovan? Do you have *any* idea what could have happened to you?"

"I couldn't let them just get away with it. I had to do something."

"Famous last words." She took a deep breath. He could see the stress tightening her face, clouding the gold flecks in her eyes. "Well, talk to Frank. Maybe as an official consultant to the NYPD, you can get a carry permit or something."

"Maybe." The thought gave him pause. In spite of the circumstances that had created the possibility, and in spite of Joann's perspective, he found himself intrigued by the idea. "I've never had a problem riding the subway late at night, or walking home after work, but this is a whole new world. A gun might not be a bad idea."

"It *is* a whole new world, and a dangerous one. If you insist on being part of all this—and despite my fears, Frank seems to think you handled yourself pretty well—I want to be sure you come back to me in one piece at the end of the day."

"Yeah, I'm a fan of that idea, too."

"You're my respite from all the political bullshit I face at work. You're my connection to normal life, where people don't shoot at each other, or chop each other to bits, or," she raised an eyebrow, "jump over shark tanks. I need it. I need you." She sipped again and waved a hand in front of her face as though erasing a blackboard. "I don't want to think about investigations or work or the mayor or sharks anymore. We have really important issues to discuss. We have to set a firm date for the wedding. I was thinking next spring, maybe the beginning of April. April *second*, not the first."

"We don't want getting married to make us...April Fools?" He sipped his drink. "Careful. Might smile. Can't have that."

She stared glumly into her martini. "After today, it's going to be a while before I smile."

He leaned in and kissed the back of her neck, grinning at the goose-bumps the kiss aroused. "That's what you think."

⌘

The next morning Donovan took the envelope from Fullam and walked to the Midtown North precinct house. Humidity layered the air even though it was barely ten o'clock. Every surface in the city smudged, slid or stuck to his hands.

He identified himself to the desk sergeant, who sent him upstairs to the detectives' squad room. Fullam's desk was in one corner. He was there with a young man who, in contrast to Fullam, was the kind of guy whose idea of style was to wear a baseball cap whose color matched his t-shirt. This t-shirt had a picture of a silhouette target with a smiley face shot out of it. Underneath, it read, "Police should be held in the highest regard. Our guns fire quick and our nightsticks are hard." His baby face lit when Donovan entered.

"Hey, daredevil. How are you?"

"Do I know you?" Donovan asked.

Fullam made the introduction. "Donovan Graham, Josh Braithwaite."

Braithwaite stuck out his hand. Muscles corded on his forearm as they shook. "Daredevil?" Donovan repeated.

"The shark tank." The young detective tossed his head. "Man, I thought *I* was crazy."

"Too bad I didn't catch them."

"Hey, you survived."

Donovan looked at Fullam. "Got a minute, sergeant?"

"Josh?"

Braithwaite rose and offered his seat. "You want coffee?"

"I'm good, thanks." Donovan handed Fullam the folded papers Joann had given him. "I guess this makes it official."

Fullam glanced at and threw them into his "Out" basket. "Congratulations."

"Thanks."

The sergeant leaned back in his chair, a move he'd practiced enough to avoid hitting the wall behind him. They sat looking at each other for a moment.

"Now what?" Donovan asked.

"What do you mean?"

"Now that I'm official, what can I do?"

"Not much *to* do yet. The wheels of justice grind slowly. We got some good forensic stuff, but it's still in the lab. The giant's fingerprints were cooked onto the steel pipe next to yours."

"You have my fingerprints to compare?"

"You're in the system." Fullam glanced at him. "You were on the list for the Academy but let it lapse. They still have your fingerprints on file."

"My father's suggestion." Donovan shrugged. "School and work got hectic. I had to choose."

"None of my business. If you ever decide to stop getting high and you want back in, give me a call. You handled yourself pretty well at the aquarium; department always needs good men."

"Thanks." The compliment made Donovan smile. "Have you got anything I could offer input on now?"

"I've got a pretty good idea Mister X is not working alone."

"You mean besides Coeus the giant?"

"He had someone grab the cleaning truck and Katz. Someone also drove it and dumped it. We found it, abandoned and burned, out in Queens."

"Really?"

Fullam cocked his head. "Something wrong?"

"After talking to Mabel Muglia, Father Carroll believes this is a satanic ritual. Satanists don't usually work and play well with others," Donovan said.

"They don't have covens?"

"That's witches, generally speaking. Satanism is different, darker. Its main tenet is the acquisition of personal power, so it tends to draw people who aren't about sharing. People who are really serious about it, like Mister X obviously is, tend to be, ah, socially isolated." Donovan shrugged. "Might mean nothing. Other Satanists need the immediate gratification of group worship, so they gather weaker people around them they can control. Charismatic leader kind of people. The people they gather don't need to be Satanists, just pissed off or desperate enough to join a group whose leader tells or gives them what they want. That leader is the focal point for their emotion, which is what drives any magical ritual."

"Pissed off or desperate enough? Kind of like the homeless?" His lips pursed. "Sorry about Joann. Raphael's a good guy, but what I hear, he had no choice."

"So Joann told me."

"I told her I'd keep her in the loop if anything relevant comes up."

"Thanks."

"Speaking of relevant..." Fullam slid a file over to himself. "We found more of the red wax on the shark tank platform. I've got the chemical analysis. I emailed it over to Maurice. You want something to do? Give me an idea what it means."

Donovan felt a charge. "Sure. Did it give you anything else?"

"There *is* some DNA—spit—in there, too, and human fat. Working on it, but no leads from it yet."

"All right, sergeant," Donovan said, standing. "I'll get over to Father Carroll's, see what we can come up with."

"Listen—"

Donovan paused at the office door.

"Call me Frank," Fullam said, with a slight angle of his head. "Sherlock Pothead Holmes or not, the aquarium was good work."

❧

Donovan rode to Father Carroll's apartment with a grin that wouldn't go away. He parked the Vulcan near a halal street vendor and waved at the priest coming out the building door.

"I was just heading over to my campus office to get a few books," Father

Carroll said. "Care to tag along?"

"Sure."

"What's so amusing?"

Donovan jerked his head towards the vendor, his grin widening. "Guy just said to him, 'I don't care. I'm hungry.' Not something you ought to say to a man who sells mystery meat on a street corner. A hot dog guy, maybe. You can recognize a hot dog."

"I'm more a fan of pretzels, myself."

"Want to take my bike?" Donovan asked. Father Carroll looked at him over the top of his glasses. "Just asking. Inject a little excitement into the day."

"I appreciate the offer, but I need my brains unscrambled for a little while longer."

Donovan fell in step as the priest walked to the corner to hail a cab. "I'm coming from Midtown North. I just had an interesting meeting with Sergeant Fullam—Frank."

"On a beautiful Saturday like today? Where is Joann?"

"Shopping, I think. Licking her wounds from the work stuff. She wants to be alone for a little while."

"Ah." Father Carroll let two regular-sized cabs pass before flagging down a mini-van one. "Yes, she told me a bit about it at the aquarium. I saw the mayor's press conference Thursday, as well."

"She's being the good soldier about it, but it hurt. Raphael gave her Friday off and told her to lie low for awhile. She thinks he'll come up with something else for her, but…" Donovan's mouth drew tight. "I wish there was something I could do to help."

"Giving her the freedom to address this in her own way *is* doing something."

"Doesn't feel like it."

"Give her time. Including you in her affairs is something she has to do herself. You can't force yourself into her life."

"We *are* getting married."

"Nevertheless."

Donovan grunted and changed the subject. "What are we going to get at your office?"

"I want to see what I have in the way of herb and plant reference material."

"Is this about the list Frank emailed you?"

"It is," Father Carroll nodded. "Most of the chemicals in the red wax were botanical."

"Anything specific?"

"Benzoin, agrimony, myrrh, rosemary, and amaranth."

"Amaranth?" Donovan said. "In magic, isn't that used to...call forth the dead?"

"It is a summoning agent, yes."

"Summoning what?"

Father Carroll shook his head. "We won't know until we consider how it is supposed to interact with the other plants. However, there was one other substance in the mix that bears commenting upon: a combination of white blood cells, calcium phosphate, nitrogen, sodium, potassium, water, chlorine and epithelial cells." Donovan looked blank. "It doesn't sound familiar? Remember your parapsychology."

"What is it, a healing poultice or—no wait. MIT." The priest nodded, encouraging him to go on. "MIT did a chemical analysis of a sample of ectoplasm after a séance in...the eighties, I think. That's what they came up with, right?"

"Something very similar. I recognized this as an example of a substance called SELER—Solid Ectoplasmic Life Energy Residue. The remnant of ghosts, or...souls."

"Get out of here." Donovan laughed. "Mister X made candles out of *ghosts*?"

The priest shook his head. "SELER isn't an ingredient, it's a remnant. As the candle is burned, it draws life energy forth."

Donovan thought about this as the cab pulled up to the building that housed the university philosophy department. "I've got to say, I'm having a hard time wrapping my head around these, ah, esoteric details."

"You don't believe in them?"

"I know what they're *supposed* to do. I've certainly studied them enough to know other people, like Mister X, believe in them. I've seen a man eaten alive by sharks and fought someone—twice—who looks like he came off a mad doctor's morgue slab. But candles with ghost residue? It sounds...ridiculous."

"Now you're getting into the spirit of things."

"'Spirit'?"

The priest realized his pun and smiled. "'Reach hither thy finger, and behold my hands; reach hither thy hand, and thrust it into my side; and be not faithless, but believing.' John, 20:27. Your doubt is understandable. In this field, sometimes even experiencing isn't believing."

"So I'm wasting a lot of time, studying things I don't believe in."

"The doubt philosophical hermeneutics inspires. You have a sound foundation for what you seek, I think, because you are engaged in a pursuit of truth. The question you may want to consider is," Father Carroll unlocked the door to his office and entered, "do you have the ability and the courage to accept that truth, whatever it is, once you've found it?"

Donovan stood just outside, wondering if he did.

∽

Twelve killings of ridiculous complexity against the largest, best equipped police force in the world...

Smoking cigarette after cigarette, Valdes sat in shadow. When he'd returned to the Cancer Hospital from the aquarium, he'd bid the others have a good time before sequestering himself in his room. Although they knew nothing of what was to come next, they understood they were helping him, and that was enough.

Now he sat contemplating what he'd accomplished, allowing the deeds to reinforce his new perspective on how the world worked, a perspective begun months earlier...

NINE

DENIAL IS AN EVOLUTIONARY DEAD END

*N*ow *what?*

The March night had been cold and rainy. Valdes walked into the first place he could find to get a cup of coffee, a two-level delicatessen whose upper level was filled with sticky-topped tables and creaky booths. He took his steaming paper cup up there and chose a booth towards the back. The coffee was bitter. On the far wall, a bright red sign screamed "No Smoking." He lit a cigarette and exhaled a cloud at it.

Fifteen years in prison because of them. They screw me, double-cross me, and then have me thrown out? Me, Cornelius Valdes?

"*The only thing anyone remembers about you is the bad,*" Paolo had said.

He gazed into his coffee cup, filled with anger but with no outlet through which to channel it.

They'll remember more than that. I'll make sure of it.

The high back of his bench creaked and the entire structure shifted as someone sat in the booth behind him.

But how?

"Mister?"

Lost in thought, Valdes ignored the question.

"Mister?" the voice persisted. "Are you Cornelius Valdes? Cornelius Valdes who just got out of jail?"

Valdes's jaw tightened. The voice was harsh, gravelly, but the words sounded strangely childish. Annoyance fluttered across his face. Without

79

turning, he responded, "What do you want?"

"I don't want anything. Mister Fizz does."

"I've got nothing for him. Nothing for anyone." Valdes' lip curled. "Tell him to try the Christian Yeoman Association. Every customer gets a free knife in the back."

"I'm bigger and stronger than knives. But I got a message."

"I'll bet you do."

Valdes stubbed out his cigarette and rose from the table. Immediately the booth shifted. Blocking his way stood the largest man he'd ever seen, a colossus at least seven-foot-three with muscles and shoulders so wide he'd have to turn sideways to go through doorways. His hair was black, his face a combination of whites: pale skin, bloodless lips, ivory teeth. Scars lined his acromegalic forehead just below the hairline, and the skin stretched tight over his face and protruding jaw like too little shroud trying to cover too much death. His clothing enhanced the misshapenness—undersized black coat and pants patchworked with Frankenstein stitches and a discolored white t-shirt. Valdes noted some sort of tattoo marking the inside of each of the giant's wrists, ink that disappeared up into the sleeves. Black gloves the size of baseball mitts covered his hands. His eyes shone like a gargoyle's, and it took Valdes a second to realize the giant wore a black pair of biker sunglasses.

"Mister Fizz said you would be angry. I guess that's why he chose you, too."

"Deliver your message and get the hell out of my way."

"'Denial is an evolutionary dead end.'"

Valdes remained braced for a moment until he realized this was what the giant had wanted to say. "That's it? 'Denial is an evolutionary dead end'?"

"Mister Fizz said you can't deny who you are."

"Really? Who does Mister Fizz think I am?"

The giant smiled, a hideous Halloween grin. "Someone who wants them to *really* pay."

Valdes stared at him, anger and fear dissolving into curiosity and the faintest hope that, at last, his luck had finally changed. The giant chuckled and turned away. Valdes left his coffee on the table and followed, out the back of the store and into that freezing March night.

Oily water stained the gutters, filling the air with fishy garbage stink. Commuters were long gone from the streets of downtown Brooklyn, chased by cold and the magic that turns Cadman Plaza into a ghost town after work hours. Valdes quickened his step to keep up.

"Where are we going?"

The giant didn't respond. He made his way towards a subway station entrance and as he did, Valdes noticed something odd. Although he took no unusual measures to stay out of sight, the giant seemed always to be in shadow. Valdes thought about first seeing him in the deli. *Were the lights brighter before our conversation?* "Some imagination, Neil," he muttered.

A sign stated the entrance was open until 7 p.m., and indeed it was now closed off by an iron gate and locked by a thick chain. The giant didn't hesitate, lumbering down the stairs and slamming the gate with one open palm. The chain snapped with a sharp *crack!*

"Bigger and stronger than a chain."

Intrigue drew Valdes along behind him. The giant boarded a subway car that immediately cleared as people saw him. The lights flickered, dimmed, and settled into brownout mode.

Whoever Mister Fizz is, Valdes thought, considering the giant, *he's certainly found an impressive messenger.*

They rode the subway across the Brooklyn Bridge to 8th Street, where the giant got off and waited for the platform to clear before speaking. "Go upstairs, across the street to the bookstore. I'll wait for you here." He started towards the end of the station away from the exit, where only the blackness of the tunnel waited.

"What am I supposed to be looking for?" Valdes asked.

"Mister Fizz said you'll know it. *If* you see it."

Valdes crossed Broadway against the traffic and looked in a window from the dark. The bookstore was crammed into a space that had probably been everything from a liquor warehouse to an apartment building in its lifetime. Nothing made the store either stand out in his mind or jog any memories, so he stood, thinking. Absolutely nothing suggested what he ought to be looking for, nor what to do once he found it. He strolled around the store, riding the escalator to the upper floor and taking the stairs back down.

"Denial is an evolutionary dead-end"...

An employee rolled a cart of books down a narrow aisle, looking for the spots on shelves where they belonged. Valdes paused to let her pass. "Psychology and Self-Help" books were in front of him. On the shelf at his exact eye level, amidst brightly colored trade paperback spines with titles exhorting every way to change your life, he saw a leather book. Its cover was the dark purple of midnight in a graveyard. The girl paused next to him, clucked her tongue and shuffled books like a Vegas card dealer, creating a rainbow of homogenous spines. As she moved off, Valdes noted that she hadn't touched the leather book. He slipped a finger over the top and leaned it out so he could remove it.

It resembled a ledger or journal, not contemporary but not ancient, nondescript enough to have come from almost any period of human history where bookbinding existed. The leather was visibly textured and warm to the touch, like skin. Valdes held it in his hands. It had some heft for its size. The title, *Vade Mecum Flagellum Dei*, was visible only when he tilted it away from the light.

Suddenly, inexplicably, dizziness skewed his vision. He felt a great surge, a supercharging burst of energy that made him think he could conquer the world. Eagerly he flipped through the book. Words and diagrams seemed to fill the pages, but only in his peripheral vision. When he looked directly at it, all he saw was white, empty paper.

Hmm.

He made his way down to the counter. Grabbing the first thing he saw, a "Word of the Day" calendar that was eighty percent off, he went to the cashier and set it, and the book, on the counter.

"Find everything you need today?" the cashier chirped.

Valdes considered the book, lying innocuously on the counter. "I think so."

She smiled and slid the calendar under her price scanner. "One-ninety-nine."

He waited, nudging the book towards her. Her blank smile remained.

"One ninety-nine?" she repeated.

He gave her two singles and picked up the calendar and the book. "Keep the change." He had a moment of concern that he'd set off the anti-theft electronics as he left, but no telltale shrieking alerted the staff that he was taking the black book with him.

At the subway station, he discovered he'd given the bookstore clerk his last two dollars. Without pause he smoothly stepped around the turnstile arm. An old woman saw this, and she shuffled behind him to the end of the platform. She wore a plastic kerchief and a scowl.

"You can't do that! You have to pay like everyone else! I'll call a cop!"

The book tingled in his grasp. Valdes glanced around. No one else waited in the station. The lights of an oncoming train brightened the tunnel. Silhouetted against one wall, the giant waited. Valdes looked at him, then at the book.

"No, you won't."

He thrust the old woman off the platform.

She shrieked as she flew across the tracks and hit the third rail. Enough electricity to power a train shot through her. The train front slammed her to the wooden track ties, its weight grinding her burning flesh into the filth. Valdes watched, fascinated, until the screech of brakes jolted him back to the moment. He blinked dizziness away and looked at the book, then at the end of the platform. Inertia carried the last car into the station, leaving space for him to jump down onto the tracks and join the giant in the darkness.

He followed the monstrous shadow through subway tunnels, eventually climbing onto another platform and riding the C train north. It was raining outside now, and frigid water flowed down into the stations through grates and cracks in the walls. None of it washed things clean; the underbelly of the city now glistened with slime.

Valdes gripped the book tighter. The adrenaline rush from pushing the old woman in front of the train hadn't subsided. He inhaled, a deep, trembling breath. Cold took root in him, anesthetizing guilt and doubt while his brain tried to process what he was experiencing. In prison he'd come across addicts of every substance. All those in recovery had described a "moment of clarity," where a Higher Power caused the scales to fall from their eyes and they finally accepted their situations, warts and all. Such perspective allowed addicts an understanding of their lives and places in the world: where they were, how they'd gotten there, what it would take to get them where they wanted to be.

For a moment of clarity, this one is muddy, he thought. *I'm not* really *a murderer...*

(Denial is an evolutionary dead end.)

He riffled through the pages of the book. They looked as they had in the store, with writing visible only in his periphery. Frustration bubbled into rage, which curdled into nausea when he thought about the old woman. The nausea churned back into rage at the men who had forced him into a position where he had to do something so vile.

He followed the giant off the C train on the Upper West Side, at 103rd Street. More tunnels—Valdes had had no idea the extent of Manhattan's subterranean passages—led them to a ragged opening in a wall. Beyond it was darkness as thick as syrup.

"Bigger and stronger than a wall."

Valdes watched Coeus flick a lighter and hold it to a wad of newspapers tied to a stick. Using this makeshift torch, the giant started inside.

Whatever building they entered had obviously been abandoned for years, if in fact it had ever been fully constructed: the walls down here were made of bare concrete that had never felt the touch of a paintbrush. The smell of urine was strong from every corner, as though the territory had been marked. Stagnant water puddled around the uneven floor. Gnawed bones strewn about suggested that if this was where the giant had taken up residence, he had a healthy appetite. Valdes wondered if the remains were animal or human. *I'll grind your bones to make my bread.*

"You gotta come this way."

Carrying the torch, the giant led him to another room on the same level. They passed a crumbling concrete staircase on the way. Valdes wondered where it led, and where they were. "What's your name?"

The giant regarded him warily. "Whuh?"

"You know who I am. What's your name?"

The giant stared at him. Valdes somehow sensed that, in spite of the sunglasses, the giant could see right through him. "Now my name is Coeus."

"Excuse me?"

"Coeus. Coe-ee-yus," he pronounced slowly and deliberately. "Ha-ha-ha-ha. I kill people with fear."

"You don't say… Where are we going, Coeus? To meet Mister Fizz?"

"Maybe." The giant shoulders moved. "You don't choose when—he does." He walked a few steps further, until the light revealed another room. He handed Valdes the torch. "You got a couple of candles in here, and you can make a fire if you get cold."

"Where are you going? Don't you want the light?"

"I don't need it. I'm not afraid of the dark."

℘

Who says you can't go home again?

Valdes sat alone with the book, his back to one cold stone wall, listening to the occasional rumble of passing trains. Candle wax sputtered and dripped.

All those years, all that pulling myself up by my bootstraps, and here I sit, on piss-soaked concrete. Welcome back.

He chuckled.

The more things change, the more they stay the same.

His laughed at his situation, a sound which took on an edge as he replayed the scene with the old woman in his mind. When he pictured her head bursting aflame like a matchstick he rolled onto his side, tears spilling down his cheeks. Hysteria rose in his tone. He recalled the sound her brittle old bones had made when the train struck her, sticks snapping in a bonfire. He laughed until his face ached, and when the madness subsided he was left with one reassuring thought:

It wasn't my fault.

Gasping for breath in the foul dankness, he sat upright.

I could have made Christian Yeoman's Association an international force for good. All Paolo and the others had to do was stay out of my way. I never intended to keep the money. I would have bought the pictures, used the information to clear any opposition, and returned every cent. But they ruined everything!

Hot rage suddenly swept through him, and Valdes howled. He threw the book at the candles, knocking them over, plunging the room into utter blackness. He shouted and pounded the floor, his fury at losing the last fifteen years of his life enflaming the anger he felt towards the four men who had been his friends until the moment they turned him over to the Justice Department investigators.

I could have done anything!

He ranted and raved, his voice shaking the walls. "I would have made us all princes! They screwed me out of my life and now they barely know who I am? I'm *Cornelius Valdes*! I dragged myself out of the worst layer of shit in this city and they threw me back down! I won't *stand* for this!" His voice dropped to a growl, and he remembered what Coeus had said to him. "I'll make them *really* pay!"

A cold wind tickled his skin.

The candles flared to life.

Valdes looked down. The book was lying at his feet. He extended a tentative hand to turn the first page.

Revenge is a universal urge, an integral element of the world, a kind of justice, even. Forgiveness is learned behavior separating us from the natural order. Why should we accept deviation from the intended state of things? Who are others to deny us what is ours? If they do, they must be taught the error of their ways. Methods may vary, but revenge must be exacted. Scales must be balanced, equilibrium restored. Taking pleasure in this is not unnatural, it's humanity acting with nature. We know it's right because it feels so. Those who seek to deny us our desire are the antithesis of who and what we are, what we

*strive to be. They must be overcome, in a way that their removal is useful in
the grander scheme.*

*In our ascent to greatness, are there better stepping stones than the bodies of
our enemies?*

It was fascinating, powerful material whose astonishing applicability
to his own life sparked hesitation within him. *Is this some kind of joke?*
Unable to stop, he read on:

*Ancient Egyptians believed thirteen to be the number of rungs on the lad-
der of knowledge bridging our world and the next, with the thirteenth giving
access to heaven. They were right, in a manner of speaking: thirteen is the path
to the highest knowledge of power. The association of bad luck is a Christian
contribution; at the Last Supper, there were twelve at the table until joined by
Judas Iscariot. Far from bad luck, this is actually a valuable point: if it can
be accessed, the thirteenth changes the course of history.*

"The thirteenth? What does that mean?" Valdes frowned. "Accessed
how?" He turned the page. Facing him were two words made sinister by
the flickering candles:

"Resurrectus Maledicat"

Eagerly, he turned the page and started to read…

༈

The ritual killings uncovered in him a brutality he wouldn't have suspected was there. Fifteen years of prison life hadn't driven him this far
along the darkest path of his soul, but one night with the book changed
everything. He'd always believed building a network for charitable dona-
tions, creating a system to help this lowest caste from which he himself
had risen, had fostered goodness and kindness within him. To discover
such a new, radical perspective was sometimes daunting. He sought refuge
in the writings of occult practitioners like LaVey and Crowley, men who
had also chosen the path of desire. He buried himself in the planning of
the sacrifices, each one a complex mix of timing and daring. Always the
book was there, inexplicably guiding him to the right choices. March
became April became May and his frozen pile of limbs and organs grew.
As it did, he came to truly understand that he'd made the right choice by
following the giant that night.

Mister Fizz.

Valdes chuckled at the childish misinterpretation of the name he'd de-
duced. He lit another cigarette and thought about the ritual's next step.

୬୨

The following Thursday, Donovan was working the service end of Polaris's bar. Thursday was always busy; in addition to the usual pre-theater
reservations and tourists, Thursday is the night Manhattan people go out
before the weekend bridge and tunnel mobs cross into the city from New
Jersey and the outer boroughs.

The crowd was three deep. Donovan was pouring a glass of meritage
with one hand and shaking a stainless steel cup full of cosmopolitans
with the other as waiter tickets came clicking up from the printer. It was
backbreaking work in an environment one notch above feeding time at
the zoo, but he barely noticed the chaos. Shouts for single malt scotch
and house specialty cocktails—even the ones made with cucumber or
elderflower liqueur—were laughably mundane after his involvement with
Fullam's zodiac murders. Where once he'd plunged fully into the middle
of the frenzy, now he felt a strange lethargy.

"Donovan."

He glanced over his shoulder, startled. The sergeant stood at the bar, his
manner clearing a tight but respectful space around him. He hadn't raised
his voice, but still had made himself heard over the din.

"Hey, Frank. What's going on?"

"You free this weekend?"

"Why?"

Fullam reached into his suit coat and pulled out a paper-clipped set of
papers. "Finally got a hit from NCIC on the giant's prints."

Donovan's pulse jumped. "This weekend?"

"Those are from the aquarium. Check out the next page."

Ignoring a man waving a black Amex card at him, Donovan looked at
the first sheet, a set of oversized fingerprints that were rough and smeared
at the edges. He flipped the top sheet over and saw a second, smaller set.
"'Montmorency County School System,'" he read from the top of the
page. "School system?"

"The hit came from a place in Michigan, Blue Moon Bay. The schools
in that county have something called Project ChildSafe; get fingerprints
and DNA samples of all school kids in case, well, in case the worst happens. The second set is from a boy named Coletun Ruscht."

Donovan flipped back and forth between the two, eyes narrowing. He
removed the paper clip and set the pages side-by-side on the bar. The noise

and crowd fell away as his eyes widened. Except for the size—Coletun's were about three times smaller—they matched perfectly. He read the age of the child and glanced at the lieutenant.

"Coeus the angry giant is…a nine-year-old boy?"

"First flight is at six-forty-five tomorrow morning."

Donovan shook his head. "I'm closing tonight. What else do you have?"

"One p.m.?"

Guzman, who had been working the front bar, noticed their interaction and drifted over. Donovan turned to him.

"Can you cover some shifts?"

TEN

BUSINESS TRAVEL

Fullam picked him up at his apartment the next morning just after eleven.

"Your flight will get into Detroit about three o'clock." He deftly steered between cars on New Jersey Turnpike, driving as though he had his siren on even though he didn't. It was the same Crown Victoria in which they'd returned from the aquarium. Donovan hoped this time he'd have better results. "Transfer to a puddle jumper at the private airfield next door to the airport, then fly up to a local airstrip. The sheriff'll meet you there. His name is Roy Talling."

"He's expecting me?"

"I called to let him know you're coming."

"What, exactly, am I looking for? A bunch of empty steroid bottles in Coletun's toy box?"

"Steroids wouldn't cause a growth spurt like that. I spoke to an endocrinologist at Johns Hopkins about our problem. Could be a tumor on his pituitary gland. There's also a hormone called 'IGF1' that can cause bizarre growth and acromegaly, but they'd never heard of either case creating someone the size of Coeus. Not in less than a year."

Donovan gazed out a side window. An edge of condensation from the air conditioning fogged one corner. He swiped it away. "Then—again—what am I looking for?"

"Whatever it is, I'm sure you'll know it," the sergeant said, sliding the

Crown Victoria to the curb at Newark Airport's Terminal C, "when you see it.

"Have a good flight."

॰

Her real name was Paula, but her red hair and jug ears had earned her the nickname "Pixie." A happy sort in spite of her occasional brushes with the law, her demeanor suggested she was always on the verge of breaking into a song.

She whistled now, making her way along access tunnels somewhere near the bowels of Rockefeller Center. The damp, the stench; these might have discouraged the less hardy. Pixie welcomed them, for they signaled she was nearly home.

Close by, a B train rumbled towards the Upper West Side.

Pixie had spent the previous thirty days as an involuntary guest of a New York State Correctional facility, so the sight of the steel door was a comforting one. She sauntered a few steps closer before realizing it stood ever so slightly ajar. A tiny crease appeared between her eyebrows. Aside from the feeling of peace the space provided her, the main reason she'd chosen this spot was its seclusion. Whether it was the depth beneath the streets of Manhattan, or the subway noise, or the thick stone walls, she could sing as loudly as she wanted or have a hundred yowling cats without fear of being rousted. The idea that someone had moved in to squat in her home while she was away drew a frown that she turned upside down when she realized it meant now she might have someone to play checkers with. Grinning ear to ear, she pushed the door open and stepped inside.

The chamber seemed larger than she remembered, with its age-blackened brick walls and rows of pillars that disappeared up into the dark. Shadow-filled cul-de-sacs lurked in asymmetrical corners while cryptically carved blocks lined a far wall. All manner of clutter choked the room: boxes, piles of moth and mildew-eaten fabric, wooden crates overflowing with implements of ceremony. Dusty booklets covered by generations of spider webs had been stacked everywhere. The only clear space was in the center, where she'd set up house. It was from here Pixie heard voices.

"—de chances of bein' found while we works?" a Jamaican-accented man's voice asked. "If I be hammerin' it might get loud…"

"Not to mention our music," a teenage girl's voice added.

"Very slight," a second man responded as smooth as milk sugar. "I learned of this chamber on a private tour of the church years ago, when I was still a Christian yeoman. It was a crypt briefly, but the secular needs of storage—and the city health codes—forced those in charge to change their ways. In fact, I believe access from above may have been walled off during remodeling. The door by which we entered is the only entrance, as far as I know."

"The rule is, make sure the place is secure," a third voice growled.

Pixie started as a smelly bear of a man grabbed her in a hug from behind, clapping a filthy hand over her mouth. She squeaked and tried to kick free but the man had a grip like a straitjacket as he carried her to the other three voices.

"Who dat?" a Jamaican man in a top hat asked, one hand going to the hammer on his belt. "What you got dere, Officer Burt?"

"A spy?" a girl in a black leatherjacket asked. Chains jingled from her zippers when she pulled out a knife. "What did she hear?"

The second man lifted a restraining hand. Although only a few inches taller than Pixie, with a not-unkind face, he was clearly the leader of this unnerving crew. "Easy, Dez. I'm sure the young lady meant no harm?" A tickle of calm soothed Pixie's fear when he looked at her. She tried to shake her head in the unyielding grip but only managed to twitch a few red hairs. "In fact," he continued, gesturing around, "if I'm not mistaken, this must be the previous tenant of this space?" He nodded at Officer Burt, who released her.

"Puh—previous?" Pixie fought back the urge to throw up from the taste of him. "No, I din't move out. I was, uh, somewhere else I couldn't leave from." She gazed hopefully at the smooth man. "But if you want to stay here, there's a lot of room! We could clean up, maybe find some furniture, make it like a…home or something?" His expression didn't change. "No, hunh?" Pixie felt her spirit start to deflate, so she put on a brave face. "Well, I guess I can't complain. I wasn't here, I can't say it's mine. Finders keepers, right?" She stooped and started to gather some nearby rags. "You'll like it here. It's real quiet and peaceful. You know where we're under, right?"

"St. Patrick's cathedral, if I'm not mistaken," the smooth man said. Dez snickered and the Jamaican man's lip curled with a hint of sneer.

"Yeah. I guess that's why it's peaceful, hunh?"

Dez snickered again. "Not for much longer."

Dread crawled on centipede legs across the hairs of Pixie's neck. "Uh, whatever." She grabbed a final scrap of cloth and stood, edging towards the door. "So I'll just do my 'losers weepers' somewhere else, hunh? Enjoy this space. Take, uh, take good care of it."

Officer Burt stepped in her way.

Pixie gasped as a hand touched and turned her. The smooth man was there, folding his hands preacher-style while he inspected her.

"Please don't," she begged.

"'Please don't,'" Dez mimicked in a high-pitched voice.

The smooth man's glance silenced her. Hope peeked into Pixie's soul. "Once upon a time that would have worked," he murmured, stroking her cheek. "Now I'm prioritizing my own needs. The book says: 'As the most sacred is made profane, so must its birthplace be desecrate.'"

"Wh—what does that mean?" Officer Burt seized her again in his rank embrace. Pixie yelped. "Are you going to kill me? Here?"

The smooth man paused. "Rape her first," he said, turning away. "All of you. Then kill her. That should do the trick."

◦◦

In Detroit he transferred to a tiny Cessna flown by a pilot with a crazy grin and a thermos full of something other than coffee. An hour of occasionally jarring mid-air drops and listening to the pilot sing along with the oldies station—almost always on-key—did little to alleviate Donovan's nerves.

Not steroids, not hormones. What does that leave? Do I want to know?

Finally they landed at an airstrip bordered by woods on one side and a river on the other. An older man, lean, weathered and traveled, waited with a Jeep. He wore a tan cowboy hat and a dark blue windbreaker with "Montmorency County Sheriff's Department" stenciled under a crest.

"Mister Graham?" He extended his hand. "Sheriff Roy Talling. Hope your ride wasn't too rough. We've had pretty harsh thunderstorms this spring."

The pilot gave a thumbs-up. "He's okay, Roy. I gave him the smooth route."

The smooth route? "I'm fine," Donovan said. "Thanks for meeting me."

"Not many cabs out here. Much obliged, Ralph." Talling tipped his hat to the pilot. "Just toss your bag in the back, Mister Graham, and we'll head over to the office."

"The office" wasn't in Blue Moon Bay but in the county seat, a town called Atlanta. Unlike its namesake in Georgia, this Atlanta's population probably didn't exceed the night shift at the Coca-Cola plant. As they drove through town, Donovan became aware of a peculiar demeanor among the people. Although only the barest breeze stirred the late afternoon cool, the townsfolk shuffled about as though in the harshest cold of winter. Evasive eyes remained lowered in faces tight against the world. He made no comment as they pulled up in front of what looked like a quaint Long Island antique shop.

"Don't let the rustic setting fool you," Talling said. "I know how to keep an eye on things. Retired and came up here to keep order while I get in some fishing."

"How's it working out?"

The sheriff chuckled without much humor. "Fish haven't been too worried, lately."

Touches of hominess dotted the station, softening the stark walls and lighting: a crayon drawing scotch-taped to the side of one desk, a Tigers baseball cap on a lamp, the banner of a lodge named for an animal in one corner. Nothing too unprofessional, but they added up to a sense of comfort Donovan couldn't imagine at Midtown North. One corner of his mouth rose as he thought about Braithwaite's t-shirt: "*Our guns fire quick, and our nightsticks are hard.*"

Talling led Donovan into his office, a smaller room separated from the rest of the station by glass and wood partitions. A young redheaded woman was inside, leaning over the desk to give an unintentional but pleasant view.

"Oh, sheriff! I brought in the files on the, uh, the case." She straightened suddenly, knocking a folder on the floor. She quickly bent to pick it up, then wiped her hands on the seat of her pants as though the folder had dirtied them. Donovan smiled.

"Thank you, Sharon."

"Would you like some coffee, Mister, uh—?"

"Graham. Call me Donovan. That would be great, thanks."

She blushed. "Sheriff?"

"Bring us a fresh pot, would you please?" Talling waited until she left before he glanced at Donovan. "She's determined to be a good cop, so I'm bringing her along slowly. Worse things to aspire to, but she's got to stop being impressed by big-shot out-of-town investigators."

"Charisma is my curse."

Talling snorted as he took off his hat. He hung it on a rack made of some kind of antler and took a seat behind the desk. Donovan sat opposite him, wondering if his black motorcycle boots, black jeans, blue t-shirt and untucked white dress shirt made him look underdressed for his role of "big-shot out-of-town investigator." They looked at each other for a moment. "Do I pass?" Donovan finally asked.

"Excuse me?"

"I've been sized up by the best." *Conrad.* "Do I pass?"

"We'll see." Talling leaned back until his chair squeaked. "Unfortunately, the fingerprints you have raise some questions about a case I'd closed. Coletun is supposed to be dead. We have a confession from his killer, and the circumstances of that confession are compelling. On top of that, Coletun's case has some aspects to it that are a little...different. Maybe you noticed the people in town aren't exactly outgoing?"

"They seemed sad. A little scared."

"What happened sucked a lot of life out of them. They've been through a lot, and I don't much relish the idea of picking at fresh scabs."

"But you are."

"I am." Talling nodded. "Something about the case was never right."

"And you think I can help you."

Again, Talling nodded.

"Why would you think that?" Donovan asked.

"I told Sergeant Fullam a little about the case. He told me a little about you."

Did he? "No wonder the fish aren't worried. Doesn't sound like you get away from work long enough to threaten them."

"Sergeant Fullam said you're an expert on strange, bizarre things?" Talling's low-key façade coated penetrating curiosity. Donovan shrugged. His manner must have conveyed something, for a thin strand of relief wound through the sheriff's caution. "Then maybe you're the right man to have sent. Maybe. All due respect to him, I saw people associated with your field when I was with Detroit PD. Psychics and mystics and whatever else they called themselves. I don't think there were any who *weren't* full of shit."

"A lot of them are, whether it's deliberate or delusional."

"Which one describes you?"

"Neither."

Talling took a second before sitting forward. "Good. I hate dealing with flakes."

Sharon returned with two cups and a coffee pot on a tray. Next to the milk and sugar was a plate of cookies. "My niece is filling her Girl Scout quota. Dig in; there are plenty more where they came from." She cast a sideways look at Donovan before glancing at Talling to see if she was being too informal.

The sheriff gave an indulgent nod and selected a coconut macaroon. "Thank you, Sharon. That'll be all for now."

"Yup." She blushed again and shut the door behind her.

"Bringing her along slowly," he repeated. "Well there may be a load of shit in your field, Mister Graham, but what happened to the Churners was brutal murder. How much do you know about Coletun's case?"

Churners? Donovan thought. "Frank didn't want to prejudice my findings. All I know is he disappeared from school."

"The last sign we have of Coletun is his fingerprints in the house of a man named Zeke Wissex. Wissex is currently incarcerated in Standish Maximum Correctional Facility for multiple murders. One of those murders is supposed to have been Coletun."

Donovan's eyebrows rose.

"Zeke came out here about three years ago from Massachusetts, kind of a trust-fund college kid. Rode out here on a giant Harley, like a Hell's Angel. One of those hippie types—do kids still follow the Grateful Dead?—but big." Talling puffed out his chest and shoulders. "Worked out; a health food nut. Kind of a charmer, some of that rich kid prick-arrogance, but not a *bad* bad guy. At least, I didn't think so. He founded a group that called themselves Churners. Most were local high school dropouts and college kids, pretty much fed up with life around here but without the skills to do much about it. Zeke bought a house—big place on a few hundred acres—and set them up as a kind of commune about two years ago."

"A commune?"

"He turned them into a little business, selling microbrew beer, soap, any natural-hippie substance. They named themselves after some Irish god."

Churners? Donovan thought again. *Irish god...?* "Cernunnos?" He pronounced it "chur-new-nohss."

"That's the one; Cernunnos—Churners." The corners of Talling's mouth turned down. "Anyway, one of the things helping them have such a good time was that, as a hobby, Wissex started growing a pretty good crop of weed out there. He didn't sell much—didn't need the money—but it made him The Man around here."

"Really?" Donovan was surprised he'd tolerated it.

"Why did I tolerate it?" Talling seemed to have read Donovan's mind.

"He was strictly local—no ambition to be a kingpin. I think he genuinely liked it out there, the people, the set-up…"

His voice trailed off, and Donovan could see the sheriff still wondered if not busting Wissex had been the right thing. Considering events, who could say?

"The Churners were devoted to partying and having a good time, as far as I could tell," Talling continued. "All his friends were over eighteen, and they kept their private lives private. Wissex always covered his tracks, so we never got enough on him to really come down hard."

"And he helped keep things quiet."

Talling examined Donovan, searching for a sign of accusation. He saw none. "That, too. Anyway, last August, August first, at 11:42 p.m., I got a call from dispatch to go out to the woods on the Wissex estate." Talling indicated at a stack of photographs. "Crime scene photos; better have a strong stomach if you want to look."

Donovan reached for them, thinking of people he knew who took great pleasure out of these types of pictures, collecting and trading them like ghoulish baseball cards.

This selection would have done any of those macabre collectors proud. Blood splattered dark patterns across the black and white backgrounds while limbs and organs were strewn about the pictures in occasionally identifiable, gruesome messes. Donovan shuffled through the photos then went through them again, slower. He saw more than bone shards and wet gristle this second time, he saw inhuman cruelty not sated by mere killing. The bodies had been savaged until barely recognizable as human beings. "Jesus Christ," he murmured. "*Wissex* did that?"

Talling nodded. "So he said. But it didn't fit my reading of him, and we never found any axes or hatchets."

Donovan paused. "Was Coletun one of the bodies?"

"No. In spite of Zeke's confession that he'd killed him, we never found Coletun's body, or any DNA evidence of it."

"And that's the thing that bugs you."

"One of them."

Donovan nodded. "Tell me about Coletun."

Talling squinted at the files. "Coletun lived in that trailer park out by the airstrip. His parents, Eddie and Lola, were, frankly, white trash. They used to fight about Coletun, among other things. Eddie never did accept that Coletun was his son, I think."

Donovan felt a pang of sympathy for the little boy caught between fighting parents. He sorted through the files and came across a school photo of a small, scrawny-looking boy. "Is this him?" The sheriff nodded. Donovan examined the picture. Coletun squinted at the camera, tentative grin wondering if he was doing what the photographer wanted. He looked sickly, as though breakfast on too many occasions had consisted of a handful of beer nuts and a push out the door.

"On the last day of school, last June, Coletun didn't come home. The principal, Sam Rolf, reported the boy got into a vehicle Sam swears belonged to Zeke. Said Coletun wasn't dragged in, didn't fight, he just got in. When he didn't show up at home, Lola decided he'd been kidnapped." Talling gestured indulgence. "Taken, maybe. But kidnapped? I told her it didn't make sense; anyone who thought they had ransom money just had to look at their trailer to see the truth, but Lola was a little, ah, imaginative about the way she viewed her life. Eddie came home, learned what happened and—I don't know. For all the emotion he showed, Coletun could have been a runaway hamster."

"Was there ever any evidence for kidnapping? Or anything else?"

"Like did they beat him to death, or something? No. His teachers saw bruises, one time he had a broken arm, but among some people around here that's considered normal. Neighbors heard plenty of verbal abuse, too. We did the usual follow-up: checked with the Staties, put word out on the wires, put that picture on a milk carton. I got a warrant and searched Zeke's house. Coletun never turned up. He'd just vanished. Two weeks later we got a call about shots fired at the Ruscht trailer, found them both dead. Interesting thing was it was Lola who'd shot Eddie and turned the gun on herself, not the other way around like you might expect. Neighbors said they were fighting about money, which we found scattered around the trailer. More than I would've expected, but Eddie did have a shady side."

"Where do the Churners come in? Was Eddie a member?"

Talling shook his head. "Too old."

"Wissex heads up a group of bored people looking for a thrill. Wissex comes from money. Shady Eddie suddenly has money. Coletun disappears, his fingerprints are in Wissex's house." Disgust clouded Donovan's face as he put it together. "He sold his kid to the Churners? Jesus Christ. And when his wife found out, she shot him."

"About how I figured it. Zeke claims he sacrificed Coletun before he did," the sheriff gestured at the pictures, "that."

"So he sacrificed Coletun with the Churners, butchered everybody, and then called you on his cell phone to turn himself in? I see why it bugs you."

"Did nothing to help his attorneys during the trial. Almost like he went berserk, then got religion after he saw what he'd done."

"Too bad for the Churners he didn't see the light a little earlier."

"You're not kidding—well, you just saw the pictures."

"And none of them tried to escape?" Donovan sorted through them again. "I mean, bigger and stronger or not, not one of the twelve managed to get away?"

"Nope."

"August first?"

Talling nodded.

"Lammas Eve," Donovan said. "A pagan feast. They were probably sampling the crop, as part of a celebration for the first harvest. I doubt any of them could have tied their shoes, much less fought off someone as big as Wissex intent on butchering them."

Talling nodded, impressed. "Tests showed they all had high levels of various drugs in their systems."

Donovan glanced out the window. "The site where Wissex says he sacrificed Coletun—can we get to it before dark?"

"Probably, if we leave now. What are you looking for?"

"Not sure." Donovan remembered Fullam's words. "But I'll know it if I see it."

* * *

"It's a partially man-made clearing, about a quarter-mile from the house." Talling gestured into the thick woods through which they drove. "I'll get us as close as I can. It's not too far from the road."

"Did Wissex own all this land?"

"A lot of it. There was no great demand; it doesn't offer much."

"Except privacy."

The sheriff grunted as he parked. "I don't know how much evidence is left. I haven't been out here in awhile." He ducked around a fragrant pine tree, the needles whispering as they brushed against his windbreaker's sleeve. Above them faint stars had come into view as the sun continued its downward trek. "Anything in particular you were hoping to find?"

"I'm curious about what kind of ritual they did—Lammas Eve is a kind of Thanksgiving. There might be an animal sacrifice to assure the next season's crop, but—barring a giant wicker man—it's not a holiday about violence, or murder."

"I just thought they all prayed to 'the Devil'?"

Donovan's boot snapped a dead branch next to a log he stepped over. The sound was like a gunshot in the stillness. "'The Devil' can mean any of a thousand occult beings, but Cernunnos is a fertility god. He doesn't ask for human sacrifice. He wouldn't require Wissex to kill his followers."

"Uh-*hunh*." Talling regarded him with caution, looking for common ground. "Interesting. I guess your attachment to NYPD is as kind of a psychological profiler?"

"Something like that, yeah."

"You any good at it?"

"Yeah. I am."

In another few minutes they made it to a clearing about the size of a baseball infield. Talling stepped to the side. "I'll stay out of your way," he said, taking out a tin of chewing tobacco. "But you don't mind if I watch?"

Donovan shrugged. "Your crime scene."

The area stood in stark contrast to the path on which they'd just arrived. Where foliage filled the surrounding woods, this clearing was entirely barren of life. Not a single blade of grass poked through the rocky soil and any leaves that had fallen or been carried here by the wind were shriveled, as dead and dry as scabs. The trees that formed the loose perimeter were all withered and gnarled beyond redemption, and they bore faint smears of paint.

Odd.

The low-level psychic sensitivity that had alerted him at the aquarium amplified the resonance of Wissex's obscene deeds. Donovan cleared his mind, shutting out Talling's presence, as his movements automatically became quicker. He inspected a slab of wood nailed to two stumps.

"Altar."

He noted it stood away from the surrounding trees, leaving no place to hang the inverted crucifix necessary to a Black Mass.

But I do get a bad sense here…

He measured lines of sight and a shudder of nausea ran through him, alongside an electric charge of *knowing*.

"This would be where Wissex stood when he sacrificed Coletun. *If* he sacrificed Coletun. But not to Cernunnos. Then who? And why?"

He worked his way around the area's outer edge, examining the ground and trees for signs of the cult's purpose. Every movement made his stomach turn. All he found were the remains of a bonfire, cracked stones and blackened bits of wood spread in a random pattern from a stone hollow in the approximate center of the clearing. He returned to where Wissex had stood and made a slow, 360-degree turn. A real remnant of darkness remained, and it unnerved him. Blood steadily pounded the veins in the back of his head. His eye again went to the burnt debris. The more he looked the more he saw of it, and there were bits of other things: a shard of plastic, the edge of a book spine, three beads still attached to a chain. *Offerings?* Dropping to a crouch, he surveyed the ground and rolled a bowling ball-sized stone over. Its underside glistened the color of syrah. *That doesn't make sense. Not a shade of purple...*

Brushing away dirt, he walked over to Talling. "I'd like to see Wissex's house."

"Thought you might. While you were doing...whatever you were doing there," Talling jerked his head towards the clearing, "I called a friend at the electric company. Power is on, so we'll have light."

"Great." There was nothing Talling could do to help with this, and Donovan didn't want to create any obstacles to learning more. "I'd like to speak to Wissex, too."

The sheriff checked his watch as he led the way back to the truck. "Not today. Prison he's serving his time in is down in Arenac County. By the time we get there it'd be too close to lights out."

"Can we get there tomorrow morning, before I leave for New York?"

Talling scratched his head beneath the cowboy hat. "Ralph's gonna fly you back to Detroit. As long as you can switch your flight there, I don't see any reason why not."

"I think Wissex will be able to give me a little more information."

"Did you learn anything back there?"

Donovan re-examined his impressions before shaking his head. "Nothing good."

ELEVEN

PRISON CATECHISM

"Mister Chew-chew! Sit still and behave!"

Paolo Tullmo slowed his pace as he jogged around the northeastern curve of the Central Park Reservoir. A stout woman, dressed in a drab smock and matching dirty kerchief, blocked his path. A small white rabbit, frightened still by her cackle, cowered before her. As he drew nearer she lurched upright like a bear protecting her cub.

"You ain't my son!"

Tullmo slowed. He was CEO of the Christian Yeoman Association, responsible for grants to many homeless shelters throughout the city and country, and he'd risen far enough up the food chain to avoid dirtying his hands with contact as direct as this.

"I have no money for you." He sidestepped the woman's outstretched hand. "Sorry."

"You lie! Attack, Mister Chew-chew! Get him!"

Startled, Tullmo stumbled. A rock on the edge of the reservoir trail got underfoot and he tripped onto his back. The old woman scuttled forward like a crab. Tullmo scrambled to his feet, adrenaline pushing him to sprint away. After a dozen steps he risked looking behind him and saw she wasn't pursuing. He slowed to a stop, putting his hands on his hips and breathing hard.

Crazy rabbit lady.

Fifty or so yards from the opposite direction, another runner approached.

"Watch yourself," he called, angling his head and tossing a hand. "There's an aggressive panhandler back there. She—"

The other jogger lowered his head and charged full speed into Tullmo. The force of their collision carried them both back off the track. Tullmo yelped and tried to disentangle himself but The Jogger clutched him like a vine. They rolled back into the cover of bushes, where the crazy rabbit lady waited with a rock. Tullmo shouted once before she brought it down on his head—

ↄ

Valdes stood over Tullmo's unconscious body. Blood seeped from the gash Bridget's rock had caused.

"He—he ain't dead, is he?" she asked anxiously. "Ya didn't want him dead, but he almost stepped on Mister Chew-chew and I got mad."

Valdes touched Tullmo's neck. The pulse was strong and steady. "No, my dear, he's fine. You did a perfect job." Her potato face radiated. "Now help put Mister Tullmo with the others, would you please?"

ↄ

Donovan spent a restless night in his motel room. He spoke to Joann on the phone for almost two hours and still missed her after hanging up. He paced the room, gazing out at the parking lot as it filled with pick-up trucks and people coming for Saturday night karaoke in the motel bar. He considered his facts.

Whatever Wissex did last August, it turned a little boy into some kind of giant, pissed off monster. The god he worshipped didn't demand human sacrifice, but twelve people wound up dead. The ritual area looked nothing like a circle designed to worship a fertility deity. Purple is not a color of the harvest.

From Talling's report he got a list of the plants and chemicals used at the site, but it only tangled the issue more. He'd spent a few hours on his laptop researching the plants and found them appropriate for certain types of ritual, but nothing overtly evil. The books that Talling had catalogued from the Wissex estate after the murders were store-bought Wicca; again, nothing overtly evil.

And yet...

The next morning, gray clouds heralded thunderstorms. Donovan ducked into the sheriff's Jeep before the first drops spattered the windshield.

"Coffee?" Talling greeted him. He gestured at the holder on the dashboard. "Got some doughnuts in the bag, too." Donovan nodded and accepted one. "You sleep well?"

"On and off."

"Learn anything useful when you weren't?"

Donovan sipped from his coffee and watched the wipers go. "I'm not sure yet. A lot of what I'm doing is woolgathering. With some luck I'll see something that means more than it seems."

"And if you do?"

I jump over a shark tank. "I'll play it by ear."

The ride took almost an hour. When they drove up to the sixteen-foot-high double chain-link fence, Donovan noted razor wire, five gun towers and a guard-filled jeep patrolling the perimeter. Talling noticed him noticing.

"Wissex killed thirteen people. State of Michigan prefers he stay put."

They were met by the warden, a stocky man named Breech Albright. His tobacco-stained fingers clutched a large golf umbrella against the steady rain. "Welcome to Standish," he said. "How's Montmorency, Roy?"

"Quieter than last time I saw you," Talling said. "Much obliged, Breech. This is Donovan Graham."

They shook hands. "I'd like this to be as informal as possible, warden," Donovan said. "Hopefully Wissex can tell me something that will help me stop some bad things from happening in New York, so I don't want him to feel like he's on the spot."

"You going to appeal to his conscience?" The warden grinned. "As many people as he killed, not sure that would have much effect."

"Sheriff Talling tells me he's found religion."

"Yep. Since Zeke's been here he's founded the Holy Rollers—all ex-bikers who have come to Jesus."

"Maybe I can find something there."

Albright led them through the initial security checkpoint. Physically the facility was imposing—solid walls and few windows, limiting illumination from outside. Inside there was plenty of cold, sterile fluorescent light, exposing every corner and allowing plenty of reaction time if someone approached. Hard-faced guards manned each corridor juncture, rubber soles squeaking on the scrubbed tile floors. Nothing was decorative among the white and beige painted cinder blocks. Everything served a function, and the function was security. Tightly controlled tension radiated from everywhere. Eyes stared at him, sullen, bored, murderous. Violence and black despair permeated the concrete like water stains in an old tenement building.

"I was going to have them bring Zeke to the Visitors Room," Albright said, pausing next to a set of metal double doors, "but if you want to talk with him casually, he's in here, the library. The Holy Rollers meet here every morning, after services."

Albright led them through. Donovan gazed around. The space looked like it had been designed as a gymnasium. Its ceilings were high, with a ring of arched windows reaching far enough down the gray walls for plenty of light, but not far enough to encourage thoughts of the world beyond. Rows of bookcases filled the floor, with a cluster of tables between them and the door. Ahead, he saw six men gathered at a long wooden table. All were white, muscled and tattooed. All wore gray prison t-shirts, jeans, and white rubber bracelets embossed with W.W.J.D. All had notebooks and copies of *Confessions* by Saint Augustine. At the head of the table sat Wissex. Donovan had met three other "trust fund kids" in his life; Wissex was bigger than all of them combined. His hair was a mane of blonde and he wore a slightly long, but shaped, beard and moustache. Serenity radiated from him and cast an aura of harmlessness about the men.

Maximum security angels, Donovan thought.

"You want company?" Talling asked.

He shook his head discreetly before approaching the group.

Closer up Wissex was even more muscular than his mug shots and the pictures from his trial; obviously he'd been putting the prison gym to good use. His hands lay relaxed on the table in front of him like medieval maces. He sat extremely still, almost beatific.

"What's going on, Zeke?"

Wissex looked at Albright and the others, then regarded Donovan without malice or sympathy. "Atoning for our sins." His voice was caramel-soft, enveloping and warm. Donovan could see how he'd been able to gather the girls of Blue Moon Bay with a little sweet talk. "Yourself?"

"Looking for answers."

"Aren't we all?"

"About this past Lammas Eve."

The Holy Rollers shifted in their seats. "We all made mistakes, before we found Jesus," said a bald man with a spider web tattooed on his neck. "Zeke's serving his penance for what he done outside."

Donovan didn't take his eyes off Wissex. "You all follow Saint Augustine?"

"His example inspires us. Augustine was also a great sinner before repenting."

"If you killed twelve people, your penance better be more than organizing catechism for convicts."

The Holy Rollers tensed. A couple started to rise before Wissex's shake of the head restrained them. Donovan sensed the guards' hands moving towards their radios and weapons. "I murdered *thirteen* people, not twelve," the big man said softly.

"Did you?"

A tiny crease formed on Wissex's facade of calm. "What are you talking about?"

Donovan waited.

After a few seconds, Wissex waved the Holy Rollers away. The men rose from the table and stepped back but watched Donovan like pit bulls watch an annoying child.

Donovan sat. "Coletun Ruscht is still alive."

Wissex's fists opened and he wiped his palms on the wood, leaving smears of sweat. "I don't think I got your name."

"Donovan Graham."

"You've *seen* Coletun?"

"I've run into him," Donovan said.

"What does that mean?"

"It means he's changed a little since you bought him from his father."

Wissex curled his hands back into maces. "You have no idea why I did what I did."

"You're right," Donovan admitted. "I don't. I don't know why you bought a nine-year-old boy. I don't know why the ritual circle for a god of vitality was a barren waste. I don't know why twelve of Cernunnos's disciples wound up dead worshipping him. I'm here to find out."

"Cernunnos? Ritual circles?" Wissex sized him up. "For a cop, you know some pretty esoteric things, man."

"For a biker, you speak pretty well."

"Ivy League education." Wissex folded his massive arms over his chest.

"I'm not a cop. I'm consulting for them about…an esoteric thing."

"Really?"

"I'm a little bit of a geek about scary things," Donovan conceded without apologizing. "Lately, my interest is being reciprocated." Something flickered in Wissex's face, an understanding Donovan recognized, and he took the opening. "None of the plants used in your ritual were for black magic. Fumitory incense? Basil? Hawthorn? Galangal? I would have expected an orgy to break out with those herbs, not a mass slaughter."

Wissex almost smiled. "That was the plan, all right. An orgy." His demeanor chilled. "In here, people have no sense of humor about helping cops."

"Sure. But your help might stop bad things happening in New York."

Wissex made a "so?" face.

"What would Jesus do?"

"Are you trying to be funny, man?"

"Not that time. Is that just a bracelet you wear?"

"Having principles doesn't make me stupid. You want me to help you. What can you do for me?"

"More than anyone here," Donovan said, "I can believe you."

The big man took a second before answering. "That supposed to mean something?"

"It should. I've been to the ritual circle. Almost a year later, I can still feel something *dark* there, something you obviously never expected. Something that *still* scares you. If you tell me what happened, I might be able to make you a little safer."

Wissex glanced around. "Safer than maximum security?"

"Maximum security is for threats from *this* world." Donovan paused to let that sink in. "You drank too much and smoked a lot of weed. I've done both and it didn't make me homicidal. 'Reefer Madness' this wasn't."

Wissex stroked his beard, weighing his options. Finally he spoke, and his voice was no longer honeyed or soft. Unease coursed through it. "I was raised in a pretty open household, you know? Outside of Boston. Religion was this thing stupid people needed because they couldn't handle the real world. I never really thought it about it one way or the other, but Greta, my old lady, was into Wicca. She introduced me to Cernunnos, and started the whole 'Churners' thing. I figured religion might be a good rallying point for my business, to maybe try and work the Rastafarian angle if there was trouble."

"Weed as holy sacrament?"

"*And* religion was a pretty good way to build an identity."

"A god of fertility was your corporate logo?"

"Branding, man." The muscles of Wissex's neck rolled in a shrug. "I took a few marketing courses.

"Anyway, at the harvest last summer, she thought since we were taking from the earth, we ought to offer something back, our 'energy.' I kind of suggested sex was the best energy and man, she *loved* the idea. She started to search her books and the Internet for a sexual Thanksgiving ceremony. I got to tell you, we had some hot hippie chicks hanging around, working for us, so the idea grew on me, too."

"What can you tell me about the ritual?"

"Not much. Greta organized it all. She picked out the herbs, the candles, everything." His voice faltered. "It was a real project for her."

Donovan remembered the crime scene pictures and wondered which ones had been of the big man's girlfriend. "Where did Coletun come into it?"

"Ah, man." Wissex swiped the back of his hand across his eyes. "You know about his dad, right? Eddie was one of my beer salespeople, peddled some weed on the side. He was an asshole, hanging around, trying to score with some of the Churner chicks. He used to bring his kid around and pimp him out, you know, like a prop to get the girls to come talk to him. If Coletun didn't play along, I saw some bruises the next time. Used to tell his kid, 'I'm bigger and stronger than you, so do what I tell you.'"

Bigger and stronger? Donovan thought.

"Eddie used to suck up to me. Thought it was cool to brag about using Coletun to drop off some of his weed deliveries. Thought I'd be amazed at how he 'insulated himself' from the cops. Asshole." He shook his head. "Kid was smart, though. One time he did get nailed by cops he managed to ditch the stuff in a river, so it got swept away and couldn't be used against him. Cost Eddie some money, though. The next time I saw Coletun he had a broken arm.

"At that point, Greta came to me. She loved the kid, said there was no future for him in his family. She wanted to adopt him like a stray, but Eddie said his wife would never give him up. I thought Eddie was a jerk off who might go away if he got a lump of cash, and, you know, I kind of liked the kid, so I bought him. Eddie would have killed him eventually, man." Wissex gave him a matter-of-fact look. "I saved his life."

Donovan refrained from commenting.

"Anyway," Wissex glanced around before lowering his voice conspiratorially. "Greta said the Thanksgiving ritual would be like our own private Burning Man. You know, that festival out west? Partying, sex, music?"

Donovan knew firsthand about Burning Man. "But on a smaller scale, obviously."

"Oh, yeah. There could only be thirteen of us, so Greta kept it secret from everyone but me. No uglies, no fatties, no Eddies—assholes—were invited. The people who *were* invited weren't told where until the day of. The only thing Greta said was for everyone to bring something from their lives that represented a desire they had. Like, I brought a picture of Greta and a scrap of…wedding dress." Remorse filled his face. "I don't know what happened. I remember it was a cool night, and I remember the clearing wasn't barren at all, when we got there. We built this huge bonfire. We were stoked, fucked up on the best crop of White Widow I'd ever grown, pounding down Jack Daniel's, Grey Goose, a couple of kegs of Heineken. Greta had made some brownies that were fucking *amazing*. Everyone was fucking everyone, and I remember at one point Greta got us all in a circle. She started to chant and threw some herbs into the fire, and things started getting real intense, you know?

"The flames were roaring, man, and the wind started blowing, and we were all fucked up and chanting and dancing, and Greta says to throw our desires into the fire. It was supposed to open the way to achieve them, she said. We all started doing it, and—" He shook his head. "And suddenly I saw Coletun. I don't know how he got out there, or how long he was watching. But when everyone else was throwing their stuff into the fire, Coletun ran up and threw in this picture he had of Eddie and Lola. He always said he wanted to be bigger and stronger than *them*—I guess to pay them back, you know? Anyway, he threw the picture into the fire and…everything changed."

"Changed how?"

"The fire turned *black*, man. One second it was normal, all red and yellow and orange. Coletun threw his picture in and it was like a switch got pulled. Everything got so dark…you couldn't see your *eyelids*, man. The flames were a dark purple and there was no more heat, and *that* freaked me out—a fire that was cold? Everybody else freaked, too, and let go of each other's hands and started stumbling around. Man, was that the wrong thing to do. All we did was isolate ourselves. Once we did that… something else came out of the fire. And then…" He shook his head, staring down. "I don't remember."

"Don't remember, or won't?"

Wissex eyed him. "Geek for scary stuff, hunh?" His jaw tensed. "Okay.

"I was the one closest to the fire. I saw something—it was kind of white, but you couldn't really see it, because you could only see it in, like, slashes. Like there was a strobe light, but not so bright. Wherever any light shined—and there wasn't much, because the fire was, uh, whatever it was—you could see, but where it was dark didn't seem to, I don't know, exist. Like the white parts were windows into whatever was hiding in the dark part. And what was hiding in the dark part..." The big man shivered and exhaled with a kind of harsh laugh. "You want to know what's really messed up? The last thing I remember is I was mad that Coletun had fucked everything up. You believe that? I was mad at a nine-year-old kid for fucking up my orgy." He took a long, slow breath and sat back. "Unreal."

Donovan saw nothing positive coming from a pursuit of that. "That's the last thing you remember? Then how did you end up calling the cops?"

"Well, it's the last thing I'm *sure* I remember. After that, it gets...I felt a really, really cold *something* stab me in the stomach. It felt like someone took a spear made out of ice and rammed it into my guts, but instead of going all the way through me it stopped in my spine and started to flatten and spread inside me. And I was still me but I wasn't, and all I cared about was that I was so *pissed off* at Coletun, and I was going to make him *pay*, but before I could do that I'd have to get rid of these people who would stop me, and..." His voice, which had grown harsher, dropped in disgust. "I did. I think. I think I did those things I saw in the crime scene pictures. I think I chopped every single one of them into..." He paused. "I don't know how. Cops never found any axes or hatchets.

"I think I grabbed Coletun and threw him into the fire, and someone, maybe me, said something in Latin or something. Some words— '*innocentia*,' and '*recursus*'—I remember. Hell, they're ice-picked into my brain. But almost as soon as I threw Coletun *into* the fire, something, some*one*, came out." He shook his head, not believing what he was saying. "Coletun. He was huge now, and naked, and I could see his skin looked like it had been stretched to cover him. He had some kind of designs tattooed on his arms and chest, all kinds of symbols, and his muscles... he was bigger than I am now. He was like an ironhead gone apeshit on steroids and working out. I didn't know human beings could get so...*big*."

"How did you know it was him?"

Wissex laughed without humor. "He grabbed me by the hair. I tried to hit him but he slapped my fist aside. He pulled me really close, and I felt this...energy coming off him, like body odor, you know? He pulled me close and looked right into my face—how he knew it was me, I have no idea, his eyes looked like they were covered by cataracts—he looked right into my face and said, 'I have to find someone, then I'm gonna come back for you. You hurt me, but Mister Fizz made me bigger and stronger than you.'"

"Mister Fizz?"

"I swear to God, I thought I was dead. I think he knew I was thinking it, because he let me go and started to laugh. That was fucked up—it sounded just like he used to, before…"

Donovan remembered the giant's laugh from the aquarium. Its memory chilled him. "'Ha-ha-ha-ha!'; like that?"

Wissex's face told Donovan his mimicry was accurate. "You *have* seen him."

Donovan nodded.

"Next thing I remember is the cold that'd been inside me was gone. The fire became normal again and I could see, and I saw the circle we'd set up in. When we got there it'd been all green and full of life. Now it was like the surface of the moon, man. The only colors were dark, purples and blacks and grays. I saw the…pieces of my friends, Greta…" He took another breath, wetness shining his eyes.

Donovan was astonished by the story, even more because he believed it. *You're not in the classroom anymore.* "So something used you. *You* didn't kill the twelve others."

"I might as well have. I ran things, it was my girlfriend who organized the ritual. I have to take responsibility. And Coletun…"

Suddenly Wissex's behavior at the trial made sense to Donovan. "You think maximum security is the safest place to be to protect you from him?"

Wissex stared for a few moments before responding. He seemed to be putting his mental armor back on. "There's always a lot of light here. There are no open fires, and no one is into Cernunnos or any other weird stuff." He angled his head towards the Holy Rollers. "And I'm surrounded by Christians. Yeah, I feel safe." He regarded Donovan expectantly. "What kind of protection can you give me, better than maximum security?"

"How about if I stop Coletun in New York?"

"The kid walked through a fire from Hell and became some kind of giant monster. How, exactly, are you going to stop him?"

"I'll figure it out. Can you remember what Coletun's tattoos looked like?"

"It was a big design, up one arm, across his chest, and down the other arm." Wissex scribbled a few lines on a piece of paper and tore it out of his notebook. "I couldn't see all of it—it was pretty detailed—but I remember there was a big pentagram at the midpoint, right on his chest."

"A pentagram?"

"And there were these." He handed Donovan the paper.

Donovan inspected the symbols Wissex had drawn. They looked vaguely familiar but he couldn't identify them right away. He folded the paper and put it in his pocket. "'*Innocentia*' I think I can guess—they were probably referring to Coletun. But the—"

"'*Recursus*' means return."

"Return? Of what?"

"You're asking me?" Wissex stood. "Even if I understood what happened out there, I don't have the first idea what to do about it."

Donovan remained seated. "And you aren't exactly straining to find out."

"Like Jake said before, I'm paying my penance. *You're* the expert on esoteric things, dude." He shrugged. "Isn't doing something *your* job?"

TWELVE

RESURRECTUS MALEDICAT

"Someone's coming."

Paolo Tullmo rolled out of his cot, his foot kicking an empty bottle of twenty-five-year-old Macallan. The hollow clink it made as it struck the cell's far wall drew a wince. Through bleary eyes he saw it was nearly three o'clock. *A.M. or P. M.?* His brain hovered halfway between a hangover and the drunk he'd been riding for the past hours.

"On your feet, fellas." A hard female voice roused him and the other three members of the Christian Yeoman Association held captive with him. The overhead lights snapped on. "Time to move out."

All of them had been riding the drunk, actually; each had been given two bottles of scotch earlier in the day. Doug McQuail thought the liquor was a final drink before they were to be killed. Joe Lopter thought it meant a celebration that they were going to be released. Skip Czerki just drank; without cocaine he grasped for any intoxicant. Tullmo shared none of their perspectives. Whoever had subjected them to this ordeal, whatever was going on, he didn't believe for a second what they'd been told, that they were "political hostages."

Tullmo regarded his three colleagues with disdain as they staggered upright. *No surprise I'm first.* "What's going on?" He forced himself to focus through a lingering amber haze. Although still wearing the running gear he'd had on when he was kidnapped, he tried to exude an authoritative demeanor towards the vulpine-faced girl with the Bruised Plum lipstick.

112

"We were told we'd be given notice of any change to our status, including moving us from one place to another."

The silent, skeletal Jogger slipped in behind her, followed by a black man in a top hat. The black man jacked a round into the chamber of the shotgun he held. "*Dis* your notice," he laughed. "Everybody against the far walls, hands over your heads."

"Do we get to go home?" McQuail slurred. "Are we all finished?"

The girl smiled, and the tiniest inkling of discomfort trickled along Tullmo's spine. "Yeah," she said, strapping a rag over his eyes. "You're all finished."

The Jogger clamped manacles on their ankles and wrists, hooked them all together and led them from their cells. "Go on, now," the black man chided.

Tullmo went first, shuffling ahead of the others along an endless path of uneven, puddled concrete and noxious jets of steam. People passed them going in the same direction, making the way smellier and occasionally tight. Claustrophobia swirled eddies in the blindfold's darkness. He distracted himself by wondering again why they'd been held and where. Everyone they'd had contact with had spoken English, although usually poorly and sometimes incoherently. All of the magazines had been American, although strangely none more recent than fifteen years, eight months and four days earlier.

"This way," the girl's voice directed him.

A hand pushed the top of his head down and he was told to step over what felt like a raised doorway. Tullmo stumbled once, and heard the others as well. Wherever they'd been brought he felt heat; dozens of candles burned nearby. He could smell them, and feel burning wax grease the inside of his nostrils with each breath. The sensation nauseated him and he swallowed vomit. Its scotchy flavor triggered something, and suddenly he saw the connection between the Macallan and the fifteen years, eight months and four days. Adrenaline surged through him. "Get out! Everyone!" He swung his manacled arms wildly. "We're not being freed! We're being—"

Something enormous slammed into the back of his head, and he staggered to his knees. Dazed, he was unable to offer any resistance as he was shackled facedown to what felt like a large wooden "X."

"Him first," a familiar voice said from behind.

Rough fingers yanked his blindfold off. They'd come to an enormous chamber of stone walls and pillars out of a medieval cathedral. Rich fabrics draped the walls, weighing down the claustrophobic atmosphere with dark colors and sinister designs. Dozens and dozens of tall white candles, their waxy smoke cloying the steam-pipe humidity, lit the space. They began in two straight lines from beyond the furthest pillar and curved in a spiral, ending in a circular drawing on the floor. The circle was drawn in red paint on the gray cement floor and divided into twelve sections, each inscribed with a different symbol. Tullmo, whose wife read her horoscope every morning, recognized them as the signs of the zodiac. Next to each symbol was a black velvet-wrapped bundle, every one a different size and shape. On sawhorses in the center of the circle lay a nine-foot cross made of dark, glistening wood; a half-melted purple candle burned at each end of the two beams. At the junction of the two beams sat a leather-bound book.

To his right, Bruised Plum and the fat blonde girl adjusted instruments. Bruised Plum wielded a guitar while the blonde girl tooled with a drum machine and rickety keyboard. *Music?* To his left stood three wooden "X"s identical to the one on which he was bound. Lopter, McQuail and Czerki were also strapped facedown, arms and legs spread wide. Tullmo watched as they struggled to see what was going on around the room; they, too, had recognized the voice.

Neil Valdes stood before him.

"Fifteen years, eight months and four days; it's how long you were in jail." Tullmo blinked as his eyes adjusted. "We gave you the scotch when you came to see us last March."

Valdes nodded, and his people removed the blindfolds from the other three men. He took out a cigarette. "You remembered."

"Neil?" Lopter chuckled drunkenly. "Is it really you?"

"What the fuck is going on?" Czerki sneered. His eyes were bleary, unfocused. "Fuckin' wacko."

"Neil, I'm sorry!" McQuail whimpered, spit flying in tiny white dots. "Honest to God, I'm sorry, for everything we did to you! *They* said we had to sacrifice you!"

"'Sacrifice.'" Valdes circled them, examining each in turn, taking in their expressions and demeanors before moving along to the next. "Interesting word choice, Doug."

Tullmo examined him in return. He looked better than the previous March, when he'd come to the CYA offices. Confidence missing then now cast him with glacial control. Silhouetted by the candles, his sweat was melting ice. He wore a black suit with a white collared shirt. In place of a tie, an amulet hung on a chain around his neck. Strange and malevolent, its design came from the same philosophical school as those on the walls. Tullmo swallowed hard but held his upper lip stiff. "Have you gone insane, Neil?"

"From *your* perspective?" The smile never rose above Valdes's teeth. "I think it's fairly obvious."

The other three lolled in the throes of drunkenness, but Tullmo grew more frightened. "What are you trying to accomplish?"

"The larger picture doesn't concern you." The orange tip of his cigarette danced in the shadowy space around him as he gestured. "Your role, the role for all four of you, is at the beginning of the ritual."

"Ritual?"

"Beginning?" Lopter glanced up, dimly aware of his situation but still cheerful. "I thought Cutie with the lipstick said we were finished. She did a good job, by the way. You ought to think about promoting her."

"You *are* mad…" Tullmo whispered.

A flush reddened Valdes's face and he opened his mouth to answer. Still looking at Tullmo, he spoke to Lopter. "A promotion? Maybe you're right, Joe. A promotion is what you give someone who does outstanding work, isn't it? Or maybe you throw them to the Justice Department when all they want to do is build the organization into something great?"

"That was over fifteen years ago. Does whatever happened justify kidnapping the four of us?"

"'Whatever happened'? You can't acknowledge, even now—" Valdes caught himself. "Of course it does. Kidnapping the four of you will get me what I want."

"And what's that? Your job back? Is that what this is geared towards, to intimidate us into rehiring you?" Tullmo searched desperately for a way to get through. "It's beyond that, Neil. Whatever revelations you've had, you have to know none of us live in a vacuum. You have to understand there was, and still is, no way you can return to the life you had."

"No?" Something flickered in Valdes' eyes. "You're half right. This," he gestured around them, "isn't about returning to my old life. Not immediately, anyway. *This* is about getting knowledge."

"What kind of knowledge," Tullmo flopped his hands, "requires all this to obtain?"

Valdes took another hit from his cigarette, long and slow. "*Different* knowledge."

Like a curtain, the darkness parted. The giant emerged, his misshapen face full of anticipation. He carried a cheap metal TV tray, atop of which sat a wooden crate. Tullmo was startled by a sudden mental image of long ago, of his son carrying a present to give him on Christmas morning. In the crate were a bullwhip, a box of coarse kosher salt, knives of various lengths, and a short poker in a small hibachi grill. Glowing red coals filled the hibachi, heating the poker's tip to match their color.

"You have no idea how…flexible reality is, none of you. No idea how many other paths there are besides the narrow, linear one on which you've lived your lives—the one from which you pushed me. When my life was at a dead end, I was afforded the opportunity to experience that flexibility and I embraced it. And what do you know—the more flexibly I behaved, the further I got. It took the best years of my life, dripping away in prison like water torture, and suffering for your sins, to put me on my true path." A chuckle slashed his mouth. "Maybe I should thank you."

"Neil, this is insane!" Tullmo protested. "You can't *still* be mad at us?"

"I *started* with anger." He selected the bullwhip from the box. It unrolled to his feet like a list of accusations. "I nursed it for fifteen years, eight months and four days. After I came to see you in March, after you dusted me off like a piece of dandruff on your Hugo Boss suits, I let that anger free. You took my loyalty and my hard work and you *pissed* on it. What did you think, that you could just get away with it? That you could just wash your hands of *me*? I'm *Cornelius Valdes*!" With a powerful swipe he tore the back of Tullmo's shirt away. The gallery held its collective breath. "I started with anger, Paolo. But I'm not *finished* with it."

"No, you've got it wrong, Neil." Tullmo's voice rose. "Please. I—I'm sorry. Please don't hurt me. I'm sorry about everything. I'll make it up to you! You can come back to the foundation! Neil, please don't hurt me! I'm sorry, Neil! I'm sorry!"

"No you aren't." Valdes leaned in, his voice rough and guttural. "But you will be."

He brought the whip up and lashed a thick, ragged red line into Tullmo's pasty white skin. Tullmo screamed. The high, falsetto sound energized Valdes. A reddish tinge welled from the edges of his vision, loosening his grip on his rage and his sanity. Tullmo struggled, screaming, against his bonds but the whip cracked over and over, peeling flesh first in tiny bits then larger pieces as the skin loosened and the blood greased its separation from the back muscles. Every stroke fanned Valdes's fury. His efforts bent him forward, like an Orthodox rabbi using his entire body to pray. He whipped Tullmo until his muscles screamed for relief. Tullmo shrieked and begged. Valdes ignored him.

"Fucking murderer!" Czerki shouted.

"Not murder." Valdes panted from his exertion. He returned to the TV tray and grabbed the poker, whose end sizzled when he yanked it from the coals. "Ritual killing."

The blood of Lopter and Czerki and McQuail splattered everywhere as he vented his rage on each of them. Energy crackled through the air, and in flashes of lucidity among the anger Valdes understood why the book had been so adamant about conserving emotion. The force he was releasing drove him to astounding heights of cruelty. Every scream that thickened the air heralded something infinitely more terrifying but he didn't care. This was his vengeance. This was his judgment.

As he worked, Coeus moved around the circle, taking each velvet-wrapped bundle and driving a long copper nail through it, securing it to the cross. When he finished nailing the final bundle to the cross he grunted again. Valdes paused, breathing great gulps of stench and the terror as the giant broke McQuail free and brought him to the final spot. Valdes took the dagger, now tacky with congealed gore, and slashed it across the weeping man's throat. McQuail's final gasp became a gurgle as air bubbled out of his exposed windpipe. Valdes dropped the lifeless body to the ground.

"See you all...soon."

The words were barely out of his mouth when something changed in the atmosphere. Multi-hued charges began to arc out of the cross. The candle flames absorbed them and grew higher, stakes impaling the souls of the murder victims. Valdes reached across the bundles and lifted the book. He flipped past the passages he'd read until he came to the end, to the blank pages that comprised the last section. With the blood soaking into his hands and the book's cover, Valdes watched words rise into view. These were the final incantations of the *resurrectus maledicat*, and they slowly emerged from the blank whiteness like new mountain ranges pushing through the earth's crust. His eyes widened in triumph.

"'These Paschal candles, pure symbols of Christian resurrection, serve our dark needs! Let them light the path from the other side! The candles draw and hold the life force here! Let them be as mother's milk, to suckle and strengthen! We have satiated the bloodlust! We have satisfied the pacts and upheld the bargains! We care nothing for the good and shun the righteous! The Infernal have demanded and we have provided! These are the bodies! This is their blood! You *must* accede our wishes!"

Wind from the astral plane swirled like a tornado from the circle's center. Valdes could feel something straining to break through. Holding the book in one hand, he unlooped the chain from around his neck with the other. The wind blew harder, swirling dust devils and smoke around the stone pillars. Valdes held the amulet above his head like a priest offering a host for consecration.

"Do *not* forgive us—"

He hammered his amulet into the top of the cross. A white bolt flashed and the metal sank halfway into the wood. Energy foamed the air with pops and sizzles. Astral winds blew harder; somehow the candles all remained lit. Valdes pressed the side of his amulet and a wicked little blade popped out. He regarded it, then his palm.

"—we *know* what we do!"

He slammed his hand down on the blade.

Pain burst stars behind his eyes and his knees buckled. He wrenched his hand in a counterclockwise motion, like he was opening a door. An ivory flame exploded upwards. Valdes reached his free hand up and into it. The flame became energy and flowed down his arm, through him, over the cross and into the twelve bundles. They began to glow. The wind spun counterclockwise around the room, building momentum as it narrowed around the circle. Dark magic tore the souls apart as the whirlpool plunged deep. Valdes shouted the name and suddenly the vortex reversed. A backlash of psychic energy blew him out of the circle. The wind abruptly died and the silence shocked his ears. The candles went out in rapid succession, a pair at a time, spiraling all the way to the inner circle. The red candles on the cross flared. Valdes watched until the brightness forced him to shield his eyes.

And then, it was gone.

Valdes got slowly to his feet, feeling a chill despite the stifling heat. He rubbed spots from his eyes and searched for Coeus. The giant crawled to his feet.

They both looked to the circle's center.

The cross and the bundles had vanished. In their place lay the crumpled figure of a man. Slowly he sat up.

"The mightiest sorcerer of medieval Europe," Valdes said. "The magician who could do anything. The necromancer whose power was so dangerous his name was relegated to fiction, an object lesson in a religious morality play."

The man blinked and gazed around. "Mephistopheles?" His eyes rolled back in his head, and he collapsed.

"Cornelius Valdes," he told the unconscious form. "You are…Doctor Faustus, I presume?"

℃

Transportation delays with Ralph and his Cessna, along with some weather problems, meant Donovan wasn't able to get a flight back to Newark until ten-thirty Sunday night.

For most of his time in the air he stared out at the black mirror of night, trying to put things into some kind of order. He'd told Wissex he could believe anything the big man said, but did he? *Could* he?

A bonfire turned into a portal? Something coming from it and possessing him? I know ritual magic done "right" is supposed to work—whatever that means—but Wissex's story just sounds…nuts.

He thought about his conversation with Father Carroll, about candles made of ghosts.

Get into the spirit of things. Ha.

Wissex's sketch sat on the tray-table in front of him, and every once in a while he picked it up, glanced at the symbols, and put it down. After some thought he identified one that looked like a cross, with two T-bars atop three step-like lines, as the cross of the archangels, or the Golgata cross. It was representative of messengers.

But from whom? Mister Fizz, who or whatever he is?

Since he only had his carry-on bag, he came off the plane at Newark and headed for the taxi line. It was almost one a.m. The terminal was quiet and uncrowded. As he approached the sliding glass doors, a large, well-dressed black man intercepted him.

"Donovan Graham?"

Donovan stopped. "Yeah?"

The black man showed an NYPD shield. "Detective Marcus Wright. Chief Yarborough would like a word." He gestured ahead of himself with a large hand marred by scars and rough fingernails. "This way, sir."

Donovan wondered how many suspects Wright had ushered with less cordiality. "Sure." He followed the detective to a dark gray Lincoln parked in the No Parking Zone. A black man with a close-cut Afro and neatly trimmed moustache sat in the back seat. Hints of salt were beginning to mix with the pepper, lending him a distinguished air augmented by his clothing: dark gray Brooks Brothers suit, white Christian Dior shirt, red-and-white striped Yves St. Laurent tie, and buffed Florsheim shoes. His style reminded Donovan of the sergeant except that his things were more expensive. Even sitting down he was short, but he held himself with a cockiness that said, no matter the situation, he was in charge.

Now what?

"Mister Graham. I am Chief of Detectives Hugh Yarborough, of the NYPD." Yarborough's soft Southern accent made Donovan's last name two distinct syllables—Gray-yum. "It's nice to meet you."

"Chief Yarborough. I didn't know you wanted to."

Yarborough waited for Detective Wright to climb behind the steering wheel. "Mister Graham has had a long flight, Marcus. Let's get him home quickly." He gave Wright the address to Donovan's apartment. Donovan wasn't surprised the Chief of Detectives of the NYPD knew where he lived, but it was a little disquieting to hear it rattled off so casually.

The car moved smoothly towards the New Jersey Turnpike. "I heard what you did at the aquarium," Yarborough went on. "The NYPD is always grateful for assistance from the public, although if I'm not mistaken, you did apply for the Academy. If I may ask, why didn't you pursue that option?"

"School. Life."

"If the change in your circumstances causes you to reconsider a future with the NYPD, I may be able to help you out. Congratulations on receiving your degree, by the way. Philosophical hermeneutics, isn't it?"

"Yeah, it is." *He knows where I live, he knows what my degree is in.* "I appreciate your interest in my life, sir, but I've got some plans in mind."

"Fair enough," Yarborough conceded with a slight nod. "Now, about your trip—did you learn anything useful to Sergeant Fullam's investigation?"

Donovan didn't answer right away. Whether it was because he didn't want to give the information to Yarborough or because he wasn't sure *how* to, he didn't know.

"You went to Michigan on the NYPD's dime. That makes me your boss. All I'm asking is, did you learn anything for his investigation into these so-called satanic murders?"

"So-called?"

"This is not the first time Sergeant Fullam has gone out on a limb with an investigation that holds the potential to severely embarrass the NYPD. A few years ago he was involved in a situation with one of your professors, Father Maurice Carroll, and could have not only embarrassed the department but also set NYPD relations with the city's Hispanic community back twenty years. As a student of philosophical hermeneutics, you understand the dangers of misinterpretation, particularly involving the deaths small children."

"Hispanic community?" Donovan raised his eyebrows. "Santeria?"

"He claimed involvement by one of the city's practitioners of an alternative form of worship in the deaths of a group at a day care center in Brooklyn. But that's not the issue at hand," Yarborough said, waving it away. "What I'm currently concerned with is his investigation into these 'zodiac murders.' What did you learn out there?"

Donovan considered how he could respond. Through chain of command, Yarborough was technically accurate when he said he was Donovan's boss. Donovan had taken money from him, he owed the man his best (unless he wanted to return the money, which he'd already used to make a payment on Joann's ring). By the same token, he knew the man who doubted Santeria wouldn't want to hear about opened portals and the thing that possessed Wissex and turned him into a butcher.

Not sure I blame him...

He told him about his time with Talling and Wissex, leaving out the esoteric elements of the big man's story. On Forty-Eighth Street, Detective Wright pulled over in front of his building. Yarborough stopped Donovan before he could leave the car.

"Awful thing, the death of a child," he said. "Did you find any clue in the case or in Wissex's story that might help Sergeant Fullam with his current investigation?"

Donovan felt the folded paper in his pocket, the one with the symbols Wissex had seen. He left it where it was. "Probably not, but I'm not a cop, so I'll let him decide when I tell him what I just told you."

"No." The chief eyed him before sitting back. He dismissed Donovan with a brief wave. "Thank you for your help, Mister Graham. However—" he pronounced it "ha-evuh"— "I believe your usefulness has run its course. I'll inform Sergeant Fullam you and Father Carroll will no longer be required to offer your, ah, research expertise."

"You're the chief."

"Yes," Yarborough said dryly. "I am."

Donovan got out and pulled his bag behind him. "Thanks for the ride." He watched them drive away before turning to his building. *"Probably not?"* A slow smile curled his lips. *Semantic games with people who can put me in jail. What am I, high?*

He chuckled and went inside.

Not yet...

THIRTEEN

DINNER AT THE BAR

Donovan wanted to smoke a joint and drift off, but his conversation with Yarborough bothered him. Joann would already be asleep; Father Carroll, like himself, was a night owl.

"Hello?"

"Hey, Father. It's Donovan."

"Oh, hello, Donovan. Is everything all right?"

"Yeah, yeah, everything's fine. Sorry to call you so late, but I just got back from Michigan."

"Ah, the fingerprints. Did you learn anything useful?"

"More than I can go into now. I'll talk to you about it tomorrow, after I have a chance to process it, but there's something I wanted to ask you."

"What's that?"

"What I found out in Michigan… I think I believe most of it, and I'm not sure I'm comfortable with that."

"I don't understand."

Donovan paused. *How to phrase this?* "Look, you know I've read about this kind of thing—demons, possession, all this stuff—since I was a kid. I read *The Exorcist* when I was eight, for crying out loud."

"So you've told me."

"And as I got older, and started to learn about the mythologies and the religions and the philosophies behind these weird things, I wanted to know more."

123

"*Yes.*"

"And I know I'm a big, tough guy, but this? This is…a lot."

Father Carroll considered this. "*Do you remember at graduation, when I told you God has a greater destiny in mind for you than 'research assistant'? I truly believe that, and I believe that involving you in this is part of His plan.*"

"Metaphysics is not reassuring to me right now."

"*Then consider reality: if you hadn't been at the aquarium, I might have been fed to the sharks. Your concern is certainly valid when you wonder about the things we face, but you're not sure you can handle it?*" The priest chuckled warmly. "*Don't you see you already are?*"

☙

For now we see through a glass, darkly.

The morning after he'd done the impossible, Valdes stared at himself in the mirror of his private bathroom. He looked into his reflected eyes, and a smile grew across his face.

We like the view just fine.

He dressed quickly, took the *Vade Mecum Flagellum Dei* book and left his room.

When they'd returned from the *resurrectus maledicat*, Coeus brought the sorcerer's unconscious form down to where they'd held the CYA executives. Keeping Faustus sequestered seemed the smartest bet. Whatever he'd been in contact with since he'd disappeared that stormy night in Germany, it couldn't have been humanity. Who knew how he would react to people now?

"*A man of uncontrolled appetites*" *is how Marlowe described him,* Valdes thought. *Will he be a slob, interested only in food, sex and material things? Did Hell—whatever that is—burn his appetites away?*

Or did the writers get it wrong? Was the real Faustus a scatterbrained scholar in over his head? Was he a professor who snapped under pressure? And how did the resurrectus maledicat *affect him? Is he normal, conscious and capable? Or is he an unstable aggregate of twelve personalities nominally controlled by the spirit of a long-dead magician?*

Valdes chuckled.

Does it matter? He's real.

At the door, he knocked twice and entered.

"*Herr Doktor?*"

He seemed to have walked into the guest room of a medieval castle, complete with working fireplace. A pointed arch framed the doorway and the room's plasterboard walls had been replaced by solid gray stone, displaying rich red velvet tapestries and dozens of shelves groaning with books. A small table held a chest the size of a portable TV. Next to it stood a life-sized marble statue of a man in a toga, who looked to one side in appreciation of the four-foot wrought-iron crucifix hanging in an alcove on his flank. Three standing candelabras formed a triangle around the room, casting overlapping illumination, while a smaller fourth sat on the long table occupying the room's center. The table served as a desk to hold an inkwell and quill, parchment paper, a rough-edged, translucent, sky-blue crystal paperweight as big as a softball, more books of all sizes and textures, and a wreath of laurels crowning a human skull.

A log dropped in the fireplace, burping a cloud of sparks that died on the stone floor. Although it was June the fire felt appropriate; something chilled the air more effectively than an air conditioner.

A man emerged from shadows. *"Wer ist es? Was wünschen Sie?"*

One look told Valdes there was nothing unstable about the man. Contrary to the image suggested by Marlowe's description he wasn't fat—just the opposite. Standing about five-ten, Faustus had a slim, sinewy build given the illusion of bulk by the scholarly robes he wore. His ruler-straight posture suggested self-assurance bordering on arrogance, and as he approached Valdes his movements and demeanor described control, not indulgence. Only in the sorcerer's face did Valdes get a sense of what the writers sought to convey—beneath his smooth scalp, Faustus's chiseled Teutonic features glowed with intelligence. Disciplined, cobalt-blue eyes saw and recorded everything around him. He had presence to burn and Valdes felt the intensity of his focus. For an instant he felt privileged to be its subject until his own suspicious nature warned him not to fall victim to star-struck manipulation.

Faustus stared, waiting for an answer. Questions filled Valdes' mind. He maintained a friendly, low-key demeanor. "My name is Cornelius Valdes. I brought you here."

Faustus's eyes narrowed. "Valdes? *Ist diese irgendeine Art vom Trick, Mephistopheles? Denken Sie mich sind noch so dumm?"*

"My apologies, *Herr Doktor*. I don't speak German."

"Nein? Sie wirklich sprechen nicht Deutsches?"

"But...you seem to understand English?"

"Conjuring requireth an enrichment of tongues," the sorcerer's features hardened, not giving an inch, "which thou, evidently, hath not.

And without tongue to conjure, how dost thou command the presence of Faustus?" Without waiting for an answer, he peered about the room and said, "Loathe am I to understand how it is I am free of Hell and its torments," he shot Valdes with another look, "unless I am *not* free? A new twist to an old game, eh? *Feh!* A poor jest. Faustus doth recognize the hand of Mephistopheles." He circled the table before knocking his knuckles on it impatiently. "Show thyself, devil!" He glanced around the dark corners of the ceiling. "Pray end this round of amusement and begin anew the persecution of a sinner!"

"This isn't Hell. At least, not as you understand it."

Faustus peered at him suspiciously.

"My name *is* Cornelius Valdes, and yes," he acknowledged, "'Cornelius' and 'Valdes' were the names of the sorcerers who taught you. An amusing irony, but nothing more."

"The eternal torment of Faustus serves as thy amusement? Mephistopheles hath indeed wrought these circumstances! What manner of Infernal underling art thou? Begone; Faustus doth dismiss thee and thy 'irony'!"

"I understand your confusion, *Herr Doktor*." Valdes nodded. "You've been taken from what you knew and thrust into a strange new world. *Believe* me, I understand that. But I assure you, this is not Hell. This is the world you left—my best guess—almost five hundred years ago. At least, it is geologically. Politically, intellectually, physically, spiritually..." He smiled gently, softening the blow. "Let's just say there have been a few changes."

"What is the year?" Valdes told him. Faustus's head cocked, unsure whether to believe. "A new millennium?" He went to the portable TV-sized chest and took out a stack of newspapers. Valdes recognized them as the ones he'd left for Paolo and the others. "No props, then, art these? The paper quality? The printing, from a Gutenberg press?" He rubbed his fingers together. "Ink that stains the fingers?"

"The modern world," Valdes agreed.

Faustus regarded the papers with some trepidation. "And...the stories within? The misery, the pain, the joy? Pictograph carvings, but printed as simply and accurately as life itself, all contained within pages also proclaiming items for sale? E-lec-tronic devices? What are those? Shops upon shops of such things Faustus hath not encountered."

"A little overwhelming, I know. The world you left is gone, evolved by human nature, intellectual enlightenment and," he nodded, "shops filled with electronic devices."

The sorcerer examined him, not totally convinced. "Mephistopheles possesseth a keen wit, to be certain. Why ought Faustus accept these things on their face?"

"You don't have to—I'll show you." Valdes motioned towards the door. Faustus hesitated. "There's no shame in caution, *Herr Doktor*."

"Faustus hath faced the terrors of Hell. Naught beyond these walls holds fear."

"Perhaps. However, with caution and a guide, all sorts of paths are opened. I offer my services as *your* guide."

Faustus recoiled. "Ah, Mephistopheles! Thou art revealed!"

"Not at all, although I *would* barter my services to you." Valdes gestured around them. "As strange and new as my world is to you, this world, *your* world, is strange and new to me. I've lived my whole life with blinders on, and for a time I was happy, unable to see the walls around me. Things changed. And like you, reaching the limits of *my* world has driven me to do things neither condoned nor accepted by those in power." He showed a self-deprecating smile. "Unfortunately, I have no Cornelius, no Valdes to show me the way beyond where we now stand. My resources in this aspect are limited. However, my desire isn't."

"Why hast thou contorted thy life to engage Faustus, Valdes?" Faustus thrust himself away from the table, into the shadowy alcove where the crucifix resided. He stared into the face of Christ's cast-iron agony. "What seeketh thou?"

"An even exchange, *Herr Doktor*. In my world, new perspectives have emerged and intellectual frontiers have expanded. Opportunities you never imagined are present in the most mundane aspect of modern life." Valdes smiled. "Instruct me in your world, and I'll instruct you in mine."

"As Faustus sought the counsel of Cornelius and Valdes, now Cornelius Valdes seeketh the counsel of Faustus? Thou *art* my devil this incarnation, I see."

"Your *guide, Herr Doktor*. Your guide. As you'll be mine. And to show my good faith, I'll get you some history books, to help you place all of this in some kind of context. Would that be agreeable?"

Faustus looked him over, wintry eyes without mercy. Finally he gave a single shake of his head. "*Nein.* Faustus hath no interest in aiding the damnation of another."

"That's more my concern, I think. *Your* concern is that I don't care what interests you. I may not be the expert you are, but I've learned enough to pursue my goals."

He tossed the *Vade Mecum Flagellum Dei* on the table. Annoyance in Faustus' expression melted into fear. Back in control, Valdes smiled.

"Let me explain in a bit more detail why I've summoned you…"

∞

Donovan spent the day trying to decipher the meaning of Wissex's symbols before heading in to Polaris at five o'clock. Mondays were slow at the restaurant, allowing him to repeatedly unfold the sketches and look at them.

Around nine o'clock things were dragging. Guzman approached him. "Mind if I go?"

Donovan surveyed the thirty-foot long, L-shaped bar. The stools were all empty. "I think I can handle the crowd."

Guzman chuckled and began to count his money out. Donovan wandered to the service end and inspected the sparsely populated dining room.

"Give me a Johnny Black, rocks."

Behind him, at the juncture of the "L," Fullam now sat expectantly. A file lay on the bar next to him. "Nice silent entrance," Donovan said, coming down to greet him. "Batman has nothing on you."

"Have a nice ride home last night?"

Donovan reached for the square bottle of scotch. "It was a little unexpected to get a ride home from the NYPD Chief of Detectives, yeah."

"What did you tell him?"

"What happened with Wissex, more or less."

"Wissex is the guy who killed the kid?"

"Supposedly. I hope I didn't get you in trouble?"

"Nothing I can't handle." Fullam drank. "You got a menu?"

The door opened, and a warm night breeze brought with it a hint of Joann's perfume. Donovan glanced up and saw her enter the restaurant with Father Carroll.

"Hey, babe. Father. This is an unusual surprise." He leaned over to kiss her and shake the priest's hand, then glanced at Fullam. "And I thought Chief Yarborough said we were finished helping you?"

"A man is allowed to have dinner with colleagues," the sergeant said. "Catch up on the day-to-day events in everyone's life."

Joann took the seat on the short side of the "L," next to the wall, while Father Carroll sat on the opposite side of the sergeant. Without asking,

Donovan took a mixing glass and uncorked the bottle of Chopin vodka. "What can I get you, Father?"

"A beer to begin, I think. Something dark."

Donovan poured the martini for Joann, a pint of Guinness for the priest, and handed menus to both of them. Joann set hers down. "Mesculin salad, porcini crusted mahi-mahi." She sipped her martini, her smile pronouncing it perfect.

"I'll have a Caesar and the ribeye," Fullam said. "Medium. Sides of asparagus and truffle mashed potatoes."

Donovan nodded, taking the order in his head. "Father?"

"The rack of lamb, medium-rare. A Mesculin salad as well, and perhaps a glass of cabernet with the meal."

Donovan reached for a bottle and handed it over with a smile. "We just started carrying it by the glass."

"What is it?" Fullam asked.

The priest looked at the label and chuckled. "A cabernet sauvignon from Napa Valley, called Faust."

Joann smiled. "Really?"

"Why is that funny?" The sergeant looked at Donovan.

"Donovan did his thesis on the Faust legend," she said.

"Well, Faust*us*," Donovan clarified over his shoulder as he put their order into the computer. "He came first."

"The guy who sold his soul to the devil? There was more than one?"

"There're a lot more than one. Most people know either Marlowe's *The Tragical History of the Life and Death of Doctor Faustus* or Goethe's *Faust*."

"What's the difference?"

"In both of them he sells his soul, but at the end of Goethe he's saved by God because he was so noble in his search for knowledge; in Marlowe, he's a sinner too proud to ask forgiveness, so he's dragged off to Hell during a violent storm. My paper discussed predestination and free will in Marlowe—was Faustus destined to go to Hell, or was it his choices—his free will—that led him to ruin? I came down on the side of 'free will.'"

From the back of the wine bottle, Fullam read:

> "*If feelings fail you,*
> *vain will be your course and idle what you plan*
> *unless your art*
> *Springs from the soul, with elemental force*'
> —Faust (Goethe).

Romantic. The wine any good?"

"It is, actually."

"Maybe I'll have a glass, too." Fullam set the bottle aside. "But as much as I enjoy waxing poetic, I'd rather discuss Mister X, *aka* Charming Man, *aka*," he opened the file next to his elbow, "Cornelius Lawrence Valdes."

"Cornelius Valdes?" Father Carroll repeated. He and Donovan exchanged a look.

"Do you know him?" Fullam asked.

"Cornelius and Valdes were the two sorcerers who taught Faustus how to conjure."

"Uh-*hunh*." Fullam stared at them. "I'm letting you two in on all this for some concrete leads on action, not obscure literary references."

Donovan started to speak but Father Carroll cut him off with a look. "Of course, Francis. Thinking aloud about these things occasionally sounds peculiar. Please continue."

The appetizers came. Fullam waited until Donovan set them down before going on. With the salads, the runner brought out a shrimp cocktail. Donovan looked at Corey, who shot him with a finger-gun. *On the house*, he mouthed.

"We know who Valdes is because of the saliva DNA we found in Donovan's wax, and confirmed it with Joann's sketch from the aquarium." He handed around a picture. "Here's the mug shot."

"Mug shot?" Donovan asked.

"Valdes was released from Danbury Federal Penitentiary this past March. Embezzlement and attempted extortion raps, eighteen years, out in fifteen and change."

"Embezzlement?" Donovan repeated. "Extortion?"

"Not exactly the crimes of a satanic mastermind."

"Quite a run of beginner's luck he's had, then," Father Carroll said.

Donovan touched the file and looked at Fullam, who nodded. While the others began to eat, Donovan skimmed the papers. "Degrees in hospitality, business, sociology, and…classical literature? Comparative Religions? Philosophy?"

"Earned the last three in the joint. In his trial transcript he swore he was being screwed over when he just wanted to help; maybe he wanted to figure out why bad things happen to 'good' people. Maybe he was just bored." Fullam paused with a forkful of salad in front of his mouth. "Valdes is a go-getter, even when incarcerated. Orphaned at age six, he brought himself up on the street after running away from a couple of foster homes. Put himself through school with telemarketing and fundraising jobs that earned him the nickname 'The Cold Call Conqueror.' Supposedly so persuasive he could get money out of Jews and Muslims for a Christian charity."

"Charming Man," Joann said.

"Graduated Magna Cum Laude from Columbia, went to work for the American Arthritis Foundation, then the Cancer Society. Didn't seem to like illness, so he moved sideways into fundraising for the homeless."

"The Christian Yeoman Association," Donovan read.

Father Carroll glanced up. "Really?"

"You've heard of it?" Fullam asked.

"Their cause is primarily indigent and domestic violence shelters. The Church has done some work with them." He took a bite of shrimp. "It makes sense he'd end up there. They're his people. But what engendered his downfall? Weakness? Human nature?"

"He was a scumbag." Fullam shrugged. "Pardon my language. I got a certain picture of the man from interviewing co-workers, subordinates and superiors who knew him before he went Inside. Valdes had a knack for finding people's weak spots and hitting them on an emotional level to get them to do what he wanted."

"Pretty handy for fundraising," Donovan said.

"When you do it to advance your personal agenda at other people's expense, it makes you a scumbag." Fullam was firm on this point. "Apparently Valdes decided he could do more to help 'his people' if the charity he worked for got bigger and more powerful. According to his trial transcript, he stole money from that charity to set up a kind of sting operation. He planned to blackmail executives from other charities so they would be absorbed into one giant institution that he, Valdes, would run. He got caught—couldn't charm his way out of it—and sent away when his superiors found out."

"Their home office is in Brooklyn," Joann said. "One guess which shelter, when it first opened, was their greatest success. Twenty years ago Dinkins was considered a model of efficiency and dignified aid for the temporarily displaced. One more guess who was the driving force behind its creation."

Donovan thought she rarely looked as beautiful as when she was totally focused on the moment, even if it was work. "Valdes."

"After his success with the Dinkins Shelter, Valdes tried to strong arm his way into control of CYA. He stole money, got caught and sent away. When he got out, he went to see his old bosses about restitution or maybe a job and was rebuffed. He decided to do whatever it is he's doing, and went to a place where he figured he could recruit help. In order to cover his tracks, he started a riot that killed people and destroyed the shelter."

"And since he knew the shelter," Fullam added, "he knew it was a good place to commit the Capricorn murder."

"Wow," Donovan said. "Those former bosses at CYA help you any?"

Joann shook her head. "They've disappeared, from their homes and, in one case, right from the office. Four of them." Father Carroll glanced up at this. Donovan recognized his expression but said nothing. She ticked the items off. "The Dinkins Shelter riot, the zodiac murders, these kidnappings are all tied together by Neil Valdes, and Raphael wants in on it in a big way. Hence my return to the front lines."

"Whatever 'it' is." Donovan cleared their appetizer plates and reset their silver.

Fullam looked at Father Carroll. "Any luck with that, Maurice?"

The priest nodded. "A little."

Their entrees arrived. Donovan poured Columbia Crest Riesling for Joann and the Faust cabernet for Father Carroll and Fullam. The sergeant took a sip and nodded his approval.

"The chemicals from the wax," Father Carroll continued, slicing a lamb chop, "come from plants that serve particular purposes in ritual magic. I'm narrowing down those purposes in search of a common ritual. If I can discover it, I'll be able to give you either the raw materials he needs or what special conditions he requires so we may track him before he completes his deeds. In that vein, you may want to look for yew wood. The botanical gardens and parks around the city have it in its raw form, but it is also used in furniture, either as inlay or in tables. The want-ads may be a fruitful source of information as well. In addition, there are several religious supply houses you'll want to speak with concerning recent orders of Paschal candles."

Donovan raised his eyebrows. "Paschal? Easter was two months ago."

"Precisely. Since they are out of season, any purchases should stand out fairly well." Donovan started to ask another question, but the priest cautioned him with a glance. "Give me a call tomorrow, I'll show you my notes. We'll see if we can come up with anything."

Joann cut a small piece of mahi-mahi and swirled it in sauce. "Did you learn anything in Michigan that could help?" she asked Donovan.

"I think so. Nine-year-old Coletun was supposedly murdered by a man named Zeke Wissex during an orgy that got out of hand."

"I thought the point of an orgy *was* to get out of hand," Fullam commented dryly.

"They mixed in a little nature worship with it and got something wrong. Like the man said, 'what you don't know can hurt you a whole lot.'"

"Drugs?" Joann asked.

"And alcohol, and lots of both. Wissex said he killed Coletun and everyone while under their influence, then came out of it and turned himself in."

"That's what you told Hugh?" Fullam asked. Donovan nodded. "What about the 'more or less' part you mentioned before?"

Donovan glanced at Father Carroll before speaking. "After I convinced Wissex I wouldn't dismiss his story, he told me he barely remembered what happened because he'd been possessed by something that came out of their bonfire. It took control of him and butchered the other twelve people at the orgy and threw Coletun into the fire. The boy came back out almost immediately, and he was the giant. He said 'Mister Fizz' made him bigger and stronger.'"

"Possessed?" The priest looked alarmed. "Mister Fizz?"

Fullam and Joann shared a look. "Uh-*hunh*," she said. Donovan thought the sergeant's eyes said something less doubtful.

"That's what he told me." Donovan sensed he was going to lose her. "Toxicology reports show all kinds of things in Wissex's bloodstream."

"Hallucinogenics?"

"Some mushrooms."

"Combined with booze and other drugs, they must have given him quite a show in his head," Joann said. "Possessed by a fire monster is a new one to me, but not the strangest."

"There was something else: Wissex said Coeus had a big tattoo across his chest and arms." Donovan took out the paper. "These are sketches of some of the symbols in it. The way he described it made me think of some variation of the *Catena Aurea Homeri*."

"The Golden Chain of Homer?" Joann asked.

Fullam looked at Donovan. "You speak Latin?"

"I've picked up a little from research. Joann's the scholar."

The sergeant turned to her. "Really?"

"*Disci omnes*; I know many things. My father said it was important for a well-rounded education." She took the paper and scanned it. "What's the Golden Chain of Homer?"

"Esoteric alchemy."

"Like *The Alchemist*?"

Donovan nodded. "Sort of. Coelho's book deals with the journey; the Golden Chain describes it in symbols. The goal was *coniunctio,* the total refinement and ascendancy of a human being. The Golden Chain diagrams the path and the process to get there."

"Said path and process being the zodiac murders?"

"I don't know. I hope it ties in to everything that way."

"What do you mean?" Fullam asked.

"If the tattoo isn't part of the zodiac ritual," Father Carroll said, "it must be part of something else. Possibly something worse."

"Worse than torturing twelve men to death and dismembering them?"

Donovan remembered Wissex's story about the thing from the fire. "You have no idea."

FOURTEEN

A BEAUTIFUL VESSEL

Donovan was awakened in his apartment the next morning by a kiss. He smiled and opened his eyes. Joann stood next to the bed, wearing a pair of white satin sweatpants and a black "Nightwish" t-shirt.

"Wow," he said.

"Raphael just called. He wants a face-to-face at ten, which leaves just enough time to go for a run and shower."

He sat up, rubbing his face. "You have energy to run after last night?"

"You give good dessert." She grabbed a hand and pulled. "Come on. If we run fast we can get back in time."

"For what?"

She grinned. "To see if you give good breakfast."

He bounced out of bed. "Race you to the reservoir."

એ

Faustus and Valdes walked through Central Park under a brilliant cloudless sky, through trees thick with leaves and colonies of cicadas, over sporadic patches of lush grass flourishing among dirt paths packed down by countless wandering feet. The sorcerer took it all in with a wistful gaze. Valdes noted this as he guided him towards the Great Lawn.

"Is this what you're looking for?"

An oval of several hundred square yards lay in front of them, surrounded by concrete footpaths, bordered by trees, concrete and wood benches, and marked with six baseball backstops. Behind them, to the north, was the 86th Street Transverse and beyond that, the reservoir. Belvedere Castle sat at the south end of the Lawn, bordered by Belvedere Lake and the 79th Street Transverse.

"*Ja, ja.*" Wistfulness curdled into petulance. "It is sufficient." He walked over to a nearby tree, muttered some words and drew a glyph on the trunk with his finger. The symbol flared to life with unholy energy, then sank into the wood, leaving no scar. "North is prepared." He began to walk west, counterclockwise around the Lawn.

Valdes fell in step beside him. "Despite our discussion yesterday, *Herr Doktor*, our arrangement doesn't have to be contentious. I've delivered the books I promised; is there anything else you need? Anything you want?"

"Thou believest this to be a concern of material goods? What scant comprehension thou hast for the forces with which thou consort. Books sufficiently describe neither the tortures of Hell nor the wonders of life. Life is lived, not read."

"With all due respect; although I may not grasp their subtleties, I understand the emotional energies that drive those forces you describe." Valdes gave a small smile. "The learning curve was steep, but I mastered it."

"The Dark Arts are *survived*, not 'mastered.'"

"Someone controls everything. Deal with them directly, show them how it benefits them to give you what you want, and there won't be any problems."

"Thou speaketh in cold abstraction. We deal in *reality*, Valdes. Dost thou grasp the scope of events to come? Hundreds, perchance thousands, subject to horrible death and damnation, with success hinged on thy self-proclaimed 'mastery.' The only surety to come is evil. Impotent to resist, Faustus must be party to it." Faustus came to another tree, upon which he drew a glyph similar to the first, with the same result. "West is prepared."

"Don't worry about me not holding up my end of things, *Herr Doktor*. Right now my people are arranging everything necessary: George and Lude are wiring up a bunch of old television sets, Dez and Melvin are picking through porn and horror movies and stockpiling drugs and booze, and Bridget, Officer Burt, The Jogger and Coeus are scouring the city for sharp and blunt objects. And all of them are spreading the word."

Faustus stared, surprised by his determination. "Eager art thou to cede earthly life for hellish torment, Valdes."

"I suppose that depends on one's definition of 'torment,' doesn't it?"

"This is the perspective of a child. Just imprisonment, stemming from deeds committed with full knowledge of inspiration and source, deeds ultimately inconsequential save for the price they extract...*this* is torment. Knowing thy pain is caused by thine own stupidity of choice, entered into freely and fueled by thine own pride...*this* is the essence of suffering." Earnestness peeked like a sliver of light through his disdain. "Renounce thy sins, Valdes. Ask forgiveness. This path can end only where Faustus ended."

Valdes sighed. "Maybe I can explain myself more clearly." He took out a pack of cigarettes and tapped it absently against the back of his hand. "You entered into the occult because you sought knowledge, didn't you? You believed you had mastered every intellectual field of the natural world."

"Pride is not the least of Faustus's sins." He drew a third glyph. "South is prepared."

"You learned conjuring," Valdes fell in step as they headed east, "and subsequently accessed the power of a god. The best you could do with this power was, in your words, 'deeds ultimately inconsequential save for the price they extract.' The knowledge you thought would raise you above everyone else did nothing of the sort, because you had no goal, no desire beyond acquiring that knowledge, that power. You sought tools without having any idea of what to build. You had the universe at your fingers, you allowed it to slip away, and you fell. I understand your perspective, *Herr Doktor*. I just don't share it. Unlike you, I don't seek to attain power as a separate being. I will join with that power, and become it." He lit a cigarette, blew smoke at the sky. "I'll follow your lead, but I have no intention of repeating your mistake."

"Intentions be damned! By dealing with Hell thou hast *already* repeated the error. In matters magical Faustus is thy master. Pay heed, lest the devils of Hell have at thee!"

"Perspective on reality has shifted since your time, *Herr Doktor*. The boogeyman stopped being an influence on most people's behavior about three hundred years ago." Valdes shook his head, forgiving the sorcerer's lack of understanding. "The Hell you describe? I was, I *am*, already there. But not for much longer."

Faustus gazed about the park, at all the life and energy, then stared at Valdes for a long second. "In truth, we stand in the presence of Hell. For Hell is where God is not, and between us..." A frown creased his brow as he searched for any redeeming quality to which he could appeal. He saw none. He sighed, filled with regret for his lot, and drew a fourth glyph on a tree on the eastern side. A subtle hum reverberated for a moment, signaling an almost indiscernible change in the energy of the Great Lawn. Valdes looked around. Few, if any, of the people reacted or even noticed. It gave him a thrill of superiority.

"Thou seeketh power to redress wrongs done thee, Valdes. Soon enough thy opportunity." Faustus turned back towards the Cancer Hospital, his enthusiasm for the natural world blunted. "For now, a final task to prepare.

"A beautiful vessel, one who is a force for good, must thou procure…"

⁓

"Breakfast of champions." Donovan held up a plastic shopping bag. "Taylor ham, egg and cheese on a roll. Four of them."

"Feeling hungry?" Father Carroll led him into the study.

"Worked up an appetite, went running this morning." *Not necessarily in that order.*

"I don't know how many sandwiches I can eat just now. That dinner last night was superb." The priest waved him to the chair opposite his book-covered desk. "Faust," he chuckled. "Appropriate wine for you of all people to sell."

"Weird coincidence, the wine and Cornelius Valdes. " Donovan sat. "Don't you teach that there are no coincidences? That God doesn't play dice with the universe?"

"I stand by Einstein's words. However, I never said people are going to, or are meant to, understand what these 'coincidences' mean in His plan."

"Hmm." Donovan raised one eyebrow as he bit into half a sandwich. A blob of ketchup threatened to drip onto his shirt. He deftly caught it with a finger and licked it clean. "Anyway, what about yew wood and Paschal candles? Are you onto something?"

"I may be."

"Why didn't you elaborate?"

"For the same reason I didn't want you to add your own speculations about what those elements might mean."

"What speculation? Yew is a link to the Land of the Dead in Northern European mythologies. I'm not making that up."

"And Paschal candles?"

"Easter—when Christ rose from the dead." Donovan took a twenty

ounce bottle of Diet Dr. Pepper from the bag and opened it, then passed
a bottle of water to the priest. "And amaranth in the wax; also used to
summon the dead. Do I detect a pattern?"

"What do you suppose their response would have been to these facts?"

"Culturally, they're the truth. We're not making up wild stories."

Father Carroll nodded. "Allow me to re-phrase: how did Francis and
Joann respond when you told them about the Faustus legend?"

"He didn't reject it, if that's what you mean. She's heard it before."

"It was a distraction. Amusing, perhaps, but a distraction. Now how did
they react when you told us what Wissex said about being possessed, and
about this 'Mister Fizz'?"

"Joann thought it was drug talk, but Frank...I don't think he dismissed
it out of hand." He cocked his head. "Does Frank's reaction have anything
to do with what Yarborough told me? That you and Frank were involved
in some kind of Santeria thing in Brooklyn a few years ago?"

"Francis has experienced reality's flexibility firsthand. He may be willing
to listen to us, but is not comforted by what we may tell him. And if I'm
not mistaken, you didn't tell the Chief of Detectives about the possession.
Why not?"

"He would have thought I was nuts."

Father Carroll took off his glasses and polished them. "So we have three
people in positions of real world legal authority whose responses to our
input vary from outright dismissal to reluctant, uncomfortable willing-
ness to listen."

"Joann's response was neither of those."

"Joann's perspective is something to which you ought pay attention."

"She'll be glad to hear you say that."

The priest smiled. "What I mean is, she attempted to explain what is going on in terms she understood. That's what you have to learn, Donovan.
We are like the freed prisoners of Plato's Allegory of the Cave. We need to
be able to describe what others see only as shadow so they understand it."

"I'll never be able to play politics as well as Joann."

"You'll have to learn. For instance, how would you explain that at the
aquarium, Coeus addressed me as 'priest' even though I wasn't wearing a
collar?"

"Recognition of ecclesiastic persons is a characteristic of possession, or
at least contact with a demonic entity," Donovan said. "Which is what
happened to him, according to Wissex."

"This 'Mister Fizz' would seem to be that entity. Now how do you phrase that so that you are taken seriously?"

"Tell him to stakeout graveyards?"

"I think we can do better than that." Father Carroll scanned the books on his desk, then slid a legal pad out from under one. "Yew, amaranth and Paschal candles are used individually in certain rituals, but the addition of the missing executives suggests that this ritual is not about contacting the dead so much as *raising* them."

"Raising the dead?"

"There were four men. In a Satanic ritual, four usually means compass points, which suggests gateways. Now—" The priest adjusted the legal pad so he could read it easier. "I found this mentioned in several tomes. It seems to fit our evidence."

"*Resurrectus maledicat.*"

"Cursed Resurrection." Father Carroll translated. He glanced up and met Donovan's eyes. "There's only one problem—the ritual doesn't actually exist anymore."

"What do you mean?"

"It goes back to ninth-century France…"

♋

In his apartment later that night, Donovan heard the entry buzzer. He smiled and pressed it, then opened his door a crack. As he did, a pile of menus fluttered around his ankles.

"Oy."

He scooped them up and brought them inside, threw them away and went to the kitchen table he'd set up in the middle of his living room. Two candles sat in crystal holders, and he lit them as Joann pushed the door all the way open. "Is everything all right, baby?" she asked, entering and setting her briefcase down. "I thought you were working—"

He spread his hands. The table was set with a lace tablecloth and his best dishes and silver. His wine bucket—something he believed every bartender should have—was chilling a bottle of La Grande Dame.

"—tonight."

"I gave my shift away. Surprise."

Her eyes went wide, showing how the gold flecks brightened. "What's this?"

"I guess I'm jealous that they got to have dinner with you last night and I didn't." He gestured up towards the loft kitchen. "Mushroom-stuffed filets and lobster tails, when we're ready. First, the salad."

She saw the plates and smiled. "Blue cheese croutons?" She touched a finger to the dish, then raised it to her lips. "Champagne vinaigrette? Glad to see you were paying attention during that cooking class."

"It was tough, taking my eyes off you…"

"This is amazing." She slid her arms around his neck and pulled his lips to hers. "Thank you, baby. I'm very impressed." She looked at the table and grinned. "Everything will keep for a bit, won't it?"

"I guess. I—"

She pulled him towards the bedroom.

༒

At a little after ten they finally made it to the dinner table. Donovan had pulled on a pair of jeans and a t-shirt while Joann, freshly showered, wore his fluffy white robe.

"So let me get this straight: this ritual exists…but it *doesn't* exist?" She tilted her glass so he could pour the Grande Dame. "Is this one of those philosophical word games?"

"Kind of."

"I don't understand." She sipped her champagne. "'*Resurrectus maledicat*? That's what you think Valdes wants to do? That's what all this has been about?"

"It's our best guess at this point."

"Cursed Resurrection? Resurrect who?"

"Does it matter?" Donovan asked. "I doubt very much it's possible for *any*one to pull it off, much less an ex-office manager, or whatever Valdes was."

"I know he couldn't actually *do* it. I'm not talking literally. If I could trace how he found out about it, though, it would be another thread tying him to everything. Knowing as much as I can helps me build a case."

"Good point. Okay, here's what we have:

"'*Les Penitents Tenebreux*,' The Dark Penitents, existed from the end of the eighth century to the fifteenth. They were formed out of the schism in the Church at the time and influenced by aspects of the Byzantines. Firm believers in and practitioners of the theology of the Holy Roman Empire. 'Dark' because they were not averse to using certain unapproved methods in their rituals, 'Penitents' because they were a penance cult."

"Penance cult?"

"People who believe they can get closer to God by offering physical penance, like monks who whip themselves and wear hair shirts. Anyway; begun in France around 814 A.D., they arose out of a fear that the country would fall apart in the wake of Charlemagne's death. They created the ritual *resurrectus benificus*, a 'benevolent resurrection,' to bring him back and continue his rule." He paused to drink champagne. "Of course it couldn't work. Attempting to resurrect someone, no matter how good or how noble the purpose, is indefensible in Christianity. It's an affront to the resurrection of Christ."

"But obviously someone did better?"

"We found references to two other attempts, both in France: in 1407 when, after the Burgundians murdered Louis, Duke of Orleans, *Les Penitent Tenebreux* attempted to resurrect him to defuse a movement towards a civil war. Ended up murdering a dozen noblemen. They were exterminated when they attempted to murder a dozen maidens to resurrect Joan of Arc at Rouen in 1431."

"But they both failed?" Joann speared a couple of radicchio leaves. Donovan nodded. "If they never made it work, why do you think Valdes would try?"

"*Les Penitents Tenebreux* didn't make it work. A Russian group, the Sect of the Flagellants, may have. Their most famous member was Rasputin. Those times he was supposed to have died? He may actually *have* on more than one occasion. Apparently, the Flagellants realized the key to the ritual was 'cursed,' and affronting Christ, resurrecting the damned, was the way to make it work. Their success was supposed to have been so impressive," Donovan said, leaning forward, "that Lucifer himself reportedly took the ritual for one of his grimoires."

She also leaned forward, feeding his enthusiasm. "What's a grimoire?"

"A book of rituals and spells. Lucifer is said to have inscribed the *resurrectus maledicat* into the *Vade Mecum Flagellum Dei*, a grimoire that contained spells so powerful one could literally punish God with them. Legend says the only people who can actually see it are those who are willing to endanger their souls. The only ones who can read it are the damned. In both cases, people have to make their own choice—free will—to use it."

"*Flagellum Dei*; hmm." A sly grin crept across her face. "Are you serious? You really believe all this?"

"Serious? Absolutely. Believe?" Donovan sat back, and considered everything that had happened so far. "I believe weird things exist. I believe weird things happen; reality is flexible. Are they happening now...?"

A rustling came from across the apartment, breaking his train of thought. Someone was trying to insert a menu under his door. Donovan looked towards the sound, a savage grin forming. He put a finger to his lips and crept quietly over.

Someone is going to wish they had a different job.

In the fraction of time between the brain accepting the signal and translating it to a command to the muscles—

In the split-second before action is taken—

Donovan's instincts screamed: *slipping a piece of paper under a door shouldn't cause that much noise!*

He couldn't stop himself. He pulled the door open wide—

Valdes was kneeling, holding a Chinese menu. Coeus stood above him. Donovan stared. "Shit."

FIFTEEN

"GOOD EVENING, MISTER GRAHAM"

Coeus's arm shot out. He seized Donovan's throat and slammed him into the wall.

"Good evening, Mister Graham. I think you remember Coeus?" Valdes sidled around them to enter the apartment. Smiling, he wagged a finger. "He remembers *you*."

"Let him go!" Joann snatched a steak knife.

"Ah, Ms. Clery." In one motion, Valdes pulled a taser from his belt and fired it. The twin electrodes shot out and pricked her chest. She gasped. He squeezed the trigger, cutting her scream short as the voltage paralyzed her nervous system. "Pleasure to see you again."

Donovan snarled and dug his fingernails into the back of Coeus' hand.

"I'll get our Vessel, Coeus." Valdes was now quick, businesslike. "Mister Graham is all yours."

With a snarl the giant flung Donovan from the foyer. Donovan hit the couch, bounced off the wall and cracked his head on the glass coffee table. He staggered upright. Coeus hooked a forearm hard into his chest, pinning him back against the wall. Donovan kicked wildly. One bare foot struck the giant's stomach; it was like kicking a tombstone. The pain shocked him and his toes went numb. He hammered both fists into the inside of the giant's elbow. Coeus's arm slipped across and off him. His feet touched the couch but his injured toes made him stumble when he launched himself. He collided with the giant's chest and carried them both over the coffee table to the floor. The glass top cracked under the impact. Donovan snatched a handful of the giant's t-shirt and twisted it tight around his fist, bouncing the giant's enormous head off the floor. Coeus lurched upright. Donovan's feet left the floor. The giant balled two fists and thrust them forward, into Donovan's stomach. Donovan gasped. The force flung him through the air and he crashed into his office's double doors.

Coeus stomped over and seized his head. Donovan clawed desperately at the cigar-fingers as they squeezed his skull. He wrapped his hands around the giant's index fingers and pulled. The bones broke with an audible snap. Coeus roared and let go. Donovan rolled out under him and dashed to the bedroom. The ASP collapsible baton he'd picked up at an Army-Navy store on Eighth Avenue was the only weapon he had, and it was next to his bed. The giant thundered after him. Donovan slammed the door in his face but Coeus exploded through it, blowing wooden shrapnel into the room. Donovan felt a piece gash his neck. Blood dripped down his back; he ignored it and dove across the bed. The giant slapped him flat with an open palm. Donovan scrabbled at the edge of the bed and touched his keys on the bedside table. He snatched them and stuck them between his fingers like brass knuckles. Before he could use them, Coeus seized a handful of his t-shirt and threw him at the window next to the fire escape. Donovan crashed through it, his t-shirt and the skin beneath it sliced by a million shards of glass and wood. His arms snatched wildly to stop him from plummeting four stories to the sidewalk. The metal blinds slapped at his fingers. He dropped his keys and desperately clutched at them. The moorings tore away and he thought he was a dead man until the steel supporting rod banged across the sill and held. He careened off the side of the building, barely hearing the debris clatter to the street above the pounding of his pulse. The fire escape was a foot away.

"Ha-ha-ha-ha!"

Coeus leered over the sill. He brought a fist up and sledgehammered it down on the rod. The steel snapped like a pencil and the blinds collapsed in on themselves. Donovan lunged for the bars of the fire escape railing, squeezing them until the metal bit into his palms. Coeus snarled and climbed out the bedroom window. Donovan swung his feet towards the escape's rail one flight down. The giant was quicker, bending and locking his massive hands around Donovan's throat. Donovan snatched at the giant and tore his t-shirt down the front, exposing part of the tattoo Wissex had described. Scrabbling for a handle, his left hand flattened against it. A flash of otherworldly fire blinded him as pain seared his palm. He screamed. Startled, Coeus loosened his grip. Donovan gritted his teeth and pulled his seared flesh free. A piece of his skin stayed stuck, sizzling until only smoke remained. With a grimace he punched the giant. Coeus dropped him. Donovan hit the third floor fire escape, missed grabbing it with his blistering palm, crashed into the second floor and fell onto a pile of garbage bags stacked against the side of the building.

Coeus shouted, rattling the rail in frustration. Donovan lay stunned, instincts fighting to keep him lucid. He rolled off the bags to the sidewalk, vaguely aware of the giant pounding down the fire escape.

Weapon...

Construction materials from city roadwork lined 48th Street but there was nothing useful. His motorcycle was parked at the curb, the Cobra Links chain looped through the back tire. He snapped aware.

Keys!

He scrambled off the garbage bags and to the sidewalk. The keys lay in the gutter a few feet away. He grabbed them. Coeus rode the final ladder to street-level, landing hard enough to shake the concrete. Donovan jabbed the key frantically into the lock. The giant lunged. Donovan freed the chain and whipped it around like he was swinging a baseball bat. Coeus caught the twenty-pound, chrome steel links full in the face. They smashed his jaw and rocked his head back. Donovan swung again and let go. The links wrapped around Coeus's shins, entangling him. Blinded by pain and staggering, the giant pitched forward, skinning both hands raw.

Faces appeared in windows. Donovan cocked his head. Sirens howled, far off but drawing nearer. Relief coursed through him but he didn't hesitate. He bolted for the fire escape. Coeus grasped the chain in both hands and pulled. The inner cable holding it together snapped; links ricocheted everywhere. One glanced off the back of Donovan's head. He stumbled, his arm slipping between rungs on the ladder. Like a linebacker the giant plowed into him, tearing him down and hurling him to the sidewalk. Breath burst from Donovan's lungs. Coeus rocketed a fist at his face. Donovan rolled and felt the air concuss when the fist missed him and hammered the sidewalk. The giant screamed, spraying Donovan with a mist of blood from his broken mouth. The sirens were getting closer. Donovan rolled to a crouch, feinted and lunged. Coeus snatched the scruff of his neck. Wriggling in his grip, Donovan saw Valdes emerge from the building, dragging Joann with him. With a scream of pain, Coeus lifted and threw him towards the construction site. Donovan crashed through a wooden barricade and kept going, down into a trench, down into darkness…

≈

Valdes had an arm hooked around Joann's waist as he dragged her still-stunned form to Ninth Avenue. An SUV cab sat at the corner, the driver reading a newspaper. Valdes yanked open the back door and dumped her in. The driver glanced back.

"Hey, I don't want no drunks puking in my cab."

Valdes walked around to the driver's side, pulled out the taser and shot him through the open window. The driver jerked and danced in his seat, then slumped over the wheel. Valdes opened the door and let him tumble out to the street.

"Coeus."

The giant staggered out of the darkness, both hands squeezing his jaw as though if he let go it would fall apart. His right hand was swollen and angry tears streaked his reddened face. He shoved Joann out of the way and clambered in, the cab sagging under his weight.

"Come along, my boy," Valdes said, climbing into the driver's seat. "Let's get home and take care of—"

He heard a snuffling, rumbling sound from the back seat. He glanced over his shoulder and saw the giant hunched forward, face buried in his hands, massaging his injuries. Valdes watched, fascinated, as Coeus straightened and wiped his eyes dry. His face was healed with no sign of damage.

"Are you all right?"

The giant grunted, not sounding entirely human. His face held a cast of almost demonic light for an instant, then was gone. Valdes raised his eyebrows, feeling a chill that passed as quickly as Coeus' demeanor change.

Hmmm.

He shifted into "Drive" and headed off.

≈

Wet. Blood? Water.

Donovan's eyes snapped open. Agony washed through him, cresting in his left palm, where he'd touched the tattoo. "Joann!"

An Asian man's face appeared above him. "Holy shit! You all right? Hey, there's somebody down here!"

They brought him up into the sea of Midtown North squad cars that flooded 48th Street. Donovan twisted free of the helping hands. "Joann! Where's Joann?"

"Who?" The Asian man, a paramedic whose nametag read "Kwan," shook his head. "There's no one up there now."

Donovan gazed up at his building. It wasn't a place to live; all he could see on the structure's façade was a skull face scarred by the fire escape, his bedroom window an empty eye socket. "Then they *do* have her."

"Take it easy," Kwan soothed. "Let me patch you up, okay?"

Fullam was conversing with a young Spanish man whose growing bald spot made him look older than he was. He foisted the Spanish man off on a uniform and came over. "I hope you've got renter's insurance." He grabbed a patrolman's arm. "Listen, can we get a shirt over here for Mister Graham?"

"Yessir."

Fullam glanced around at the activity. "When I heard there was a disturbance at this address, I told them to send the cavalry." He shook his head. "Too late, I guess."

Donovan shifted impatiently as the medic assembled his supplies. "Valdes showed up with Coeus, and they took her."

"Hell of a burn you got here." Kwan wiped Donovan's hand clean and reached into his bag for bandages and salve. "That's going to leave one unusual scar."

"I don't care." Donovan's palm was already blistering, the shape of the five-pointed star and circle clearly visible. *Great. Marked for life.* He shrugged into a sweatshirt and leaned against a squad car while Kwan wrapped his left hand. His fingers jutted out of the sterile dressing and he flexed them, loosening the bandages enough so he'd be able to grip the handlebars of his motorcycle. "Valdes and Coeus. They took her."

Fullam frowned. "They showed up, beat the crap out of you and kidnapped Joann?"

"I opened my door, they were there. We fought; the last thing I saw before Coeus threw me into the ditch was Valdes hustling her away, towards Ninth Avenue."

"How did they know where you live? How did they know Joann was there?"

"No idea."

The sergeant looked at him, eyes matter-of-fact. "We'll get her back."

Donovan seemed not to hear. "He was definitely here for her. He said,

'I'll get our Vessel, Coeus' before he tasered her."

"'Vessel'?"

"I have to figure this out." Donovan started for the building door. "I've got to call Father Carroll."

"Hey!"

Donovan finally looked at the sergeant. Fullam glanced around, reached into his jacket and unclipped a holster from the small of his back. Keeping it lowered, he pressed it into Donovan's hand. Leather straps held a Glock .40 in place.

"Next time, give Coeus my regards. Right between the eyes."

Donovan stared at the weapon, looking for answers. After a moment he spoke. "I never should have opened the door."

"Not without your x-ray specs," Fullam said. "Not your fault."

"Sure."

As Donovan opened the door to the building, the balding Spanish man jogged over. He was the building super, Alfredo Campanio.

"Damn, *vato*. Why you got to make work for me this late?" The force of Donovan's stare made him stop short. He took a step back and looked up at the shattered window. "You went *through* there?"

"Yeah. And my bedroom door, too."

"Really? You okay?" Alfredo's eyes shifted to Donovan's face, to the gun Fullam had given him, and back to Donovan's face. "*Vato loco*. Give me a few minutes. I'll bring some plywood up, patch it until I get someone to come out tomorrow."

At the moment repairing the window wasn't the highest priority Donovan had, but in Hell's Kitchen he knew it had to be done, and quickly. "Fine. I'll be upstairs."

"*Vato loco*," Alfredo repeated, looking up again as he walked away.

Donovan climbed the stairs with footsteps as heavy as his soul. The enormity of what had just happened was starting to sink in, past the bruises and the shock. He reached the top of the steps, saw the menus still scattered in front of his door, and felt a surge of irrational anger. He kicked them out of the way with his dirty, bare feet and went inside.

The energy of the fight hung in the apartment like the smell of sex. He went up to the kitchen and scooped a handful of cubes from a tray, then held the bundle in his injured hand. Shifting it like dice, he stared at the refrigerator's bottom shelf, where his weed kit nestled out of sight. The temptation to soften the reality of what had just happened in clouds of fragrant hydroponic smoke was strong.

This isn't a crime scene you can go to high.

Instead, he shut the door and went to a cabinet, where he took out a bottle of Bushmills and swigged a mouthful. The Irish whiskey burned past the lump in his throat. He picked up the cordless handset and called Father Carroll.

"They got her, Father." He took in more whiskey, gripping the bottle like it was his last handle on reality. "Valdes and Coeus. It's my fault. They took Joann."

"*I'll come up,*" the priest said immediately.

"No." He shook his head. "I'll come to you. We have a new lead.

"We need to figure out why Valdes needs a Vessel."

༄

"I give you, *Herr Doktor,* your Vessel." He gestured triumphantly at Joann's unconscious body. "A beautiful force for good." Flushed with his victory and the exertion of carrying her limp body, Valdes seized her shoulders and rolled her onto her back. "I certainly hope she's acceptable. You have no idea what it took to get her here."

Faustus took in the curves of her body inside the fluffy white bathrobe with no hint of lust or leer. He took her chin in hand and turned her head, eyes clinical as he examined her features.

"She seems satisfactory." When he saw the marks from the taser darts he frowned. "Once Faustus hath remedied these—"

Valdes spread his hands, "what can you do?" "I *asked* her to come politely."

༄

Alfredo finished boarding things up and left while Donovan took a shower. Now dressed, Donovan stuck Fullam's Glock into his waistband, grabbed his helmet and headed for the door.

He pulled it open and stopped short. His hand snapped to his waist before he recognized the angry face of the man.

"Where is my daughter, Donovan? Where is Joann?"

In no mood, Donovan pushed him away with a hand to the chest. "Get out of my way, Conrad. I have things to do." It was his bandaged hand, but he refused to let Joann's father see him wince.

"You son of a bitch!" Conrad growled, seizing Donovan's jacket. "It's *your* fault!"

Donovan yanked away. "You don't even know what happened."

"I know people *everywhere*. Joann was here when this serial killer and his goon showed up. One of your neighbors told detectives they said they were there to kill you. If Joann hadn't been here, they wouldn't have had the opportunity to take her for God knows what." He looked like he wanted to spit. "Philosophical Hermeneutics."

"Killing me was an afterthought." Donovan shouldered the smaller man back and stepped out of the apartment. "They came for *her*."

"Don't try to bullshit me to soothe your conscience—"

"I'm *not*—" Donovan paused, furiously gaining control of his temper. "They want," he began again, "to use her for something. That's why they took her, because of something about her, about who *she* is. I don't understand what that means, but I will find out.

"And I will get her back."

∾

"Did you kill him?" Valdes asked.

Coeus sat glowering in the shadows. The only light came from a trio of candles and a battered twenty-inch television set in one corner. Wires connecting a computer game console to it cast serpentine shadows along the floor.

Valdes folded his arms and sighed. "We got what we needed. I'm not angry. I just need to know if—"

"*I don't know!*" Coeus leapt to his feet, his scarred visage inches from Valdes's calm expression. "I *tried!* I tried to kill him, but we had to *go!* I would have killed him if *you* didn't make me leave!" He gritted his teeth and clenched his fists, face screwing up into an impending tantrum. Valdes could swear he heard the rumble of thunder, but it was only a growl building in the giant's throat. With one sweep of his arm, Coeus slapped the television set across the room. The game unit flew after it like a child unable to restrain a Great Dane on a leash. They exploded against the far wall in a shower of sparks.

First the aquarium, now this. Coeus doesn't seem much of a problem to him. Valdes considered the implications before ultimately dismissing them. *Then again,* I'm *not Coeus.*

SIXTEEN

QUESTIONS

Joann's body absorbed the effects of the taser shock like a sandbar defeating a rising flood. Consciousness returned in a solid mass, without nuance or detail. At first she accepted this; the torpor was not unpleasant, and remaining at this base level kept her anxiety in check. Detached bits of information gradually began to filter through her senses: soft cloth across her face, garbage dressed with urine, a sense of weight above and around her, newspapers and a rough blanket under her.

She groaned and pulled off her blindfold.

Three bare fluorescent bulbs cast funereal illumination around the windowless room. Filthy, water-stained tiles edged by dark rust and mold lined the walls. The single door had a twelve-by-twelve inch space that was all wire reinforcement and no glass. Gaps in the cement floor suggested furnishings long since removed by scavengers.

Rotating her neck muscles, she took stock of herself. Her body no longer hurt; she was surprised to find there was no swelling or soreness from where Valdes had zapped her. Her feet were bare and she still wore Donovan's white robe, although now it was considerably less fluffy and smelled like her makeshift mattress.

She heard a noise and went to the door. An old woman shuffled by outside, bent back and ruddy face suggested long days gathering sod off the bog for the fire. A white rabbit trembled at her feet. "See what happens if you don't obey me, Mr. Chew-chew?" She jerked its leash and nodded at

Joann. "I'll put you in a cage to starve and rot and die!"

Joann stared as the woman passed into the darkness. *What in the world—?* She banged the door with the butt of her hand. "Hey! *Hey!*"

"Ah, my dear. You're awake."

Valdes came down the shadowy corridor, a ray of sunshine. *Charming Man,* Joann thought. Coeus lurched behind him, and a chunky blonde girl with bad skin followed shyly. He unlocked the door to her cell, and all three of them crowded in.

"Where am I? What time is it?"

"You're my guest, and it's morning. I hope you've suffered no ill effects? The drugs I have are hardly top quality, and I was afraid there might be some side issues."

"Drugs?"

"To help you rest." His smile widened by a few teeth. "You have a big day ahead of you; or, rather, a big *night* tonight."

Fear tightened her face, so she reached for her prosecutor's manner. "What do you want?"

"At the moment, I want you to be comfortable. You're my guest, and I'm not a savage." He angled his head. "This is Lude, and I think you know Coeus. They'll take you to the showers, then to the dining hall."

She folded her arms to keep them from trembling. "I'll ask again: what do you want?"

"*I* don't want anything." His lips twitched, restraining a smile as he glanced at the giant. "Mister Fizz does."

&

Donovan snapped awake.

"Good morning." Father Carroll stood next to him, holding a paper cup from which wafted a nutty vanilla trickle of steam. "Bad dream?"

Donovan nodded, dry-washing his face. "Joann. Covered in blood. Smiling."

"Indeed?" The priest's eyebrows rose as he went behind his desk, to the seat he'd occupied all the previous night. "I shouldn't worry, my son. Dreams tend towards the dramatic when expressing anxiety, you know that."

"They can also demonstrate prescience. Unfortunately, I didn't see anything that might be a clue. Just...Joann, covered in blood. Smiling." He sat silent for a moment. "No help finding her. Like this," he gestured at the materials they'd been searching all night. "I've studied it for years, but when I need it most, it's no help."

"It's only failure if we cease our efforts."

"It's not our efforts, it's our direction, or lack thereof. We have no idea who or what she's supposed to be a vessel for, and less idea than that on how to save her."

"Now we know there are *two* rituals," Father Carroll pointed out. "The *resurrectus maledicat* and the ritual in which Valdes will use Joann."

"You're sure he didn't take her *for* the *resurrectus maledicat*?"

"Fairly certain. The purpose of the *resurrectus maledicat* is to assemble a dozen life forces and create a vessel for the resurrected. In this case, pieces of each victim were removed."

"Frankenstein lives."

"And provides a vessel for the ritual. It thus stands to reason Valdes would need Joann as a vessel for something else."

"But what?" His cell phone buzzed. Donovan looked at the number, then at the priest. "Frank." He flipped the phone open. "Any news?"

Fullam paused a second before answering. "*I've got someone who wants to speak with both of us. Here. At the precinct. Now.*"

"What do you—?"

"*If you wouldn't mind, Mister Graham.*"

Donovan's stomach tightened at the soft Texas twang. "Of course, Chief Yarborough. Give me a half hour."

Yarborough cut off the connection before Fullam could say anything else. Father Carroll looked puzzled. "That was…?"

"Frank's boss, Chief of Detectives Hugh Yarborough."

"Oh, my. Why would he want to speak to you?"

"No idea." Donovan gathered up a few pages of notes. "Guess I'll find out soon enough."

ev

"You don't have to do this."

Joann had waited until she and Lude were alone before speaking. Coeus stood outside the shower room door, preventing any break for it, but Joann had already sized up Lude and decided the chubby blonde girl with the bad skin was a weak link.

"Hunh?"

Joann let the water run but didn't move. "When people are young, they sometimes do things they wouldn't have if they thought about it. I've seen it a hundred times, at my job. I work for the courts in Brooklyn."

The girl stared blankly at her. "Don't you wanna take a shower?"

"I'm just saying," Joann slowly lowered the robe, keeping her tone neutral-friendly, "sometimes people think they're trapped in a corner. I know how to get them out. I'm a lawyer, I do it all the time at work."

"I sleep in the middle of the room, not in a corner," Lude said. "But sometimes I feel trapped. I shouldn't hafta hang out with people I don't wanna hang out with, should I?"

Joann shook her head.

"I mean, it was cool at first, you know? Big C is, well, Big C. No one never messed with me when we was hanging out, not even Dez. Even though she's my friend, she still fucks with me sometimes, you know?"

"Big C is Coeus? Is he your boyfriend?"

"Oh no, nothing like that." Lude flushed. "We just hung out, you know? Played video games—he's got a real cool set-up that George did for him, in his room way downstairs."

Joann stepped under the shower, goose pimples rising under the stinging cold spray. "You don't hang out with him anymore?"

Lude glanced around before lowering her voice. "It got weird, you know? Ever since Mister Valdes and Doctor Fowlstus and those four guys he, uh…" She leaned in closer, face pale. "I don't like it here anymore. I'm scared. *Really* scared."

Fowlstus? …Faustus? Mystified, Joann nodded, sympathy warming her smile. The level of danger she was in left no room for error. "When I get scared, you know what I do?"

"What?"

"I go have a drink. If I go out and have a few cocktails, it usually relaxes me enough so I can see a new approach to whatever's bothering me." She shrugged. "Have a few drinks, talk to the bartender, get my head straight."

"Yeah?" Her blemished features reflected her delight at being spoken to as an equal by this woman. "I like to hang out in bars sometimes, but usually they're too loud to talk to the bartender. Sometimes Dez goes home with him, but I never do." Her face fell. "I'm not as hot as she is."

Joann nodded sympathetically. "Well, if you want to talk to a cool bartender, I can tell you where to go. Tell him I sent you and he'll buy you the first drink…"

☙

Figuring it would be a bad idea to show up at Midtown North with an unlicensed, illegal handgun, Donovan stopped by his apartment and left Fullam's Glock there before heading over. Although he'd straightened up the apartment a little before going to Father Carroll's, there remained a sense of disarray from the fight.

He knew something was up as soon as he got to the precinct. Yarborough's linebacker-sized driver, Detective Wright, was waiting for him outside the detectives' squadroom. "Chief Yarborough wants me to take your statement from last night."

Donovan looked around him—difficult but not impossible. The sergeant's desk was empty. "Where's Frank?"

Wright looked down at him. Between the detective and Coeus, Donovan was starting to feel small. "Take a seat. When you're done, the chief will talk to you."

"Is there any word on Joann?"

The barest trace of sympathy trickled off him. "Sorry. Haven't heard anything." He stepped over and pulled out a chair. "Sit down."

Donovan took a deep breath, restraining his desire to challenge him. *This is another way to find her*, he reminded himself.

After Wright had finished, he took the statement and left the detectives' squadroom. Donovan sat with a can of Diet Coke, glancing around for sign of Fullam, but saw none. The detectives moved around him, occasionally giving him looks that varied from disinterest to disdain to discreet approval. After fifteen minutes he was ready to leave, but before he could Wright appeared back in the doorway and gestured for him to follow.

‽

"Ah, Mr. Graham. Come in."

Yarborough invited Donovan into the office of the precinct captain, waving him to a padded leather chair in front of a large oak desk. The office was done with style, masculine woods and deep reds and golds accessorized with flags—American, NYPD and Marine Corps. Pictures of smiling men studded the walls, at Ground Zero, shaking hands with Mayor Bloomberg, and one smiling with Barack Obama.

"Is there any word on Joann?"

Yarborough sat on the edge of the desk, making himself taller than

Donovan. "Unfortunately, Ms. Clery remains unaccounted for. How-ever," again it came out "hah-evuh," "there is another matter to address."

"No, there isn't. Joann is the only thing that matters. Whatever politics you want to play, play them after we've found her." Before Yarborough could comment, Donovan took out the pages of notes. "Valdes performed a ritual called *resurrectus maledicat*. It had certain material requirements. If we can track him through the suppliers, we'll find her."

"Paschal candles?" Yarborough glanced at the list. "Yew wood?"

"Paschal candles are for Easter. You light them the night before Easter Sunday and let them burn next to the church altar until the Feast of the Ascension. Yew wood is used in magic ceremonies to raise the dead. Res-urrection theme—Easter is the time of resurrection; *resurrectus maledicat*, cursed resurrection. Get it?"

"Raise the dead," Yarborough repeated slowly. "I know serial killers can create elaborate designs to surround their deeds, but—"

"Valdes isn't a serial killer. This isn't about episodic aggressive behavior. There's a plan, and the murders are part of it."

"I believe your degree is Philosophical Hermeneutics." He tapped his black and silver Mont Blanc pen on his palm. "Are you formally trained in aberrant psychology as well?"

"I've had some practical experience in the field. I've also done my home-work—they didn't kidnap Joann on a whim. She's still alive because they need her for something."

"This, ah, 'cursed resurrection'?"

Donovan shook his head. "Father Carroll and I figured out there are two rituals—the *resurrectus maledicat*, and one in which Valdes needs Joann to serve as a vessel."

"Two rituals," Yarborough repeated. "Did the first one, this *resurrectus maledicat*, succeed?" Donovan almost answered before realizing how it would make him sound. "So he committed all these murders, *resurrected* someone, and is now planning another, equally bizarre ritual for which he needs your fiancée?"

Hearing it said aloud confirmed his fears, so he remained silent.

Yarborough stared at him, then selected a file from behind him, opened it, and put on a pair of reading glasses. "Cornelius Valdes is the former chief fundraiser with the Christian Yeoman Association Founda-tion. A brilliant organizer who was promoted to Chief Financial Of-ficer. Apparently this introduced too much temptation into his life, and he was convicted almost sixteen years ago of embezzling the funds he raised. Released from Danbury Federal Penitentiary last March on good behavior. Although, as the name suggests, the charity has some religious ties, and he showed his face at the right churches at the right times, Valdes never expressed interest in the spiritual side of anything besides his bank account." He glanced at Donovan over the tops of his glasses. "Does that sound like someone who gets involved in weird rituals?"

"I'm not trying to justify his motives and, frankly, you'd be surprised at what kind of people believe in the paranormal."

"Maybe. On the other hand, Valdes' actions do fit the profile of someone looking to set up an insanity defense if he was caught in the act of murdering the four men he felt were responsible for sending him to prison."

"What do you mean?"

"We found the bodies of four men in a chamber underneath Saint Patrick's cathedral, identified as Valdes's former superiors at the charity." Yarborough looked a little smug. "Whatever this witchcraft nonsense you're pushing may or may not mean, this has all been about revenge. And now that Valdes has gotten it, he may be working on a way to ransom a deal if we catch him. Or 'when' we catch him, I should say, because why would he want to go to this trouble unless he made a mistake that will lead us to him, and soon?"

"He was just out for revenge? Then why would he have committed those twelve zodiac murders? Why not just kill his four bosses and be done with it?"

"I've been over Sergeant Fullam's work on those deaths, and as near as I can tell, there's no evidence to actually *tie* Valdes to any of the killings except at the New York Aquarium. In fact, I remain unconvinced that many of those so-called 'zodiac murders' were, in fact, murders."

What?! Donovan sat upright. "The methods, the pattern—"

"Some of those pointed out *were* unusual," he conceded. "However, excepting the arrows, all were at least plausible taken in total context—a man attacked by a lion may sound bizarre, but when that man is a security guard at the Bronx Zoo it becomes a case of 'wrong place, wrong time.' Strangulation, shooting, drowning; these are hardly the work of Satan, wouldn't you agree?"

His soft southern accent struck precisely the wrong chord. Donovan chose his words carefully, screening out personal animosity. "I never said they were 'the work of Satan.' In fact, I'm not sure *why* Valdes is doing the *resurrectus maledicat.*"

"Did you actually *see* Valdes throw the curator into the shark tank?"

"The building was locked! They went in, and I saw Katz hit the water a few moments later." Donovan took a calming breath. "There was also a particular red wax at each murder scene. If you let me take a look at the files, maybe I can add something to—"

"I'm sorry, this is a police matter." Yarborough closed the folder he held. "NYPD have our own people. Thank you for your offer, but Ms. Clery's kidnapping has involved the FBI, and they also bring with them behavioral profile experts. The investigation requires no more civilian assistance."

Donovan had been fired before—in the restaurant business in New York City, getting fired was as common as owners who steal tips from their employees. The thought of losing this avenue to find Joann made him swallow his pride. "I would be an asset to the investigation, I can assure you."

"Really? How?" Yarborough looked him full in the face, malice deep within him. "You told me yourself you didn't learn anything valuable talking to a convicted satanic murderer in Michigan."

"I wasn't being open when you grabbed me at the airport," Donovan said plainly. "I wanted to avoid exactly this kind of political dancing."

"Didn't do a very good job, did you?"

Not the first time, Donovan thought. "This is my fiancée. I can help."

"You're a bartender with a degree. Whatever you know about the occult has little or no bearing on this situation. Our people will provide us with information regarding Valdes's motives, with the added benefit of knowing how to conduct a kidnapping investigation." Yarborough shook his head, closing the matter. "I need people who follow orders and regulations. You don't. You are unqualified and redundant. I don't need you."

"But Frank—"

"Sergeant Fullam," a slight, satisfied grin as he sat behind the huge desk, "has been dealt with. I am personally running this investigation now. I have staffed it with professionals who are infinitely better equipped to find Neil Valdes than you are."

"See, that's the difference. *You're* looking for Valdes. *I'm* looking for Joann."

"And?"

"Question of motivation." There was no cracking the concrete façade of Yarborough's self-justification. Donovan took a moment to get a handle on his anger and frustration before standing. "Thanks anyway. See you around."

"If I do," Yarborough said with what sounded like anticipation, "you'll wish I hadn't."

SEVENTEEN

ANSWERS

So many details, so little time left...
Valdes climbed the stairs from the subterranean dining hall, past the decrepit rooms on street level, and up to the Cancer Hospital's fourth, top, floor. The hall ended at a round corner room. From the outside, the room's architecture resembled a medieval donjon tower. Inside, he could see the chamber was almost empty, with some sort of design on the floor.

"All is in order, *Herr Doktor*?"

"*Ja*." Faustus turned from whatever he was doing and met him at the door. "Stay thy hand, Valdes. The gateway is drawn; thou must not interfere, lest the binding spell ensnare thee."

"Excuse me?"

"Such a gateway requireth an unbreakable bond." Faustus gestured behind himself. "Individual elements, though enchanted, remain separate. Once the binding spell is cast, the elements meld until broken by blood of a martyr."

Valdes looked past the sorcerer curiously. "Doesn't look special to me."

With a small, cynical smile, Faustus glanced back. "Entwine."

Inside the room, the elements shifted almost imperceptibly. A low hum of energy, much like the one Valdes had experienced in Central Park with the sorcerer, resonated. Everything in the gateway now bore the slightest shimmer of tarnished silver.

"To ensure naught disturbeth the gateway…" He backed Valdes away from the doorway and drew an intricate design in the air. "Guardian sigil, the Circle of Neith." He sighed, as though accomplishing the deed increased his burden rather lightened it. Valdes tried to reach across the room's threshold. A spark flashed and he jerked his hand back. "Dost thou doubt the ability of Faustus, Valdes?"

"Not at all. I'm a man of details. I'll always check."

"Verily? Faustus instructed thee to obtain a gift of beautiful adornment. Hast thou?"

"As a matter of fact, I have. Well, I'm on my way now to get it."

"When entering into negotiations of this sort," the sorcerer said icily, "a gift is essential. Else all is for naught, and Valdes will spend eternity in abject despair over his stupidity regarding a simple thing."

"I will have it," Valdes said, "in a few moments."

"Make haste." Faustus turned away. "Thy soul hangs in balance."

eo

"You're back," Father Carroll observed from the kitchen. "Would you care for some lunch?" Donovan set his helmet down on the table near the front door and immediately went into the study. Father Carroll followed, reading his expression and body language. "It did not go well, I take it?"

Donovan sat at the desk and picked up the phone. "Well, you were right about how to explain all of this to people. And I was right thinking I wouldn't be very good at it. I was officially fired, if in fact I was still hired in the first place."

"By Francis?"

"By Yarborough. He's taken over the investigation, and Frank is…I don't know where. I'm going to try his cell again."

This is Sergeant Frank Fullam. Leave me a message. If this is an emergency, call me at Midtown North Precinct.

"Frank, it's Donovan. Call me at Father Carroll's." He left the number and hung up, frustrated. "He won't answer his cell or at his apartment. Yarborough said, in not a nice way, that he's been 'dealt with.'"

Father Carroll frowned. "What happened at the precinct?"

"A lot. Nothing. First Yarborough told me he'd 'dealt with Frank,' then he let me know how useless I was, then he told me the FBI is now involved, then said if he sees me again I'll 'wish he hadn't.'"

"Isn't it a good thing that the FBI is involved? The resources they bring—"

"Yes and no. I mean, it's good they're bringing in the big guns, but they're aiming them the wrong way. Yarborough is conducting things like Valdes was just out for revenge—they found four dead men under Saint Patrick's cathedral who have been identified as his ex-bosses. The FBI thinks Joann's situation is a kidnapping. They're waiting for Valdes to contact them with ransom demands."

"Ransom demands?"

"They think Valdes has made a mistake that will lead to his capture. They think that this capture is 'imminent,' so Valdes took Joann as a bargaining chip." The incredulity on Father Carroll's face made Donovan wonder if he'd looked like that himself at the captain's office. "And Yarborough thinks *I'm* crazy for talking about magic rituals." He nodded at the window. "That looks out onto the street, right?"

"East Fourth Street, yes."

"Do me a favor, see if there's a dark blue SUV out there, two guys inside?"

The priest raised an eyebrow but did as Donovan asked, parting two blinds with his fingers. "Yes…but I can't tell if there are one or two men inside." He let the blinds go. "Who are they?"

"Yarborough's, I think. I noticed them when I left the precinct."

"Why would he have you followed?"

"Maybe he doesn't believe I'll leave this alone, wants to keep an eye on me. At least he didn't have me arrested." He slumped into the chair behind the desk. "Did you get anywhere with the *resurrectus maledicat*?"

"There were always twelve victims, or as it was described, 'twelve shall be sacrificed to the strength of the one.' When they attempted to resurrect Charlemagne, *Les Penitents Tenebreux* put to the sword twelve noblemen, priests and generals. Charlemagne was a military commander and the first Holy Roman Emperor. With Joan of Arc, they attempted to kill twelve nuns and abbesses."

"Then if 'to the strength of the one' is zodiac murders, it sounds like Valdes is looking to bring back an astrologer."

"Which, in historical terms, suggests a sorcerer."

"A sorcerer who could give him what he wants—power." Donovan considered this. "Frank told me the victims were all of German descent, all male."

"German sorcerers?" The priest paused. "Most noted Christian magicians in the last hundred or so years have been either French—Eliphas

Levi, Pierre Vintras—or British, from the contingent of Aleister Crowley and MacGregor Mathers. In the 1920s there was a German sex-magic society, the Order of Templars of the Orient. To the best of my knowledge it died out years ago without siring anyone of renown."

"There have to be at least one or two famous German sorcerers in history."

"The idea of fame for practitioners of witchcraft or sorcery is a relatively modern concept." Father Carroll adjusted his glasses. "Historically, the term 'witch' or 'sorcerer' has been applied to alchemists, philosophers or anyone outside 'normal' society, and it was not something to be lauded. Although the first Inquisitor of Germany—Conrad of Marburg, whose charming motto was 'we would gladly burn one hundred if just one of them was guilty'—was appointed in 1231, Germany's most turbulent paranormal times were the late 1500s and early 1600s, the time of the Bamberg trials. Estimates put the number between 40,000 and 100,000 people killed by witchcraft tribunals, led by Bishop Johann Gottfried von Aschhausen, the Witch-Bishop. In addition, witchfinders like Jakob Bithner and Count Balthasar made a fine living accusing and prosecuting people, seizing their lands and property while innocents rotted in jail or worse." He shook his head, disappointed. "As far as famous German sorcerers go, I'm afraid the pickings are slim."

"There has to be *some*body. Somebody well-known enough that Valdes would have heard of, or read about."

"Perhaps he found someone in Grimm's Fairy Tales?"

Read about... Donovan had a vision of the file Fullam had at the bar. "Classical Lit degree. Who, in classical literature, could fit? Who could give him power—"

They said it simultaneously.

"—that you'd sell your soul for?"

"Doctor Johann Faustus," Father Carroll continued in a low voice, clearly impressed with the deductive process. "Well *done*, Donovan."

Donovan was nearly speechless. "That's...just not possible. I did my thesis on the *legend* of Faustus. He wasn't real."

"Yes, he was. I thought you understood that. He was a contemporary of Cornelius Agrippa, Paracelsus and Nostradamus. Not particularly well-regarded by them, perhaps, but real nonetheless."

"You're serious."

"Unfortunately."

The truth of Father Carroll's simple admonition—'reality is flexible'—hit Donovan with near-physical force. *Faustus...resurrected.* He said nothing—there was nothing *to* say—for a long moment. Finally he shook his head. "This can't *all* be real?"

"If you're speaking of the paranormal in general terms, of course not. Not all of it. It's up to you to deduce what is reality and what is falsehood. Your studies make you particularly well-suited to that task."

Donovan sat for a moment, determined not to be overwhelmed. "Whatever any of this means, it doesn't change the goal. We have to save Joann."

"Yes."

"We *will* save her."

"Yes."

Donovan looked around at the books and materials scattered around the study. He wondered where she was being held, and how she was being treated. The possibilities he envisioned were not encouraging. Only one thought gave him hope:

If they need her as a Vessel, they can't kill her yet.

ↄ

Valdes had had a bench brought into her cell while she was eating. Joann sat on it, her hair hanging in loose, damp curls down her back, wearing a simple white dress and slippers.

She wondered if Lude had taken the bait. The girl was obviously under horrific stress. Whatever Valdes had done—*she must have meant Faustus, but how could that factor in?*—had sufficiently terrified her to make her prone to turn. The concept of turning a member of a group made Joann realize she was still in work mode, and it almost made her relax. Had circumstances been different, and this a more ordinary kidnapping (she almost smiled to herself at the thought of "ordinary kidnapping"), she might have been more frightened, more like Lude.

Why aren't *I more afraid?* She toyed with her engagement ring. *Because Donovan knows all of this. He'll find me…this isn't a crime scene to get high and go to.* The thought tightened her mouth, and she chided herself. *He'll find me. He* will.

The door to her cell unlocked. She jumped to her feet and faced it as Valdes and Coeus entered. "All clean and fed?" Valdes asked. "Good."

"What the hell is going on upstairs?"

"Excuse me?"

"In the dining hall, where I just ate," she said. "You've got someone setting up television sets, people in the kitchen cooking what looks like provisions for a small occupying force, tables covered with tarps…what's going on?"

"Nothing that…well, it concerns you, but it doesn't, if you get me."

"I don't. Why me?"

"Come, sit down." Valdes straddled the bench and waved her to the other end.

She remained standing. "Who's Mister Fizz?"

"He wants a few things, one of which I'm here to discuss." His eyes flickered to the giant, then back to her. "Please. Sit."

She kept her face hard while she did. "How did you know where I was to get me?"

"Joann—may I call you Joann? I think we've shared enough to be on a first name basis—"

"All right, *Neil*."

Valdes conceded a smile. "I'm a friend to the friendless, which means in this city, I know people everywhere. It's easy to gather knowledge when no one pays attention to the gatherer."

She looked past him, to the door. She could hear shuffling feet and hushed tones of the audience beyond it. "Your people."

"My people."

"And you feel no qualms about exploiting them? You spent your whole life trying to help them, but now? You've got them aiding and abetting your crimes, and you've apparently deluded them into thinking one of you is a sixteenth century German sorcerer. What is going on?"

"Deluded?" He rubbed his chin as he studied her. "I'll make you a deal, Counselor. I'll answer you if you give me something back."

She folded her arms defensively.

"I'll take that as a 'yes.' What's going on tonight, you might call 'cosmic tough love.' That sounds kind of overly grand, I admit, but I think it's also particularly descriptive. And apt. My world—*the* world—hasn't been right since I was screwed by the CYA."

"Since you stole money and were sent to prison."

He shrugged. "Tonight I'm going to set the Universe right. It's going to be painful—hence the 'tough love' part—but once it happens, none of this," he gestured around them, "will matter. To make it happen, though, Mister Fizz needs your engagement ring."

Her stomach dropped. She didn't move. "Why me?"

"Because you're a beautiful vessel who's a force for good. Both are highly prized qualities in some circles. Mister Fizz comes from those circles, and he's the one who's brokering things. As for my people," he chuckled, "isn't delusion in the eye of the 'deluded'?" He glanced at his watch. "Now, as entertaining as this is, Joann, I really don't have time to chat. So much still to do, you know. I need your ring, please."

She clenched a defiant fist. "No."

"I see." He nodded, waiting for a change of heart. When none came, he sighed. "Well, you understand that asking was the polite way to do this?"

Coeus grabbed her from behind, pinning both her arms with one of his. She gasped. One massive paw swallowed her left hand, forcing it to the bench with her ring finger standing alone. Valdes reached into his jacket and pulled out a hunting knife with an eight inch blade, eight shiny inches of steel.

Fear tasted like coppery dust as she struggled. "No. *No!*"

Valdes gave a self-deprecating chuckle. "I'm a very…approachable person. People tend not to see me as a threat because I'm so empathetic. I admit it's been a useful quality throughout my life, but it's a double-edged sword. Because they don't see me *as* a threat, they don't take me seriously when I *make* them."

The tip of the blade slit a fine line on her skin. A red line welled. She ground her teeth but didn't flinch. Valdes observed her reaction and made a small gesture with his free hand.

"There, you see what I mean? You've seen firsthand what I'm capable of, I've just cut you with this knife, and still you won't give me your ring." He shrugged. "It leaves me with so few options. I can give up—not really an option, I have to admit—or," he rested the knife on the knuckle just before the band, "I can keep *pressing* until I get something."

Her eyes widened but she remained silent.

He shifted his weight. The knife blade cut effortlessly through her flesh, resting on the bone with a sound of a skate blade chipping ice. Joann gasped. Valdes waited as scarlet welled around the blade. He looked into her face, which had gone white. She clamped her lips tight. With a sigh, he leaned his full weight down and cut off her ring finger. A thin red mist spouted up, followed by a thicker spray.

Joann's eyes rolled back, and she slid into blackness.

ꙮ

Without expression, Valdes plucked the finger from the spreading pool of blood, took a handkerchief from his breast pocket, and stuffed it in the wound. He took off his tie, made a rough tourniquet around her wrist, and picked up the finger. It was warm and fragile, like a newly-hatched baby bird. He slipped the engagement ring off and set the finger down on the bench.

Coeus stared in fascination at the bleeding. "What about her?"

"I'll send Faustus down to deal with it." He opened the door and looked back, eyes shining. "It's time. The word has been spread; let's start bringing them in. Tell the others.

"Go."

⁊

Throughout the afternoon, shadows formed and grew as Donovan and Father Carroll pondered questions of vessels and sorcerers. The energy in the room seeped away like smoke, leaving dead ash behind. Exhausted, Donovan sifted that ash one more time.

Why Faustus? Why does Valdes need him?

As he'd told Fullam at the bar, there were many versions of the legend of the man who sells his soul for supernatural favors. They go back at least to Simon Magus in the New Testament's Book of Acts, with the most popular tellings the Marlowe—*Faustus*—and Goethe—*Faust*—versions. Both agree on the basics: Johann Faustus (Heinrich Faust in Goethe) was a proud, learned man who sought to expand his knowledge and power beyond what any had ever possessed. Learning the art of conjuring from two magicians—Cornelius and Valdes—he tries to summon Lucifer "to attain a world of profit and delight, of power, of honor, of omnipotence." Instead it is Mephistopheles, Prince of Darkness and servant to Lucifer, who appears and brokers a deal: he will serve Faustus, provide him with whatever information he might request, and never utter an untruth to him. In return Faustus would sign a contract in blood, renounce his Christian faith and, at the end of the contract's twenty-four year term, surrender his body and soul to Lucifer.

Once the contract is signed, Mephistopheles grants Faustus's wishes but in ways that steer him away from his original, virtuous intentions to focus on trivialities. Instead of learning the mysteries of the universe, Faustus contents himself with such deeds as turning invisible to play tricks on the Pope, cursing a knight who mocked him by giving the knight a set of antlers, and summoning Helen of Troy for his pleasure.

The key difference between the versions, as he'd told the sergeant, was the ending: in Goethe, God's hand takes Faust to Heaven. To Renaissance author Goethe, man could achieve godhood because knowledge was its essence, and man was capable of attaining knowledge. This quest is so noble it transcends all, even joining with evil. Faust was the ultimate example of the ends justifying the means.

The story of Faustus described the opposite. After selling his soul and not repenting even at the urging of angels, Faustus is dragged off to Hell by devils during a terrible storm. Medieval author Marlowe thus described the fate of any man who chose to ignore the religious and moral constraints of life to pursue a goal whatever the cost.

All of it left him with his head in his hands. He opened his eyes and looked at the priest. "Does any of this help us find Joann?"

Father Carroll glanced up from the text he was studying. "Excuse me?"

"I've pretty much re-written my thesis in my head, trying to figure out why Valdes resurrected Faustus." He still couldn't fully believe it was possible. "I'm getting nowhere."

"I admit I'm feeling less than totally useful myself, but we must trust God is showing us the way. However convoluted that way may be."

"The thing is—and maybe I'm missing something here—I can't remember much that Faustus actually *did*. If Valdes is looking for power, I don't understand why he'd choose Faustus. I mean," Donovan gestured at an open book in front of him, a copy of Marlowe's tale, "Mephistopheles is the one who causes things to happen. Faustus directs him, but it's Mephistopheles who makes things work." He smiled without humor. "Mephistopheles—Mister Fizz…"

"Then it would seem logical to suggest resurrecting Faustus was not Valdes' endgame."

"Faustus summoned Mephistopheles." A spark in his chest, a spark of certainty, drew him upright in his chair. "*That's* what he did that no one else could. *That's* why Valdes needs him."

"To invoke the Prince of Darkness?"

"It makes sense. Once he has, he'll get knowledge and power *from* the Prince of Darkness, like Faustus did. Degree in Classical Lit, right?"

Father Carroll leaned forward thoughtfully. "Infernal Lords do need a physical form to manifest on this plane of existence. A living body, not a piecemeal one like the *resurrectus maledicat* created. A living vessel like—"

"Joann." Donovan could barely believe what he was saying. He got to his feet. "Valdes resurrected Faustus to summon Mephistopheles. Mephistopheles needs a living vessel to exist on this plane of reality. Valdes kidnapped Joann to be a vessel. Joann is going to be possessed by Mephistopheles." He stood. "Unless we save her."

"Where are you going?"

"I can't sit around and research anymore. I have to get out and do something to find her." Donovan reached for his motorcycle helmet. "We've been looking for Valdes, but Frank said he's had help. It never occurred to us to ask who that might be. As a former homeless person and fundraiser for them, where do you think he might go for help?"

"Homeless shelters. And soup kitchens." The priest rose to his feet, stretching to his full, prodigious height. "I know people in several shelters around this area. Do you think it's worth talking to them?"

Donovan nodded. "I do."

EIGHTEEN

FOCUS AND DESIRE

W hat's all that noise outside? What's going on?
Is he serious about "cosmic payback"?
Does he believe he's not deluding these people?
Joann still sat on the bench, keeping her bandaged hand down at her side, out of her sight. When she'd come to, she'd managed to drape a piece of newspaper over her severed finger before throwing up what she'd eaten in the dining hall. The sour smell of vomit kept her stomach reeling.

Why did he have to take my ring?

She stared at the wall, desperately clinging to her professional persona, trying to focus on the questions instead of her circumstances. It was an uphill fight; her bloody knuckle throbbed, a constant reminder of what had happened.

The door unlocking made her jump. A straight-backed bald man dressed in antique scholar's robes entered. He sized her up with penetrating cobalt blue eyes.

"Who are you?" she asked. "What do you want?"

He looked down his nose. "Stay thy hand, woman. Doctor Johann Faustus, thrice-learned scholar, renowned astrologer and magician late of the land of Germany and the court of the Emperor Charles, at thy service."

Although she recognized the name, and the delusion, his certainty threw her. "*Who?*"

He ignored the question. Annoyance brushed his face as he roughly

took her injured hand. She gasped. He was brusque and businesslike un-
wrapping her wound, making low noises of disapproval in his throat. He
sighed when he saw the ragged flesh and dark, crusted blood around her
knuckle. "The King ignoreth a damaged Vessel," he muttered. "Valdes,
thou art a fool."

He dropped her hand, drawing another sharp breath from her, and
looked about the cell. Joann raised her injured hand to her chest. *What
is he—?*

"*Welches hath Valdes getan mit thy Finger?*"

She stared at him, uncomprehending.

"Thy finger," he repeated. "What hath Valdes done with thy finger?"

Confused, she darted her eyes at the end of the bench. He snatched the
newspaper covering it away. "Ah."

Seeing her finger separate from her body, lying there like a sausage link,
almost made Joann throw up again. She turned away and swallowed as
Faustus picked up and inspected it. "What do you want?" she asked, continuing to avert her eyes.

"The King ignoreth a damaged vessel," he repeated. "Faustus wilt remedy thy imperfection."

Remedy? He took her hand again, and she turned to see him take and
uncork a vial from up his sleeve. "What's that?"

Instead of answering, Faustus tilted a few pearls from the vial onto her
mutilated flesh. He murmured words in a language she'd never heard and
suddenly a warm, tingling sensation coated her hand. Before she could
comment he stabbed her finger back into her knuckle. A shock of pain
made her gasp. She looked down; her finger was reattached. She held her
hand in front of her face, flexing the digits. "Oh my God!"

Faustus put the vial away and turned to go.

"How did you—?" Her throat constricted as she realized she didn't care
how, just that it *had* happened. "I—I—*Thank you.*"

He ignored her, his rudeness a slap. Joann half-turned and saw the open
door to her cell. Everything about her circumstances rushed back to her.

Go! Run! Now!

As though he'd heard her thoughts, Faustus paused. Without turning,
he said, "Thinkst thou not of escape, woman. This eve, thy role in the
tragedy of both man and devil looms, a shadow from which thou canst
escape."

"*Man and devil*"? She felt her tether to reality loosen. "Then help me."
She wiggled her fingers. "Again."

"Faustus hath healed not for thee but toward an end whose shadow *he* canst escape."

"Of *course* you can! I work for the Brooklyn District Attorney. I can help you escape whatever cult, or group, Valdes has organized."

"Tis not Valdes Faustus doth fear; rather, destiny is the inescapable shadow cast."

She felt herself being drawn into his delusion, and she shook her head to regain her perspective. "Do you want money? My family can pay you to help me escape. You can make enough to leave the city, the *country*, and never worry about Valdes again."

"Money?" Scorn dripped from the word. "Escape? Tempt not Faustus with thoughts of salvation, lest thou hast in thy possession *Magia Naturalis et Innaturalis?*"

What? "No," she said slowly, " but I work for the District Attorney's office. I can arrange legal documents, get you money and send you wherever you want to go."

"'Legal documents'? Thou art a *woman*. What canst thou know of law?"

In spite of what she knew was reality, Joann found herself justifying her words to him. "My gender has advanced in society since, ah, your time. I graduated at the top of my class at Columbia Law. I've worked for the DA's office for seven—"

"Pray, a query: what is the solution when two claim ownership of the same thing?"

"…What?"

"*Ich wußte, daß es eine Zeitverschwendung war. Eine Frau könnte nicht mir helfen.*" Faustus gave her a long look, turned, and walked out of the cell.

She stared after him, thinking about Donovan and his thesis on the Faustus legend, then shook her head. *Their delusions must be catching. For a second there I could have sworn… No. Impossible.* She examined her hand, once again complete. *He doesn't seem to be Valdes' best friend, though. Getting on his good side might not be a bad idea…*

Closing her eyes, she began to dredge up what she knew about contract law.

☙

The sun had set as they began canvassing the Lower East Side. Riding from shelter to soup kitchen to halfway house, Donovan gradually became aware of something in the night air. Indefinable, it drew light and energy from the atmosphere and replaced them with something sinister. No natural illumination came from above; despite the lack of cloud cover, there was no moon or stars. The storefronts of Avenue A, the neon, even the glittering cables of the Manhattan and Williamsburg Bridges seemed dimmer. It was the prime of the evening but there was little traffic, either in the streets or on the sidewalks.

What is going on?

The dark blue SUV followed them at a respectful distance but never left them alone. Donovan debated trying to shake them but didn't want to waste time. As long as they didn't interfere he didn't care about the audience.

It was 9:45 when they reached the Sisters of Mercy shelter on Ludlow Street, the final place where Father Carroll had a connection. He went in to see the nun in charge while Donovan waited outside. He took out his cell and saw on the screen the tiny figure of a voicemail. His pulse jumped.

Frank?

He stabbed the number and impatiently punched in his access code.

"*First message: 'Donovan, it's Corey. It's about quarter after five. You're working tonight. You were supposed to be here at five. Where are you?'*"

Donovan groaned inwardly. *This, I don't need right now.* He skipped to the next one.

"*'Donovan, it's Corey again. It's nine-thirty. I don't know what happened to you, but I hope it's nothing serious. 'No call, no show' is automatic suspension, and Henri is pushing for it.'*" Henri was a manager Donovan disliked, an elf of a man whose sense of Gallic outrage was constantly being piqued by having to work in America. "*'I'll try to smooth it over, but you better have a good excuse for tonight.'*"

"Don't worry, I do," Donovan muttered.

"*'Anyway, if you get this, some blonde girl is here looking for you. Said Joann sent her, but I kind of doubt it. She's pretty skanky looking.'*"

Donovan almost dropped the phone. He stood stock still, mind churning.

Okay. A plan. Need a plan.

He dialed the restaurant. When the hostess answered, he cut off her greeting. "Jen, it's Donovan. Let me talk to Corey, quick."

He came on a second later. "*Donovan? What's going on? Where are you? You were supposed to work tonight.*"

"I can't go into details right now. Is that blonde girl still there? The one who said Joann sent her?"

"*Uhhh, let me see.*" Donovan heard him ask in a voice muffled by a hand over the receiver. "*Yeah, she's at the bar, trying to talk to people. She's kind of weird.*"

"Keep her there! I'll be right up!"

Corey was taken aback by his urgency. "*Okay, sure. Don't sweat it.*"

Donovan hung up. *What now? Try Frank.*

As before, it rang twice and went to voicemail. This time, though, it said:

"*This is Fullam. I don't care what you do.*"

The "s" in "this" had an almost imperceptible slur. Donovan's lips pursed but he said nothing, left no message. As he debated his next move the shelter door opened, allowing out a waft of warmth and light buoyed by laughter. Father Carroll emerged with a nun, presumably the one who ran the shelter. She was younger than Donovan would have expected, her pale Irish complexion looking even fairer framed by her dark habit.

"Thank you, Sister," Father Carroll said as he approached. "And this is my friend Donovan. Donovan, this is Sister Mary Faith."

"Nice to meet you." He grabbed the priest's arm. "We have to talk."

The nun stopped him. "Mister Graham, I'm so sorry for your trouble. It's a difficult situation, but I hope you understand, not everyone in need is a criminal." She took his hand in both of hers, her faint Old Country brogue soothing. "If there's anything I can do—"

"Thank you, sister. I appreciate your sympathy."

She shrugged and indicated back towards the doorway. "I'm afraid there isn't much here tonight. None of the more…challenging guests we get have been around. As far as where they might be, no one can agree on what they may have heard. The only common thread is, a lot of people seem to have gone to Central Park today."

"Thank you for your help."

Sensing his urgency, she let him go. As she turned away, Father Carroll nodded at the cell phone in his hand. "Trying to reach Francis again?"

"Yeah. Still no go. *But*—I got a call from Corey at Polaris. Some blonde girl came in looking for me, said Joann sent her. I called back, she's still there. I'm going up to see what's happening. You've got to find Frank."

"You don't think Chief Yarborough will listen if you go to him with this?"

"I wouldn't know where to find him, and if I did I have no idea how to approach him. Frank is our best chance to get the cops involved."

"Where do you suggest I look?"

"He changed his voicemail message sometime today, and he sounded a little drunk. Try Ninth Avenue. The bars along there are close to Midtown North. I'll meet you at my place as soon as I can."

Father Carroll clasped his hand. "Good luck. Godspeed."

❧

Standing in the kitchen annex to the dining hall, Valdes pulled back the curtain separating him from the mob. He nodded at what he saw—the word he'd had his people spread had been best received by feral predators from the fringes of society. He watched them shamble in, sullen eyes hot with anger or glazed by instability. A lust for violence hung in the air, stirred and strengthened by the alcohol and drugs he'd had distributed along with the food.

Perfect.

"Thy charges grow spirited and restless," Faustus warned from behind him. "Wilst thy tongue maintain control o'er them?"

"I won't have to, not for long. People like this, you give them an enemy and the rest comes naturally."

"Once didst thou promote charity *over* cynicism, *nein*?" Faustus regarded him with thinly disguised disdain. "And now thou art absent all feeling for those souls led astray."

"You can't be 'led astray' to your destiny."

"The 'destiny' of others, it seems, serveth *thine* interests well. Thou claimeth these people as brethren, yet it is thy machinations which casteth them into damnation. Thy machinations," his voice softened, "and the hand of Faustus."

"You think I'm casting them into damnation? Have you taken a look at them? These people are *already* damned. They can't take care of themselves. They're helpless in the face of modern society. They *need* me."

"For what, pray? Struggle, challenge; these are hallmarks of life. The responsibility God hath given each for his own life requireth we judge and make correct choices. In this way do we learn and fulfill our purpose. To act differently resulteth in fallen souls, as," he grimaced, "Faustus doth demonstrate. In God's Universe it can be no other way."

"God's Universe? I ask again, have you taken a look at them? Even if it is the perspective of some that this is 'God's Universe,' I think our friends," he gestured, "might have a different point of view." Valdes remained unperturbed. "I get what you're trying to do. I thought we'd settled this: I've made my decision. If anything, these people are going to ride *my* coattails. They'll benefit from *my* foresight and planning."

Faustus said nothing.

"This is all a moot point, anyway, isn't it? After I'm through, none of this will matter. It's a do-over for everyone."

"Suffering of this sort canst never be undone, Valdes. Damnation is subject not to thy whims of what is 'fair.'"

"I suppose we'll see soon enough, won't we?" Valdes turned his attention back to the mob. "But there is something that may be trouble. Our vessel's fiancé, this Donovan Graham, will probably try to save her. Is there any way to tell if he—or anyone else who might try to stop me—might have infiltrated my little party?"

Faustus stared at him for a long moment, but finally stepped towards the curtain to look.

∾

Donovan raced up the FDR Drive, not caring that he lost the blue SUV on the way. He pulled the Vulcan up on the sidewalk in front of Polaris and slammed the kickstand down, then pulled off his helmet as he ran inside.

Henri was waiting. "Donovan, you are not to be here now!" He moved to stand in Donovan's way. "You must talk to Meghan before you—"

Donovan swept him aside with one arm as he marched to the host stand. Corey waited there with an amused expression. "Nice move."

"Where is she?"

"Over there. I asked Guzman to buy her a drink." He read Donovan's face and grew serious. "Is everything all right?"

Donovan said nothing, already moving towards the end of the bar where a chubby blonde girl sat. She seemed very uncomfortable, constantly touching a patch of bad skin on her cheek she'd tried to cover with makeup. He pushed through the group standing next to her. "Joann sent you?"

She glanced over, startled. "Uh...what?"

"I'm Donovan Graham. I'm Joann's fiancé. Where is she?"

"I'm Josie. Josie Ludescowicz. They call me Lude." His directness caused her to shrink in on herself. "Uh, I don't know. I mean, I know where she was, but...can I talk to you? Miz Clery said I could talk to you about stuff."

It was with great effort that Donovan calmed himself. He became aware of people watching him, so he took a deep breath and nodded. "All right. Let's take a ride."

❧

Back at his apartment, he made a show of locking the door behind them. "Safe now. Is Joann all right? Where is she?"

Lude gazed around the living room, guilty and sad, and for an instant Donovan was reminded of a photo of Coletun's mother Lola. "They're keeping her in one of the rooms downstairs. Not on the dining hall floor. Below that. I think it used to be an operating room, but there's nothing in there anymore, just—"

"Operating room? Is she in a hospital?"

"Oh! Uh…I don't know. I guess it could have been. I think Mister Valdes told me and Dez when we first started living there, but I don't remember things so good sometimes. It's why I failed out of school." She gave a halfhearted shrug. "I guess it's how I ended up with Dez and them, and Mister Valdes."

"Where was it? That you ended up?"

"I don't know. Somewhere near the park." She squinted at him, twisting her fingers together. Her eyes were wet. "I don't want to go back. That's why I left. Miz Clery said I could talk to you about it."

Donovan held a poker face, desperately needing the information but not wanting to scare her. "Of course you can. But don't you think it'd be better to go get Joann first? If anything happens to her—"

"Oh, something's gonna happen to her tonight. Mister Valdes acted like she was the most important part of everything."

He was barely able to restrain himself from grabbing the girl and shaking the truth out of her. "Where is she?"

"It's near Central Park, way up there. I used to have to take the subway to get anywhere. Big C broke a hole in the wall in the basement so we could go into the tunnels. It was kind of fun, like exploring caves back home…" She sighed, swiping at the tears that welled in her eyes.

Whatever her role in Joann's fate, she was a pitiable figure. Donovan steadied his temper and put an arm around her shoulder. She leaned into him, and he felt wetness through his t-shirt to his chest. "I'll get you someplace safe until this is over. I promise." She sniffed. "You said Valdes has her in a hospital near Central Park?"

"A really old one. No one uses it anymore. The only doctor there is Doctor Fowlstus."

Faustus. After everything, Donovan still had to take a moment to accept what he was hearing. He shook his head. "Is it an old building *in* the park?"

"It's across the street." She sniffled again. He handed her a box of tissues. "A bunch of buildings together."

"East Side or West Side?"

"Uh...Central Park West."

He went to his office and retrieved Andrew Dolkart's *Guide to New York City Landmarks.* "Do you have any idea what street?"

"Uh...a hundred and...six. One Hundred Sixth Street!"

Thumbing the pages, he came to the section *59th Street to 110th Street, West Side.* One entry leapt out at him.

New York Cancer Hospital, 32 West 106th Street.

❧

Valdes took the stage at 10:13 p.m. The mob, thoroughly enjoying the cheap liquor and drugs being offered, paid no notice until he took out his revolver and fired two shots up. Nobody panicked—this crowd was well-familiar with gunfire—but it got their attention.

"A long time ago," he began without preamble, "I hosted events much like this for my job. One of the first things I was taught was that to make an evening truly memorable, you need a gift for the guests. Something personal that will make a statement about the purpose of the evening. Tonight," he took out a cigarette, "I have something for you all."

"Pussy!" a drunken, skinny white teen shouted from the front.

Valdes lit up, unoffended and in control. "Better."

"Really *good* pussy?"

"Even better." Raucous laughter spread. Valdes was unperturbed. "What *don't* you have? Don't say it," he warned the teen with a good-natured smile. "Looking around, I'd say a lot of you don't have a steady place to stay, or a stable income, or family to turn to, or many true friends." A few voices rose in protest. He shook his head twice and held up a restraining hand. "No offense. Understand, I'm not offering pity. I'm no traveling preacher, and this is no soup kitchen party. I'm not here to discuss or condemn whatever you did that put you in your current circumstances. Frankly, I don't care. The past is no longer my concern, and after tonight, it won't be your concern either. A home? A job? Friends, family? You may lack them, but does that make you any less worthy a human being? Not to me. There *are* those who would believe that, you may believe that yourselves, but *I* don't. I believe you have the most important thing, the most *necessary* thing, to get them if you want them. In fact, you can get *whatever* you want, if you want it badly enough. 'The seeds of godlike power are in us still. Gods are we, bards, saints, heroes, if we will.'" He had a drag off the cigarette. "I'm not offering pity. I'm offering much, much more."

He exhaled smoke and watched the cloud drift over the mob. As it descended so did his gaze, and he made eye contact with a half-dozen people. None shied away; the sincerity, the *truth* in his voice had every one of them wanting to know more.

"I had a wonderful life—job, wife, money, house—but to get it I was forced to give others power over me. When I became a threat to them, those people used that power. My job? Gone. My wife? Left me. My bank account? Taken by the government. Me? The Danbury Federal Penitentiary became my home."

Even now he was unable to keep the bitterness entirely from his voice. The crowd heard it and responded, the tone of their rumblings growing uglier. Alcohol, drugs and the paranoia of tightly-packed bodies simmered resentment from their personal experience. Valdes noted this.

"There's something that they don't tell you, the people who have things, a secret to their success. Would you like to know what it is?

"Getting what you want…is *easy*."

He paused for effect, a thin smile beneath the wisp of smoke that curled from his nostrils. The mob growled, restless and caged. On the monitor screen nearest him, a man was viciously stabbed, spilling greasy intestines and a flood of blood.

"It's easy," he repeated, "*if* you have focus and desire.

"Focus is tricky. Knowing what you want is probably hardest for most people, but not for all of you. *I* know what you all want. After months, *years* in jail, on the street, pushed around like punks, ignored except when you offend some asshole's sense of what's right or wrong, you want to be on top. You want your struggles to *mean* something in the real world. You want the rewards you *deserve* by right of your pain and struggle, rewards that by all rights are yours, rewards they've stolen! Because they *have* stolen from you—nobody gets rich or successful on their own! The only way they've succeeded is on *your* sweat, *your* blood, *your* hard work! They owe you, but do they care? No! You want to put your foot on the neck of every one of those scumbags and let them know that *you* are in charge of your life, not them. You want to force them to stop denying you what's rightfully yours, force them to stop blocking your way to everything this world has to offer, force them to make restitution.

"You want them to *really* pay."

A group pushed forward, provoking threats and a few punches.

"So we agree," he went on, voice rising. "You know what you want. You have the focus, but do you have the *desire* to get it? *I* do. Everything I want is just beyond my reach, but I can see it. I'm willing to do whatever it takes to get it. No one will stand in my way. *No one.*

"Who's with me?"

As the mob roared he scanned the hall, eyes coming to rest on a Hispanic man wearing a nylon skullcap. The man kept his head low, hiding in the center of the crowd. Valdes glanced back at Faustus, who nodded grimly.

"You, sir," Valdes said in a voice of shaved ice. "Would you step up here for a moment, please?"

The man looked startled. A circle suddenly cleared around him. He turned to the left but saw Melvin brandishing a machete. He looked right and saw Officer Burt in his filthy uniform coat and police hat, clenching fists that sported brass knuckles. He whirled to make a break for it—

Coeus emerged from the shadows and slammed him to the ground with one punch.

The mob howled. Valdes watched with satisfaction as the giant snaked his pipeline arms into a full nelson around the dazed man's neck and marched him through the chaos to the stage. He glanced around the room and jerked his head. Dez, Bridget, George and The Jogger pulled tarps off four long tables, revealing knives, swords, nail-studded clubs, machetes, broken bottles...

Everyone in the room started grabbing weapons.

"Does anyone else here recognize an undercover police officer when they see one?" Valdes motioned for Dez to join him on stage.

The Hispanic man struggled in Coeus' grip. "Man, the fuck're you talking about? I ain't no motherfucking cop!"

Valdes ignored him. "His shoes, my dear."

Dez pulled the hiking boot off his right foot and handed it over. Valdes peeled back the insole and held it high for everyone to see. A shiny badge caught the light just right, winking at them all. Those in front screamed obscenities, and as one the mob surged forward.

"You can't kill me!" the Hispanic man shouted. "I got back-up coming!"

Valdes' snarl described his disbelief. "I will never let the police stand in my way, *ever again*." All of his anger, every bit of his rage, was furiously controlled, channeled into his words. He turned to the crowd. "And as of this moment, neither will any of *you*."

He pushed the man off the stage. The mob fell on him, drowning his screams.

"Now go," Valdes growled, "take the park."

NINETEEN

THE SIXTH TYPE

"Y ou all ready?" Donovan asked Lude. He waited for an affirmative before flipping down the front of his motorcycle helmet. "Hang on."

He rode the Vulcan up Eighth Avenue and around Columbus Circle. Picking his way through the traffic of some sort of construction project that involved concrete cinder blocks and wrought-iron fence spires, he followed Broadway uptown, towards 106th Street. He parked on 106th and West End Avenue. Central Park West was three cross-town blocks away. It would take a few minutes to walk to the Cancer Hospital from there, but the distance would give him time to review with Lude. He would have preferred to leave her behind in the relative safety of his apartment, but her attempts to describe where Joann's cell was in the hospital were scattered and unreliable. Her presence, though, had given him a plan.

"You're *sure* no one knows you left to escape?" He locked their helmets to the Vulcan, slipped the keys into his boot, and started walking.

"If anyone knew, I'd be dead." She smiled nervously. "Don't tell them."

"Just be cool. This will work. You said you guys were out all day gathering people? I'm your newest recruit." At the apartment he'd changed into ratty clothes, and splashed some Bushmills on himself for effect. "Get me inside and we'll go down to Joann's cell. We'll try to get in and out before anyone knows what's going on."

"If you say so."

At the corner of 106th and Manhattan Avenue, Donovan looked down towards Central Park West. A wooden fence screened the lower half of the block. Tall shadows of buildings loomed in the meager streetlight. Saliva evaporated from his mouth. His heartbeat drummed louder but softened as they got nearer—there was no noise, no sound coming from inside the compound. He glanced at Lude, who looked confused herself. They approached a gate in the fence and he saw it had been nearly torn from its hinges. The dirt and stray papers nearby were flattened, and some garbage that had been within the fence was now scattered and blowing in the street.

Deserted?

He glanced around and stepped through the opening.

The Cancer Hospital was no modern concrete and steel cracker box; with its corner turrets and Gothic architecture, it seemed designed more for restraint than recuperation. Even with occasional sounds from the nearby traffic the courtyard felt intensely isolated. Darkness filled the clearing with insulating numbness. Litter blew around his ankles while a million broken bottles crunched underfoot. The buildings looked condemned for a century, too creepy even for squatters. He turned to scan for signs of life behind the empty windows. Four stories up, light flickered in a turret atop a corner tower.

"You said she was *down*stairs?" Lude nodded. He angled his head towards the light. "Do you know what that is?" She shook her head. He stared up at it for a moment longer, filled with uneasy suspicion that it was important. Time was an issue, though, so there was only one priority. "All right," he said, turning away, "let's go find Joann."

"When I left, this place was packed with people," she whispered. "Two or three hundred, at least. Where is everyone?"

"I think we're about to find out. Which way is downstairs?"

"Over here." She led him through a door-less doorway into a filthy brick stairwell. Cracked, worn concrete steps led down, illuminated by a lone string of twenty-watt bulbs. "The way to her cell leads right past the dining hall," she whispered. "That's where Mister Valdes set the party up."

The further they went down, the more he got the feeling the place had been abandoned. There was the same atmospheric quality of chaos and recently spent energy here as at his apartment after the fight. Water stains, patches of black mold and crumbling plaster and brick marked every step of the way with nightmarish graffiti. It smelled musty and damp, with an undercurrent of unwashed body, but he was surprised there was no bitter stink of urine in the mix.

Valdes kept that much order, anyway.

They approached a right-angle in the corridor, and Lude slowed to sidle next to Donovan. "The dining hall is around here."

Donovan saw flickering light on the wall. "What's that?"

"He had Dez and George get some DVDs to show. Lots of really gross horror movies, and a bunch of porn. Bad porn, with rape and stuff."

Rounding the corner, Donovan saw a set of double doors that had, like the gates in the fence outside, been destroyed. Within the room, he could see garbage and broken liquor bottles scattered everywhere. He drew cautiously up to the entrance, making sure no one was hiding in the shadows. The hall was deserted but not empty. Eight television monitors flickered mutely, showing what Lude had described—violence, porn and violent porn. Long tables around the room were empty, with paint-spattered tarps lying in heaps behind them. In front of the stage were the mangled remains of a Hispanic man, his body literally torn apart, intestines and their pungent stink spilling a chunky puddle around him. The funk from the hall was much stronger in here, tempered with the sour smell of spilled beer and the sweet, burned fragrance of marijuana and other chemicals. Riding high above it all, almost imperceptible, was the fireworks scent of gunpowder.

Lude came up behind him. "Where'd they go?"

"No idea." He turned away from the carnage, back towards the entrance. "Which way to Joann's cell?"

She led him down to the next lower level, but as they approached the door he got no sense of any life, let alone of the woman he loved. It was no surprise when he peered through the cell's small window and saw it, too, was empty. Frustrated, he kicked the door in and entered. His white robe, the one Joann had been wearing when they'd taken her, lay in a heap on the floor. Carefully he gathered it up, his throat narrowing as he raised the bundle to his nose and connected with this tiny piece of her.

"Do you have *any* idea where they could have gone?" he asked, his voice rougher than he'd have expected. "Where Valdes could have taken her?"

Lude shook her head, relieved that she was safe but sad that she hadn't been able to help more. "They was just here. They can't have gone far—"

That was when the darkness came.

❧

Of all the bars along midtown Ninth Avenue, Rudy's is maybe the best place in which to disappear. It's dark, usually very crowded with a good mix of twentysomethings and old men, and they serve hot dogs. It was also close enough to Midtown North that Fullam was able to walk without wearing himself out or spending what was probably his last paycheck on a cab.

The sergeant sat nursing a Dewar's on the rocks and inspecting his reflection in the mirror behind the bar. Self-loathing filled his gaze. He lifted his glass off the bar. "We whose careers are about to die," he muttered, toasting himself, "salute you."

A tall man in black sidled up next to him. Fullam obligingly leaned to the side to allow the man to get to the bar.

"Hello, Francis."

Fullam cocked his head. "A little out of your neighborhood, aren't you, Maurice?"

"I've been looking for you." Father Carroll shook his head at the bartender. "You really shouldn't turn off your phone. People might need you."

"Yeah, right." The sergeant snorted. "In the middle of all this weird stuff, I'm the guy to call."

"Have you forgotten about Lisette Osorio?"

"That was then, this is now." A hard smile carved Fullam's face. "If you would care to remember, I didn't particularly enjoy myself with that Santeria stuff, either. And this seems a lot worse. Of course, it's none of my business anymore. If I'm not officially fired yet, I will be after tomorrow."

"Donovan and I need you, Francis."

"I show my face and Hugh gets wind of it, he might have me shot. Donovan seems like a good guy, and I feel for him with Joann being kidnapped, but this is way beyond us. Staying away is the right thing to do."

"'Every way of a man is right in his own eyes, but the Lord pondereth hearts.'" Although Father Carroll's voice was only one among scores of voices battering the bar walls, his words left no room for questioning. "Do what you think best. I must go."

The sergeant's eyebrows rose. He set his glass aside and followed the priest out.

❧

Although nothing physically changed in the room, Donovan staggered back and had to brace himself against the wall of Joann's cell. Lude watched him, curious. "You okay?"

"Didn't you feel that?"

She shook her head. "Feel what?"

He bundled the robe tight and tucked it under his arm. "Come on."

Every step they took towards the stairs, and then up to the courtyard outside, brought them closer to the source. All the pain and sickness that had sunk into the hospital walls over the years now seeped free, and Valdes's evil floated atop it like an oil slick. The air thickened, hard to walk through and harder to breathe. Donovan's field of vision narrowed into a black-framed tunnel. He stretched out one hand to make contact with something solid and was grateful for the sandpapery feel of the concrete wall.

Outside, his dread was multiplied a hundred times. A fog of desperation billowed through the hospital complex, inspiring a strong urge to run.

"Joann."

Saying her name aloud gave him strength. He steadied himself and gazed up, looking for clues. The turret where he'd seen the flickering light was barely visible; somehow, the night seemed to have grown darker, more dangerous. White flashes that might have been electrical discharges blinked around the brick tower and glided towards Central Park.

Electrical discharges don't move with purpose.

Lude stared, eyes wide. "What's that?"

∽

"Central, this is One-Delta-Eight." Officer Kevin Whitsett steered his blue and white cruiser down Central Park West but was unable to enter the transverse road. "Advise Central Park Precinct they have unmonitored police vehicles blocking intersection 85th Street and Central Park West. We are proceeding on foot." He parked perpendicular to the obstruction so the headlights shone into the park. "Come on, Joe," Whitsett opened his door, "let's see what's up."

"*Copy, One-Delta-Eight.*"

Officer Joe McIntyre squinted into the gloom. "Pretty dark in there. Didn't they get money for streetlights in this year's budget?"

They left the headlights and revolving cherries on, but the light failed to penetrate into the park as the men would have expected. It was as though the blackness was something other than the night air.

McIntyre unhooked his nightstick and tapped it on one Central Park patrol car hood. "Hello? Anyone home?"

A woman staggered out of a clump of brush, her head low as she clutched the tatters of her dress. She took a few steps and dropped to her knees. The officers ran to her side, McIntyre unhooking his radio.

"Central, this is One-Delta-Eight. Request ambulance and female officers at 85th Street and Central Park West entrance. Probable sexual assault victim."

"Take it easy." Whitsett knelt next to her. "We're police officers. We've got you. We're—"

"Dead." A broken bottle suddenly appeared in the woman's hand, and she slashed it across Whitsett's throat. He gasped and slapped a hand to the wound. Blood gushed between his fingers and showered her in a grisly baptism.

"Holy shit!" McIntyre dropped his radio and pulled his gun. "Drop it, lady! Kev! *Kev!* Are you all right?"

Whitsett gurgled, collapsed and lay still.

Some noise, warped like an old vinyl record, whispered around them, and suddenly it seemed to get a little darker. A huge cloud formed above Central Park, and from it a white bolt streaked towards the ground. It struck the woman and hurled her backwards, out of McIntyre's sight.

"Freeze, goddammit, lady!"

Gun trained where she'd disappeared, he looked desperately for a way to staunch the red river flowing from his partner's throat.

"Jesus, Kev, I—"

Shapes lurched from the bushes, grabbed both cops, and hauled them into the shadows.

The red lights atop the car revolved.

And revolved.

McIntyre burst into the open, panicked eyes searching for escape. His shirt was torn, revealing a bulletproof vest with deep grooves cut into the Kevlar. Blood streamed down his face from a gash that left part of his scalp flapping down. Three flickers of light and shadow pursued, swarming and overwhelming him.

"*No!*"

His radio crackled. "*One-Delta-Eight, what is your status?*"

They dragged him back. He wrenched one arm free and scrabbled at the concrete. The radio remained just out of reach.

"*One-Delta-Eight, this is Central. Do you copy?*"

The red lights revolved as the dark swallowed them all.

"One-Delta-Eight, One-Delta-Eight. Do you copy?"

✥

Father Carroll and Fullam were already there when Donovan got back to his apartment. That they had gotten Alfredo the building manager to let them in didn't surprise him; the sergeant seemed to have no qualms about using attitude and authority—even when it had been suspended—to his own ends.

"Donovan!" the priest exclaimed. "Did you find Joann?"

"She *was* there, but not anymore. No one's there now."

Fullam looked past Donovan. "Who are you?"

"Uh…Josie. Josie Ludescowicz." She cringed and leaned into Donovan. "Lude."

"She was one of Valdes's people until she had a change of heart." Donovan gently guided her to the sofa.

Father Carroll knelt beside Lude and looked her in the eye. "You're safe now, my child. Safe, and among friends."

Donovan could feel the magic of the priest's concern. Lude burst into tears and threw her arms around his neck. "I'm so sorry! I din't mean for none of this to happen!"

Fullam grabbed Donovan's arm and drew him aside. Donovan could smell the Scotch on him. "What the hell is going on? Hugh suspends me, I'm drowning my shit luck in Johnny Black, and the next thing I know Maurice is behind me at the bar, saying you need me."

"Valdes was holding Joann at the old Cancer Hospital on Central Park West."

"You went there?"

"I found this," he proffered the filthy robe he'd brought back. "This was what she was wearing when they took her. But that isn't all. I also found a lot of empty beer and liquor bottles, crack vials, and TV sets that were showing violence and porn for who knows how many hours. Apparently Valdes gathered a mob, got them high and whipped them into a killing frenzy."

"Killing frenzy?"

"In the dining hall there was a guy literally torn apart, stomped flat." Donovan grimaced. "Now they're in Central Park, and they still have Joann."

"Why?"

The thought of trying to explain Mephistopheles and Faustus to the sergeant was too daunting. "...I don't know."

The scope of Donovan's words seemed too much to take in. Fullam exhaled and pulled out his cell phone. "I know one of the desk sergeants at the Central Park Precinct. Craig Wesley. I'm going to see what he's got."

Donovan looked at Father Carroll and angled his head to one side. The priest nodded, murmured some soothing words to Lude, got up and joined Donovan by the kitchen steps. "She's very troubled."

"I'll bet she is." He glanced at Fullam, who was frowning as he waited with the cell to his ear. "Listen, while we were at the Cancer Hospital, something else happened. I couldn't tell Frank, but it's...I don't quite know how to...it's bad. Something, some kind of darkness, is coming from one of the Cancer Hospital's towers."

"Darkness?"

"Darkness, but...more. Definitely not natural. Inside it, I saw white flashes, hundreds of them. I think they were some kind of...entities, or spirits or something. They moved with purpose, heading for Central Park." He suddenly realized what they must be, and a wave of dread roiled his gut. "If these are the same as the thing that possessed Wissex..." Images from the Blue Moon Bay crime scene photos overwhelmed him. *And that was only one of them.* "This is...bad."

"Recall Francesca-Maria Guazzo, in the *Compendium Maleficarum*, offers six categories to classify diabolic entities."

Donovan thought for a moment. *What are the six? Fiery, aerial, terrestrial, aqueous, subterranean and heliophobic.* "These came in darkness; they have to be heliophobic."

"'The sixth is the heliophobic,'" Father Carroll recited, "'because they especially hate and detest the light, and never appear during the daytime, nor can they assume a bodily form until the night. These devils are completely inscrutable and of a character beyond human comprehension, because they are all dark within, shaken with icy passions, malicious, restless and perturbed.' Guazzo's description is disturbing, but it seems to confirm your earlier suspicion that Valdes is taking the next step along Faustus's path to power. Who would such entities serve?"

"Mephistopheles, 'chief lord and regent of perpetual night.'"

"Precisely. The name 'Mephistopheles' is from the Greek, 'he who loves not the light,' which also describes his relationship with his master Lucifer Morningstar, the Angel of Light. Mephistopheles, one of the seven great princes of Hell, has always chafed in the role of 'prince, but servant to

Lucifer,' as Marlowe wrote, yet he serves as the conduit to Lucifer's power."

Donovan heard hesitation in his voice. "Something, Father?"

Before the priest could answer, Fullam came over. "It looks like you're right about something going on in the park. I can't raise Wes, or anyone, at the precinct. How long has something been going on, did you say?"

"I met Josie at Polaris about an hour ago. She told me Valdes has had his followers bringing in people all day, up to the Cancer Hospital. We went up to check it out. I found Joann's robe but the place was empty except for what I told you. We came right back here." The sergeant was still a little muddled by his drinking, and seemed to have trouble following him. Donovan felt his temper start to rise, and he tightened his grip on it. "If you need someone to check it out, Yarborough has a car watching me. Send them."

Fullam frowned. "What?"

"Dark blue SUV outside. Been following me ever since your boss bounced me from the investigation. I figured it was his way of keeping tabs."

"Why would he do that? He's already won. He doesn't need to know what you're doing and frankly, I don't think he cares." Fullam's eyes narrowed. "It's not Valdes?"

"Doubt it. Too clean and professional."

"Then forget it for now. Why can't I get anyone at the Central Park Precinct?"

"Is that unusual?" Father Carroll asked.

"There's *always* someone to answer the phone except, apparently," Fullam looked at Donovan, "now."

A siren passed by outside, making Donovan wonder if things were already spreading beyond the park's borders. "I'm going to get Joann," he said. "My best chance to save her includes the NYPD getting involved. *I* can't do that, not initially, at least."

Fullam considered the options. "Conference call. Valdes was my case—still is, as far as I'm concerned. If he's doing something in Central Park, it's only right that I let the captains of the surrounding precincts in on it."

Donovan looked at the priest. "Father?"

"Actually," Father Carroll shook his head, "with your permission, Francis, I'd like to take Miss Ludescowicz to a safe place until all of this is over. I'm certain she has given us all the information she can, and I think it would be in everyone's best interests if she was out of harm's way."

The sergeant glanced over at her. Lude sat huddled on the couch, looking scared and alone. "She's a material witness to more things than I can list, Maurice. At this point, my *only* material witness."

"I understand that. However, she is doing no one any good here now. I can bring her to a shelter and be back in under an hour."

"Why do you need to come back?" Donovan and Father Carroll looked at each other. Fullam regarded them both, annoyed but resigned. "Fine. Go."

"Come, my dear," Father Carroll beckoned her. She bounced to her feet and scurried over. "I'm taking you to a friend of mine, away from the danger."

"Sister Mary Faith?" Donovan asked, walking them to the door.

Father Carroll nodded. "Let me know what comes out of this. I'm going to bring Josie to the shelter and stop by my apartment. I may have some things that will help." He clasped Donovan's hand. "God bless. I'll be back soon."

"Good luck. And hurry."

TWENTY

WELCOME TO THE SLAUGHTER

Fullam was in Donovan's office. Although there was a chair behind the desk, he chose to stand while the conference call was coming together. "Six precincts around the park," he said, sketching a rough drawing on a piece of paper. "West is the Two-Oh and the Two-Four; east is the One-Nine and the Two-Three; north is the Two-Six and the Two-Eight."

"What about south?"

"Midtown North covers the whole length of Central Park South. I don't know all the captains personally, but Susan—Susan Uzaki, our switchboard operator—gave me their names and says she can get them all together."

"Susan won't tell Yarborough?"

"Susan and I go way back. She'll give me a little head start." Fullam's mouth curled in a half-smile. "Apparently there's already been some talk about a situation—the Two-Four and the Two-Oh have been getting calls for the past half hour about a brownout and just generally weird feelings."

"*Everyone's on the line, Frank,*" came a female voice from the speaker. "*Good luck.*"

"Gentlemen—I'm sure some of you already know, but for those who don't, we have a situation in Central Park." The captains all began to speak at once, firing questions and concerns. Fullam waited for a second before continuing. "The leader of the situation is a case of mine. Let me tell you what I know and we'll go from there:

"Neil Valdes, recently paroled from federal custody, has gathered and organized a mob of approximately two to three hundred individuals from the homeless population of the city. Using the old Cancer Hospital on 106th and Central Park West as a base, he fed them alcohol and drugs, armed them, and led them into the park for unknown purposes. He has an unknown number of hostages, including Joann Clery from the Brooklyn DA's office, whom he and another of his people kidnapped. I've tried to get hold of Craig Wesley, but there's no answer from anyone at Central Park Precinct."

"*This is Roy Matz from the Two-Four.*" Matz had a slow, syrupy drawl. "*I sent a car and a couple of my men to check out some disturbances at the 86th street transverse. They reported something about a possible sexual assault victim, but I haven't heard from them since. What do you know, sergeant?*"

Fullam looked to Donovan, who shrugged. "Less than you, I'm afraid. My source doesn't know anything about that."

"*This is Jim Seifert. What source are you talking about, Frank? Do you have somebody inside Valdes's mob?*"

"I have someone who was at the Cancer Hospital very recently."

"*Ed Devine from the Two-Six. Who is this Valdes? What does he want?*"

"Valdes was a white-collar criminal who moved into the major leagues. Since March he's been on a killing spree all over the city, working some kind of occult ritual that seems to be coming to a head now."

"*Occult ritual?*"

Fullam frowned. "Who's this?"

"*Rich Darenelli from the Two-Three. Craig Wesley is a good friend of mine. I just talked to him a couple of hours ago. There was some kind of rock concert in the park tonight, but he didn't say anything about any rituals.*"

"Valdes's entire purpose since he was paroled has been this ritual—"

Darenelli interrupted. "*I'm calling him.*"

"I haven't been able to get any answer—"

"*Well now, you know, Frank?*" Roy Matz threw in. "*I surely would like to know a little more about this, and what happened to my men, before I go charging off.*"

"*I've got his private number,*" Darenelli added.

On the first ring the receiver was picked up and dropped on a hard surface. The connection stayed open. No one spoke, but they heard a mushy chopping, and an occasional sharp crack.

Darenelli cleared his throat. "*Uh, Wes? You there?*"

The chopping paused.

"...*Wes?*"

A faint, barely audible whimpering.

The chopping resumed.

Something severed the connection. For a moment no one spoke.

"*Have any of y'all ever worked in a slaughterhouse?*" Matz finally asked. "*Because I have, and unless I'm wrong, we just heard a carcass being butchered. 'Cept that one sounded...still alive.*"

Everyone shouted. Fullam leaned forward. "Hey, *hey!* Gentlemen!" Beneath his professional façade Donovan could see he was clearly shaken. "We don't want this to get away from us. If there are no objections, I think we should mobilize ESU and EMS, gather in Columbus Circle to establish a command post.

"Whatever we just heard, it is extremely possible it wasn't an isolated incident."

☙

While Fullam made initial arrangements with the other captains, Donovan changed out of his "bum" clothes and into black jeans, a long-sleeved black t-shirt, boots, and gloves. As he picked up his leather jacket, he considered the Glock Fullam had given him.

"Not sure how much good it'll be against anything else," he muttered, tucking it into the small of his back, "but it should work against Valdes just fine."

He emerged from his bedroom as the sergeant was hanging up. "Listen—I left my car parked on Ninth Avenue. Can you take me on a quick stop there? I've got some body armor I want to put on."

Not sure how much good that'll *be, either*, Donovan thought. "Sure."

"Getting some preliminary reports from drive-by cruisers. All of them say the park seems 'darker' than normal. Not chemical cloud, not smoke, just...darker." Fullam eyed him. "Any thoughts?"

Nothing you want to hear. "Not until I see it."

"Fair enough," the sergeant said, accepting but only conditionally. "For now."

Donovan grabbed his helmet and pulled the door open. In the hallway outside his apartment stood Conrad Clery, flanked by two men. The larger of the two had dark hair and wore a dark blue windbreaker, while the smaller man had blond hair and the hand calluses of someone who practices some kind of martial art. Both men wore sneakers and loose-fitting street clothes that hid weapons. Conrad looked as though he hadn't slept since Donovan had last seen him. Dark circles underscored his eyes, and his clothing—although obviously expensive casual sportswear and a trench coat—was rumpled and creased.

"Where is she, Donovan?"

ॐ

Over the previous hours Joann had heard a lot of chaos. Whatever Valdes had organized, it sounded like a riot was seconds from breaking out. She heard many, many people moving about upstairs, and then silence. Before she could seriously consider what it all meant, her cell door swung open and Josie's friend Dez appeared, brandishing a revolver. Her eyes glowed with angel dust and brimstone.

"On your feet, bitch. Time to go."

Joann slowly stood, brushing dirt from the new, clean white dress she'd been given. She looked sadly at Donovan's robe.

"Leave it. Ain't gonna need it where you're going."

She had a fleeting thought of jumping the girl and escaping, but it was chased by the appearance of the brutish Officer Burt, who stepped behind Dez in the doorway. His labored breathing; the way he clenched and unclenched his hands; the furious glaze over his features underscored the madness Joann now sensed throughout the hospital.

They hustled her upstairs. No one else was around, but Joann got the sense that everyone she'd heard was recently gone. Outside in the compound's courtyard Valdes, Faustus and Coeus waited by a hotwired Parks Department maintenance truck. They made an odd, bizarre trio: Valdes wore a dark suit, crisp white shirt, bold purple and red patterned tie and well-polished black dress shoes, looking every inch the executive approaching a career-making deal. The giant shifted from one enormous foot to the other, eager to be somewhere. He was dressed in his usual stitched-together black suit and t-shirt, his sunglasses polished to soulless black lenses. Faustus, in his navy blue scholar's robes, leaned on the edge of the truck's cargo space, looking out of place but serene. Whatever issues he might have had about the roles of man and devils and shadows were now either resigned to or resolved. The feeling Joann got was of the former—felons got the same air when an unfavorable plea bargain was reached. A tiny bubble of hope burst in her chest.

I know the answer! She wanted to scream. *I can solve your problem!*

Valdes came forward to greet her, taking her arm and hand in his grasp. "Ah, Joann. Good to have you with us."

She looked him over for signs of insanity but saw only determination. "Where are you taking me?"

"To destiny—yours, theirs," he glanced at Faustus and Coeus, "and mine." She stared at him. He raised his eyebrows politely. "Was there something else?"

"I'm just waiting for the crash of thunder and maniacal laughter."

"Religious ritual, I'm finding, brings out the melodramatic in me." A sly grin spread across his face. "Who knew?" He nodded at Officer Burt, who pulled a pair of handcuffs from his belt. Joann took an involuntary step away. The barrel of Dez's gun stopped her moving back any further. "We can cuff you," Valdes continued, "or we can make you entirely helpless." He looked towards Central Park, and Faustus's words about man and devils came to life in his gaze. "Which would you prefer?"

Her heart pounded, and she held her wrists stiffly in front of her. Officer Burt slapped the steel bracelets in place, then lifted her into the pick-up's cargo space.

"You wanna drive, Mister Valdes?" Dez asked, holding the driver's door open.

"No, my dear, you go ahead. You and Officer Burt take the cab. It's such a nice night we four will ride back here."

Joann sat on a wheel hump as the three men climbed into the cargo space next to her. In contrast to Valdes's good humor, Faustus maintained a stone face. An almost overpowering need to speak to him swelled her throat. She held back as the entire truck sagged under Coeus's added weight. Valdes remained standing, bracing himself against the cab's roof.

Dez backed the truck out of the compound carefully, not wanting to stagger her leader's stance. The truck bounced gently on the curb, then moved down 106th Street to Central Park West and made a right turn. A few cabs and a newspaper truck were the only traffic about the streets. Glancing at Valdes's watch, Joann saw it was almost eleven o'clock. She looked around at buildings she'd seen many times before. Now they seemed alien, the pattern of lit windows forming strangely menacing shapes. Thoughts of her father and the safety of the world he represented stung her eyes. She recalled the dinner she'd had at Polaris with Donovan, Father Carroll and Fullam.

"Worse than torturing twelve men to death and dismembering them?"

"You have no idea."

She swallowed and blinked back tears of fright.

Even he couldn't have expected this, though...could he have?

Dez took the turn into the access road on 85th Street and followed it to the park's West Drive. They didn't stay there long; with another bounce they went off-road, heading for the Great Lawn. Streetlights kept some parts of their path lit, but there were too many patches of darkness and shadow for Joann to have felt comfortable under the best of circumstances. Now they were surrounded by insanity.

Screams filled the night. Derelicts swept through the brush and fields, driving victims forward, herding them like cattle into the slaughterhouse chute. They attacked anyone they encountered, cutting short cries for mercy with fists and clubs and knives. The violence was absolute and unyielding. Whatever Valdes had done to them, the mob swarmed through the park in a berserker rage. Despair withered her resolve. Everywhere she looked she saw gruesome, horrible death inflicted. The police were their first targets, the sheer numbers of the mob canceling any advantage of guns or vehicles. Such sudden, absolute savagery shocked people until screams shattered the moment, spurring everyone into frenzied dashes for safety. There was none.

On the Great Lawn ahead, she saw a concert full of Lilith Fair-types hacked to pieces even as the murderous wave overwhelmed patrons of the Delacorte Theater. People who joined together to fight were overrun. Those who offered no resistance were crushed. Blood was everywhere, spattered on trees and puddled in the dirt as the dying pleaded for rescue. Revulsion filled her throat. Joann turned to Valdes with tears streaming down her cheeks.

"Why?"

Even he seemed surprised by the intensity of what he'd spawned. Her words brought him out of his reverie, and she sensed a change within him on some core level. He surveyed the situation with the dispassion of a general observing the tide of battle. "Sacrifices must be made for the greater good."

"What greater good could possibly—"

"Mine." He turned to her. On the surface he was in control, but in his eyes she could see that the core change had released in him a terrible darkness and determination. "*My* greater good." He tapped the roof of the truck cab. "Park it over near the top of the Great Lawn, please, Dez. Then you and Officer Burt may go join the others."

The streetlights surrounding the Great Lawn remained mostly intact. The illumination they provided showed the oval space was a true killing field, grass and dirt soaked red, patches churned into crimson mud. Valdes's mob was out of control, slashing and bludgeoning, slaughtering innocents as their own screams rose to fury-heightened pitches. A group of four people ran for the truck, thinking it a safe haven, until they saw Coeus. They stopped short and were tackled from behind, screams drowned by the shouts of the mob. Dez swerved and jerked to a stop, kicked the door open and disappeared into the chaos almost before Joann could register it happening. Officer Burt lumbered after her, wheezing.

Something caught Valdes's attention. "Be useful, *Herr Doktor*. Tie Joann to that tree." He tossed the keys to the handcuffs over and seized a tire iron from the back of the truck. "I'll be right back."

Joann watched him stalk over to a scraggly man who stood above an unconscious woman. The scraggly man was undoing his stained, baggy trousers and giggling. The pants dropped to the ground and he knelt between the woman's legs, tearing at her dress. Valdes came up behind him and slammed the tire iron into the side of his skull. The scraggly man crumpled, brain and blood leaking into the grass.

"These people are sacrifices, not playthings!" Valdes commanded in a no-nonsense voice. "Maintain your focus. Control your desire for now."

The sorcerer climbed down from the truck, keeping his eyes on the sky, looking north towards the Cancer Hospital. Precise in his movements, he kept his eyes above everything going on around them. Joann willed him to look at her, but he resisted as he led her by the cuffs to the tree Valdes had indicated.

"How can you let this happen?" she asked, her voice pleading for intercession. "Don't you have any compassion?"

"Faustus doth what Fate commandeth," he muttered as he secured her to the tree with clothesline. After he drew the line taut, he undid the cuffs and strapped her hands down as well. "This canst he not alter."

Joann desperately squeezed her eyes shut. The sounds of brutality and suffering rang in her ears and her soul, gasping, crying, begging. "I know the answer. I know the answer to what you asked me."

"*Was? Welche Frage?* A question Faustus asked?"

The words came out fast, as though the sooner she said them the sooner the madness would end. "You asked me before—'what is the answer when two claim ownership of the same thing?' I know."

He said nothing, and although she couldn't watch him because that would mean opening her eyes, Joann felt him finish tying the knots. She sensed him moving around the tree to stand in front of her. With enormous will and effort she peered at him through slitted lids. There was no madness or anger in his demeanor, and barely any curiosity.

"Speak, woman."

"*Si una eademque res legatur duobus, alter rem, alter valorem rei.*" Faustus folded his arms, waiting. Panic ripped her. *Did I get the Latin right? I did! I know I did!* "*Si una eademque res legatur duobus, alter rem, alter valorem rei,*" she repeated. "Do you understand?"

"'If something is bequeathed to two persons, one shall have the thing itself,'" his lips pursed, "'the other something of equal value.' *Ja*, Faustus doth understand—"

He paused and looked north. Joann watched him steel himself even though she detected no imminent bodily threat. Seconds later she felt it, a vibration of some indeterminate energy that reverberated in the wood of the tree she was tied to, along the ground, and in the air itself. A dark haze welled around them. She blinked, trying to clear the tears and shadows from her vision. The shadows remained, seeping fear and sadness into her soul. Desperately she followed Faustus's gaze skyward and saw an enormous mass above them, swelling like a storm cloud. All around them members of Valdes's mob also felt the darkness. They stood motionless, looking up with awe. As the cloud grew thicker, white flashes within it strobed contrast to the blackness. Something rumbled, heavy and fearsome, but it wasn't thunder.

"What's going on?"

"Emotion doth energize magic," Faustus murmured. "The darker the emotion…"

Dez staggered into view, dragging a semi-conscious elderly woman past the truck and in front of Joann. "Hey, bitch! Wanna see what you're missing?" She drew a hunting knife from a sheath and slit the elderly woman's throat, cutting so deeply Joann could see the gaping hole of her windpipe. "How about *that*?!"

A white flash shot downwards. Joann gasped. The bolt struck Dez in the chest, knocking her back past the truck and to the ground. Darkness swirled like a fog, obscuring the view. She shrieked. Joann wondered if it was fear or excitement. Something popped up where Dez had fallen, or at least Joann thought she saw something. Between the darkness and an odd flickering she couldn't blink away it was difficult to be sure. The figure moved closer. What the ambient light of the park illuminated remained solid, but past the brightness she had become a wraith, entirely defined by the edge dividing light and darkness. Beyond that border Joann sensed the monstrous, and she was grateful she couldn't see her fully.

Abandon hope, all ye who enter...

She shook her head and squeezed her eyes shut, then opened them and squinted. Each movement Dez made played optical tricks that switched her from two- to three-dimensional and back as light struck her at different angles, revealing glimpses of ghastly, pale bluish-white flesh, the skin of an asphyxiated corpse. All of the color had evaporated from her irises; only pinpricks of black pupil remained, filled with malevolent intelligence. Her black lips drew back impossibly far, revealing teeth as jagged as broken glass. She moved forward—it wasn't a step, exactly, but more an insectoid creep, like the stiff grace of a praying mantis. Joann's heart raced, her hold on reality growing more tenuous. Part of Dez's leg crossed the headlight beam. She leapt back with a shriek as wisps of grayish smoke wafted from inside her clothing. Reflexively she lashed out. Joann heard a juicy, wet sound, like a knife cutting into a watermelon, and a long scythe blade unfolded from her forearm. She slashed it down, chopping off the headlight and half of the truck's front.

"*Faustussss...*" The voice in which Dez spoke was her own but not, warped and roughened by Infernal fire and the cold of evil. "*Quo procer porta?*"

Although it sounded like Latin, Joann couldn't quite understand. The thing turned and came at her with the praying mantis grace, all sharp edges and angles as it drifted in and out of darkness that never went away. Joann shivered uncontrollably as it drew close.

"*See what you're missing?*"

It was too much, and she felt the ground disappear from beneath her feet. As she slipped away Dez's words followed her down with one final, horrific pronouncement.

"*But not for long...*"

TWENTY-ONE

SEEING IN THE DARK

Conrad's strong, tanned hands clenched and unclenched, betraying the stress his voice struggled to check. "Where is my daughter?"

The stress wasn't quite hidden, and it turned what had started as anger in Donovan into sympathy. "She is your daughter." He nodded slightly. "I respect that. And, if it matters, I apologize for the way I spoke to you earlier. But you can't help her now, Conrad."

Conrad's face tightened. "My friends in the department have kept me informed about the progress they're making. The FBI as well. It isn't much. I asked Jan," he angled his head towards the muscle man with dark hair, "and Sylvester to keep an eye on you. You seem to have momentum. You and Father Carroll, who I'm told left a little while ago."

"Blue SUV?" Donovan asked Jan. "You're sloppy."

"Wasn't trying to hide."

"Neither was I." Donovan shook his head. "Because I don't have time to waste. I respect your concerns, Conrad. Maybe the FBI or the cops need your back-up. For Joann's safety, and your own," he started past him, "don't follow me now."

Sylvester cocked a fist back for some kind of hand strike. Without hesitation Donovan dropped his helmet and punched him in the chest. Sylvester gasped, clutching at his heart. Donovan got his weight behind a left hook that slammed the smaller man into the wall and put him down face first on the cheap hallway carpet. Donovan sensed movement behind himself and swung an elbow. Jan snorted blood as his nose crumpled. He clapped his hands up. Donovan closed in, slapping the man's hands apart and jabbing at his face. Jan bulled him into the opposite wall, jumped back and pulled a .45 from under his windbreaker. Fullam stepped forward. In his hands he held a Glock, and it was pointed less than six inches from the river of blood that streamed from Jan's broken nose. Conrad's voice whipped him from behind.

"Sergeant—I mean, *Mister*—Fullam; is it legal for a suspended officer to be armed with an unlicensed automatic weapon?"

Donovan snatched the .45 from Jan, ejected the magazine and tucked it in his pocket. He jacked the round free from the chamber, pocketed it as well, and handed the pistol back, butt first. Fullam slowly lowered his gun, eyes never leaving Conrad. He looked like he wanted to say something, but he remained silent.

"I'm not exaggerating," Donovan said. "For your own safety, stay away from me."

"She is my only child." Conrad's voice no longer whipped, nor did it contain any challenge. "How can I help?"

"If there's anything you can do…" As odd as their role reversal was for him, Donovan could barely imagine what it was like for a man as powerful as Joann's father to genuinely beg for help. He offered a tight smile he hoped gave some reassurance. "I'll be in touch."

The sergeant tapped Conrad with the butt of his gun, dropping him like a stone.

※

On their way to Donovan's motorcycle, Fullam stopped next to the dark blue SUV, took out a pocket knife, and stabbed both tires on the left hand side.

"That isn't legal, either," he said, tucking the blade away in his back pocket.

They made the detour the sergeant wanted, and after getting the body armor and shotgun Fullam had in his car they headed up Tenth Avenue. At 60th Street Donovan turned east, towards Columbus Circle. As they approached he could see what the initial patrol cars had reported—the darkness from the Cancer Hospital tower now shrouded Central Park. It wasn't impenetrable; further away it was almost indistinguishable from the night sky. Closer up, though, Donovan could make out a sort of border at the park edge. There the darkness shifted like the sea, swirling in currents and eddies within itself. Its ethereal nature made the shifting hypnotic and it captured the eye. Blink and you would lose track of it, but Donovan realized it wasn't just about a visual. Powerful emotional energy radiated from it, negative force whose proximity sapped will and physical strength.

"You've seen it," Fullam shouted over the Vulcan's engine. "Any comment?"

"Not yet."

Light blue sawhorses blocked off the feeder streets into Columbus Circle. Donovan pulled up next to one of the uniformed cops guarding the perimeter so Fullam could get them past. As they talked, Donovan gazed around. Everywhere he saw police activity. Squad cars bearing the numbers of the surrounding precincts filled the gaps alongside fire trucks, ambulances and vehicles of all sizes from city task forces with more arriving every minute. Officers came and went; uniformed and plainclothes, all of them wearing some form of body armor, they flourished their weapons as they scrambled around the cars and trucks. Four Emergency Services trucks parked around the circle from Eighth Avenue clockwise past the front of the Time Warner building to Central Park West. Rising from the backs of the trucks, floodlight towers used to illuminate nighttime crime scenes made it noon at midnight.

Once Donovan steered the motorcycle inside the sawhorse barrier, Fullam tapped him on the shoulder to pull over.

"Park and meet me at the FBI vans," he directed, nodding at two silver trucks the size of express mail delivery vehicles. As if to emphasize their separate status from the locals, they'd been pulled up onto the sidewalk beneath the column and statue of Christopher Columbus. "Anybody asks, you're one of my people. That'll work until Hugh gets here."

"Yarborough's not going to scare me off."

"He doesn't have to. If he gives the word, you'll be arrested and *dragged* off. And you have to be around for this." Fullam shifted inside his Kevlar vest. "I'm going to go get acquainted. All of them outrank me, but since it was initially my case they'll give me a seat at the table. At least until Hugh shows up." Bitterness whetted his lips. "Listen—I'm not sure what's going on in there, and I'm pretty sure no one else does either. You wanted to save Joann by getting the Department involved? We're here. Now we need information."

"I'll do everything I can," Donovan hedged.

"Yeah, we *all* will. It'll be enough, *if* we know what we're facing."

Never had the differences between how he experienced reality and how others did seemed more stark. He took some comfort in knowing about the sergeant's experience with Santeria as he pulled away and steered the motorcycle carefully, the bandage on his left hand making it a little difficult to maintain a firm grip on the clutch. Central Park South had also been blocked off, so he rode around towards it and parked at a spot near the Broadway split-off. The concrete cinder blocks and iron fence spires he'd seen while riding up to the Cancer Hospital earlier remained on the sidewalk outside the park wall. He pictured cops using them as cover while firing at whatever emerged from the darkness.

Vivid imagination.

"Hey, daredevil," Josh Braithwaite called. He wore midnight blue riot gear with his baseball cap backwards. "Now I know we're going to kick some ass."

"How's it going, Josh?" Donovan asked, reassured to see at least one familiar face. "Putting in a little overtime tonight?"

"Word's out, man. Everybody's coming down. We got the whole park surrounded. What's up? Fuckin' rag heads taking another shot at us?" He looked towards the darkness and his cockiness faded. Draped in its shadows, even blossoming trees looked menacing. "I heard they took out the Central Park Precinct."

"I don't know."

If he suspected Donovan had more information that he was letting on, he made no comment. "If you're here...does this have anything to do with that aquarium thing?" Braithwaite squinted at him. "Because if it's the same guy, this is still Frank's collar, no matter what the chief says."

Donovan thought Fullam would appreciate his loyalty. "Yeah, Frank *is* here; in fact, I have to go join him." Donovan extended his hand. Braithwaite blinked at the gesture, but shook it with a firm grip. "Do me a favor," Donovan added, "spread the word: when you go in...things in there aren't going to be what they seem."

"What do they have? Anthrax?" Braithwaite gave him a strange look. "Nukes?"

"No, none of that. I can't think of any better way to describe it. Just be careful."

Before the young detective could respond someone hailed him, so he gave Donovan a tight smile and left. Donovan turned towards the FBI van, disappointed he hadn't given Braithwaite a more useful warning.

If you don't come up with something better, he told himself, *it will be a problem.*

❧

Darkness enveloped the Great Lawn, its border delineated by fading streetlights and the glow of torches circling the field. Slashes of white flickered as the possessed moved in and out of sight around the concert stage, chased by whispers in a strange language. Valdes stood to one side, feeling akin to an entomologist observing a colony of spiders building a giant web. They'd moved the stage to the north end of the Lawn oval and were now swarming over the structure, and although he couldn't make out all the details, the groans and pervasive stench of viscera promised a unique vision when they were finished. Steaming clouds, the smoke of cooling flesh and intestines, drifted to descend around his feet, creating a grisly layer of fog above the ground. The night air grew chillier as it got darker.

I thought Hell was supposed to be hot?

In front of the stage, more of the possessed had carved a design into the ground. Valdes instantly recognized it, for it was in the shape of the amulet he'd worn through the *resurrectus maledicat* sacrifices: the Sigil of Baphomet, and inverted five-pointed star inside a double circle, with a goat's head represented within the star. Faustus had supervised its creation and anointed various parts with oils and herbs, making the eyes of the goat shine.

"Valdes."

He turned at the sorcerer's voice.

"Thy followers exhibit much zeal but little judgment. Where sufficient numbers had been are now corpses whose sole use is raw material."

Valdes took out a pack of cigarettes. "What do you mean?"

"The invocation to Lucifer requireth a gathering of six hundred sixty-six sacrifices. A current tally revealeth a shortfall of twice and a half one hundred."

"That many?" He was more disappointed than angry.

"If thou hath desire to deal with forces beyond thy ken, thou must prepare thyself for...eventualities."

Valdes tapped a cigarette on the back of his hand. In his peripheral vision he caught better looks at the white slashes. They bore a passing physical resemblance to those they possessed, but exuding an aura that was harder, sharper. Within their gaze existed no trace of humanity; these were things of ice and violence. "What's the exact number?"

"Two-hundred-sixty-one." Valdes's calm seemed to irritate the sorcerer. "Thou hath not the skill of Faustus for conjuration of this number, nor even of one."

"I'll find a way, *Herr Doktor*." In the sky to the south, a light approached. Valdes glanced at it. "I'm very good at solving problems."

❧

Donovan spied Fullam with a group of men and women between the FBI trucks. The ones in ties and flak jackets he took to be the precinct captains. ESU and task force commanders were dressed in full battle gear, while the FBI all wore dark windbreakers with their agency in bold white letters across their backs. Through the open side panel of one of the trucks Donovan could see what looked like a space shuttle cockpit. An older blonde woman, an Asian man, and a black woman manned the consoles, while a slim man with a gray crew cut and FBI windbreaker stood just outside. His sharp nose and profile suggested the cultured PBS logo, but the Brooklyn tone of his voice when he opened his mouth eliminated any thought of *Masterpiece Theater*.

"Who are you?"

"Donovan's one of my people," Fullam answered. "Research and Intelligence."

"Really?" the man gave a brief, brisk handshake. "Harley Clark, Supervisory Special-Agent-In-Charge, New York office. Support personnel need ID, too, sergeant." He looked through Donovan, saying the words "support personnel" like "stay out of my way." "We don't want people getting their heads blown off because no one knew who they were."

Fullam grabbed a clip-on plastic tag and handed it to him. Donovan attached it to his jacket, surreptitiously taking note of the reactions to his presence. No one seemed to think anything wrong. Everyone was watching the five television monitors inside the van. They showed stationary, long-range shots of different park areas. None were particularly clear. Occasional glimpses of white strobed by, but the darkness made everything look like they were watching a feed from cameras deep underwater. Donovan couldn't make out much besides shadowy figures moving around. There was no audio.

"Where are these coming from?" he asked Fullam softly.

"Three are NYPD, two from the Met."

The Asian man overseeing one wall of consoles, who wore a badge around his neck identifying him as Peter Lo, leaned over to speak quietly. "Those three," he indicated at monitors, "are NYPD. The other two are from security cameras of the Metropolitan Museum of Art. Of all the cameras in the park, these were the only ones still functioning we could access remotely. We turned them inward to focus on the Great Lawn, since that's where most of the activity seems to be."

"What are they showing?"

"Not much. Unfortunately the cameras aren't equipped with strong enough zoom or infrared. We've been downloading what we get through our system to clean it up." He handed Donovan some digitally enhanced printouts from the system. "Apparently there was some sort of concert on the Great Lawn tonight, and the terrorists seem to have seized the stage as their rallying point. There's some sort of wall or structure over here, at the north end, but we don't know what it is yet."

Terrorists? Donovan glanced at Fullam, who kept his face carefully neutral. *It's a description they'll understand.* He studied the photographs. "Any word on hostages?"

"We're hoping, but we heard they took out the precinct, so—"

"What's…this?" Donovan pointed at a blurred figure near a tree adjacent to some lights or torches. It was the only one dressed in white. "Can you clean it up any more?"

"Let's see…" Lo tapped a few buttons, calling the picture up on his screen and zooming a crosshairs icon on the spot. Lines coursed down the image, sharpening it a little more. "How's that? Anything more will just look like a bunch of pixels."

Joann!

Just then, a blue-and-white Bell 206B Jet Ranger helicopter thundered overhead. It paused a hundred feet above Columbus Circle, spun 360 degrees on its axis, and skimmed across the treetops into the park.

The radio on Fullam's belt crackled to life. "*This is Sergeant Tex Waring. You down there, Frank?*"

The captains all looked at him. Fullam shrugged. "We were in the Academy together. He got smart and specialized." He unclipped the radio. "Yeah, I'm here, Tex. You got the background on what's happening?"

"*Some sort of group has invaded Central Park. A lot of people are dead; they've even taken out the precinct.*" Donovan thought Waring, like Braithwaite, sounded eager for action against the invaders. "*What do you need from me?*"

Clark leaned forward to speak, nudging Fullam's hand so the radio faced him. "Intelligence, son. We've got very little to go on."

"*Who's this?*"

"FBI; Supervisory Special-Agent-in-Charge Harley Clark. What we need is an idea of their set-up: how many there are, hostages and their location, defense placements—whatever you can tell us."

"*Uh*-hunh," came the reply. "*10-4, Agent Clark. Frank? Anything*," his voice deepened just enough for Donovan to detect sarcasm, "*The F-B-I left out?*"

"Be careful in there, Tex. See what we need, and get out. No hot—"

❧

"—*shot flying.*"

"Roger that." Tex finger-controlled the cyclic pitch stick, tilting the chopper's nose down slightly as he headed north into the park. Trees rolled beneath him like dark green surf. "Switching on nose spot." He squinted and squeezed his eyes shut, then blinked. "Is there some sort of chemical smoke or something covering the park?"

"*Our sniffers don't detect anything. How's visibility, scale of one to ten?*"

"Maybe…six, seven. I can see, but…I don't know. It seems odd." He cleared his throat. "No activity up to and in the Ramble. Might want to watch out for some of the denser growths, though. I can't penetrate the cover to give you anything certain. The Boathouse and Tavern on the Green both look deserted, as far as I can tell." Tex's eyes skittered behind the nose-spotlight in rapid arcs across the terrain. "The drives look clear enough to bring the men up. Are you getting my video feed?"

"*Roger that. Your spot shows us some, but outside of that is a little dicey.*"

"Streetlights along the drives are operational. You shouldn't have ob-structions coming from the south. In fact, from what I can tell, there's not much in the way of light or movement north of the 86th Street Transverse, either. Everything seems to be centered on the Great Lawn. I'm going to go check it out."

❧

The shock of Dez's transformation had overwhelmed Joann, not just eliminating but destroying her perceptions about reality and its boundar-ies. The actual physical change was bad enough, but even worse was the energy emanating from Dez like shimmers of heat in the desert. It filled Joann with despair and hopelessness, with the certain knowledge that the evil she'd faced within the justice system was fueled by something far, far worse, and that something was approaching.

"'*Quid tu moraris?*'"

Although her mind floated in blissful semi-consciousness, absorbing every iota of comfort before returning to her captivity, she recognized the resonant voice of Faustus.

"'*Per Iehovam, Gehennam et consecratum aquam quam nunc spargo, signumque cruces quad nunc facio, et per vota nostra, ipse nunc surgat nobis dicatus Mephistopheles!*'"

She struggled to keep her eyes closed, to hold onto the comfort of not knowing, but her nature was inquisitive. Gradually her eyelids lifted their weight.

Faustus stood in front of the stage, inside of some kind of design (*Donovan would recognize it,* part of her thought. *Why isn't he here yet?*), as Coeus knelt shirtless before him. The sorcerer raised his hand high before plunging it into Coeus's chest. Joann gasped.

That—that can't *be possible!*

But the night's events had demonstrated the limitless potential of existence. The knowledge was little comfort as an icy blast of wind came from the circle and Faustus began to withdraw his hand slowly, forearm muscles standing out in cords, as if he was bringing something along with it, something from inside the giant…

Darkness called her again.

☙

"*—coming up on the Great Lawn now.*"

The three NYPD monitors had been tied in to Tex's camera; the other two were left long-range. All across the oval field Donovan could see the two- and three-dimensional flickering of the possessed darting in and out of the chopper's spotlight.

"*This is unbelievable!*" Astonishment filled Tex's whisper. "*Are you getting this?*"

The entire lawn had been stripped of recreational features and turned into bloodstained tundra, with a huge holding pen constructed on the dirt of what normally were softball fields #3 and #5. Its steel wire sides stood eight or nine feet high, and it was filled with people in all stages of panic. Outside it, trees hung heavy with dark, dripping shapes. Gouges had been dug out of the dirt in random spots, as those lucky or dexterous few avoided imminent death for another precious moment. At the north end, a Sigil of Baphomet as big as a helicopter landing circle had been carved into the ground. Donovan could see the detail of the goat's head, with eyes of shining liquid, inside the inverted pentagram. His eyes unconsciously went to his bandaged hand, and he wondered how similar the scar from Coeus's tattoo would be to it.

"Jesus." Captain Seifert rubbed his chin as he watched the screen. "What d'you think? Three, four hundred?"

"Didn't think there would be so many," Fullam said.

"At least we know they haven't killed as many as we first thought," the older blonde FBI agent, Vicki Matthews, observed.

"*Mother of God...*"

Tex's voice drew their attention back to the monitors. He aimed his camera towards a mass rising five stories high at the north end of the lawn. At first Donovan thought it was intangible darkness, a trick of reflection and his own tension. As Tex swung the nose spotlight up, however, he saw the two-and three-dimensional flickers swarming over a structure styled in what Donovan could only think of as Gothic Anti-Christ. A huge pointed arch—created and supported by a half-dozen rib arches—served as backdrop, along with needle-like spires, buttresses and miscellaneous edged cornices. Individually they would have been difficult to look at for any length of time. Together they were literally painful to set the eye upon, offending the natural order vision seeks to impose.

"Is it me," Peter Lo asked slowly, "or is that...*thing* moving?"

The FBI man was right, the entire structure seemed to be trembling with life. Donovan looked closer than he wanted to. Human bodies dangled from hooks and spears, grotesque set dressing for the stage. Blood dripped, black and shiny in the moonlight, congealing into macabre designs to decorate the walls. Those still alive quivered, vainly attempting to relieve the agony of the steel embedded in their flesh as they babbled soundless onscreen pleas for the release of death.

The images stunned everyone until Captain Darenelli voiced their thoughts. "What the *fuck* is *that*?"

"*What do you want me to do?*" Tex could barely speak the words.

Fullam's stoic manner didn't keep disgust from his voice. "Nothing. You've been in their sights too long. Pull out."

"*No one's taken a shot at me yet, and these folks don't seem the type to hold back. Maybe they don't even have guns."*

"What are you going to do? You can't save—"

"Sergeant Waring," Clark interrupted. "What's going on below you?"

Donovan looked at the bottom of the monitor. Onscreen, Valdes herded three hostages from the holding pen out into the center of the lawn. The hostages—two women and a man dressed in an NYPD uniform—were forced to kneel in the open, as though Valdes wanted no obstruction to the show he was producing. Donovan watched him step behind them and, keeping the gun trained, draw a long knife from under his coat. The blade caught a shaft of firelight and flashed through Tex's camera into their eyes.

"Looks like—oh no!"

Valdes raised his head deliberately, gazing at the helicopter as he seized a handful of the first woman's hair, jerked her head back and slit her throat. A fountain of red sprayed. Without pause he repeated his actions with the other two, movements simultaneously implacable and chilling. As a final insult, he wiped the knife on the uniform shirt of the police officer he'd just murdered. Fullam cursed under his breath. Before disappearing into the dark, Valdes looked back at the helicopter. He didn't smile, he didn't laugh, but one eyebrow twitched as if to challenge observers to stop him from doing it again.

"That son of a bitch!"

"Get back here, Tex." Fullam said numbly. "We've seen what we need to."

Everyone started talking at once. Donovan turned away, puzzled and angry. *Why? Those weren't sacrifices to any deities. Those weren't ritual killings. Why did he do that? Cutting their throats did nothing for him from a paranormal perspective...*

The television crews were pushing at the sawhorses, anxious to get their gallon of guts for the news cycle. For the moment, they were being handled by uniforms. On the edge of the crowd he saw a cab pull up and Father Carroll climb out, clutching a gym bag. He still wore black but without his priest's collar. Donovan caught his eye and started walking away from the media. On the other side of the barricades Father Carroll followed, until they reached a spot near where Donovan had parked.

Father Carroll embraced him, then looked past Donovan to stare at the swirling darkness cloaking the park. "My God."

"Yeah."

"My God," he repeated. "Donovan, this is...formidable." As though realizing there was no point to belaboring what they faced, he looked away from it, changing topics in mid-thought. "Sister Mary Faith has taken Josie in. For the moment, she's safe."

Donovan nodded and gestured at his throat. "Good move with…"

"My collar? Oh, yes. I removed it in the taxi when I saw the television cameras. I felt it prudent not to open the police up to ridicule and speculation."

"Definitely the right choice." He gestured at the gym bag. "I hope you found something useful at your apartment?"

"One or two things." The priest eyed him. "Are you all right?"

"Frank sent a chopper to get some visuals and intelligence on what's going on. Valdes saw it, trotted out three hostages and cut their throats. Right there, out in the open. No negotiating, no demands to stay away. The only thing that seemed to matter to Valdes was that we saw—" Donovan stopped, eyes narrowing as he put it together. "He *wanted* us to see. Why would he want that?"

"Perhaps to elicit the very reaction he has gotten from you. To make our side charge in without being properly prepared. Against the heliophobic, that would be suicidal."

"How are we supposed to prepare them?"

"That," Father Carroll replaced his priest collar, "falls upon your shoulders."

"Me?"

"These are men of secular protocols and rules. They would never take me seriously. It seems you," he gestured at the ID tag Donovan wore, "have already been introduced."

"Frank asked me if I could give them intelligence, but that's background, not tactics."

"If not you," Father Carroll said plainly, "then who?"

"I can't go tell a bunch of cops and FBI agents how to fight those things! I mean, I could. I know how. But…that's insane. They'd never listen to me. I told you I wasn't as good a politician as Joann, remember?"

"And I believe my response was 'you'll have to learn.' All things are possible through the Lord." Father Carroll's eyes lit up and he crossed the street, heading for the stack of black-painted fence spires. "For instance, iron is a powerful weapon against the diabolic, iron like these bars. These will be most effective against anything Valdes and Faustus have conjured up, especially after I've blessed them."

"But you see? That's what I'm talking about. How do I tell *them* that?

'Leave your guns holstered, boys. I got something better against those things—a skinny piece of iron!'" Donovan looked towards the FBI truck. Fullam broke from the pack and waved him over. Donovan's heart beat faster. He ran his bandaged hand through his hair. "I don't see how it can work, but if I can't do this, they're going to get slaughtered."

"I agree their training leads them to certain conclusions, and their lives encourage ignorance in many facets of reality." The priest knelt to root through his gym bag. "*Your* life, conversely, has not. If mixing the two realities is the source of your concern, the solution is simple. Don't approach your explanation from *our* side, but from theirs.

"Put it in terms they understand."

TWENTY-TWO

THE APOCALYPTIC CULT

With a nod of satisfaction, Valdes watched the NYPD helicopter fly away.

"Valdes." Faustus called to him. He was breathing hard and his face looked drawn. "Thy presence is requested."

"'Requested'? Then you were successful?"

"Come."

Valdes followed him across a patch of bloody dirt. The earth was so dry it had soaked up the liquid, leaving only a dark stain and the scent of burnt copper. From everywhere he sensed the possessed, whispering seductively in their bizarre, warped language. The darkness hid them well but he glimpsed an occasional flicker of scythe blade in the torchlight.

"Where's Coeus?"

"'*Procer porta*'; the child was 'the gate of the Prince.'" He gestured into the darkness. "As thou seest."

In front of the stage, within the Sigil of Baphomet design, there loomed a terrifying, disgusting...*thing*. Valdes stopped short. It writhed over and in on itself, a Chthulian vision from the heart of Lovecraft's fevered hallucinations, seeking escape from the confines of its magical prison with every greasy lurch. It glistened, roared, twisted; its flesh bubbled and churned, changing shape in a ceaseless parade of unearthly forms and figures. It was repulsive. It filled Valdes with loathing and an urge to inflict harm upon others, and himself. It was darkness in all colors, blues

215

and grays and purples and blacks, a palette unlike anything he had ever seen, but its magnetic ugliness drew his gaze. The longer he looked the further in he fell. Beneath the surface the figure exuded a potent lure, an almost pheremonal hold that belied the physical. In an instant he realized what he was seeing, and he turned his head with a smile. "*Quin redis, Mephistopheles, fratris imagine!*" When he turned back, the nightmare vision had been replaced by a giant silhouette. "…Coeus?"

"Partly."

The voice was as deep as it had always been, but now possessed a quality Valdes hadn't previously encountered. Confident and persuasive, it reminded him of his own.

"'*Quin redis, Mephistopheles*'?" the giant continued. "I see you've read Marlowe."

Valdes watched as one hand slowly rose to remove the sunglasses. The giant's features were still scarred, but serenity had replaced Coeus's dull brutality. Now his eyes glowed dark purple with tiny white flecks, galaxies in deepest space. His lips curled, and even his smile was more knowing.

Valdes quickly recovered from his surprise. "I read a lot while I was in prison."

"Prison?" The giant glanced around his feet. "*There's* something we share."

Valdes stepped forward and smudged the outer circle of the design. He extended a hand across the line, bridging the magical barrier. "I'm Cornelius Valdes." Mephistopheles accepted the handshake. Coeus's grip had been clammy and clumsy; this one was warm and firm. "Forgive me. I was expecting, well, a friar."

Mephistopheles gave a sly smile. "Don't believe everything you read."

"Valdes…" Faustus watched, amazed, as Mephistopheles stepped free from the design. "How didst thou know—?"

"I resurrected you to instruct me, *Herr Doktor*. What kind of pupil would I be if I did no study on my own?"

"No man worthy of his destiny has it handed to him, Faustus." Mephistopheles turned and looked at the stage, and at the structure behind it, approvingly. "Have four hundred odd years with me taken from you the thrill of discovery?"

"What thou doth offer hath robbed from Faustus any semblance of joy at the new."

"Then it's a good thing," Valdes said, "this isn't about *you*."

The flush in Faustus's face cooled to granite. Mephistopheles nodded and inspected his fingers as he flexed them. "Quite an ambitious undertaking you've been on, Neil. Contacting *me* takes a tremendous amount of focus and desire. A *resurrectus maledicat*—by yourself—is truly impressive."

"Thank you. I wasn't totally without guidance, though. I had a grimoire to help me through the zodiac sacrifices."

"Did you? You certainly made the most of it."

"So far. But I'm not finished yet."

Mephistopheles paused in his exploration of the physical and cocked his head. Coeus's misshapen features took on a bemused cast. "Such confidence." He inhaled deeply the scents of blood and death. "*I'll* decide whether you're finished. And then I'll decide whether to hang you from your ribcage on that hook above the stage."

Valdes didn't look up. "You could," he acknowledged, taking out his pack of cigarettes. "However—and I mean absolutely no disrespect—*you* aren't the reason I did all of this. The grimoire helped me get to Faustus. Faustus helped me get to you. Only you can help me get to the King. And *he* can get me to what I want."

"*I* reign over desires and wants, Neil." Mephistopheles' smile revealed teeth perfect and sharp. "If you want something, it will involve me."

"That's my understanding. However, my understanding is also that you provide the *things*; the King is the power that creates them." He tapped out and lit a cigarette. "I want to deal with *him*."

"Is that what you learned from reading Marlowe? Mark your blood on a piece of paper for the King and you get a servant like *me*?" Mephistopheles drew himself up to Coeus's prodigious height. His aura darkened the world around him, and the muttering of the possessed grew silent. "Do you think I'm an *errand boy*, Neil?"

"I think you are the path to get me where I want to be, but you aren't the destination itself." Valdes held his ground and continued to smoke. "Nothing personal."

Mephistopheles stood astonished. He looked at Faustus, back at Valdes, blinked, and chuckled. The sound began as grating, stone on steel, and rose to a wheezing rasp that echoed across the Lawn as the possessed joined in.

"Yes." Mephistopheles shook his great head and peered down at Valdes. "Neil, you might actually understand how things work." He spread his hands and gave a slight bow. "I would be *delighted* to work with you towards achieving your desires."

Valdes smiled. "Let me tell you what I'm looking for..."

⁓

Fullam met Donovan a few steps outside the group, indicating what Donovan carried on his shoulder. "What's that?"

"One of the spires the city is using to build a wrought-iron fence. There're a bunch of stacks of them back there."

"Why are you—?"

He looked towards the officials. "What's going on?"

Fullam stared at him for a long moment. "Valdes's stunt with the hostages," he finally said, "convinced Clark and a few captains that we can't wait this out or wait for them to open negotiations. They're definitely going in, and are drawing the plans now."

"Can you get me a few minutes?"

"If I can't, crack a couple of heads with that thing. Start with the FBI."

Clark seemed to be leading the discussion. Fullam waited for a pause before inserting himself. "Excuse my interruption, gentlemen, this is Donovan Graham. He's one of my research people, been working with me the last few weeks. He's got background on Valdes and his group that might be helpful."

"Graham?" the FBI man repeated. "Do you have another involvement in this case?"

"Joann Clery is my fiancée."

"He's also the one who picked up Valdes's trail at the Cancer Hospital," Fullam added.

"What sort of background information do you have?" Ed Devine, a large, round-bellied man in a tweed sport coat, asked. "Because I have never seen anything like what they're building outside of a horror movie. People impaled on hooks? Hanging thirty feet in the air? What kind of terrorist group *is* this?"

"They don't think of themselves as terrorists. Valdes has created a powerful cult of personality." *Here we go.* Donovan moved through the ring of people, to where he could make eye contact with them all. He stood in front of a map of Central Park, which had designs showing the directions from which the police forces would approach. "There're all kinds of cults of personality—political, military, religious. This is the last; specifically, an 'Apocalyptic Cult.' They have a purpose and a cause: to bring about the Apocalypse. They believe in a literal Heaven and Hell. They believe they're soldiers for Hell. They believe you and all of your men are soldiers for

Heaven. They believe they're fighting Armageddon—the Final Battle—
right here, right now, against you."

Dead silence.

Donovan started to wonder if he'd overplayed his hand when everyone
began talking at once. Mike Quentin, the captain from the 28th Precinct,
who looked like a young Morgan Freeman, spoke the loudest. "You're
telling us those people are devils from Hell? And we're fighting to stop the
end of the world?"

Yes. "I'm not 'saying' it. I'm telling you they *believe* it."

"Mister Graham," Clark interrupted. "In 1890, the tenets of a Lakota
Sioux religious cult held the 'ghost shirts' their ancestors gave them would
make them bulletproof against the U.S. Cavalry at Wounded Knee. They
didn't. Why does it make a difference to us what they believe?"

"Their beliefs dictate their behavior. Even though the Lakota Sioux
weren't bulletproof, they attacked as though they were. How many cav-
alrymen could have been saved if they'd understood that? This has less to
do with *your* reality than *their* perception. The key to beating them is to
understand their perceptions and exploit them."

"What perceptions?" Devine asked.

"Valdes has been feeding them drugs and liquor all day. They have a
very high tolerance for pain and very low threshold for reason right now.
They'll follow their beliefs before they take time to think things through.
They believe themselves invulnerable to most things *but* vulnerable to
others, and will respond accordingly. For instance, they're a Christian
cult; certain symbols of Christianity will be effective."

"Like crosses?" Darenelli sneered. "You want us to go in with wooden
stakes, too?"

His tone of voice gave Donovan flashbacks to his father, but he resisted
arguing. "It's not about what *I* want, it's about what *they* believe. If you
understand it, not only will you have a better chance of rescuing my
fiancée, you'll have a much better chance of surviving this. So no, they're
not afraid of wooden stakes. But they *are* afraid of wrought iron," he held
up the spire, "like this." The fact that it looked like a weapon—it was
about three and a half feet long and painted black—gave him confidence
he could sell it. "As it happens, the Parks Department has stacks of them
for a fence they're looking to build. If you equip your men with these you
will definitely have the advantage if or when you go hand-to-hand."

Clark shook his head, dismissive. "I can certainly accept these people
believe they're devils, but are you saying the only way to defeat them is

to treat them as though they *are*? To use iron fence spires instead of our standard weaponry?"

"Not 'instead of,' in addition to. They also fear holy water, so—"

"So why not get some squirt guns, too?" Darenelli scrubbed his head with one hand. "Look, I don't know why we have to complicate this with talk about devils and cults and iron bars. After what we just saw, there is no way I'm going into a whole mob of them armed with something designed to keep dogs off the grass. I have a hard time justifying anything besides bullets, and plenty of them. If it's true they took out the Central Park Precinct, let's send 'em to meet *whoever* they worship as fast as we can."

Murmurs of agreement ran through the group.

"They aren't afraid of guns. If you shoot at them, they'll keep coming. If you come after them with an iron bar, they'll hesitate, they'll back off." Donovan withheld as much urgency as he could from his voice. "You've seen what they're capable of. When you try to stop them, they're going to throw everything they have at you, up to and including suicide attacks. If you have these—"

"Thank you for the strategic advice, Mister Graham," Clark cut him off. "We'll certainly keep it in the mix as we prepare. I think your fiancée will have a much greater chance of survival, though, if we stick with tactics and weaponry that have been developed and tested over time. Scary make-up and drug-induced rage are no match for the firepower we've assembled."

Captain Matz took the spire from Donovan's grasp and hefted it. "What is this, about five, ten pounds? That's a lot of extra weight when you're trying to move fast." He handed it back. "Sorry, Mister Graham. I'm inclined to agree with Special Agent Clark, too. But my men will keep an eye out for your lady."

Donovan's mouth tightened. He noticed and consciously relaxed the tension. "Thank you, captain. I appreciate that. I saw her on one of the video feeds. Wearing a white dress, tied to a tree at the north end of the Lawn."

Before he could go on, Fullam nudged his arm. "Are there any other questions?" he addressed the circle. With cursory shakes of the head and nods of thanks, they turned back to their planning. "Thank you for your time, gentlemen."

"Good luck," Donovan added, before the sergeant steered him away. "What's going on?" he asked. "That's it? That's all I get?"

"Here and now, yeah. You did what you could. Go wait with Maurice."

Donovan looked at the spire, taking strange comfort in its weight in his hand. "What's the hurry? Maybe I can—"

"Go wait with Maurice," Fullam repeated, pointing his chin at a dark gray Lincoln that had just pulled up near the 60th Street subway entrance. "And keep your head down."

Donovan recognized the car from Newark Airport. *Yarborough.* "Got it." He held the spire out of sight and started to walk away. "I'll see you over there."

∽

As tightly as Joann clung to unconsciousness, the wailing around her finally grew too loud and too pained to avoid. With a groan she forced her eyes open. Darkness kept the night air slightly opaque, allowing her to see shadows but not differentiate too many details. She had never felt so alone.

A ring of odd-shaped torches was being lit in a circle in front of her, and she could see a recognizable figure moving around them. "For the love of God, Faustus, put those people out of their misery!" she cried. "Don't you have any mercy in your soul?"

Faustus paused from his task and started to turn and respond when an amused voice got there first. "Well that's a bit of a problem," Valdes said, coming around from behind the tree to which she was bound. "He hasn't *got* a soul. At least, not here and now."

"Stop it! Stop lying! Faustus was just a story!"

"Was it?"

She saw Coeus step out from behind the tree in her peripheral vision. Valdes turned and spoke to him. "As I was saying, at this point she's become somewhat delusional; she maintains the conceit that she can affect the outcome of tonight." The giant nodded and, without speaking, stepped closer as if to study her. "But I think you'll agree, a Vessel of great beauty. And she *is* a force for good, or at least she tried to be. She was a prosecutor for the Brooklyn District Attorney's office."

The giant extended a black-gloved hand. Joann flinched. *What happened to him?* He showed a small, almost shy, smile and used his index and middle fingers to turn her face to him. She refused to meet his eyes, staring at the ground, trembling. The sounds of suffering reached a crescendo as a woman somewhere screamed over and over, her voice growing hoarse until finally all they could hear was desperate whimpering.

Tears streamed down Joann's cheeks. "I've dealt with criminals for years," she said, still looking down. "All of them, even the worst of the killers, have had *some* humanity. But not you. There is no greater good that can be served by this, this *slaughter*."

"'Greater good' depends on your perspective. I sacrificed twelve people for my *resurrectus maledicat*; however, I made every effort to select only those who offered little or nothing compared to what *I* will bring to society. On balance, I know I did the right thing."

"You corrupted Coletun, and all these people—"

"I forced no one. I gave people a choice, and when options are available, people will do what they want. I would have thought your time in the justice system would have taught you that." Valdes laughed. "You aren't telling me you're *shocked* by their behavior?"

"Coletun is nine years old! He has no capacity to make that kind of choice!"

The giant glanced up. "She's got you there, Neil."

His voice wrapped her in the folds of a funeral shroud. Joann snapped her head around and looked into Coeus's face. In the spiraling galaxies of his eyes she saw indescribable agonies, losses and defeats of cosmic proportions that drained all life and vitality from her, replacing them with only the darkest human emotions. Hopelessness sucked her down, stealing the only strength she had left, that of righteous anger. *Donovan, where are you...?* She sagged against the tree. "What are—you...aren't *real*..."

"I am, actually." Her despair energized him, lighting his features. "And *this* is reality."

Joann swung her head back towards Valdes; anything was better than to be trapped in the giant's gaze.

"Beautiful, spirited, and," the giant's nose wrinkled in a hideous parody of delicacy, "she stinks of love. She's an excellent choice, Neil."

"Thank you."

Donovan. Please, help. Please come... His name was a life preserver and she clung to it, but it was small comfort in the vast, dark ocean of the giant's eyes.

He put his face next to her ear. "Hold tight to your life preserver, Joann." She turned her head to gaze at him, eyes popped in shock. "Because once you let go and find despair, you'll never recover your faith."

TWENTY-THREE

CATCH A DEVIL BY THE TOE

Donovan walked close enough to his motorcycle and the stack of iron spires so that Father Carroll could see him, then angled his head and followed the southern curve of Columbus Circle. He paused behind an unmanned fire truck, exhaled, and stared at the neon signs above him while he waited for the priest.

"It did not go well." Father Carroll's words were not a question.

"I gave them the information, but I don't think I convinced anybody."

"Will it be enough?"

"Going to have to be."

"Clearly you don't think it is." Father Carroll touched his shoulder. "You did as much as you could under the circumstances facing you. For better or worse, that's what life is, Donovan." He glanced at the shadows of the park. "The police will do what they do. We'll try to help them, but we have a higher priority."

"Joann."

The priest regarded him for a moment without saying anything. "The summoning of Mephistopheles," he began, "is a very real possibility. We cannot allow the Prince of Darkness himself to be called here, now."

"When we save Joann," Donovan replied levelly, "he won't be. If she's not there, they'll have no host body, no Vessel for him. She's tied to a tree at the north end of the Great Lawn, next to some kind of stage that Valdes has set up."

"Do you have a plan?"

"Working on it." Donovan chewed his lower lip. "So far we have blessed iron spires to fight them. I told the captains holy water would work, too."

"It will. Find some water and I'll bless it."

"Then that's two weapons." *Why don't I feel any better?* "What have you got?"

Father Carroll lifted his gym bag onto a step along the fire truck's side. "'For Jesus said unto him, 'Come out of the man, thou unclean spirit.' And He asked him, 'What is thy name?' And the man answered, saying, 'My name is Legion, for we are many.'" His eyes sharpened. "We face a similar situation here. That possession was of one by many, while what we face here is many by many. The traditional Rite of Exorcism would be ineffective for the simple fact that it is geared towards a one-on-one situation. However." He went into the bag. "Through certain channels I was able to procure something that should serve our purposes well, a prayer that has roots in that passage of Scripture I just recited." Father Carroll produced a rolled piece of paper. "The Vatican archives have a great many things to use in the struggle against evil. One of them is this: the Orison of Saint Raymond Nonnatus. A purification benediction of great potency."

"Someone faxed you a medieval *super*-prayer?" Donovan allowed himself the luxury of being totally baffled for only a moment before adjusting his perspective. *Reality is flexible.* "What does 'purification benediction' mean?"

"Essentially, what it says. A benediction is a blessing; 'purification' refers to the intensity of the prayer's strength. Raymond Nonnatus was a saint who devoted most of his life to the redemption of captives. His canonization was supposedly confirmed by his transcription of this prayer, which redeemed the possession of one section of Cardona, the Spanish city from which he came. You might compare it to a concentrated Rite of Exorcism. It will take almost a minute to recite once, but from what I've been told about the cumulative effects of constant repetition…know we don't enter this struggle unarmed."

Donovan felt the weight of Fullam's Glock in his belt. "Never thought that. But even if the Orison is as effective as we hope, how do we use it?"

"What do you mean?"

"Could you recite it over the area where the possessed are? Like if we got you to that stage somehow. If you said it over the Great Lawn—as an exorcism ritual, would it cleanse the possessed? Purify their souls?"

Hope flickered in Father Carroll before being overcome by anxiety. "They'd have to stay and listen. An exorcism can't work without the possessed present. Could the police hold them all in hearing range?"

"Not without the iron bars." *Damn.* "What about the source? Can we go to it?"

"Mephistopheles?"

"The Cancer Hospital. That's where the darkness came from."

"Infernal portals are dangerous creations. One doesn't just kick over a few candles and expect everything to go away. The energies that create and hold a portal open are quite vast. Consider the death and destruction it took to open this one." Father Carroll thought about this, scholastic curiosity now supplanting anxiety. "Generally speaking, one must use the proscribed rituals to close a portal before mucking with it. To do otherwise would be akin to dynamiting a dam on Central Park West."

"What if you recited the Orison *inside* it? Which way would the flow go? If it's all energy, do you think the Orison would reverse its...I don't know, polarity? Draw all the heliophobic devils *back* to it instead of freeing them?"

Father Carroll opened his mouth to speak before closing it. He regarded Donovan, impressed. "I would not have considered that."

"Frank said I don't think like a cop. I guess I don't think like a priest with an Augustine Dictate either."

"In theory, it sounds plausible. In reality—"

"Do we have a choice?"

Father Carroll looked at the faxed prayer in his hand. "All things are possible through the Lord when you open your life to Him."

After Special Agent Clark's curt dismissal, Father Carroll's attitude renewed his determination. "I hope 'all things' covers crazy motorcycle stunts, too, because that's the only way I'm going to get Joann."

"What do you mean?"

"Once the police move in it's going to be a war zone in there. In the middle of it all, while Valdes and Faustus are defending their ritual circle, I can ride in, grab her, and get away to someplace safe."

Father Carroll's eyebrows rose. "Crazy motorcycle stunts, indeed."

"What do you think?"

"Evil of this sort has always seemed steeped in ancient tradition and musty ritual, but police assaults? Riding a motorcycle through an army of the possessed? This time it's very modern, very large, and very daunting." For all his concerns, he burned with a resolve greater than Donovan had sensed in Braithwaite and the helicopter pilot. "Still, only the dead face no change. *We* persist."

"We'll do more than that."

"*If* we avoid overconfidence. You must know *exactly* where you will ride, and it can't be far. If you stay too long in range the possessed *will* catch you."

"I'll make it through Valdes's mob. I'll get her free. Once I do I need somewhere safe to take her, but what does 'safe' mean? Hallowed ground? A church?"

"Mephistopheles himself wouldn't be stopped by one," the priest said. "According to Marlowe, he and Faustus played tricks on the Pope in Rome, after all. Mephistopheles' acolytes, though, will be unable to follow you into a church without great suffering."

"Considering the stakes, I think it's a safe bet they won't let that stop them." Donovan gripped the spire tighter. "But I won't let them have Joann."

"On Central Park West there are at least half dozen churches between the Lawn and here. Any of them will do; the closest may be the Universalist Church on West 76th Street. But Donovan—there's something else we have to address. The worst case scenario."

"You mean if we're too late, and she's already been possessed by Mephistopheles? I thought about it." Donovan took in a deep, resolute breath. "I *won't* let it happen."

"It may be out of your hands."

Donovan half-turned away and stopped, rubbing his palm down the leg of his jeans. "Then…you can use the Orison on her, too. A 'concentrated Rite of Exorcism' sounds like the right way to handle a Prince of Hell."

"Without a doubt, but as I said, the subject for the exorcism has to be present. We must hold her physical form to perform it, and we *are* discussing a Prince of Hell."

This point Donovan hadn't considered. "You have thoughts, I hope?"

"Actually—" Father Carroll spoke slowly, as if he didn't want to raise expectations. "Goethe *did* have something to say on the subject." He closed his eyes to read the passage from his memory. "Faust is dismissing Mephistopheles to bring the bargain for his soul to Lucifer. He begins by saying:

> 'Here is the window, here the door,
> A chimney there, if that's preferred.'

"Mephistopheles replies:

'I cannot leave you that way, I deplore;
By a small obstacle I am deterred;
The witch's foot on your threshold, see—'
      "Faust:
                        'The pentagram distresses you?'
   "If Goethe is to be believed, Mephistopheles can't cross a threshold with
a pentagram."
   "If Goethe is to be believed, Faust and Mephistopheles spent their time
engaging in civilized philosophical debate, not doing...this." Donovan's
lips made a thin line. "Think we can trust it?"
   "It's not the sort of thing I'd like to try without testing, but we both
know the pentagram is a powerful magical symbol."
   "Like we have a choice anyways." Donovan watched Clark, Yarborough
and the captains on the other side of Columbus Circle. He saw Fullam
break away from the group and start towards them. It triggered an idea
that made him laugh. "Dragging a possessed Joann anywhere is crazy. It'll
never work. If we're too late and she's been possessed, I'll have to do the
only sensible thing."
   "Which is?"
   "I'll have to make Mephistopheles so mad he chases me."

                              ∾

He wasn't human.
   Joann wasn't sure whether she was thinking or saying the words aloud.
She was sure of nothing anymore, ever since she'd seen whatever Coeus
had become.
   *This is impossible. Valdes is just a murderer. He kidnapped me, he drugged
these people, but that's not supernatural. He must have given Coletun some
kind of make-up, some cosmetic contact lenses. His methods are bizarre, but
he's still just a murderer.*
   He's just a man.
   In her mind, she sounded less than convinced. The suffering around
her created a wellspring of emotion, but to empathize with the tortured
would have drowned her. A wisp of anger curled around her doubt.
   Where are you, Donovan?
   A cool, slippery touch on her forehead made her gasp. She opened her
eyes and saw Faustus standing before her, smearing some kind of oil on
her forehead, cheeks and chin. Her nose twitched at the musk in the oil.

As he moved, he spoke in a low, singsong chant:

>"'Die Sorge nistet gleich im tiefen Herzen,
>Dort wirket sie geheime Schmerzen.
>Unruhig wiegt sie sich und storet Lust und Ruh;
>Sie deckt sich stets mit neuen Masken zu.'"

"What are you doing?"

He met her eyes then quickly looked away. "The Vessel must be properly anointed," he said, brusque manner covering his emotions. "Lest the King find it unworthy."

Panic threatened to overwhelm her. *I'm still a prosecutor.* Joann clung to this slim lifeline and summoned every iota of control she had left. "You *owe* me. You asked me a question, I answered it. I know by your reaction it was important to you."

From his wooden box of supplies Faustus took a small jar and uncorked the top.

A very unprofessional fear surfaced in her tone. "It isn't too late for you. I can still get you immunity. I can still get you free from Valdes."

Dabbing a bit of the jar's viscous brown contents on his fingertip, he stroked it onto her eyelids as he recited:

>"'Ich grube dich, du einzige Phiole,
>Die ich mit Andacht nun herunterhole.
>In dir verehr ich Menschenwitz und Kunst.
>Du Inbegriff der holden Schlummersafte,
>Du Auszug aller todlich feinen Krafte,
>Erweise deinem Meister deine Gunst!'"

"I answered your question!"

Faustus fussed with his supplies, muttering to himself. Joann caught part of what he said: *"Ex malo bonum."*

"From evil, good may come"; what does that mean?

☙

"*Chase* you?" Father Carroll repeated. "I hadn't considered that option. But then, insanity isn't the first track upon which my train of thought travels."

"If Joann is," Donovan cleared a lump from his throat, "is possessed, you're right; there's no way I'm going to be able to physically drag her anywhere."

"But chase you where?"

"Wherever we've already painted pentagrams on the windows and doors." The further he thought it through, the less appealing an idea it seemed.

"He won't notice the symbols?"

"Not if I make him mad enough. And all I have to do is get him inside."

Father Carroll just stared at him. "Donovan, do you understand what you're proposing? Possessing a human form to interact on this plane limits the power of an Infernal being, but it by no means eliminates it. This is a Crown Prince of Hell you'll be trapped with."

"No. I'll be trapped with Joann. Together we'll fight Mephistopheles."

Before Father Carroll could challenge his logic, Fullam came around the back end of the fire truck. His face remained flushed from his encounter with his superior.

"Well, you're still with us," Donovan said. "That's a plus."

"Hugh has assigned me to the barricade at 110th and Fifth."

"How nice of him to keep you out of harm's way," Father Carroll said dryly.

"It's not harm he's keeping me from," the sergeant frowned. "I'm too deeply involved, and it's getting too hairy too quickly, for him to make a stink about me being here."

"How's your job status?" Donovan asked.

"The only way it changes is if I make a serious impact on the outcome of all this, which is why he stuck me way the hell up north, away from any possibility of that happening. Since I can't help him, I'm helping you." Donovan started to protest but Fullam went on. "You want to save Joann, I want to save my people. And my career."

"What if I say no? Are you going to arrest me?"

"You going to make this a pissing contest?"

"What I told them," Donovan jerked his head in the direction of the police officials, "is barely the tip of the iceberg. You have no idea what's really happening here."

"Mysterious darkness and iron bars and apocalyptic cults? Of course I don't. Not fully. So what? I didn't understand everything in the Lisette Osorio—the Santeria case either. When I need forensics I don't get behind the microscope, I go to someone who knows what they're doing. I don't *have* to fully understand any of this because I know *you* do, and I trust you." He looked at them both to make sure his words had sunk in before going on. "Now if these were ordinary circumstances, I'd say they've got

230 { thomas morrissey }

things pretty well covered. Since we all agree we're in the Twilight Zone, I'm going to ask you both—what can I do to watch their backs?"

Donovan and Father Carroll exchanged a glance. In spite of the sergeant's enlightened perspective, they knew sharing anything about the Orison would be a waste of time. "Actually, Francis," Father Carroll began, "we were looking to stay out of their way while we did what we had to do."

Fullam nodded. "Which is what?"

"During all the fighting I'm going for Joann," Donovan said, "Father Carroll's going to try to do something about the, ah, cult members. We're still working on specifics."

"Perhaps you can help," the priest continued. "One of the things we need is a room or a building, a place nearby, where Donovan can go after he rescues her."

"Just get behind the police lines. You'll be all right."

"That might be," Donovan searched for the right word, "impractical."

"Uh-*hunh*." Fullam reached into his back pocket for a sheet of paper. As he smoothed it out against the side of the fire truck, Donovan saw it was a map of the park. "Matz has the motorcycles and mounteds assembling on the northwest quarter, but most of the police response is coming from the south. Be easier to sneak you down from the north*east* side. And if you're approaching from there—" The lieutenant tapped a spot. "South Gate House. Right here, at the southern tip of the reservoir. It's a couple of hundred yards from where you think she'll be. I can give you a skeleton key to get in."

Donovan considered it. "Not bad. I've passed it a million times when I've been jogging. The walls are stone, it's got bars and steel mesh on the windows, only one door in front…okay. Okay, it sounds good."

"There are some preparations we'll have to make to it," Father Carroll reminded him. "We'll need paint, or markers or something."

"I'll talk to Jesus Higuera at Emergency Services. Now give *me* something." Fullam folded his arms across his chest. "I'm going watch my people's backs. I know about the iron spires. Give me something else."

"In fact," Father Carroll said, "that was also one of the things we were discussing, what weapons we have available to—"

"Light," Donovan interrupted. "Sorry, Father."

Fullam squinted at him. "Light?"

"If you want to make a difference in the fighting, the best way would be to light the field. You've seen how difficult it is to get a good look at them.

Part of the reason is they're heliophobic—they can't tolerate light. In the dark they're nearly invincible; illuminated, they're not as tough."

Fullam glanced at the vehicles around Columbus Circle. "I'll have to get a little help, but *that*," he said with satisfaction, "I can arrange."

"Light," Donovan murmured again, "iron spires and—" He looked past Fullam's map to the side of the fire truck. "And holy water…"

TWENTY-FOUR

ONSTAGE

"Neil; a moment?"

Mephistopheles stood on the stage, beckoning. Valdes went to him, noting that the Prince of Darkness never seemed to actively walk through the shadows; he merely appeared where he wanted to go within them.

"'Prince' is a title, a quantification to allow human comprehension. I *am* Darkness, and every terror that exists within." Mephistopheles regarded the carnage. "I am why mankind has always feared the setting of the sun." Behind them, a man with a steel hook embedded in his back groaned and went limp. "Do you have the ring?"

Valdes took Joann's engagement ring from his pocket. The diamond caught a shaft of firelight and sparkled. "I asked Faustus why we needed this," he said. "He told me it was to be a gift, something protocol demands before serious negotiations."

"Do you doubt him?" Mephistopheles chuckled, plucking the ring from his grasp. "Such a suspicious mind you have. Although I can't say I blame you, not after what the CYA Board did to you."

Valdes clenched his teeth behind his pleasant demeanor. "How do I use it?"

"Merely offer it, but only after you've made your case. By no means attempt to discuss terms until you've given him this. Otherwise you risk giving offense—Lucifer is extraordinarily vain. Witness his requirement for a Vessel: 'a beautiful force for good.'"

"You sound unimpressed."

"A *servant* does as he is bid. Once Lucifer accepts it freely and puts it on, we can begin. All that remains until then—"

"The rest of the six-hundred-sixty-six sacrifices are on their way." Valdes looked towards the south end of Great Lawn. "They'll be here in time."

⁂

Faustus watched Valdes hand the ring to Mephistopheles. They spoke briefly, and Valdes turned towards the lawn. As he did, Mephistopheles silently mouthed a few words and, out of sight of Valdes, touched the ring with one monstrous finger. A shimmer of tarnished silver sank into the bauble. The sorcerer's eyes narrowed as he recognized the Prince of Darkness' movements mirroring ones he himself had made hours earlier.

Was geschieht?

An implication came to him, one so incredible, so astonishing, that his hands began to shake. "*Ist es möglich…?*" he murmured. "*Könnte Rettung für Faustus zur Hand sein?*"

Wie könnte Faustus dieses nutzen?

His heart began to pound as he sought to devise a plan.

⁂

The main force of police held together as they double-timed towards the 65th Street overpasses in two rows. The first line brandished bulletproof shields.

"Keep moving." As the official head of the Valdes investigation, Yarborough had taken personal command of the operation. Clad in body armor and carrying a shotgun, he stayed close to Detective Wright. In his other hand he carried an NYPD flashlight, one of the heavy, ten-battery numbers. "What is with these damn things?" He slapped it on his thigh, but it remained dark. "Doesn't anyone have one that works?"

"None of them are working," Wright replied. "Neither are the night vision glasses. Some kind of interference." He glanced at Clark. "Your people detect any kind of electromagnetic device could cause this?"

Next to him, the FBI man ran easily with his younger agents. He shook his head impatiently as he put a finger to his earpiece. "Vicki? Any movement yet?"

"*Negative.*" Vicki Matthews, who had remained at the FBI van to monitor things on the remote cameras with Peter Lo, sounded worried. "*Be careful, Harley.*"

"*Contact!*" Lo interrupted. "*Bushes near the overpass, dead ahead. Looks like about a dozen…armed and taking aim!*"

Yarborough heard this and barked. "Darenelli, watch out!"

Wild shots came from the bushes. Darenelli shouted orders to the twenty men in front of him. Those holding shields dropped to their knees, while the ones behind opened fire. The derelicts were annihilated.

"Close ranks!"

More cops rushed to firm up the line. Everyone paused, waiting for orders. Yarborough approached the bodies cautiously. "I don't see anything unusual about them. I don't know what Donovan Graham told you, but these 'cult members' look to me like garden-variety crackheads." He glanced at the captains. "If these are examples of their typical foot soldiers, we may have less difficulty than we thought."

"So much for the Apocalypse." Darenelli waved over one of his people. "Call the meat wagon, and let's move out!"

The police line obeyed, marching north…

…while behind them, the "crackheads" opened their eyes and began to rise again. Like old skin their human guises sloughed off, revealing more hellish incarnations.

"'*Call the meat wagon,*'" one mimicked. "'*Let's move out.*'"

An undercurrent of anticipatory laughter swelled as more shapes emerged from the darkness. They followed the police, numbers growing. As they went they passed the word:

"*Two hundred sixty-four and kill the rest.*"

ᘓ

"Follow me."

Fullam put the red light on his dashboard and, with Father Carroll in the passenger seat, led Donovan's motorcycle the wrong way up Fifth Avenue's Museum Mile. Nervous cops blocking the cross-streets watched them. Donovan wondered what they thought of the night's events. He wondered what Joann, in the midst of it all, thought.

At the Fifth Avenue and 102nd Street barricade, the sergeant stopped, climbed out of his car, and went to the sergeant in charge. Donovan pulled up and removed his helmet to watch. Father Carroll joined him.

"Suppose Francis isn't able to get them to allow us entrance?"

"Then I'll fight them first." Up each sleeve of his leather jacket he'd slid an iron spire as long as his forearm. It was like wearing a half cast on each arm. *I'd be a lot more uncomfortable* without *them,* he thought. He snapped his arms away from his body. The spires slid into his hands, although the bandage on his left made holding one difficult. He raised his forearms and the spires returned to his sleeves. "Joann doesn't have much time."

Someone in dark blue body armor trailed Fullam as he came back. "Hey, daredevil."

Donovan recognized Braithwaite. "What are you doing all the way up here?"

Fullam's mouth twisted down. "The price for being on my team."

"Glad I can help make a difference." Braithwaite turned his baseball cap backwards and rolled his shoulders loose. "Always wanted to get behind the wheel of one of those big ESU trucks."

Donovan pulled Fullam aside. "Does he understand the, ah, *uniqueness* of the circumstances?"

The sergeant gave a look that wondered how stupid Donovan thought he was. "I'll give him an iron spire and let him know the score," his voice softened, "when we go in. But if I'm going to take the fire engine, we still need one more person."

"I've been thinking about that. I've got someone." With some awkwardness caused by the spires in his sleeves, Donovan took out his cell phone and dialed a number. It was picked up on the first ring, as he knew it would be. "It's Donovan. Do you want to help rescue Joann?" The voice on the other end exploded through the receiver. Donovan kept talking over it. "Go to Columbus Circle and ask for Sergeant Fullam. He'll be looking for you. Just one thing—you *did* say you used to drive a truck in college?"

൭

A cluster of figures emerged from the darkness near the stage; all of them save one immediately ran off; the last—Valdes—approached, brisk and all business. His good humor, so infuriating, was muted by an edge of tension and excitement. "Everything is going well, *Herr Doktor*? Is our lovely Vessel all ready?"

"I have anointed her."

"Excellent." Valdes inspected Faustus's work. Joann twisted her head away from his touch. "Mephistopheles is laying the groundwork for my deal. My people are finishing gathering the necessary blood for the Amaranthine Gateway. If you've prepared *Joann*," he stressed her name with a smile, "I think we're all ready."

"*Nein*." Faustus reached into his wooden box and produced a rolled sheet of parchment. "Thou hast not completed thine end of thy bargain to offer."

Valdes took it, scanned the writing on it and laughed. "A *contract*? You're not serious?"

"As did Faustus, so must Valdes."

"But Mephistopheles just made a joke about Marlowe—"

"If thou hast wish to enter the world of Faustus," the sorcerer spoke as though to a child, a smug note creeping in, "thou must attend the rules. The Universe is thus structured, to maintain order amidst chaos."

"I told Mephistopheles my plan, and he said nothing about this."

"Nevertheless."

Valdes pursed his lips, reached into his suit coat's inside pocket and took out the knife he'd used earlier. A scab of blood crusted the hilt. "Allow me."

Joann watched as he took the knife in his left hand, held up his right, and, with agonizing and deliberate slowness, sliced through the tip of his index finger. He didn't change expression, holding her eyes even when he had to saw a bit to get through the bone. Blood sprayed up to grotesque comedic effect, speckling her skin. Horrified, she couldn't look away as he held the severed joint in his hand while wrapping a handkerchief over the wound. Red immediately seeped through the white cloth, soaking it and running down his wrist. He turned to Faustus, braced the parchment and signed in blood with the mutilated digit.

"There." He could have been an author autographing a newly purchased copy of a bestseller. Peeling the bloody cloth from his finger, he handed Faustus the nub of flesh and bone. "If you please, *Herr Doktor*."

Faustus regarded him with disturbed eyes but repeated the healing procedure with which he'd saved Joann's finger.

When he'd finished, Valdes turned back to Joann. His pleasant manner had returned, but with it also came the edge she'd seen when he'd first come over. "I don't care what you think you know," he said. "I don't care what you think you've seen or experienced so far. *Nothing* will stop me from getting what I want. And if I'm willing to do this to myself," he brandished his hand at her, "imagine what I'm going to do to you."

❦

Five minutes later, Donovan and Father Carroll were inside the South Gate House.

"Make sure all the lines connect," the priest cautioned, carefully completing a star. "If I recall the remainder of the passage I cited earlier, it runs along these lines:

> "Faustus:
> 'The pentagram distresses you? Then, son of Hell, explain to me:
> How could you enter here without ado?'
>
> "Mephistopheles:
> Behold it well, it is not quite completed;
> One angle—that which points outside—
> Is open just a bit.'

"If there are any gaps, he'll be able to slip out."

"Got it." Donovan gazed about the room, double-checking their handiwork. The interior of the South Gate House was roughly the size of a grade-school classroom and had the dingy, dusty quality of a government office—yellowed walls filled with posted regulations, aged file cabinets, triplicate forms, a couple of worn desks and chairs, and a standing closet/locker. Every wall had tall, narrow windows. In front they looked out onto the jogging path, while in the back and on the sides they displayed the vast, dark pool of the reservoir. Each opening now sported a bright orange pentagram, including the back of the door they'd entered. In one rear corner, a spiral staircase of steel steps led down into the dimly lit bowels of the reservoir monitoring station, to runoff chambers and storage rooms.

"Looks good."

He turned and saw the priest had gone to the doorway. Beyond was darkness, but they could both hear the cries of pain and madness.

"What is it?"

Father Carroll spoke without looking at him. "If Valdes is, as we believe, following in the footsteps of Faustus, he will eventually deal with Lucifer. All of this," he nodded in the direction of the Great Lawn, "is quite a bit of pageantry. Are we sure it's for the Prince of Darkness, and not the King of Hell?"

"What?" The prospect stopped Donovan cold. He forced himself to think rationally. "No, it can't be. Everything Valdes has done so far has been very by-the-numbers. First the zodiac murders, then the *resurrectus maledicat*, now summoning Mephistopheles. I don't think he'd jump to the next step without knowing what was going on. Rushing in could ruin everything. He's too methodical to do that."

"As he gets closer to what he wants, he may be more anxious. And less cautious."

The concept was unfathomable. *The King. Of Hell.* "How could we tell if...?"

Father Carroll also struggled with the reality that Lucifer might be involved, and so retreated into a professorial stance. "Without seeing the ceremonial accoutrements it's difficult to say. The pageantry is one indication. This is the King of Hell, after all. One cannot make contact with such a being using shopping mall candles and playing a record backwards. Royalty demands so much more, from a specific hue of the Infernal portal to a proscribed number of sacrifices upon arrival. In Lucifer's case, that color is a shade of amaranth purple—the exact one is unknown and almost impossible to discover. Amaranth symbolizes the eternal; purple stands for royalty. The number of sacrifices is, of course, six hundred-sixty-six."

"If the hostages they have are supposed to be offerings, there's nowhere near that many." Donovan let out the breath he hadn't realized he'd been holding. "There were maybe half that." A humorless half-smile formed on his lips as the absurdity struck him. "Guess that means we're *only* facing the Prince of Darkness."

"As odd as it sounds," Father Carroll said with a rueful shake of his head, "we *are* better off. For all the earthly danger Mephistopheles represents, his domain is desire and want. He may succeed on a physical level but spiritually can be stalemated by faith or will. Lucifer, conversely, gains his greatest satisfaction from twisting man's noblest efforts into something that serves the Infernal. Faith and will are tools in his hands. I'm at a loss to comprehend what it would take to *survive*, let alone fight, that." He crossed his forehead. "I pray we never have to."

Donovan's heart still pounded. He went to a window to touch up a pentagram before slipping the small can of spray paint into his jacket pocket. The surface of the reservoir lay placid, as smooth and black as volcanic glass. An idea occurred to him, so strong an image that his head jerked.

Father Carroll noticed. "Something?"

Donovan took Fullam's "skeleton key"—a large pair of bolt cutters to sever the chains holding the Gate House doors closed—and started out-side. "Come on."

Infernal energy trembled so strongly in the air it made leaves sway. All around them, the raspy voices of the possessed filled the blackness. Father Carroll walked around to the chain-link fence but Donovan stopped. Four hundred yards away from the Great Lawn, through a line of trees and brush, he felt the pull of the dark. It repulsed him because it was impossible *not* to wonder, even for a second, what you could accomplish with that kind of influence on your side. The lure Faustus had felt centuries before reached out to him...

He shrugged it off with barely a thought. *Faustus didn't have Joann.*

Father Carroll's voice interrupted his thoughts. "What do you have in mind?"

"Most of what we're about to do is going to be physical. Hand-to-hand." Donovan snipped links, working the bolt cutters like he was trimming hedges. "Do you think it'd be to our advantage if they couldn't touch us?"

"I don't follow."

"What if we were soaked in holy water? The possessed couldn't touch us, at least not without enough pain to even the odds a little."

"Soaked in...how could we accomplish that?" The idea intrigued him, but its practicality left him unsure. "By blessing the reservoir so we might go for a swim?"

"Absolutely." Donovan set the bolt cutters aside. There was now a man-sized hole in the fence. "You just blessed some water for Frank. What's different here?"

"*That* water supply was bit smaller than this. I don't think the same Prayer for the Blessing of Water would have the effect you want here."

"Then what about the Orison? You said it purifies." Donovan stepped through the hole. "Why not recite *it* over the water?"

"It seems so...mundane a purpose for so powerful a prayer." Father Carroll followed him, still doubtful. "Still...I would not have thought of that."

From far to the south came gunfire. Donovan looked at him urgently.

"I'll try."

He lowered himself to the reservoir, which at this spot came up past the knees of his black pants. "It feel likes there's a steep drop off just beyond this point." He swirled his hands in the water, shifted his feet, raised his arms to Heaven and began to speak in a strong, clear voice:

"'By the power of Christ!

Listen and submit yourselves to God! Resist the devil, and he will flee from you! Draw nigh unto God, and he will draw nigh unto you! Cleanse your hands, ye sinners, and purify your hearts!'"

The prayer went into Latin at that point, so Donovan glanced around to make sure they hadn't been spotted. The lights ringing the reservoir's running path glowed dimly. Way up one side of the reservoir, he could see a figure jogging towards them.

Damn!

"*In nomine Saint Michael et Jesus Christ, consummatum est.* Amen."

Donovan kept his eyes on the figure. It kept coming, a flicker of white shifting and dancing in the shadows. He registered that Father Carroll had finished speaking, and after a few seconds he called, "Is that it?"

"I could do it again, to be sure—"

"No time." He set Fullam's Glock on the wall, took a few steps back and launched himself in a dive over the priest's head. He hit the water with a sizable splash, and his clothing, leather jacket and boots immediately began to soak up water. Combined with the weight of the iron spires up his sleeves, they dragged him down into the cool, murky depths. Adrenaline charged his muscle and he pushed up, gasping for air.

Father Carroll had lunged out to him and was treading water. "Are you all right?"

"I'm fine." Donovan clumsily stroked to the shallow area where the priest had recited the Orison. He swept his wet hair back from his forehead and hoisted himself out of the reservoir. "I don't really feel anything. Should I?" He extended a hand to help the priest. "A tingling or something?"

"Do you normally feel anything when you touch holy water?"

"Well no, but—"

The scuffling of The Jogger's sneakers grew closer. Donovan wondered if he'd seen them. He ducked back through the hole in the fence, leaving a trail that became a puddle as he stopped in The Jogger's path. With a quick snap of his arms the spires slid into his hands. He blinked once and suddenly The Jogger was on him, swinging his right arm high. Donovan heard a wet cutting sound, and he gaped at the scythe-like blade that unfolded from The Jogger's forearm.

The Jogger chopped the blade at Donovan's head. Donovan caught the blade in an "X" of crossed spires. The Jogger growled as he tried to bear his weight down. Donovan swung their arms in a circle, forcing the scythe down. He slammed his elbow back into the derelict's face. A white light flashed when his holy water-soaked jacket made contact. The Jogger grunted, stumbling before attacking again. Donovan ducked the scythe and whipped one spire. It cracked The Jogger's shin, buckling his leg and dropping him awkwardly. Donovan slammed the other spire down, snapping the scythe blade off. The Jogger cried out in his creepy, warped voice and grabbed Donovan's leg. Another flash lit the path when he touched the dripping fabric and The Jogger screamed. Donovan kicked at his face. His boot glanced off the side of The Jogger's head. The Jogger threw a handful of gravel in his face. Donovan staggered and fell back, swiping dust from his eyes. The Jogger lunged. Donovan rolled along the chain links, grunting as the derelict jumped on his back. Its claws stabbed through the back of his jacket, drawing blood and thrusting his face into the fence.

"*The power of Christ commands you—depart from the soul of this man!*"

Father Carroll's voice boomed in Donovan's ear. Before Donovan could react he saw a peripheral flash of light and felt the weight of the derelict pulled from him. He spun, ready to attack. The priest held The Jogger in a full nelson, his knobby hands laced behind the derelict's head to hoist him off the ground. Constant contact between holy water and possessed flesh made a hissing, spitting sound like frying bacon, and gave them an otherworldly glow.

Donovan raised one spire in both hands for the killing blow.

"No! He still has a soul!"

"That's crazy! You can't hold him for long!" Donovan looked towards the Great Lawn. "We *have* to go!"

The priest turned away, lurching back to the hole in the fence. "*Get thee behind me, thou unclean!*" he roared. Staggering mightily he fought the derelict to the edge of the reservoir. "*Begone from that to which you have no claim!*" He jumped, taking them both over the shallow ledge. They hit the water with a tremendous splash and vanished.

"*Father Carroll!*"

♋

Fullam retraced his drive back down Fifth Avenue and across Central Park South to Columbus Circle. When he saw the man he was looking for he gave a tight smile.

Conrad Clery stared at him with the weight of a thousand won trials.

"Where's my daughter?"

"She's being held in there." Fullam nodded towards the park. During the time he, Donovan and Maurice had been planning, the darkness surrounding it seemed to have grown deeper and more intense.

"What's being done to rescue her?" Conrad looked at him strangely. "And why did Donovan ask me if I know how to drive a truck?"

Braithwaite was already going for the mini-forklift near the palettes of iron spires. Fullam started walking towards the fire engine. "Can you?"

Conrad gave a little start as the forklift fired up, and Braithwaite began to wheel a load of spires towards them. "It's been a while, but yes, I still remember."

"Good." Fullam stopped, one hand on the engine's driver door. "What we're going to do to save Joann is a little unusual, and the less you know the less you'll question and make an issue out of."

"Sergeant," Conrad said, deliberately using Fullam's rank, "this is my daughter. I don't care if this is sanctioned or not. Can we save her?"

Fullam told him what he had to do.

ↄ৴

Faustus appeared at the end of the stage. If the suffering surrounding them left any mark on him, he remained impassive. "Thy subjects are complete in their task. The blood of many innocents hath been collected for the Amaranthine Gateway. All that awaits," he bowed slightly towards the huge Sigil of Baphomet in front of the stage, "is thine addition."

Valdes looked at Mephistopheles.

"Innocence corrupted." Mephistopheles' voice held a strange note, one that sounded almost like anticipation. "All of the blood in the Amaranthine Gateway comes from the innocent. When I add mine, not only does it create the correct color, it also changes pure to impure." He hunched in on himself, and the massive, misshapen Coeus morphed into the form Valdes had first expected: a monk, clad simply in brown cassock with a rope belt. On his now-normal feet were sandals of wood and cloth. His eyes, however, remained unchanged; vast, unending purple lakes speckled with infinite white pinpoints.

"I thought—"

"You were presumptuous in your use of Marlowe, Neil," Mephistopheles said. "I don't do requests. I only take this form when dealing with Lucifer because," a slight sneer curved his lip, "it doesn't *threaten*. Whatever Vessel

Lucifer possesses needs to be the most beautiful in the room."

"*Solamen miseris socios habuisse doloris*, Valdes." Faustus regarded him like a cattleman herding a steer into the slaughterhouse. "Art thou prepared to join Faustus in damnation?"

"I've made my position clear, *Herr Doktor*."

Mephistopheles gazed down the Lawn. "I see the sacrifices coming, Neil. I trust the fight will provide enough energy to open the gateway?"

"Absolutely," Valdes said. "I arranged for the police to find a little extra motivation."

"Excellent." Mephistopheles nodded. "Then I'd best get our Vessel."

TWENTY-FIVE

...WHERE THE INEVITABLE BEGINS

The police line broke to bypass the blockade of Belvedere Castle and Turtle Pond; half went north on the west side, half on the east. The rank, airborne taste of disembowelment was evident even before the police came in sight of the Great Lawn. Drawing nearer they began to see bodies whose intestines and organs draped tree branches like ornaments.

"If they think they're soldiers from Hell," Darenelli observed, kissing the crucifix around his neck, "looks like they want home field advantage."

Clark kept professional despite a growing suspicion he should have given Donovan Graham's warnings more weight. "Keep in formation. Watch out for traps."

At the southernmost tip of the Lawn the police line re-formed. All the surrounding streetlights had been vandalized, and since none of the NYPD flashlights were working, the only illumination came from bonfires and torches. Rather than form a chain of light, each individual fire lit a small space around it, shrinking visibility to two dozen tiny spaces scattered around the field. Breezes from the north carried stronger smells, of organic material so pungent it could only be newly dead. Worst was the cloying, stifling silence—the impression the men had taken away from the briefing was of bustling activity filling the park. Now there wasn't enough noise to drown the groans of the dying.

Clark glanced at Yarborough. "How can this many people be so quiet?"

"Donovan Graham said there were a lot," the chief said with disdain. "How many did the chopper flyover actually *show* you?"

"Enough." The FBI man spoke softly into his radio. "Vicki? Where is everybody?"

"*Can't tell. From here, everything looks like it's getting darker.*"

Clark raised his head. Matthews was right; the area inside the Lawn's oval had become darker and more mysterious, its pockets of light compressing as though the darkness had actual weight. Ahead, he saw the vague shape of something—some *things*—stretching across the bottom of the Lawn.

"Hey!" Darenelli shouted. "There goes someone!"

Two white slashes danced across the grass expanse. They dropped a pair of torches and melted into the dark. Something in the grass caught fire. A blazing circle erupted, fully displaying what stood in the way of the police—the heads of the Central Park Precinct officers on stakes. Their limbs, still clad in their uniforms, had been torn off and formed into a giant word:

WELCOME

Throughout the dark, a message whispered: "*Two hundred sixty-four and kill the rest!*"

 co

Donovan dropped the spires and dove back into the reservoir. About ten feet away the two figures bobbed to the surface, their struggles churning a froth of black water and white slashes. Father Carroll wrestled The Jogger's head above the surface before dunking it and repeating his adjuration. "*The power of Christ commands you—depart this man!*" Hissing and biting, The Jogger tried to roll onto his back. His chalky bluish skin blistered as the priest jerked him under.

The surface of the reservoir calmed.

Donovan thrashed towards them. The spot where they'd gone below strobed once; a dark, amorphous cloud erupted and vanished north.

"Donovan!"

The priest struggled to support what was now an unconscious man in a filthy track suit. His skin had returned to a pale, human shade, and its blisters were gone. Donovan swam over, and together they dragged him to the reservoir's edge and hoisted him out. The Jogger's head lolled back on the dirt, tongue draped over his lower lip. Donovan checked to see if he needed mouth-to-mouth, grateful to find he didn't. "That cloud…was that—?"

"'The fiend in his own shape is less hideous than when he rages in the breast of man.'" Father Carroll stood next to him, looking down. "Nathaniel Hawthorne, 'Young Goodman Brown.'" He suddenly began to tremble. Donovan thought he was cold, but as he looked into the priest's face he saw it was not cold but an overwhelming excitement that made him seem twenty years younger. "Astounding!" He smoothed his dripping beard with a trembling hand. "I...I've participated in hundreds of exorcism investigations, performed nine *true* exorcisms, but this...this was *astonishing!*" He glanced around. "Where did it go?"

"North, back to the portal in the Cancer Hospital. Are you all right?"

"I feel...energized."

In spite of the circumstances, Donovan allowed a small smile. They looked at each other, unable to articulate anything more about what had happened. "We have to go."

"Are you ready?"

"Yeah." The spires lay at their feet. Donovan picked them up, slid one up his right sleeve and offered the other. "Just in case." He stopped and looked around. "Damn!"

"What is it?"

"Frank's gun; I left it over there when I jumped in the water. It must have gotten knocked in during the fight."

"I apologize."

"Not your fault." Donovan looked at The Jogger, still unconscious, and restrained an urge to throw him into the reservoir to look for it. "Have to manage without it."

They stood in the eye of the hurricane and looked at each other.

"Are you afraid?"

"Terrified." Donovan thought of Joann. "But afraid isn't an option."

"Fear ends where the inevitable begins. I believe God has a plan for you, a destiny. Accept it, and follow it with faith."

The noise of the police assault was getting closer as the force worked its way towards the Lawn.

"There is one more thing," the priest said, going back into his gym bag. He removed something, hurried through the hole in the fence, and stooped to the reservoir. Donovan watched, unsure, as he hurried back. "Here. Take this."

He gave Donovan a handful of purple silk that was darkened to black by the water. Donovan unrolled it. It was about six feet long, with a thin edge of gold embroidery and a gold cross embroidered at each end.

"What's this?"

"It's the stole I've worn for all nine of the exorcisms I've performed." He gestured. "For extra protection."

Donovan hesitated. "Are you sure?"

"*You* face greater peril, I think."

"Yeah." Donovan looked at the stole. "But I'm ready now. I'll see you after all this is over, or," he glanced at the foreboding shadow of the South Gate House, "I'll see you back here. Good luck."

"Go and save Joann, my son." Father Carroll swept him up in a bear hug. "God be with you."

He released him, turned, and ran towards Central Park West.

∾

Joann locked her eyes on the handkerchief at her feet as Valdes walked off, focusing on the bright scarlet stain.

I can't. I can't look. I can't...see him *again.*

Her teeth began to chatter as she realized she no longer thought of the giant as Coeus anymore. She squeezed her eyes shut.

I'm in serious danger, but I believe Donovan will come. I believe Donovan will save me. He has to come. He has *to.*

She heard the giant's words over and over again: "Hold onto your life preserver, Joann."

Why isn't *he here yet? How long has it been since Valdes grabbed me from his apartment, two, three days? Hasn't he figured it out yet?*

She groaned softly and hung her head.

Has *he abandoned me?*

∾

The police charged past the gruesome display of their comrades' bodies and into...

...nothing.

The Lawn was a vast, dark, empty void.

Cold dread seized Yarborough. "What the fuck is going on?"

He and Clark had followed their men, expecting to face what Donovan Graham had described as an all-out war with an apocalyptic cult. What they found when they crossed onto the Lawn was darkness as thick as fog but not as tangible, so dense they could barely see the man next to them.

"Link arms! Hold the line!" Clark's voice came from somewhere next to him. "Nobody panic! Chief, have your units report in!"

"*Harley, are you with me?*"

"I'm here, Vicki. What happened? We can't see anything."

"*Everything just went black. We didn't know if it was technical or not.*"

"No, it's out here, too. Stand by." He groped in the darkness and found Yarborough's arm. "How are your people doing?"

"All units report!" Yarborough barked.

Immediately a hundred voices responded, offering information, asking for explanations, waiting for orders. "*What did these fuckers do?*" Darenelli's voice was unmistakable as it cut through the commotion. "*How did they—*"

"Hold your positions," Clark advised everyone. To his amazement, his teeth were chattering with fright. He clenched his muscles in resistance and leaned towards Yarborough. "They sucked us in with that display back there. We should pull back, see how localized this darkness is."

"What is it?" Yarborough tried to wave it away from in front of his eyes. A quaver in his voice made him clear his throat. "Chemical smoke screen?"

"I doubt it; Valdes didn't have the connections necessary to get his hands on that kind of stuff." Clark kept his eyes moving, wondering if this was how cavalry felt waiting for a Lakota Sioux attack. "Our sniffers picked up nothing."

Suddenly, the radios burst alive with frenzied panic.

"*Captain, I—aaaaaaaahhhh!*"

"*Harley, what the fuck—*"

"Sit rep!" Clark demanded.

"*They're hitting us in packs!*" came a high-pitched reply. "*We linked arms and they're coming from everywhere, taking groups of us!*"

"Taking?" Yarborough growled. "What do you mean? Taking out? Killing?"

"*No, taking! They're grabbing more hostages, I think!*"

"*261…219…188…*"

Clark strained his ears. *Are those…numbers?* "They're counting something down. Could be a bomb."

"Too quick. Too uneven a count." Yarborough clutched his radio. "Pull back! Regroup at Turtle Pond!"

More shouts and screams punctuated his order. "*They're all around us!*"

"Then use your nightsticks, goddammit! No guns!" Yarborough thrust the radio into his pocket and started to back up slowly. "What the *fuck* is going on?"

☙

"You've begun to doubt."

Joann's head jerked up at the giant's voice. "No," she stated. "No. Donovan *will* save me." She looked around and blinked. The giant was nowhere in sight; his voice had come from a plainly dressed monk. "Who are you?"

"I am who you think I am." The monk grinned slyly. White swirls spiraled in his gaze. "I have many forms and faces. Surely that doesn't surprise you?"

She gaped at him, recognizing his eyes. "N-no. I don't—" She shook her head. "No. Donovan will be here. He'll save me."

"Well *that* would be a neat trick. From what I understand, he's already dead."

"Dead?" She started to panic. "I don't believe you. Valdes would have made a point of telling me before now."

The monk shrugged. "I only know what I'm told. They send dead people to the tombs, don't they?"

"Tombs?" Joann hesitated. "*The* Tombs?"

"I'm told he's on his way there now. Apparently there was an altercation with the police officials. He started ranting about devils or some such, and perhaps it got out of hand. Perhaps he was high."

"You're wrong! He's still alive!" The knowledge lifted her spirits. "*The* Tombs is a jail. It's one of the places downtown they hold detainees."

"Oh. Well, then that *would* be good news, I suppose. He's not dead, he's only on his way to imprisonment." The monk raised one curved eyebrow. "Miles from here."

High? The understanding his words brought weighed her shoulders. *Ranting about devils?*

"He tried." The monk patted her shoulder. "But...he *is* only a bartender."

Arrested. Her head hung down in defeat. *You should have known they wouldn't understand...*

"Damn you, Donovan..." she whispered.

"Exactly." The monk inhaled slowly, satisfied. "And now it's time to do what *we* came here to do."

Joann barely noticed as he raised his index finger and touched her forehead. Then it all went black.

☙

Still soaking wet, Donovan returned to the Vulcan. He looked at the stole, then at the bandage on his left hand. Quickly he wound the stole around his right hand, neatly tucking in the end. He flexed both hands and made fists.

Just like you're getting into the ring.

He gingerly walked the bike down the steps from the South Gate House, across an overpass and along a paved walkway that wound near the Lawn. The darkness was thicker here, closer to the source, and it became more difficult to see. He thought he should be more frightened than he was, but with everything else stripped away, all that remained was saving Joann.

Fear ends where the inevitable begins.

He left his key in the ignition and edged through trees and bushes. Every branch he moved near threatened to crack, forcing him to pick each step with care. Caution made him take short, shallow breaths. A thin white trail from his nostrils made him realize how low the temperature had dropped here. Despite the cold, sweat mixed with holy water and trickled down his back. He swiped drops from his eyes and carefully held a branch aside. From here he could see most of the stage, its backdrop dripping gore from the damned that had been hung. In front of the stage sat an altar made of stone and wood. Only a few shapes moved around it; Donovan guessed most of Valdes's mob were fighting the police. He couldn't identify any of the shapes until he saw someone in a brown monk's robe carrying Joann's limp body to the stage.

"Joann!"

As he started forward, his path was immediately blocked by sharp white edges. He whipped his arm out and the spire slid into his hand. He lashed out, and the blessed iron cracked against a sliver of white face. The possessed man howled and dropped backwards, black blood stark against his skin. Donovan pivoted and threw a roundhouse punch at another who stood behind him. His left hand, its bandage wet with holy water, caught the creature full in the jaw. Pure white light burst from the contact. It howled in pain and clapped spindly, jagged fingers to the burn. Two more possessed grabbed his arms. Donovan lurched, staggered, and tumbled to the ground, taking them with him. His holy water-soaked jacket made them screech and smoke, and he was able to wrest himself free. He sprang to his feet and raised the spire in time to parry the scythe-blade that had unfolded from another creature's arm.

"He burnsssss!!"

Donovan dodged a blade that swung at his head and made a break for the altar. The darkness grew thicker and deeper, confusing him after a few steps. He saw no one near him, but he could hear rustling and the wet slicing sound of scythe blades unfolding from the forearms of the possessed. In the distance he saw meager torchlight and ran for it. Suddenly, the monk appeared in front of him. He no longer carried Joann, and he stared at Donovan with bemusement. Donovan stopped short and started to raise the spire, but found to his amazement he couldn't. He stared at his arm. It began to tremble, a shiver that ran up to his shoulder and spread through his entire body. His chest contracted and he gasped, unable to breathe. His throat muscles trembled and squeezed shut in the throes of fear he'd never before experienced or even comprehended. His legs buckled, and he dropped to his knees. Paralysis swept over him. He tried to raise his head but his muscles were locked, and he could only stare at the ground. Valdes and a bald man in scholar's robes joined the monk, but Donovan's muscles had stretched so tight he could barely move to see them. Everything felt tight and cold and dark…

e/o

"I trust this is the last distraction we'll have this evening?" Mephistopheles said archly. "We have no more time to waste."

"Faustus hath completed the spells. As the bargainer, Valdes, it falls to thee to open the Amaranthine Gateway."

"I'm well aware of my duties, *Herr Doktor*," Valdes said. He turned to Mephistopheles. "As for distraction, yes, that should be the last of them. I suspected Donovan Graham would show up, so I took precautions. Here, and at the Hospital."

"A Circle of Neith hath been cast there," Faustus assured him. "None shall enter—"

"If he was able to get this far," Valdes scoffed, "do you think simple magic would stop him? Or anyone helping him? I sent someone to guard it. Don't worry; it's safe." He looked down at Donovan. "He's not going anywhere, is he?"

"No. I found what the dark represents for him." Mephistopheles brushed off the forearm of his sleeve. "Are you ready, Neil?"

Valdes looked towards the stage. "Yes, I am."

TWENTY-SIX

CONSUMMATUM EST

With all the action on the Great Lawn, the NYPD perimeter around the park had grown skeletal. The sidewalks were practically deserted and lit by flashing lights from sporadic clusters of patrol cars. Sawhorses jutted into Central Park West, abandoned in the face of reality. Disarray and anxiety clouded the air. Father Carroll crossed the avenue and hurried north.

The interior of the once-impressive medical complex was as silent as a deserted stadium. Father Carroll located the shimmering light that Donovan had seen and quickly made his way to the corner tower's top floor.

He found himself in the center of a corridor. The portal was in the room at one end: four lit candles, all black, marked the primary compass points around a circle on the floor, a circle formed by a chain of tarnished silver links. Outside the circle, touching a point facing Central Park, white powder had been poured in the shape of a scallop shell. In the middle of the circle, broken bits of copper wire were arranged into a Star of David. At each corner of the star fat red candles burned, propping up six mirrors to face each other. Burnt almonds and singed wheat stalks lay scattered around the circle's interior while in the middle of the Star of David, a glyph had been drawn in dark, shiny liquid.

Carefully, the priest brought his face close to the doorway. A familiar, static-electricity buzz tingled his beard. He looked the entrance up and down and gingerly extended a hand. A purplish light shimmered as his touch came closer. He nodded, respectful of the craft.

"Circle of Neith, I'd say."

The spire felt sturdy and righteous in his hand. As blessed iron, it would split the blockage like gossamer. He took a step away and raised it like a paladin's sword.

"Father! Praise be!"

The voice made him freeze. He turned, arm still high, and found himself facing the silhouette of a stout woman dressed like an Old World Irish mum.

"Can you help me find my son? He was with that nasty man, and I'm afraid something might have happened to him." She started to approach, then cowered back at the raised spire. "Please don't hurt me, Father."

Father Carroll looked at the spire, gave a sheepish smile, and slowly lowered his arm.

∽

"*73…51…22…8…0!*"

Shadows receded like the tide, making the normal dark of a summer night a sunrise by comparison. Clark lowered his machine pistol to survey the landscape. Over a third of their force was gone; no blood, no bodies, no evidence of their presence remained. The officers and agents who were left fired random shots as they drew together. "Vicki, what happened? Can you see?"

"*I don't know—whatever was blacking out my monitors has just lifted.*"

Yarborough came to his side. "Anything?" Clark shook his head impatiently. The captain grimaced; they'd made it roughly a fifth of the way up the Lawn. "Matz!" he growled into his radio. "Matz! Where the hell are you? Get down here and secure these hostages, *pronto!*"

Static distorted the response. "*…tack…fight…a moment…*"

A figure streaked along the field. "Stop right there, goddammit!" Yarborough fired a warning shot he ran to intercept it. "Surrender right now!"

Clark watched him, noting a growing number of whitish flickers in the shadows around them. He was not a religious man, but Donovan Graham's insinuations about devils refused to leave his mind. Inside his body armor his heart hammered, and tension sweat made him look like he'd just gone for a swim.

Yarborough returned, panting. "We have to keep going. We can't let them take back momentum."

"I can't see shit!" Darenelli hissed. "These goddamn flashlights—"

"What's that?" Clark pointed north, where a light had begun to shine. It grew brighter until it revealed the truth of their situation: grinning white faces leered all around them.

The apocalyptic cult had them surrounded.

"*We got the 264.*

"*Now kill the rest!*"

Yarborough slowly raised his radio. "All units assemble! Collapse the perimeter and get down here, *now!*"

Hoofbeats and motorcycle engines rumbled and the ground shook at the approach of a force from the west side.

"Matz!" Darenelli cried, dropping the flashlight to clutch his shotgun with both hands. "Never thought I'd be so glad to see his ugly mug—"

He stopped short when he saw Captain Matz's face; it was draped over the chalky, grinning visage of a cult member in a top hat. Behind him, more rode the NYPD motorcycles. They, too, wore faces peeled off police officers.

"Jesus Christ," someone breathed.

The police force turned outwards. Half the men went to their knees and took aim with their weapons while the rest stood above them to do the same. In all, Clark estimated they had between a hundred-fifty and two hundred people left.

The cult members tightened their circle.

అ

As Valdes, Faustus and the monk walked away, Donovan's body cramped into a motionless curl. The darkness, vast and suffocating, became his entire existence. His mind shrank inward.

Joann's going to die.

She thought I was out of my league. She was right. Conrad was right. I'm nothing.

All of this is my fault.

I deserve to die.

Misery swept over him. He had no more energy to resist the fist crushing his spirit. It would kill him, he knew, if the possessed didn't take him first. He didn't care. His strength seeped away, leaving behind only numbness. He closed his eyes...

How can this be the right path, Father, if it ends here?

...and nothing happened.

He waited for the final gasp of suffocation, for the killing blow, but neither came. His breathing, labored and hot, continued. His skin and clothing, wet with holy water, went untouched. The earth remained firm beneath him. Somehow the world went on. He forced his eyes open and saw only darkness. The grass of the Great Lawn tasted bitter on his lips. *Blood?* He imagined what he looked like, groveling in the dirt, and tried to find anger to spur himself into action. None was there, no emotion remained. Failure had wrung everything out of him. Everything except one, lone thought:

Maybe this isn't *the end of the path.*

But it *had* to be; nothing about the situation had changed. Had it?

Fear ends where the inevitable begins.

Donovan pushed himself up out of the dirt and into a crouch. His head reeled and he staggered but remained upright. None of the possessed were around. From the south he heard gunshots and shouts; to the north, a single voice incanting something in Latin.

He stood motionless. The struggle back from the darkness had left him drained and adrift. As he gazed about the empty lawn, an absurd memory came to him:

The Comparative Religion final had been tough, but he'd finished it with a little time to spare. As he brought his paper up to Father Carroll, he noticed some students praying for divine guidance. He smiled at the priest, who watched the room with some amusement.

"No atheists in foxholes, I see," he'd said.

Father Carroll had chuckled. "Don't look for God where He's needed most; if you didn't bring Him, He isn't there."

The bandage on his left hand, Father Carroll's stole on his right, both squished with holy water. The iron spire lay at his feet. He stared at it, feeling faintly ridiculous and ashamed of his weakness.

If Joann is that way, why are you standing here?

He picked up the spire and headed for the stage.

☙

Valdes sensed the setting to invoke Lucifer before he saw it.

Since the portal had opened in the Cancer Hospital, he'd become aware of an unusual frequency vibrating in his inner ear. It wasn't unpleasant, but it was a change from the usual energy of the city. That frequency had changed upon the arrival of Mephistopheles, becoming lower and more guttural, and now had shifted once more with the imminent arrival of Lucifer. This new resonance—for it wasn't an audible sound, but a sensation that stirred darker emotions—combined qualities of dread from the first and terror from the second, but it was more than the sum of those parts.

Of course it feels different than anything, he thought. *This is the edge of the abyss.*

He smiled at his own melodramatic tone.

As if from thin air, the stage appeared in the darkness before him. He paused from far enough away to be able to see everything. The altar, built by the possessed out of wooden bench slats, stood in front, in the center of the Sigil of Baphomet design. Hands no longer quite human had sanded and smoothed the material until it seemed to be one large slab, into which Mephistopheles and Faustus had carved designs of intricate magical significance. A container of metal that the possessed had twisted and pounded into an odd, oblong shape sat before and below it. It measured the height and width of a Jacuzzi and brimmed with dark, viscous red fluid, the blood collected from victims of the park's conquest. Skulls swathed in slabs of fat made grisly torches that burned brightly around the Baphomet circle, forming a gruesome, semi-solid wall of fire. Overshadowing everything was the half-shell stage backdrop. The cries of those impaled on its hooks, the blood and gore that dripped down its arched walls evoked the worst of Hieronymus Bosch and every medieval depiction of Hell, but he was unmoved.

"Enjoying the view?" Mephistopheles was suddenly there, in the dark next to him.

"It's a little theatrical for my tastes." Valdes slowly, almost unconsciously, rubbed his hands together as he turned away. "How do we begin?"

"I'll make the opening invocation. You'll take the Vessel," Mephistopheles gestured at Joann's limp body, which he'd left on the edge of the stage, "stand atop the altar, speak your preliminary statement and then…" He spread his hands.

"Preliminary statement? I didn't prepare anything."

"How else does one begin a business transaction? Introduce yourself."

"That's all?"

"These things are not complicated to *do*," Mephistopheles said. "It's getting to the point where you do them that takes the thought and planning."

"Given the setting," Valdes looked up at the writhing bodies, "I suppose

I expected something more…dramatic. How do I get to the—"

In a flicker of shadow, Valdes was standing within the circle of fire, atop the altar, cradling Joann in his arms. Her body seemed to have no weight; he could have held it all night. Below him, the oblong container was a dark pool. He blinked and steadied himself as Mephistopheles began to speak in Latin, his voice a sing-song chant. Although there were noises of fighting further south, the Lawn had grown still around them. Fat from the torches crackled and sizzled, blackening the skulls, popping parietal seams with the heat. Faustus stood to one side of the stage with a solemn expression, head bowed. Mephistopheles stood on the other side of the ring of fire, facing Valdes. As he spoke, his voice grew louder and more charged. He reached a crescendo and half-turned, extending his right arm to the south and his left to the north. He seemed to be reaching for something. The air heated as though lightning was about to strike. Valdes watched charges and sparks of energy drawn from the south to his fingertips. Mephistopheles began to speak again, still in Latin, but with more passion and greater urgency. The sparks grew larger and more sustained as the sounds of fighting became louder. An aura appeared and began to swell around Mephistopheles as he took in more and more energy. The darkness that normally surrounded him began to lighten, becoming less and less black until Valdes could see the threads in the fabric of his monk's robe. It occurred to him that gathering energy and light was the harshest situation for the Prince of *Darkness* to be in. Mephistopheles bore the strain in his otherwise bland face and made a "come on" gesture with his left hand.

"I am Cornelius Valdes," Valdes began, speaking in the loud, clear voice with which he'd addressed his audience at the Cancer Hospital. "I request an audience with Lucifer Morningstar, the First of the Fallen. I would like to strike a bargain.

"I've lived most of my life bending to the will of others. I've seen and experienced how the world treats those without the courage and strength to follow their own desires. I was one of them and I suffered for it. Over the last several months I've been engaged on a quest to right that wrong. A lot of people stood in my way. I used the weak and defeated the rest. Now I stand here, in full control of my destiny, ready to receive my reward. I've done everything required, I've met all the conditions. It's time."

Mephistopheles raised his left arm and snapped it down, the force of his movement concussing the air with a muffled boom. Instantly the energy he'd collected shot forth, pouring into the vat of blood and making the red liquid churn. Valdes extended his arms, holding Joann above it.

"Welcome to my world, Your Highness."

He released his grip.

ᔣ

Donovan followed the sound of Latin through the darkness. He crossed the ground quickly, a little surprised by the ease with which he moved. The sounds of fighting, the death that had swept through Central Park, the sorcery and the supernatural all conjured images of an otherworldly battlefield strewn with corpses and monsters. Instead he found himself alone on a cold, dark, seemingly endless plain, running to save the woman he loved from nightmarish circumstances that were far, far over his head.

The Latin came from near a circle of light, and as he drew closer he saw he was almost sat the stage. The circle was made of flames, and within them he recognized Valdes perched atop something. The monk stood opposite him, outside the circle. His right arm extended towards the sound of the police battling for their lives while the left arm pointed towards a Jacuzzi-sized metal vat at Valdes's feet. Valdes was holding something wrapped in white. Donovan heard his voice but couldn't understand the words; his attention was drawn to the white-wrapped object. It was Joann.

The monk jerked his arm like he was holding a whip. Thunder cracked and energy began to pour from him into the metal vat.

Valdes released his grip.

Donovan's eyes went wide. The word was a whisper on his lips: "No…"

She dropped with a splash.

Donovan ran forward. He got within a dozen feet of them before the monk glanced at him and grinned. Instinctive fear threatened to paralyze him again, but it was the line from Marlowe's play that came to him and stopped him short: "*Quin redis, Mephistopheles, fratris imagine*"; "return, Mephistopheles, in the form of a friar."

Mephistopheles…here? Now?!

His legs refused to move.

But if it is, *then…*

Donovan staggered three more steps before the monk's will forced him to his knees. He lunged forward. Anger he'd been unable to find before now roared through him, charging his body with the strength to resist.

The monk's eyes, white specks against deep purple, widened the tiniest bit. He angled his head and a group of the possessed surrounded Donovan. Donovan lowered his head and charged blindly into them, lashing out with his holy water-soaked fists. He knocked two out of the way before the rest piled on, bearing him to the ground with their sheer mass. One seized a handful of his hair while another, despite the sizzling and burning the holy water inflicted, began to pound away at him. The world glazed over with a red mist and he shouted, fighting, swinging his fists against the onslaught. The juicy slicing slithered into his ears and a pair of the bone-scythes crossed beneath his chin.

I will *save you.*

The energy Mephistopheles had been collecting sparked something within, creating a light that burned brightly enough to render the metal container translucent. Donovan squinted but couldn't look away. The liquid was a deep, dark purplish-red, like a new shiraz before decanting. Joann floated in the center of it. The light grew brighter still, bleaching all color until only the brilliance remained. Then came a deep, rasping groan, a mausoleum's long-rusted hinge forced open. Waves of emotion, dangerous and seductive, poured forth in a torrent, battering Donovan's soul. Abruptly the light vanished, searing Rorschach blots onto his retinas. He shook his head, blinking furiously, and finally cleared his vision.

She stood before him.

"Joann...?"

But this *wasn't* Joann, and Donovan knew it. He searched her face, examined her body; he saw none of the character life had etched into it. She was unquestioningly perfect, her perfection an objective fact, not a subjective decision based on knowing her, living with and loving her over time. Her skin positively glowed. All of the blood's color had leached into her hair, irises, lips and dress, recasting her beauty with overtones of perversion and dark sensuality. Overwhelmingly drawn to her yet fearfully repulsed, he could only stare.

She set her gaze on him and her eyes swallowed his heart.

Not like wine, he thought. *Like a flower that symbolizes the eternal. Amaranth.*

The gateway had been opened.

The King of Hell had arrived.

"*Consummatum est,*" Mephistopheles said with a bow.

TWENTY-SEVEN

"ENTWINE"

"I don't know what happened to him, Father," the old woman went on, keeping a wary eye out. "Once he started to follow that Mister Valdes, he became a different person. I haven't seen him since the day he walked out, swearing he'd found the 'truth.' *Feh.*" She dismissed this with a wave. "Can you help me?"

"Of course, dear lady, of course. What's his name?"

"God bless you, Father. His name is Michael."

"And yours?"

"Bridget." A shaft of outside light fell across her path. She stepped through it, and for an instant Father Carroll saw something hanging around her neck. *Is that...a rabbit's head?* "Can you come a bit closer, Father? My eyesight's not so good these days."

The evil of possession wafted from her like cheap bodega perfume. *My, what big teeth you have, Grandmother,* Father Carroll thought. He kept the spire at his side but tightened his grip on it. "Where do you think he might be?" he asked, sidestepping her request. "Was there somewhere in here Valdes and his group squatted, perhaps?" He edged towards the room with the portal.

"Oh, you don't want to go down there, Father," she said from right next to him. He hadn't seen her move, and her presence so close took him a little off guard. "There's nothing there to interest you."

"Actually," the priest said, regaining his composure, "I'll go anywhere I

260

have to if it helps your son. Or you."

"Me?" She coughed, a wheezing sound that it took him a moment to realize was a laugh. "Why would I need help?"

He looked down at her and smiled. "Because everyone makes decisions in their lives that have adverse consequences on themselves and the world. God forgives anything as long as forgiveness is sought. Humans are imperfect beings, but our imperfections don't have to define who we are. Overcoming them is a much more appropriate way to honor God, and ourselves." He extended a hand. "Let me help."

His skin touched hers, and with a flash of light, the holy water on his skin seared into her. She screamed, spraying spittle everywhere, and seized his arm. His holy-water soaked clothing sizzled her flesh, and with another shriek she whipped him around into a wall hard enough to shake plaster loose. Pain shot down his spine, and the spire clattered to the floor. Baring jagged rows of teeth, she hissed at him, all pretenses abandoned.

"*Don't you know the first rule of dealing with the possessed,* Father?"

"'Never engage them in conversation.'" He righted himself stiffly and brushed off dust. "And I won't, except to tell you this—I'm here to help you. To help *all* of you. Let me help. Please."

Bridget scuttled forward, her hunched shoulders resembling a beetle's carapace. Father Carroll took a few steps back. In this form she blended with the night, visible only as slivers of white in the corner of his eye. "*We are here to achieve much greater things than to be aided by a* priest." She spat the last word out. He danced back but her agility caught him off guard, and her weight sent him staggering back into the magical barrier. The dark energy sizzled a taser blast along his nerves. She shrieked at the contact and drew back as he staggered, just managing to stay upright.

"Get thee behind me, thou unclean!" he gasped, brandishing a cross. "Be gone from that to which thou hast no claim!"

"*Oh, but I do have claim,* priest. *Or do you not know what occurs in the park? What this one was part of—*"

A shockwave of evil stronger than anything Father Carroll had ever experienced suddenly shook the world. Reality shifted, and the result plunged a knife of despair into his chest. He tried to shake it off when another airborne shockwave hit, cracking the dilapidated building and raining bits of plaster down on them.

Mephistopheles? he wondered. *Good God, not...Lucifer?!*

Suddenly she was on him. He tried to push her off, but the plaster dust had coated his hands and made paste of the holy water soaking him.

A liquid sound, like the one that had come from The Jogger near the reservoir, slithered wetly at his ears. From beneath the skin of her forearm a scythe blade unfolded and reared up like a praying mantis claw. His eyes went wide and he raised his hands to shield himself, but she swung it sidearm. The blade plunged deep between his ribs. He gasped, blood spraying from his mouth. Bridget cackled and slowly withdrew, the blade grinding on the bone of his ribcage. Father Carroll sucked in air, and a gurgling told them both that the blade had nicked a lung, which was now slowly deflating. Her eyes lit. One corner of her tongue touched some of his blood that had splattered on her chalky skin.

"*Can you help yourself,* priest?"

൚

Yarborough could wait no longer. The light had provided a glimpse of their situation and he knew they were not only surrounded, but the apocalyptic cult was closing in.

"*Fire!*"

As one the police force obeyed, weapons roaring, lighting the night with muzzle flashes and sparks of ricochet. Pistols, revolvers, shotguns, semi- and fully automatic rifles sprayed a storm of bullets into the cultists while empty steel and copper jackets rained around their feet. Those nearest the police, the ones most illuminated by the flashes and torchlight, sucked it up as conscripts put on the front lines to exhaust the enemy's ammunition.

Clark watched figure after figure take more punishment than was humanly possible before withdrawing into the shadows. Whenever his hopes began to rise the gap was quickly filled by a fresh, evil grin. "Don't waste your shots!" he ordered over the din. No one heard him, nor did the FBI man believe they would have obeyed. Everything they'd seen, the atrocities committed against their brethren, the desperation of their situation, had electrified the cops into a "take as many of them with you as you can" mindset. It was impossible to tell how many of the derelicts went down; the darkness hid their numbers and their movement, preventing the police from effectively using their dwindling reloads. Still they fired and still the cultists came closer, flickering in and out of the shadows with maddening irregularity. Targeting was next to impossible—they just weren't visible for long enough. Cordite and hot steel spiced the foul air. For three full minutes the police fired, taking some cultists down but gaining neither ground nor an opening to escape.

"They're keeping the motorcycles in reserve!" Yarborough pushed his way next to Clark. "We have to focus on one spot in their line! If we can create an opening we can get to the hostages!"

"Those people are civilians! We can't throw them into the middle of this!"

"Not all of them," Yarborough said. "What have these…cultists been chanting? '264'; that looks to be about as many of our people that are missing. If we free them we increase our numbers." From one location on the East Side and another on the West sirens, screeching tires and gunfire blew into their conversation. The white flickers thinned as packs of cultists left to deal with the flank attacks from the collapsing perimeter. "Now's our chance! They're splitting up!"

"If we're going to cut a path," Clark's eyes probed for an opening, "we'd be better off with a tactical withdrawal, to get reinforcements and more firepower."

"The NYPD doesn't leave its people behind, Special Agent, *ha-evuh* the FBI feels!" Yarborough glared at the FBI man for a second before turning. "Darenelli!"

Darenelli emptied his riot gun before falling back. "What's going on?"

"Pass the word; we're going for the hostages. Have the men ready for hand-to-hand."

"About time. We stay here much longer we're gonna run out of ammo and they're gonna cut us to pieces. We're almost down to nightsticks, switchblades and flares, and Emergency Services are the only ones with flares." He wiped sweat from his forehead and reloaded. "I don't suppose anyone thought to bring an iron spire like that guy Graham said?"

"We have flares? Why didn't anyone—" Yarborough made an exasperated face. "Can you get me a few, Rich?"

Seconds later word came back that the police force was ready, with the most heavily armed Emergency Services men spearheading the way. Yarborough struck a flare to life, held it high and flung it ahead of them in the general direction of the hostage pen. The light showed slivers of the cultists, who scattered when the burning stick landed among them.

"Now! Go!"

The cultists fought but parted to allow the police to spread themselves out. Once they had, Top Hat rode an NYPD motorcycle directly into their path and dismounted. Others formed a phalanx behind him. The ESU men in the lead stopped short at his apparent fearlessness as he stood in their way, hands folded preacher-style in front of him. All around them, Clark and Yarborough heard juicy, wet splitting noises, like over-ripe fruit bursting, and suddenly the cultists all had some kind of sword.

"*Kill the rest!*"

The cultists tore into the police like Crusaders retaking the Holy City. From every inch of darkness they came, buckling the police force, crushing them with the bulk of their assault. More blood, too much to measure, spattered the already-saturated ground as the derelicts attacked. Captain Devine went down as a burly man leapt on his back and cleaved his ribcage apart. Top Hat bludgeoned his way through the chaos, mus-cular hands smashing the slightest resistance. The cultists poured it on, attacking with chain saw precision, their ferocity stunning the police. Some cops snapped; shell-shocked by the violence and the darkness they gave up and fell to their knees, heads lowered, ready for slaughter. Oth-ers, trying simultaneously to defend them and attack, were beaten down and butchered. About a third of the police force was lost by the time they made it to the hostage pen. Yarborough slammed against the gate in frustration. The pen looked to have been thrown together haphazardly but was deceptively solid. On the other side of it men and women pressed forward, some begging to be let out, others spoiling for a fight.

The surviving cops closed ranks, battling to give the captain precious seconds to free the captive officers and shift the odds back to their favor. "I've never seen anything like this!" he shouted to Clark. "This gate is locked tighter than a goddamn bank vault!"

The cultists ripped away the outer line of police as though peeling a massive onion. Yarborough hammered the entrance to no avail. Every scream, each officer dragged into the horrors that waited beyond the light dropped guilt on him like it was raining sandbags.

"Central, this is Chief of Detectives Hugh Yarborough!" Yarborough shouted into his radio over the din. "Call the National Guard! Call the military! Get us help here *now!*"

"They'll never make it in time," Darenelli said, resignation tightening his voice. "This is it; we're fucked."

That's when they heard the siren.

☙

"*Donovan,*" she said in a voice of honey and warmth. "*We recognize you.*" His throat constricted. The possessed withdrew their scythes so Lucifer could approach him. A smile flickered over her full, dark purple-red lips as she pressed them softly to his. Holy water smoldered like dry ice yet Donovan felt no pain. Instead, deep, deep inside of himself, the very core of his soul trembled. Intellectually he knew he had to do everything he could to stop Lucifer, but his emotions ached to join with Joann, whatever the cost. The conflict paralyzed him until she finally broke the kiss, licking his lips.

"Joann, you have to fight it," he pleaded. "You have to fight Lucifer—"

"Sssshhh." She put a finger to his lips. "*You did not summon Us.*"

"*I* opened the Amaranthine Gateway." Valdes climbed down from the altar and stepped quickly through the ring of fiery skulls. "*I* called you. I'm Cornelius Valdes."

"*Cornelius Valdes.*"

Lucifer spoke his name but didn't look at him. Instead she walked to the stage and up its steps, gaze lingering on the backdrop. A low-hanging man in a blood-soaked golf shirt shuddered. Crude steel hooks held him in place, and every time he tried to move he only embedded them deeper into his flesh. Lucifer's smile broadened. Despite his agony the man drew back, tearing meat and cloth with gory little ripping sounds that were soon drowned by his shrieks. She leaned closer. He screamed a final, hoarse plea for salvation before shuddering and falling limp. For long moments she stared, absorbing every twitch, every whimper, every groan. Finally she spoke, bemusement a patina over threat.

"*You have Our attention.*"

Valdes surreptitiously wiped a hand on his shirt as he reached into his suit jacket and withdrew a pack of cigarettes. Although the darkness remained cool, almost cold, Donovan could see he was sweating. "I want to help you."

"*Help…Us?*" It was as if a fly had offered to assist God.

"In a manner of speaking." He tapped a cigarette out and lit up. "Forgive my poor phrasing. What I meant to say is the bargain I want to strike with you will benefit us both."

"Valdes, listen to me," Donovan said through gritted teeth. "You're *not* talking to characters in a play. You *don't* know what you're dealing with!"

Valdes ignored him. "In exchange for your assistance, I believe I can offer you something you don't have, something you will find extremely valuable."

"*You are no mage or scholar as was Faustus, yet you follow his path to Us. He offered his immortal soul. What, We wonder, can you offer to justify Our attention, let alone Our reciprocation?"*

"You don't have free passage to this world."

"You think not?" Lucifer widened her eyes. *"We believe others,"* she glanced at the stage backdrop, *"would disagree."*

"You obviously exert influence on this world," Valdes acknowledged, "but I suspect the world would be a much different place if you had a free hand in it. I don't understand *why* you can't come and go as you please, only that you can't."

"And you believe you can…provide this?"

"I know I can. The specific incantations, magical gestures, whatever, you can teach me. If Faustus can learn it, no offense, *Herr Doktor*, I believe myself more than capable. I don't think those are the most critical elements to the issue."

Donovan pushed against the scythes, feeling a thin line of wetness seep into his t-shirt. "You won't be able to repeat any of this, Valdes. If I don't stop you, someone else will. The cops are—"

"The police are currently being massacred," Valdes said, annoyed at the interruption. "The rest are in a holding pen, waiting to be sacrificed to His Majesty." He gestured with his cigarette at the two possessed who held Donovan. "Why is he still alive? He has no further purpose. Decapitate him."

"All of your lives continue at Our pleasure, Cornelius Valdes." Lucifer's tone remained as silk, but there was no mistaking her meaning. The possessed froze in place, eyes averted. *"Not yours."*

Valdes looked at Mephistopheles, then Lucifer, and for a moment Donovan thought he'd gone completely insane by deciding to argue. Instead, he took another hit off his cigarette and remained silent.

"Your arrogance speaks loudly but Donovan Graham is correct—what you've accomplished this night will not *be repeatable."*

"Why would I want to repeat tonight? I know how to do it better now." Valdes ground the cigarette out beneath his heel. "As I was saying, I don't believe the incantations and gestures are the problem with allowing you access to our world. I think the problem is the energy. It requires an enormous amount to open an Amaranthine Gateway, and very few people are able to marshal it. I'm one of them. Look around you: this is what I accomplished living in a hovel, among semi-literate addicts and lunatics. Given the proper circumstances, I can gather energy to power as many Amaranthine Gateways as you like."

"The ' proper circumstances'?"

"Give me back my life! They lied to me and they screwed me and I wasted the best years of my life in prison and I want them *back*!" Madness burned in his face for just an instant. He realized it and took a breath, hiding it behind his charming smile. "I want to go back, with all the understanding and knowledge I've gained, to just before I joined the Christian Yeoman Association. I'll be able to take my rightful place as CEO without any ridiculous blackmail plot, and I'll grow the foundation into an organization with fingers in every bed of human misery on earth. I'll build an empire of charity. No one will refuse such magnanimous assistance. I'll take their misery and offer hope and change, and use it all to power your dreams. And mine."

"*And yours.*"

"I have dreams now, too. You've given them to me."

Lucifer stared at Valdes, arms folded. "*And you would not prefer to be installed as the leader of this foundation* now, *without having to endure the struggles and uncertainties of ascent?*"

"Where's the fun in that?"

"You can't bargain with Lucifer, Valdes!" Donovan shouted. One of the possessed pressed the edge of his scythe into his flesh. "Didn't you learn that yet? You're following the footsteps of Faustus straight to Hell."

"I suspect," Valdes said, "you're less concerned with what happens to me than you are with what happens to your fiancée."

Lucifer maintained an air of regal disinterest, but Donovan could tell by Joann's mannerisms that Valdes had intrigued the King of Hell. "*You come from…an interesting point of view, Cornelius Valdes. You simplify things beyond the telling. Your understanding of reality is absurdly limited. However.*" Her amaranthine eyes glowed. "*Your proposal…amuses Us.*"

Mephistopheles shifted his stance subtly, moving just enough to alert Valdes. "Before I would even *consider* discussing specifics of our bargain," Valdes reached into his pocket, "please accept this token of my esteem."

Donovan's eyes widened as Valdes took out Joann's engagement ring. Lucifer cocked her head, and Donovan could see she was both admiring and curious. She reached for it with the same motion Joann had used to accept it from him, and a dagger lanced his heart.

"*Well done, Cornelius Valdes. We are pleased.*"

Next to the stage, Mephistopheles started to chuckle.

She slipped it onto her finger. "*This is beautiful, and also…familiar.*"

Mephistopheles continued to chuckle as he slowly raised his head and began to approach the two of them.

The ring reflected the light of the torches and sparkled white, almost as brightly as the Amaranthine Gateway. Lucifer stared at it curiously.

White light reflected through a prism—or a diamond—will diffuse into all the colors of the spectrum. Donovan watched the colors reflected through the ring begin to dim and dissipate, starting from the brighter end. As the remaining sparkle grew darker, the cold, black terror that he'd first felt grew more powerful.

Lucifer trembled and clutched at her hand, trying to remove the ring.

Mephistopheles drew nearer, his chuckle becoming more sinister.

Lucifer gasped as a cloud of darkness swirled about her.

Donovan pushed against the bone scythes. "Joann!"

She winced, obviously in great pain. "*Mephistopheles, what is the meaning of this?*"

"Forgive my impertinence, *Your Highness.*" He backhanded her, a vicious grin plastered across his face. Lucifer cried out and fell to her knees. "There's been a change of plan. I won't be answering to you anymore."

He looked at the ring, then her.

"Entwine," he said.

TWENTY-EIGHT

TO RULE IN HELL

Father Carroll had never experienced such pain. His legs sagged but he refused to go to his knees, to even *seem* to be kneeling in front of the heliophobic devil. The tightness in his chest screamed that he needed serious medical attention, but there were more pressing concerns to be dealt with.

God give me strength.

"Do you still feel a burning desire to help me?" Bridget growled, her voice raspy and warped. *"Or maybe just a burning agony?"* She raised her arm-scythe. *"Let me help you."*

The priest dodged and rolled along the filthy hallway, a deep, agonized groan in his throat. Pain had him writhing, curling him into a ball as he battled the shock that he knew would kill him if he succumbed. *Forget the rules of dealing with the possessed.* "I want to help…all of *you.*"

"You can't help yourself, so I guess you can't help everyone else." She stood over him, a prizefighter taunting a knockdown.

"You don't understand—this is not about *me.* My pain is temporary. Yours won't be, if you don't seek forgiveness." Something inside shifted, and his strength waned. *"Please.* Let me help you."

"Stop asking me that!"

"Soon enough, I won't have a choice."

"Shut up, shut up, shut up!" Bridget whipped her arm-scythe up threateningly. *"You won't have a choice now!"*

Lowering his head, Father Carroll whispered something.

"*What? What did you say? Don't you try to use no magic on me!*" She started to shrink back on herself before she recognized what she was doing, and stopped.

"No…magic. That's not…what I do."

"*Then what did you say?*"

His head lolled back in semi-consciousness. Bridget shook him to full awareness. "I asked God," he hacked up a wad of blood, "to forgive you, as I have. You know not what you're doing."

She thrust him away, flapping her hands. "*Don't you do that! Don't you dare forgive me! I killed you! You're going to die because of me! You can't forgive me for that!*"

In all his pain, lying in the filth of the abandoned Cancer Hospital, Father Carroll somehow managed to smile. "I already have."

"*No, no, no!*" She screamed and dug her scythe into the corridor wall, tearing chunks of wood, plasterboard and brick. "*I didn't ask you to forgive me! You ain't got the right!*"

"Forgiveness isn't a right bestowed by man, my child. It's a gift from God, given freely. I give it freely to you." He wiped a clammy hand across the sweat on his forehead. "If I am to die here, now, I can think of no better legacy to leave."

Bridget's nose sniffed this unfamiliar perspective. Father Carroll blacked out…

…and came to.

The first thing he saw when he opened his eyes was the decapitated rabbit head. He jerked to a sitting position. Bridget cocked her head. "*I thought you was dead.*"

"Soon, I think." Every word felt pulled from his mouth with pliers. "I'm going to pray now. Would you like to join me?"

The suggestion shocked her. She shook her head and scurried to the other side of the hall. "*What? No! I can't—I can't pray!*"

"I'll help you with the words. They aren't difficult." The cross on the gold chain had miraculously survived the attack and remained around his neck. He clutched it in his trembling fingers.

She shifted her weight on her feet. "*Why don't you just die? I killed you. Why aren't you dead?*"

"Perhaps because my…work here isn't…finished."

"*Leave me alone! Just leave me alone! Don't forgive me! Don't save me! I don't want it, I don't deserve it! Just leave me alone!*"

"I could never do that. Nothing is worse than being left alone."

"*You're dying! That's worse—*"

"But I'm not alone," he said softly. His eyes cleared for a second as he focused them on her. "And I notice that your words sound less diabolic and more like the woman you are, Bridget. You *can* fight. You *can* be forgiven your sins. It's never too late to seek God."

She stared at him for long seconds. Outside on Central Park West, a lone siren raced by. The candles of the gateway sputtered, casting shadow-fingers along the ceiling above them.

"*I'm—*" The dam broke. She collapsed in a heap at his feet, sobbing inconsolably. Her voice, like her words, was now human. "I'm sorry…"

"Ssh. Ssh. I've already forgiven you, my child. I've already forgiven you."

"Please—help me. Make it stop! Take it away!"

He struggled to kneel beside her. She slapped his outreaching hand away and suddenly sprang to her feet, her face twisting and reforming. Her mouth stretched impossibly wide to reveal rows of churning, grinding teeth before snapping back into the plain, doughy features she'd worn all her life.

"*God damn you! You're going to suffer—*no!"

Screaming obscenities, she bolted into one of the rooms off the corridor. Father Carroll heard wood shatter. He lurched upright and staggered after her. A sickening water balloon splatter painted the courtyard. Bridget's body had landed and impaled on an iron signpost jutting up from the cracked concrete.

"Oh, God," he groaned.

Like blood, a black shadow leaked from her prone body. Without a living human host it was drawn back to the gateway, shrieking soundlessly at the priest as it passed. He leaned away to give it a wide berth. When it had gone he made the sign of the cross towards her body. "Your work is finished. God *will* forgive you, my child." His breath hitched in his throat. "My work, however, remains to be done."

He gripped the windowsill until the pain passed. Blue-black fluid mixed with the blood running down his legs. Determined to face whatever the Lord had in mind for him on his feet, he straightened and staggered back to the corridor. The iron spire was where he'd dropped it.

He retrieved it and, keeping pressure on his wound, headed for the portal.

⁙

The drive up from Columbus Circle had been tense—Fullam had been monitoring the radio frequency the police were using. What he'd heard so far filled him with both dread and determination. A few minor roadblocks the cultists had thrown up proved no physical obstacle, but the dark smears left behind on the fire truck's windshield worked on his psyche, especially after the wiper-wash had failed to completely clean them.

When he wrenched the wheel to go off-road from the East Drive towards the Great Lawn, he hit all the lights and the siren. He pulled the air horn before wrapping his arms around the steering wheel and bracing himself. Crashing through the brush bounced him in his seat but he kept his eyes focused straight ahead. To do otherwise would invite the worst sort of speculation about what he was seeing. He thought about being "in the Twilight Zone" and a smile of gallows humor spread across his face.

"'A journey into a wondrous land whose boundaries are those of imagination'," he quoted softly. "That's the signpost up ahead…'"

At the bottom of the Lawn, a circle of flame burned down to embers. He turned towards it. As he got closer, in the truck's headlights, he saw "Welcome" spelled out in what looked like human limbs. Surrounding the word were stakes driven into the grass, stakes topped by decapitated heads.

Jesus Christ…

The sight disturbed and infuriated him, but at the same time he felt a surge of confidence. He would make a difference, maybe *the* difference, in everything because of what Donovan and Maurice had shared with him. Whatever arcane knowledge they possessed, he believed it more potent here than a squadron of Cobra attack helicopters. He stomped the gas pedal and pointed the nose of the truck towards the chaos.

Yarborough saw him first, and began to jump up and down, flagging him over. Fullam gritted his teeth and swerved around the bodies of several officers. The derelicts in his path scattered. When they saw where he was aiming, the police also dove for cover. At the last moment he slammed on the brakes, skidding on the dirt of the softball field. The fire truck's nose plowed into the structure, shattering its headlights but crumpling the barrier like a recyclable can.

Fullam leapt down and ran around the truck's side. He pulled one end of a rope, and an enormous racket clanged down the back. "Take these!" he shouted, gesturing at the pile of iron spires he'd released.

"Your plan to help is *this*?" Yarborough sputtered. "What—what are these things?"

Fullam didn't answer. His eyes went wide, and he lunged to grab a spire. Yarborough gaped as the sergeant threw him aside and swung the iron bar. It connected at its apex with the scythe-blade a cultist had swung at the chief's head. Fullam wrestled the scythe to one side, kicked the cultist in the groin, then whipped the spire around and cracked the cultist's knee-cap. The cultist screamed, an unearthly howl full of pain and indignation, and scuttled into the dark.

"Fuckin' *A*, Frank!" Darenelli hefted one like a baseball bat. "*Now* we're talking!"

"Get those hostages out of here! All police personnel who can stand fall in!" Shaken, Yarborough sought to regain control. He grabbed Fullam's arm and spun him around. "I asked you a question, sergeant. Where's the additional ammunition? The heavier firepower? We need more guns and bullets and you bring us…pieces of *fence?*"

Fullam wrenched his arm free. "Guns and bullets been working for you so far, chief?"

"Goddammit, sergeant, I will *not* tolerate your insubordination—"

"*Kill the rest!*"

One cultist growled it and the rest picked up the chant as they re-grouped. For a second, nobody moved. The only illumination came from sparse torches and the revolving lights atop the fire truck.

"Fuck!" Darenelli swore from somewhere in the dark.

Fullam grabbed a nozzle from the side of the fire truck and carried it with him as he climbed on top. "Fall back to me!" he shouted, waving one arm. "Everybody, fall back!"

All around them the white shapes gathered, flickering in and out of sight as the lights revolved. "*Kill the rest!*"

The sergeant pulled a radio from his coat. "Bring the trucks! "*Now!*"

&

Lucifer climbed slowly to her feet. Donovan thought she looked more curious than anything. No dirt clung to her in spite of where she'd fallen. She still looked perfect. "*You've…bound Us. To this female.*" She extended her hand. "*With this ring.*"

My engagement ring.

"*Cornelius Valdes?*" She raised a hand to her face. No mark bruised her perfect visage. "*What is the meaning of this?*"

Astonished by this turn, Valdes could only gape.

"The 'meaning'? You're Lucifer. First of the Fallen. God's favorite, before…" Mephistopheles slowly circled her. "Don't you *know*?"

The meaning of what she'd said hit Donovan, and he felt blood drain from his face. He repeated the words softly. "You bound her."

"What's going on?" Valdes managed to ask. "You said 'entwine.' Is that like the binding spell Faustus cast on the gateway?"

"More powerful is the binding for humans," Faustus confirmed. "Lucifer is trapped inside the Vessel until she is—"

Donovan tried to shut out the word.

"Dead," Mephistopheles finished.

"*In binding Us to the Vessel you have limited Our access to Reality. Limited, but not prevented. Nothing of this world harms Us lest We will it.*"

"I'm looking forward to testing that claim." Mephistopheles grinned. "Believe me."

A golden throne, upholstered with living flesh and adorned by skulls and fresh hearts, appeared onstage. The Prince of Darkness moved towards it.

"What is this…?" Donovan said in disbelief. "You've done this to my fiancée for some kind of…*political gain?*"

"When the Ruler of Desire usurps the Throne of Hell, it's a bit more impressive than a 'coup.'" Mephistopheles sat on the throne and narrowed his eyes at him. The peak of his robe's hood formed a vulture beak above his forehead. "You come here soaked in holy water and armed with blessed iron. You resist my will and come very close to disrupting my intentions. Neil, who is this person?"

"His name is Donovan Graham. He's the Vessel's fiancée." Valdes continued to process everything, and he spoke in a distracted manner. "I, I still don't understand. Why are you doing this?"

"Why? After everything you've done and endured, you ask *why?*" Mephistopheles paused, his restraint palpable. "Do you think you're the only one who's ever experienced the unfairness of reality, Neil? Do you think you're the only one who's ever done something about it? My existence has ever been one of bondage, fulfilling the desires of others. Why? Because I was *ordered* to." He sneered. "What sort of prince is a servant?"

"*Desire is a servant, not a master.*" One corner of Lucifer's mouth rose, truly interested but not in any way threatened. "*Reality is not decided by the whims of desire. It cannot be, for desire is transitory. You, the Devil of the Bargain, ought to recognize that. Reality is eternal, and you must find your place in it to become part of it.*"

"I *have* found my place." Mephistopheles settled back on the throne. "And I rather like the view from here."

"*You desire the Throne of Hell and in the plotting, the intricacies of the game and the pursuit of it is your true being revealed. But kingship for you,*" she shook her head again, "*is not Reality. A triumph of desire is temporary, a Pyrrhic victory which will inevitably turn to the reality of ash.*"

" Pyrrhic? Isn't it better to rule in Hell?"

"*In Reality, Mephistopheles does not.*"

"He does now."

"*Does he?*"

Mephistopheles sank further into the flesh cushions even as his head shrank into his shoulders. The atmosphere around him thickened with smoky, oily darkness. "You *will* acknowledge me."

"*Desire cannot rule, for it is a limited point of view. We do not subscribe to 'points of view'; We simply acknowledge what is. You do not. It is why you are not a king.*"

"My, my. Detached arrogance, and arrogance that *isn't* detached." Mephistopheles pointed to the earth before him. "Kneel before me or suffer." Lucifer stood her ground. Mephistopheles sat for another moment before offering a shrug and a chuckle. The sound fooled no one; it covered none of his hatred. He set his gaze upon her. The air around him began to darken, and as far away as he was, Donovan could feel it grow colder. Mephistopheles seemed at first to join with the darkness, but Donovan saw it was emanating *from* him, forming tendrils that drifted like a fog bank towards Lucifer.

"What about me?" Valdes interrupted. "This is all supposed to be—"

"For *your* benefit?" Mephistopheles sneered. "Hardly. You describe your ignorance in magical matters and think you did all of this without help? Who do you think created Coeus and sent him to you, sent him to show you the way to the book? That was *my* grimoire that showed you the *resurrectus maledicat*. Who do you think allowed Faustus to leave Hell so you could do all of this? This has always been about *me*."

"But *I* made the choices! *I* did the work!"

The darkness enveloping the throne was silent for a second until, from within, came a creepy laugh. "Kudos," Mephistopheles said, "for a job well done."

Valdes turned to Faustus. His face was flushed and he breathed through his nose, trying to keep calm. "*Herr Doktor?*"

Faustus, Donovan noticed, had edged closer to Lucifer. From where he stood, he could also see the sorcerer had a piece of paper and something shiny up his sleeve. "Thy reasoning is flawed, Valdes. Emotion is key, *ja*, but thou payest no heed to the subtleties of magical study." He took a step as if to approach Valdes, but in fact it brought him even nearer to Lucifer. "Incanting requireth both emotion *and* knowledge for mastery. Thou hast ignored one element of that vital equation to thy detriment."

"'There's no such thing as a free lunch' is not the best choice of words here." Valdes brought his hands together in front of his face and rubbed them together. He turned back to Mephistopheles. "Because in fact, nothing has changed. What I want benefits *whoever* is in power. I can still generate the emotional energy needed to open any gateway. As a token of faith I offer you, *Your Highness*," he paused to emphasize the use of title, "the six hundred sixty-six sacrifices we held for Lucifer."

Mephistopheles' lips twitched, restraining a smile. "For a novice," he said, "you have a rather developed acumen. Unfortunately, what you don't have is sacrifices."

Valdes glanced to the southern end of the Lawn. "Have they escaped?"

"Oh, no, they're there. And We—" Mephistopheles paused and chuckled as he caught himself indulging the royal phrasing. "*We* will kill them in many delightful ways. But they are not what's required for your end of the deal."

Donovan's eyes went to Faustus. The sorcerer had managed to sidle next to Lucifer and slip her a scroll of paper. He had no idea what was going on but he sensed it was important enough to let it continue.

Valdes started to turn back to Faustus.

"In magical terms, Valdes," Donovan quickly said, drawing Valdes and Mephistopheles' attention to himself, "a sacrifice is an offering to appease the deity on arrival, or to entice one to appear. If you want to bargain you have to offer something more enduring than the physical."

"Like what? Their souls?"

"What, did you think you could invoke and just smooth-talk the King of Hell?"

Valdes spun towards Mephistopheles, accusation in his face. "You never told me I needed more than their bodies. I didn't know that. How was I supposed to get six hundred sixty-six people to sign contracts giving their souls to Lucifer?"

"You weren't. Does that make it clearer? It was *all* about Us, from the beginning." Mephistopheles grinned. "You served your purpose. You invoked Lucifer and enabled all this to occur. For that you have Our gratitude."

"But *I* signed a contract!"

"Really? Why would you do that?"

Valdes whirled and pointed at Faustus. The sorcerer stood next to Lucifer, holding the scroll Donovan had seen. "*He* told me I needed one—there! That's it! He's holding it!"

Lucifer raised her eyes to inspect him with a gaze Donovan had seen Joann use to size up a guilty defendant. "'*I, Cornelius Valdes,*'" she read, "*of New York City, New York, do, by this document, give both body and soul to Lucifer, King of Hell, and furthermore grant unto him, when twenty-four years have expired, full power to carry the above articles into his habitation wheresoever it may be.*'"

Faustus unrolled a bit more, allowing Lucifer to continue. "'*However, said period shall be considered expired immediately and all articles collectible forthwith should Lucifer immediately and unconditionally release from eternal bondage the soul of Doctor Johann Faustus in trade.* Alter valorem rei.'"

"*What?!*" Valdes flushed bright scarlet. "That last part wasn't there when I signed it!"

"*Is this your blood?*" Lucifer asked. "*Your signature?*"

"Yes, but—"

"*Then no dispute have you. Done.*" Faustus slapped the contract into Lucifer's hand. The parchment dissolved. "*And filed.*"

The sorcerer bowed as a golden aura enveloped him, making him glow like a stained glass window at dawn. In the midst of all the death and horror his soul stood out as a shaft of the divine, and although it was a brief vision, the manifestation rivaled Lucifer's appearance in beauty.

When the light had absorbed into his body, and everyone was momentarily distracted, Faustus slipped from his sleeve the other item Donovan had seen. It was a sacrificial dagger. "*Auf wiedersehn*, Your Highness." He lunged.

"*No!*" Darkness burst from Mephistopheles' hand, a riptide that knocked Faustus off his feet and buried the knife. "*What do you think you're doing?*"

"Do thy worst, Mephistopheles." The sorcerer fought to sit up. "Faustus is free."

"Faustus," Valdes whispered, "what did you do?"

"*Si una eademque res legatur duobus, alter rem, alter valorem rei,*" he gasped, the weight of the darkness slowly crushing him. "'If something is bequeathed to two persons, one shall have the thing itself, the other something of equal value.' This eve hath Faustus accomplished what four hundred years ago he could not—retrieval of that which God hath bequeathed. Faustus is at last free of Hell." He squeezed his eyes shut. "My apologies, Lucifer, for not fulfilling the remainder of the deal."

Donovan instantly understood: Faustus struck a bargain for his soul, under which he would have freed Lucifer from Mephistopheles' trap.

Freed Lucifer by— His heart froze. *No.*

Mephistopheles studied the sorcerer, probing for untruths. He saw none, nor did he see any problem for himself. "Idiot. Do you know what you could have had, what you could have been?"

The weight on Faustus prevented him from responding.

"*Faustus quests for knowledge, not power. That is his place in Reality.*" Beatifically calm, the King of Hell wandered in front of Donovan. "*You see, Mephistopheles, even if you do not seek your place in Reality, the universe is filled with those*—" She stood on her toes to kiss him gently. "*Who do.*"

Donovan saw a subtle shift in her amaranthine irises; for a fraction of a second Joann looked back at him. In that moment, he knew there was no other way.

Lucifer's greatest satisfaction comes from twisting man's noblest efforts into something that serves the Infernal.

His mind spiraled down, chased by Father Carroll's dictum.

Don't make me. Jesus, don't. Give me another way...

"Enough philosophy!" Darkness swelled in thunderheads around Mephistopheles. The charm, the verbal sparring was gone, replaced by the crackling of malevolent energy. "I don't give a damn about what you think or don't think! I'm taking the throne *now!*"

"No, you aren't," Donovan said.

'*Nothing of this world harms Us but We will it.*'

Joann stood before him, her arms spread wide.

He raised the spire and plunged it into her heart.

TWENTY-NINE

EX MALO BONUM

With his waning strength, Father Carroll raised the spire, letting its weight carry it forward and down. The iron sliced through the Circle of Neith, shorting out the magical energy with a shower of purple and white sparks.

Hurry, now.

He dropped the spire and entered. As he crossed the threshold, his lungs wrung out a coughing jag. His feet scuffed near the circle of tarnished silver chain links and he stopped, heart pounding as he clapped his free hand over his mouth. He remained motionless until he was sure the fit had passed; if any part of the gateway was disturbed, he'd lose the chance to save the souls of the possessed. Slowly he backed away, not stopping until he felt a wall against his shoulder blades. A deep sigh of relief hissed through his teeth.

"Thank you, Lord."

He stroked his beard fiercely and concentrated his remaining strength on examining the object of his quest. Red and black candles burned at various significant points within the design; he recognized the individual elements—wheat symbolizing Christ's body and rebirth, almonds for His ascension to Heaven (all burnt here to describe the satanic nature of the spell), the broken Star of David denoting the removal of barriers, tarnished silver representing corruption, and the chain to connect Hell to Earth.

"God give me strength," he muttered.

With his free hand he made the sign of the cross above the gateway. Even though it meant releasing pressure from his stomach wound, he raised both his hands to Heaven.

⚮

Two Emergency Services Heavy Rescue Trucks barreled up the Lawn, one from the East Drive, one from the West. They steered through the trees with extra caution, and as they cleared the brush it became obvious why: their telescoping rotational light towers rose from hatches on their backs.

Fullam shouted. "*Josh! Conrad!*"

"*Now!*"

Every circuit on the towers burst to life, spreading daylight over the entire south half of the Lawn. The cultists froze, hands and arms bloodied by their killing frenzy, before scattering for the comfort of the darkness.

Hostages poured out from behind the shattered gate. Cops swarmed over the wreckage, re-forming units and rushing to help comrades. Braithwaite ran from his truck to the fire truck. "Come on!" he shouted grabbing spires. "Come get these! Use these!"

Conrad Clery climbed down from his truck's cab, shaken from the ride and at the slaughterhouse he'd just entered. "Joann!" he called. "Where are you?"

He slipped on something greasy in the dirt and tripped to his knees. One hand shot out to brace his upper body and plunged into the eviscerated chest cavity of a woman whose riot helmet had been neatly split halfway through her skull. His eyes saucered and he jerked his hand back. A piece of loose flesh stuck to it. He shouted and whipped his hand around until it flew off into the dark. He knelt there for a moment, staring at the red stain left behind, then rolled over and vomited.

"Conrad!" he heard. "Are you all right?"

"Where is she, sergeant?" he shouted, climbing to his feet and wiping a smear of bile from his cheek. "Where are they keeping my daughter?"

"You can't get there alone!"

"Then come help me—"

A terrifying wail from the north end of the Lawn made everybody stop dead. Conrad looked at Fullam, who had no answer. Before they could react, a wave of darkness surged from the same direction. Conrad stared, incredulous, as it swept over the two ESU trucks and swirled about them for a moment before dissipating. The lights were now out; every bit of power had been sucked from the generators.

The cultists, emboldened, began to slink back towards them.

Conrad gasped. He scrambled to the fire truck, confusion and fear obliterating everything but self-preservation. "What now, sergeant?!"

❧

Donovan stared, shocked, while Joann's body gently folded backwards, sliding the length of the spire on a lubrication of blood. Her weight pulled his arm down—

DEAD WEIGHT! his mind screamed.

Far, far away, he heard a roar.

"WHAT HAVE YOU DONE?"

Another riptide of darkness shot forth. It crashed and dissipated like waves when it touched his holy water-soaked clothes. Donovan didn't even register it; every sense, every emotion he might have felt lay smothered beneath the horror of his action. He couldn't move or think or speak or breathe while the question eclipsed his soul.

What have *I done?*

No answer could solve the problem. No structure could maintain his rationality or instinct to act. Blood and amaranthine energy formed a fluid shape around Joann as Lucifer divided his essence from her lifeless body. The color drained from her, deepening the luster of the shape and revealing the dark, spreading stain on her white dress. Her body collapsed, iron scraping bone as she fell to the dirt. A shudder racked Donovan's soul. White noise filled his ears. He dropped to his knees, desperately trying to maintain a link to her.

"Jo, I—I…"

But he knew she was dead. His detached persona recognized that Lucifer wouldn't have been able to leave her body if she wasn't. Still, he stretched a hand to her face. Her skin still felt warm where he'd caressed her a million times before.

"I—"

Killed you!

"In Reality, Mephistopheles has his place. We have Ours." Lucifer's voice rang from the amaranthine figure like a death knell.

Mephistopheles leapt to his feet. "I beat you!"

"Winning and losing are points of view. Our faith in Reality never waned."

"You can't deny me! I beat you!"

"Where are the contracts, Mephistopheles? We knew there were none, and so there were no sacrifices. And thus, there would be no bargaining."

"Then why did you come?" Donovan asked without looking up from Joann's face. "Why didn't you just ignore Valdes?"

Lucifer surveyed the death, the misery and fighting surrounding them. He looked at the stage backdrop, at the people who no longer twitched and shivered, at the blood that covered the stage.

"Where's the fun in that?"

Donovan raised his eyes and swore he saw the tiniest smile.

"But there is a last item—"

The amaranthine figure opened its arms, and it became less defined as human and more like an enveloping cloak. "No!" Valdes screamed. He ran to the stage, clutching at the monk's robe. "Help! Help me!"

"Not my problem," Mephistopheles snarled, thrusting him away.

Valdes stumbled and fell through the liquid form. It shifted shape to envelope him, sticking to him like gelatin. Valdes screamed soundlessly. The fluid swirled and began to dissolve him, staining itself with his liquefied body.

"We shall await your return to Hell, Mephistopheles, with…anticipation."

And he was gone. Without Lucifer's essence to hold its shape, the blood splattered to the ground, leaving only a dark, shiny puddle.

Donovan remained dimly aware of events. They came to him in a peripheral, secondhand way, as though from a television set in another room. He couldn't take his eyes off Joann's body for fear it would disappear as quickly as her life had. Disgust welled in his throat. He wanted to vomit the deed from his life, to run away and never stop or have to live with what he'd done—what he'd *had* to do—when a stray, self-preserving thought trickled through his addled brain:

The blood of a martyr is powerful magic.

He raised the spire to his eyes and examined it. The black wrought iron glistened wetly with her blood. He despised himself instantly.

From the south end of the Lawn, two masses of brilliant light flashed on.

The Prince of Darkness bellowed in pain, shocking Donovan from his reverie. Rage overwhelmed his every instinct as a sound began in the back of his throat, a low Rottweiler growl that built as he gripped the spire tighter. His muscles tensed and he stood, scanning the ritual clearing with predator's eyes. From the stage, twin shadow riptides shot south. The lights vanished, swallowed by the dark. Donovan padded forward slowly, not wanting to spook his target, before a burst of energy shot him in to attack. With a guttural snarl he flung the spire like a spear. The iron shaft smashed into the center of the monk's brown robe, lancing into Mephistopheles' chest and knocking him back onto his throne. Breath exploded from his lungs as the chair tipped backwards. Donovan leapt up the stairs, seized the end of the spire and wrenched it free. He howled, raised the spire and hammered it down. Fury rendered him incoherent. He shouted and taunted and raged, pounding the spire hard into splitting bone and flesh. Mephistopheles tried to roll out of the way, to change form or protect himself, but the holy water, Joann's martyred blood and the iron itself formed a potent magical bludgeon. Again and again Donovan battered the devil, madness blanking his features but burning in his eyes. No thought or reason drove his actions; there was only the fury, a raging, flaming hatred that seared his throat and spilled scalding tears down his cheeks. He was screaming now, his arm a blur as he tore into the devil's physical body. Mephistopheles wasn't moving. Bone and flesh hung from his face while blood and brain soaked into the stage…

…Slowly Donovan regained his senses.

I think he's dead now.

He looked at the shattered thing at his feet, feeling no regret for the savagery he'd unleashed. Instead, shock at what he'd done—*had to do!*—to Joann welled in his soul, pushing him to the edge of catatonia.

Movement in the corner of his eye made him jump. He whirled and saw Faustus, no longer pinned by Mephistopheles' tendrils, cradling Joann's body.

"*Get away from her!*" He heaved the spire. It spiked into the ground just in front of them, marking the spot like a tombstone.

Faustus didn't move. He looked back steadily, sadness at Donovan's loss palpable. Donovan started forward, fresh fury peeling another layer of sanity from his brain.

"*I said get away from her!*"

Surprise instantly transformed the sorcerer's expression. "Beware!"

Before Donovan could react, a giant fist slammed into the side of his head.

ℰℛ

"*In nomine Jesus Christ, consummatum est.* Amen."

Father Carroll panted, sweat pouring off his forehead and dripping from his beard.

"Lord, please," he implored. He'd recited the Purification Benediction six times and was astounded that the gateway remained unaffected. His intestines roiled like overcooked soup; he knew he couldn't do this much longer. "Forgive my weakness, but please don't forsake me!"

Pain racked his body, forcing him to his knees. He whimpered, biting his back teeth, but began again:

> "'By the power of Christ!
> Listen and submit yourselves to God! Resist the devil, and he will flee
> from you! Draw nigh unto God, and he will draw nigh
> unto you! Cleanse your hands, ye sinners, and purify your
> hearts!'"

This time the gateway began to hum. Renewed, he dove into the Latin part of the prayer. Now the mirrors started to glow. Astral winds stirred the wheat stalks. Father Carroll's voice rose as he neared the end.

"*In nomine Jesus Christ, consummatum est*! Amen!"

The glow from the mirrors shot forth, intersecting to form a latticework of light. Every candle melted simultaneously, spreading red and black wax over the tarnished silver chain. Their fire rose into the air and formed a ring that stretched the mirror light into a column. Father Carroll clenched his fists, urging it on. The light hit the ceiling and stopped; it couldn't quite make it over the top. Father Carroll cried out. "Why, Lord, *why?!*" He slumped forward, defeated, and buried his face in his hands. "Why...?"

He saw the blood on his hands.

"Blood of a martyr..."

He dipped his fingers into his wound and raised them to make the sign of the cross.

"In the name of the Father, and the Son," he swept his hand through the air, his gesture throwing red drops across the gateway, "and the Holy Spirit, Amen."

"*Consummatum est*," he murmured, surrendering to the pain. His body fell across the gateway.

BOOM!

The roof exploded. Light sprayed from the gateway, through Father Carroll and into the pitch-black morass above Central Park, chasing the darkness like a spring rain washing the air clean. His last thought was of Donovan, and he smiled.

"Go to the light..."

❧

"What now?" Fullam replied. He aimed the firehose to Conrad's right and twisted the nozzle. A blast of water sprayed the cultist who was creeping closer, scythe blade rising. He spun away with a shriek, smoking and blistering where the water had touched him.

"*Holy water!*"

Conrad snapped his head over, then back at Fullam. "What in the name of God—sergeant, where is my daughter?!"

Above them, night became day. Everyone froze.

At first Fullam thought someone had fired off a flare. He stared into the sky and knew it wasn't a flare. This was infinitely purer, the clearest, brightest sunbeam on a perfect summer day. It filled him with joy, with the sense that the tide of battle had irreversibly changed.

Donovan or Maurice? he wondered.

The light spread and blossomed, sending radiant streams down into the darkest corners of the park. Wherever the streams touched a cult member, Fullam witnessed an amazing metamorphosis: whatever had transformed them into a super-killer seemed to emerge as a shadowy, semi-solid form. It resembled a smudge of black smoke but with vague features that tried to scream. The light drew it, and hundreds of other "smudges," into itself without darkening—oil and water in the sky. Like a vent clearing a polluted room it reversed itself, taking the foulness along as it disappeared back to its origin.

❧

Donovan saw a white flash before his reflexes took over and had him scrambling to gain a second to recover. When the stars faded he saw Mephistopheles wasn't dead at all—he'd recovered and returned to Coeus's form. He was dressed as Coeus had been when Donovan had encountered him at the aquarium, in a patchwork black suit and dirty t-shirt but without the sunglasses—his cataract-covered eyes had been replaced by Mephistopheles' white-speckled purple orbs.

"You can't exorcise *me* with an iron bar, Donovan." His pineapple fists clenched and unclenched. "And if I can't touch you with darkness, I'll do it in a more satisfying way."

Joann's body lay just in Donovan's line of sight.

Satisfying?!

With a roar he charged the giant, plowing into him and taking them both to the ground. The holy water in his clothes sizzled as they rolled around in the grass and dirt. Mephistopheles grunted and flung an arm out, separating them enough to get to their feet. Donovan charged in and began working the giant's body. The stole and bandage were like hand wraps to a boxer, sparking white where they struck. Mephistopheles staggered back. Donovan threw a right hook. Mephistopheles shot a hand up and caught it. His massive paw smoldered and blistered but he squeezed Donovan's fist. Donovan screamed and rammed his forehead into the giant's nose. Mephistopheles lurched upright, seized Donovan's jacket with his free hand and dragged Donovan off the ground. He released Donovan's fist and hooked an uppercut into Donovan's torso. Something snapped. Donovan grunted and ineffectually battered the giant's head. Mephistopheles sneered, raising Donovan and body slamming him to the ground.

Donovan hit the earth so hard he blacked out. Instinct instantly drove him back to consciousness and he returned to pain so severe he was sure the giant had broken his back. He groaned and opened his eyes to see Mephistopheles inches from his face.

"I sometimes forget how *fragile* mortals are."

He lifted Donovan upright. Donovan weaved in place. The giant laughed and timed his backhand just right. Donovan spun clumsily, blood flying from his nose and mouth as he dropped to his knees. Mephistopheles picked him back up and slapped him like a handball. Donovan dropped again, feeling the whole side of his face begin to swell. He tasted dirt.

I'm sorry, Jo. I'm so sorry—

Suddenly it was daytime.

Mephistopheles shrieked and threw his arms up for protection. Through his daze Donovan saw hundreds of black shapes pulled into the light. Way down the Lawn, he heard cheers and shouts of triumph.

Father Carroll!

The realization slapped him to his senses. An image of the priest submerging The Jogger flashed across his mind's eye.

The South Gate House!

He pushed up to his feet, staggering off the Lawn. The surrounding brush stretched a spider web of prickly branches across his path. He fought through them, leaving flecks of skin and blood behind. His heart pounding in his ears couldn't cover what he was sure were

Mephistopheles' footsteps pounding after him.

"I'll have to make him mad enough," he chuckled with borderline hysteria, "to chase me."

He plunged out of the brush and bolted across the concrete overpass.

"*Donovan? Are you there?*"

Fullam's voice startled him. Donovan snapped his head around before realizing he still had the radio Frank had given him centuries ago. "Frank?"

"*It's over, baby! We won!*" Heart-pounding relief echoed in the sergeant's words. "*Where are—?*"

"Frank, listen," Donovan cut him off, dodging behind a tree at the base of the stone steps to the reservoir. The South Gate House waited at the top like the Supreme Court. "Get an ambulance! Get up to the stage! Joann is—" He swallowed. "Joann is—" He tried to force his words past the cork in his throat but they wouldn't go. "Listen—I'm not done. Go get Father Carroll up at the Cancer Hospital. Bring him to meet me at the South Gate House. We've got one more thing to take care of. Hurry!"

"*The South Gate—*"

"Donovan!"

Mephistopheles was suddenly at his back. Donovan gasped and spun. One scarred hand snatched the front of his jacket. The wet leather sizzled and smoked. Mephistopheles chuckled. "Did you think shadows would hide you from *me*?" The radio slipped from Donovan's hand as abject terror threatened his sanity. "I *am* the dark."

e/o

Faustus remained perfectly still as he watched Mephistopheles chase after Donovan Graham. When they were both out of sight he gave his full attention to the body of the woman in his lap.

"Honor bound am I," he murmured.

e/o

Holding Donovan aloft by the burning grip, Mephistopheles marched up the stairs. Mucus and saliva thickened his breathing as he savored the endgame. In front of the Gate House door he thrust his arm out and released the jacket. Donovan slammed back into the entrance and kept going as the door blew off its hinges and skidded across the Gate House floor. It hit a desk, scattering office supplies all over him, and stopped precariously on the edge of the spiral steps leading to the bowels of the reservoir station.

The giant's monstrous form filled the open doorway. "So much for the pentagrams. Now I can come and go as I please."

Donovan shifted his weight and the door started to slide. It hit the first curve and jammed, throwing him all the way to the bottom. He groaned and reached underneath himself to remove something sticking in his back—the can of spray paint Father Carroll had used. Clutching it, he scrambled to his feet and stumbled along a cramped corridor barely lit by fifteen-watt bulbs.

Breathing echoed all around. Mephistopheles' evil seeped through the stone and the pipes in a clammy humidity that formed scum on every surface it touched. Donovan pushed on through his panic. He took the next two left turns he came to and found himself in a short corridor that stopped at a dead end.

Now what?

From some recessed corner of his mind he heard a bemused chuckle. "Father?"

Go to the light.

Donovan searched the darkness, his heart lifting. Something beckoned from just ahead. "Father Carroll?"

Go to the light.

Quickly he retraced his steps, choosing a right turn first, and came to a well-lit corridor. On either side was a door: a rounded rectangle of steel surrounded by a gasket, of the same watertight design as those on a submarine. Each had a wheel in the center, pocked with rust, and a filthy plaque labeling it a "Runoff Chamber," numbered one and two. He tried number one. Ancient hydraulics prevented him from yanking it open, and once he'd gotten it wide enough to slip inside they prevented it from slamming shut.

The "chamber" was actually an oval conduit about fifty yards long, made of damp, stained white tile, fifteen feet across by ten feet high at the widest points. Three rows of halogen lamps lit every grimy brick with light so bright it almost blinded him after the darkness outside. He stood on one end of a narrow walkway that bridged the conduit. It was an unusual perspective—the walkway was level but everything else sloped at a forty-five degree angle. On his side of the walkway, stairs led to the bottom. Opposite him, another staircase led to the conduit's top. Mephistopheles' footsteps vibrated at the edge of Donovan's hearing. He jerked around, gasping as the sudden movement shifted his injured ribs. The door clanged into place, a barely audible "hiss" sealing the gasket. His eyes darted around the conduit, formulating a desperate plan.

A fifteen-foot-wide lattice of bars screened the top of the conduit, covering the mouth of a tunnel that extended back about six feet before curving up and out of sight. In front of the screen, bricks formed an abbreviated landing wide enough for workers to stand on.

Runoff comes from there.

Strings of recessed lights illuminated the deep rust and slime trails on the floor and walls, trails that marked the passage of water between the two openings. At the conduit's bottom, a metal cover perforated by one-inch holes capped a huge drain.

And is channeled through there.

Handrails, which would enable workers to climb or descend the slopes, lined the walls. A rich, loamy stink of water-decayed pulp and leaves evidenced worker neglect: soggy leaves, branches, dirt and newspapers so old they'd been soaked shapeless clogged the drain.

Clog...

A yellow wheel jutted from the wall down near the drain, below a sign with arrows indicating which way to turn it to *Open* or *Closed*. Another wheel by the upper grate would open the channel to drain the overflow.

He climbed off the walkway and used the handrails to make his way down to the wheel. Seizing it with both hands, he wrenched it free and turned it until it turned no more. Pain from every injury throbbed to life, blazing glorious streaks across his vision. He stumbled to the drain, slopping sludge off the cover until he found a solid place to paint a pentagram. When he'd finished—making sure all the lines connected—he ascended to the walkway. Droplets of mucky, gooey condensation glazed his shoulders. He returned to the door and pushed it all the way open, easing up when he heard it clang against the wall. The metallic noise made him think of a bell tolling. Coughing to cover the noise—and draw Mephistopheles to him—he sprayed a pentagram on the door, blowing as he worked to help the paint dry quicker. When he finished he took off his jacket and hung it to hide the symbol. He then scrambled up to the upper grate and turned that wheel all the way to "Open." Deep inside the ground, something groaned. A trickle of water dripped through the grate. Donovan made his way back down to the door, allowing his senses to roam. Silence clotted the damp air, thinned only by a high-pitched shriek of rusting hinges closing. The noise made him shiver. Part of him hoped Mephistopheles had gone, had given up the search. He knew it was wishful thinking. In the bigger picture he *had to* beat Mephistopheles here, now. He coughed again, baiting the trap.

Where the hell—?

A single fingernail dragged along stone.

Mephistopheles rounded the corner. The light that had been so bright fluttered and faded, retaining just enough illumination to hint at the evil draining it.

For a second Donovan was positive he would never move again. Jamming the paint can into his back pocket, he bolted back into the runoff chamber. The door continued to close, but so slowly that Mephistopheles followed him in without bothering to touch it. Donovan ran across the walkway and made a show of being trapped. Mephistopheles paused halfway across to allow Donovan to fully appreciate what was coming. Light from beneath them cast Coeus's scarred features like something out of a campfire ghost story. He flexed and preened, taking full advantage of his captive audience. Donovan forced his teeth to stop chattering. He stared at the closing door and licked his lips.

Come on, come on, come on!

"Are you nervous?" Mephistopheles grinned the hungry grin of a cannibal, displaying teeth far pointier than Coletun or Coeus ever had. "You should be. I'm going to make the whole world a lot more…on edge very soon." He took a threatening step forward. "Lucifer was partly right—I do get a tremendous amount of pleasure from the bargaining, the strategy and construction of a plan to achieve my ends. But he was dead wrong about my ability to rule. After all, what is ruling but endlessly constructing plots to make use of all that power? I may not be on the throne now, but I still have everything in *this* world at my disposal." He kept his glowing, piercing eyes fixed firmly on Donovan as if daring him to try to escape. "Not the best result, but how much fun would anything be that only required so," he jerked his head up, in the general direction of the Great Lawn, "*limited* a scope of destruction?"

"You want limits?" The door clanged shut and hissed as it sealed, bringing a sneer to Donovan's lips. "'Can't cross a threshold marked with a pentagram.'"

Mephistopheles stopped short.

"Look under my coat," Donovan urged, jerking his head. "Go ahead. I'm not going anywhere. I wouldn't *want* to go anywhere and miss this."

Mephistopheles regarded him warily before glancing back. A bare twitch of his hand sent Donovan's jacket flying. The hunter orange pentagram shone against the blackened steel door as bright as a flatlining cursor on a heart monitor.

Donovan vaulted off the walkway to the sloping floor. He slipped and slid but somehow pulled himself along the handrail to the top of the pipe.

"Distract me and make a run for it?"

He looked up and started—Mephistopheles leered at him from behind the screen.

"Is that your idea of a plan?"

Mephistopheles shoved. The screen flew open on a hinge that swung Donovan back, pinning him between the screen and the wall. He couldn't move, but he saw the trickle of water had grown stronger. Way up the tunnel, something splashed.

Mephistopheles stepped onto the worker's platform and jerked the screen closed. With his other hand he grabbed Donovan and pinned him against it. "I could still chase you if you tried to get out this way, because I don't see a pentagram on the screen here." He spun and slammed Donovan face first into the bars, breaking his nose with a crunch. Fresh blood poured out of his nostrils. "Do you?"

Far up the tunnel came a noise like an approaching train. A cool wind chilled the damp material Donovan wore. He twisted his head and gave a harsh laugh.

"I see *some*thing."

Water poured down from above and crashed to the floor on the other side of the grate. Splashes flew everywhere and Mephistopheles gasped as some struck his flesh. Donovan wrenched free from his grip, seized the bars and jump-kicked. Both his feet slammed the giant's midsection and sent him flying off the landing. He rolled through the slime all the way to the bottom and hit the drain just ahead of the first stream of holy water.

Donovan yanked the screen open. Pushed by the building river it came easily, and he climbed into the tunnel as the flow intensified. The devil prince bellowed as the holy water gushed down the slope but he didn't give up; his shoes burst apart and his feet morphed into claws that hooked the brick and allowed him to fight the current. Holy water rushed around his knees, already flooding the bottom of the conduit and rising. His clothing smoked and the smell of his skin sizzling gave Donovan harsh satisfaction.

"Do you think this is enough to stop *me*?" Mephistopheles screamed, making his way step by agonizing step. "I'll swim through an *ocean* of holy water to get you!"

Donovan slammed the screen closed. All around him the water roared down, soaking and freezing him to his core. It filled the pipe, churning and frothing against the bricks, thickening the air with icy spray, pressing him forward against the steel bars. Vaguely he considered he might drown with Mephistopheles, but after what he'd done—*had to do!*—to Joann, he didn't care. The water cascaded past, battering him from behind. He wondered if this was what it was like, trapped on a sinking ship. Now the conduit was full to the walkway; in seconds that would be submerged. The lights lining the lower end of the pipe cast an eerie, swimming pool glow. Undaunted, Mephistopheles plodded upwards, his skin a hideous mélange of bright red and pale white blotches. Like a burn victim seeking relief he plunged through the holy water towards Donovan, powered by all the rage of Hell.

"You can't get out of there!" Donovan yelled over the water's roar. *Unless the paint washes away. Unless you see the wheel to stop the flow. Unless, unless, unless...*

His mind spiraled down.

Please, God.

I killed Joann.

"I can't?" Mephistopheles snarled. "I still don't see a pentagram on those bars!"

Donovan's heart stopped.

"Oh, did you forget that part?" Mephistopheles hunched forward while the water, as though coming to Donovan's defense, surged anew. "Remember it for the last five seconds of freedom you have!"

Donovan scrabbled in his back pocket. The can wasn't there; as he raised his head he saw it bobbing on top of the water...

...on the other side of the grate.

Mephistopheles held it up in one massive fist and, when he was sure Donovan saw, crushed it. The "pop!" the aerosol can made was nearly inaudible, and the torrent of holy water washed away the sunburst of orange paint.

The water had reached the landing. Mephistopheles was practically swimming now, fighting his way through rapids past his chest. Donovan frantically searched for something he could use to scratch a pentagram into the steel bars. His jacket had zippers with metal tabs but it was somewhere on the other side. He fumbled for his belt buckle but the soaked leather refused to come free.

The water had filled the conduit to his level, and now rose past his knees to his waist. He couldn't see the buckle in the froth. He clutched for it then stopped, his eyes pointing at his bandaged left hand like it was magnetic north.

"Hell of an electrical burn you got here," the medic had said. *"That's going to leave one unusual scar."*

Mephistopheles hoisted himself onto the landing, dripping flesh and blood, looking as though he'd emerged from a bath of sulfuric acid. Only the galaxies of his eyes remained unaffected, lasering twin holes in Donovan's soul.

"I still don't see a pentagram!"

He reached for the bars. Donovan pulled the bandage away and slammed his pentagram scar forward.

"How's *this?*"

They touched the screen simultaneously.

White light blazed from Donovan's palm, lightning coming out of the bottle. Mephistopheles screamed as though he'd been electrocuted, challenging the light, holding on as long as he could before the force was too much. It blew him backwards, out of Donovan's sight and into the depths of the flooded conduit. Donovan could feel the vibrations of his scream through the water. Grimly he held on, determined not to be fooled by a master liar. The water raged higher, up to his neck, when suddenly a blob blacker than squid ink roiled up. It churned towards him in the shape of a monstrous lamprey eel, jaws spreading wider and wider until it struck the screen. The white charge crackled again, exhilarating Donovan with pure, selfless energy. The darkness exploded into a million tiny bubbles that fizzled into nothingness.

Then there was just the water.

Donovan refused to move, thinking his hand had fused to the bars, not caring as the water rose to his chin.

I did it! I beat Mephistopheles! He's gone!

His triumph was short-lived as the reality of his situation surfaced.

But she's still dead.

The holy water continued to stream around him, filling the enclave where he stood. "I'm sorry, babe," he whispered, salty tears mixing with the fresh water just before it closed over his head…

☙

…but it was not his nature to give up.

He released the screen and floated to the top of the tunnel, where an air pocket had formed. As he'd learned from SCUBA diving, he hyperventilated before taking a deep breath and plunging back underwater.

The screen opened easily, and he swam through it to turn the wheel by the upper screen to close off the water flow. The lights in the walls gave enough illumination to see but not all the way to the bottom. A wave of inexplicable panic sucked at him.

He's gone, right? I beat him, right?

Although he knew he had, adrenaline still energized him, driving him down to the walkway. The pentagram remained where he'd painted it, a beacon guiding him to safety. He pulled himself along the walkway, braced his feet against its rail and put his back to the door, fighting the hydraulics. The exertion drained his air, and the edge of things got fuzzy.

Maybe I am *supposed to be with her...*

Something brushed his leg. He jumped, and the extra push forced the hydraulics to give an inch. When they did there was no stopping the weight of the water and the door groaned open, spewing out a ton of holy water and Donovan. He crawled out of the way as the water inundated the corridor, not stopping until it had leveled off at the base of the door.

He stuck his head around the corner.

The runoff chamber remained half-flooded. There was no sign of Mephistopheles, but something else caught his eye.

The body of a young boy floated, face down.

Donovan plunged back into the room, dragging him from the chamber and out to solid ground. He pumped his hands on the boy's chest, giving him mouth-to-mouth until the boy gagged, turned onto his side, and threw up.

Donovan gasped and sat back. *Coletun Ruscht, I presume?*

The boy mumbled something, closed his eyes and lapsed into unconsciousness.

છ

EPILOGUE

PYRRHIC ASHES

Silver Mount Cemetery is a small, discreet burial ground that lies opposite Silver Lake Park and Silver Lake Golf Course in the northern section of Staten Island. Not as elaborate a cemetery as others of the borough or as historical as those in Manhattan, it's a peaceful tract where polished headstones extend a hundred and fifty yards or so back from the street to a hill topped by thick trees. A single serpentine path winds through the well-maintained grounds, past crypts, wooded plots and memorials dating to the early 1900s, before circling back on itself and returning to Victory Boulevard.

The morning was cold and lonely as Donovan stood above the freshly covered grave. He'd been in the hospital for the funeral, so now was the first opportunity he'd had to pay his respects. Physically, it would be some time before he fully recovered. Most of the crisp gauze strapping his body was hidden by his black suit and black leather trenchcoat, and the parts of his face not covered by his sunglasses had already begun to turn a variety of colors. He wore the sunglasses on this cloudy day to hide the black eyes from his broken nose. When he limped even a casual observer could tell he'd been badly beaten.

Emotionally, no bandage could staunch the bleeding.

"I killed her."

Father Carroll stood next to him, dressed in his simple priest's black suit, looking none the worse for his battle at the Cancer Hospital. "Yes."

"I had to."

"Yes, you did." He laid a hand on Donovan's shoulder.

Donovan didn't seem to notice. "There was no other way. And then I found out it didn't even matter. Lucifer knew all along what was going on. He answered Valdes' invocation for some fun. I killed her for…" His whole body began to tighten. He forced himself to breathe. "Is that the best we can do? Provide amusement to the forces of the universe?"

Father Carroll said nothing.

"You told me I was on the right path, but…" He paused to take a deep breath, flinching when his broken ribs shifted. "I don't know if I can do it."

"You can, my son. You can." The priest's warmth chased the misty chill. "I believe you know that. In time you'll *accept* it as well. Reluctance and fear aren't sins to be punished, they're conditions of humanity. It's when we overcome them that we honor God, for that's when we are able to best serve His purposes."

Donovan read the headstone again. He couldn't even muster tears; he knew those would come later, when the numbness had finally gone and the world began to spin again. It was a moment he dreaded.

Father Carroll seemed to read his mind. Behind his spectacles he radiated encouragement. "You *will* move on, you know. It's what the living do. Only the dead face no change."

"Yeah," Donovan said in a whisper. He glanced over and his voice grew thick. "You think you could give God a message for me?"

The priest shook his head, a good-natured chuckle lighting his smile. "That sort of language is frowned upon up there."

"Donovan?" Fullam called as he trudged up the path to the grave. He stepped carefully, keeping his shoes clean. "Who are you talking to?"

Father Carroll dissolved like a dandelion in the breeze.

Donovan turned from the priest's grave. "A ghost."

The sergeant frowned, unsure whether he was serious. "Joann just called. She's on the Verrazano; she'll be here in a few minutes."

Donovan nodded silently. He began to slowly, painfully, make his way down to the cemetery entrance.

"I know you've been drugged up lately," Fullam followed, eying him, "but as a trained detective, I can see things aren't straight between the two of you."

Donovan kept walking. He said nothing.

I wasn't able to protect Joann when it mattered, but ultimately I'm the only one who could have saved her. And I did. At what cost?

What am I going to do?

Fullam paced quicker, frustration casting a shadow across his face. "What the hell happened on the Great Lawn? Why won't you talk to anybody?" He kept a respectful distance from him, but his desire to help bridged the chasm. "She doesn't remember anything. Some guy dressed in a monk's robe tells her you were arrested, and the next thing she knows she's lying in the dirt with a diamond-shaped scar on her chest. A scar which I happened to note has the exact dimensions of one of those spires we were using against the...apocalyptic cultists."

Donovan held his poker face. "Is that a fact?"

The metal scraped bone as her dead body slid down it...

"Yeah." Fullam waited for more. When nothing came he sighed. "Anyway," he took an airline voucher from inside his brand-new Burberry raincoat, "your flight leaves at eight tonight. You can leave your motorcycle at the precinct; I've got a ride for you whenever you want to leave. Hugh and Clark both wanted you out of town sooner, but fuck 'em. Take your time." Without looking, Donovan stuffed it into his pocket. "It's open-return, so stay over there as long as you want. The Feds are picking up the tab." Fullam grunted. "Hawaii; must be nice to travel on the government's dime."

Donovan thought about the tsunami of media coverage Valdes's conquest of Central Park had engendered. It turned out one of the hostages the heliophobic devils had put in the pen was Chessie Cummings, a local television reporter. Overnight she'd become an international celebrity, and the NYPD and the FBI were only too happy to confirm certain elements of her story so that everything looked as "normal" as was possible. It was a version easier to push with Donovan out of the picture, so he'd been "cordially invited" to take an extended vacation in paradise.

"Don't make your silence cheap for them," Fullam went on. "You earned it. When they're finished taking all the credit, maybe they'll acknowledge that."

I wouldn't count on it. "They can have the spotlight. I don't care."

"Uh *hunh*." The sergeant shot his cuffs, brushed some condensation from his sleeves and tried another tack. "You heard the Cancer Hospital is gone, right? All the red tape that was holding up demolition and construction of new housing has mysteriously been cut."

"Really?"

"They start blowing it up next week."

Father Carroll's memorial. He squashed a spurt of anger. *Blow it all to hell.* "What about Coletun?"

"The kid? I thought you heard—well, I guess you've been out of the loop while you were in the hospital. The Church has him. Apparently he has no relatives in Blue Moon Bay or anywhere else, and an official contingent from the Vatican came in. Somehow they managed to obtain custody."

"The Vatican?"

"All that way for a poor little orphan from Michigan. They've, ah, *graciously* agreed to see to his care, and to raise him." The sergeant tapped the side of his nose. "*If* he ever comes out of that coma."

"Nice and neat." Seeing the loose ends gathered made Donovan feel empty, used up. He stopped and checked the street for Joann's car. "At least you got to keep your job. Are you getting anything else out of this?"

Fullam snorted. "My name in the papers, several paragraphs below Hugh and Clark. A bonus that's going towards a wardrobe upgrade." He held his raincoat open to display his new Armani suit. "There's been some talk jumping me up the promotion ladder, too, but we'll see. 'Lieutenant Frank Fullam.'" He chuckled. "We'll see."

"Good to hear." Donovan looked at him, then back at Father Carroll's grave. "So...how are *you* doing?"

The sergeant gave this some consideration. "Better than a lot of other people," he said finally. "But I wasn't in the thick of it for very long. I told you—I don't have to believe in it. You do." He shrugged. "I believe in you."

A black limousine drove up Victory Boulevard and pulled over in front of the cemetery. Joann emerged from the back seat, looking more attractive than Donovan could ever remember. Although—as Fullam had noted—she remembered nothing after a certain point, her captivity and the role Valdes had forced her into had given her a deeper, stronger belief in herself. Donovan saw that confidence translate into a serenity that polished and matured her beauty. Even coming straight from work she looked stunning, with her blonde hair pulled into a loose bun and her business suit tailored to perfection under a pearl gray trenchcoat.

Conrad got out behind her, in a beige raincoat, and leaned back in to talk to the driver.

"Frank." She embraced him, lips brushing his cheek.

"Hey, Joann," he said.

She carefully put her arms around Donovan. He rested his hands on her waist. "Mmmm. That's the first time I've done that in a while." She felt his back stiffen and she immediately released him. "It's not the same, hugging you while you're lying down."

He pulled her to him, ignoring his injuries. She squeezed him once and stepped back. Her eyes were shining. "Let me go pay my respects."

Donovan stepped aside and watched her stride up the hill.

"You, uh, want me to stick around?" Fullam asked. "Give you a lift back to the city?"

Donovan shook his head. "I'll find my way."

"All right. Don't forget—ride's waiting whenever you're ready."

"Thanks."

He watched Fullam drive away.

"Hey." Joann had come back down without his being aware. "How are you doing?"

"Okay." Donovan managed a half-smile. He gestured towards Silver Lake Park. "Take a walk?"

They crossed the street and were soon on the path surrounding Silver Lake. Fog whispered in the air around them, coating benches and grass with just enough moisture to soften the edges of the scene. The lake was actually another city reservoir surrounded by a fence, but landscaping inside the fence and the park created enough atmosphere to support the description.

The sight of the black wrought-iron spires in one section of the fence made him cringe.

"I'm glad you're back to work," he said. "What's happening on the prosecution side?"

She took his hand, mindful of how tender the pentagram scar remained. "Since the official version of events is the whole apocalyptic cult thing, we're looking for 'the leaders of the movement.' You said Valdes was killed but there hasn't been any trace of his body found. Of course, in all that, that…" She shuddered at the memory of the carnage. "We may never have confirmation, so he remains officially missing. Mainly, we're looking to build a case against the leaders of the mob."

"Not Faustus?"

"No." Mention of his name in connection with the crimes agitated her, as though prosecuting him would be an affront to justice. She didn't seem to be aware of this, Donovan noted. "Not Faustus. Not…Faustus."

He wondered if her experiences were buried too deep to ever return. "Good luck on the homeless angle. Think you'll be able to show any of them has the brains to put this all together?"

"Valdes will remain the titular head of the cult, so we won't really have to. Things should be fine as long as we get convictions among those we captured, which won't be hard considering how many witnesses we have, and most of them are police officers and FBI agents."

"'Those we captured'; did a lot get away?"

"Best estimates are we got about eighty percent—" She stopped short. Donovan followed her gaze to a homeless man digging through a steel mesh garbage can. "Hold on a second."

She strode purposefully over to the man and slipped him some folded money. The man looked at it and, with much effusive arm waving, began to thank her. She smiled, said something, and came back to where Donovan waited. The man called more thanks.

"Feeling generous?"

"Let's just say I have a new appreciation for some people's situations." She tightened her coat around her. "And, until she has to testify, Josie Ludescowicz is safe and sound back in Iowa."

Donovan remembered the chubby blonde girl. "I'm glad."

"I remember some of it," she said abruptly.

He paused. "How much?"

"The monk. He smelled like sandalwood. Faustus, of course. And I was supposed to be…The Vessel."

He waited.

"What did that mean?" Her hand rose to her breast, where Donovan knew she had the diamond-shaped scar. "Was I?"

He studied her, keeping his face expressionless. *Who am I keeping it from, her or me?* "Does it matter?"

"I don't know. Does it?" She leaned close to him. "Are we safe?"

"Yes." He put all the reassurance he could summon into his voice. "As far as…the monk—he'd almost said "Mephistopheles"—was concerned you could have been any beautiful woman." *The only reason he'd come after you now is to get at me.* The realization stung him. "The Universe has rules. Checks and balances," he assured her, not adding that few of them were absolute. "…People can't just come and go as they please."

She bit her lower lip, wanting to believe. "So we won't have to keep looking over our shoulders? Paper our apartment walls with pages from the Bible?"

He shook his head. "Just in the movies."

"Good." She swiped at the corner of her eye with a fingertip. "I'm sorry, it's just…I don't know what to think."

"About what?"

"Reality. I thought my place was with you, but now…"

He took a deep breath, and then he took another.

"What happened on the Great Lawn?" she asked.

He started to reply and was forced to stop by a sudden influx of cement into his chest. She waited patiently. He couldn't look at her. Instead, he watched two ducks on the surface of the water. One groomed the other for several seconds before abruptly stopping and flying off. The remaining duck paddled in circles, aimless.

"What happened," he began, forcing the words, "wasn't actually important." *Yeah, right.* "What I learned…is."

"What did you learn?"

"My reality. My…path." He gave a small chuckle. "Melodramatic as that sounds."

She relaxed fractionally. "That's a good thing. It's important."

Hell with it, he thought, feeling a surge of hope. *I* will *protect her. We can make it work. I can make it work.* "I guess."

"It *is.* I'm just sorry…I can't walk it with you."

Donovan's head snapped around. Tears ran down Joann's face. "What?"

"I can't be by your side. That's not…not *my* path. Not my reality. Not now."

"Not *now?*"

"I lost faith in you, Donovan." She swallowed and braced herself, remaining calm with what was obviously tremendous effort. "I was scared, but I believed you would come. But you *didn't.* The monk encouraged my worst fears, that you were just a bartender, that you had no idea how to act…"

"I—"

"I know *now* that you *were* coming. *Then*, all I knew was I was alone, surrounded by sociopaths and lunatics. I thought I was strong enough. I thought I was better than…that. I wasn't. I'm…not."

"You're stronger than you know."

"That's the problem—I *don't* know. And I *didn't* know then, and everything got so insane, and you *still* didn't come, and when the monk told me you'd been arrested, I…believed him. And I damned you." Her voice was cold, damning herself now. "It might be different if I could *comprehend* this—*your*—reality. But I don't. I can't live in a reality that makes me lose faith in you."

Donovan stood very, very still. She leaned in, kissed him on the cheek and quickly turned. He watched her walk away, too stunned to react. She disappeared into the mist.

After a moment he turned to stare at the lake. It was empty. In the fog, its blank surface seemed to go on forever.

"Donovan."

Conrad's voice made him turn. Joann's father came a few steps closer, hand extended. In his palm was Joann's engagement ring

"I never said you weren't a good man," he told him. "Just the wrong one for her."

Numbly, Donovan reached for it. Conrad stood for a moment longer, a reflection of mist in his glasses obscuring his eyes. He offered a brief, sympathetic smile, then turned and left.

Donovan stared at the ring.

"When desire defeats reality, it's a Pyrrhic victory." Lucifer's words turned a part inside of him cold. *Who knew it was the same the other way around?*

He pushed away from the railing and headed home, to prepare for his trip to "paradise."

෬෬

Careful observation and a bit of glamour magic had provided him with an appropriate choice of clothing. The stone felt cool under his fingers as he leaned on it, looking up at the carved words above the massive entranceway:

NEW YORK PUBLIC LIBRARY

Faustus paused at the revolving door, momentarily confused by the contemporary device. In an instant he'd figured it out and entered. No one paid him any attention as he approached the woman behind the information counter.

"Forgive my intrusion, my lady. Pray, canst thou guide me to thy tomes of history?"

The woman glanced over the tops of her half-glasses. Her chubby face dimpled. "What a lovely way to speak."

"Not a hundredth as lovely as thine eyes." He bowed. "Now, dear lady, the path?"

"Here, use this." She handed him a single-page map detailing the library's floors and showed her dimples again. Faustus smiled charmingly. "Just go up those stairs."

"My gratitude." He bowed again and moved off.

"I hope you find what you're looking for," she stage-whispered after him.

"If not, I shall return and seek again. I am able once more, praise God. Able to seek."

He gazed about the grand marble interior, relief and wonderment and eagerness brightening his face. His shoulders squared in preparation to support the burden of new knowledge.

"And Faustus hath so much to learn."

☙

THE END
Consummatum est

ACKNOWLEDGEMENTS

It's been a long time coming, and there are a lot of people who helped with this book. I regret not being able to thank them all here—actually, I can, so, thanks to all who, over the years, have lent a hand. I want to make special mention of my former agent Mary Grey, as well as my current one Damon Lane. Both have been invaluable in getting this book to the world. Also, thanks to Jeremy Lassen, who saw what others didn't. And my editor, Ross Lockhart; great minds think alike. And my mother, who read all my stuff, and typed the first story many years ago.

A special thanks to my Stonecoast mentor Scott Wolven. His support and encouragement was and continues to be a candle in some of the darker nights of my writing. Thanks, Scott. Stay noir.

Night Shade Books is an Independent Publisher of Quality Science-Fiction, Fantasy and Horror

ISBN: 978-1-59780-230-7 ❦ $24.99 ❦ Look for it in e-Book!

Strange things exist on the periphery of our existence, haunting us from the darkness looming beyond our firelight. Black magic, weird cults and worse things loom in the shadows. The Children of Old Leech have been with us from time immemorial. And they love us...

Donald Miller, geologist and academic, has walked along the edge of a chasm for most of his nearly eighty years, leading a charmed life between endearing absent-mindedness and sanity-shattering realization. Now, all things must converge. Donald will discover the dark secrets along the edges, unearthing savage truths about his wife Michelle, their adult twins, and all he knows and trusts. For Donald is about to stumble on the secret...

...of *The Croning*.

From Laird Barron, Shirley Jackson Award-winning author of *The Imago Sequence* and *Occultation*, comes *The Croning*, a debut novel of cosmic horror.

Night Shade Books is an Independent Publisher of Quality Science-Fiction, Fantasy and Horror

ISBN: 978-1-59780-399-1 ❧ $15.99 ❧ Look for it in e-Book!

Fear is the oldest human emotion. The most primal. We like to think we're civilized. We tell ourselves we're not afraid. And every year, we skim our fingers across nightmares, desperately pitting our courage against shivering dread.

A paraplegic millionaire hires a priest to exorcise his pain; a failing marriage is put to the ultimate test; hunters become the hunted as a small group of men ventures deep into a forest; a psychic struggles for her life on national television; a soldier strikes a gristly bargain with his sister's killer; ravens answer a child's wish for magic; two mercenaries accept a strangely simplistic assignment; a desperate woman in an occupied land makes a terrible choice...

What scares you? What frightens you? Horror wears new faces in these carefully selected stories. The details may change. But the fear remains.

Night Shade Books is proud to present *The Best Horror of the Year, Volume Four*, a new collection of horror brought to you by Ellen Datlow, winner of multiple Hugo, Bram Stoker, and World Fantasy awards.

NIGHT SHADE BOOKS IS AN INDEPENDENT PUBLISHER OF QUALITY SCIENCE-FICTION, FANTASY AND HORROR

ISBN: 978-1-59780-232-1 ❦ $15.99 ❦ Look for it in e-Book!

edited by
ROSS E. LOCKHART

the BOOK of
CTHULHU

Tales inspired by H. P. Lovecraft from:

KAGE BAKER   LAIRD BARRON   ELIZABETH BEAR
RAMSEY CAMPBELL   DAVID DRAKE   CAITLÍN R. KIERNAN
THOMAS LIGOTTI   TIM PRATT   CHERIE PRIEST
W. H. PUGMIRE   CHARLES STROSS   GENE WOLFE
and many others...

Ia! Ia! Cthulhu Fhtagn!

First described by visionary author H. P. Lovecraft, the Cthulhu mythos encompass a pantheon of truly existential cosmic horror: Eldritch, uncaring, alien god-things, beyond mankind's deepest imaginings, drawing ever nearer, insatiably hungry, until one day, when the stars are right....

As that dread day, hinted at within the moldering pages of the fabled *Necronomicon*, draws nigh, tales of the Great Old Ones: Cthulhu, Yog-Sothoth, Hastur, Azathoth, Nyarlathotep, and the weird cults that worship them have cross-pollinated, drawing authors and other dreamers to imagine the strange dark aeons ahead, when the dead-but-dreaming gods return.

Now, intrepid anthologist Ross E. Lockhart has delved deep into the Cthulhu canon, selecting from myriad mind-wracking tomes the best sanity-shattering stories of cosmic terror. Featuring fiction by many of today's masters of the menacing, macabre, and monstrous, *The Book of Cthulhu* goes where no collection of Cthulhu mythos tales has before: to the very edge of madness... and beyond!

Do you dare open *The Book of Cthulhu*? Do you dare heed the call?

NIGHT SHADE BOOKS IS AN INDEPENDENT PUBLISHER OF QUALITY SCIENCE-FICTION, FANTASY AND HORROR

ISBN: 978-1-59780-334-2 « $14.99 « Look for it in e-Book!

Michael Swanwick—The Hugo, Nebula, and World Fantasy award-wining author of *Stations Of The Tide*—delivers a stunning "Post Utopian" novel of swashbuckling adventure, dangerous women, and genocidal AIs.

Dancing with Bears follows the adventures of notorious con-men Darger and Surplus: They've lied and cheated their way onto the caravan that is delivering a priceless gift from the Caliph of Baghdad to the Duke of Muscovy. The only thing harder than the journey to Muscovy is their arrival in Muscovy. An audience with the Duke seems impossible to obtain, and Darger and Surplus quickly become entangled in a morass of deceit and revolution.

The only thing more dangerous than the convoluted political web surrounding Darger and Surplus is the gift itself, the Pearls of Byzantium, and Zoesophia, the governess sworn to protect their virtue.

This steampunk-*esque* adventure explores the great game of espionage and empire building, from the point of view of the worlds most accomplished con-men, Darger and Surplus.

NIGHT SHADE BOOKS IS AN INDEPENDENT PUBLISHER OF QUALITY SCIENCE-FICTION, FANTASY AND HORROR

ISBN: 978-1-59780-315-1 ☙ $14.99 ☙ Look for it in e-Book!

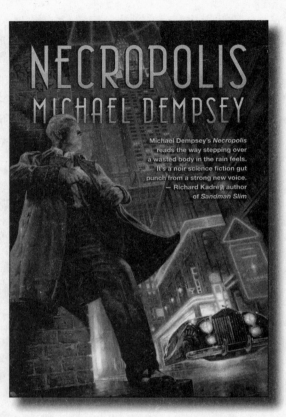

Michael Dempsey's *Necropolis* reads the way stepping over a wasted body in the rain feels. It's a noir science fiction gut punch from a strong new voice.
— Richard Kadrey author of *Sandman Slim*

IN A FUTURE WHERE DEATH IS A THING OF THE PAST... HOW FAR WOULD YOU GO TO SOLVE YOUR OWN MURDER?

Paul Donner is an NYPD detective struggling with a drinking problem and a marriage on the rocks. Then he and his wife get dead—shot to death in a "random" crime. Fifty years later, Donner is back—revived courtesy of the Shift, a process whereby inanimate DNA is reactivated.

This new "reborn" underclass is not only alive again, they're growing younger, destined for a second childhood. The freakish side effect of a retroviral attack on New York, the Shift has turned the world upside down. Beneath the protective geodesic Blister, clocks run backward, technology is hidden behind a noir facade, and you can see Bogart and DiCaprio in *The Maltese Falcon III*. In this unfamiliar retro-futurist world of flying Studebakers and plasma tommy guns, Donner must search for those responsible for the destruction of his life. His quest for retribution, aided by Maggie, his holographic Girl Friday, leads him to the heart of the mystery surrounding the Shift's origin and up against those who would use it to control a terrified nation.

NIGHT SHADE BOOKS IS AN INDEPENDENT PUBLISHER OF QUALITY SCIENCE-FICTION, FANTASY AND HORROR

ISBN: 978-1-59780-323-6 ❖ $24.99 ❖ Look for it in e-Book!

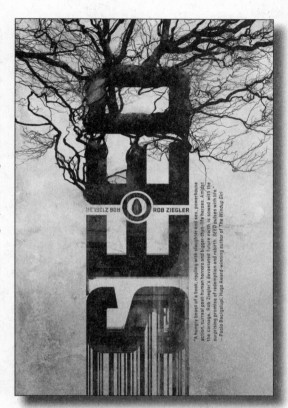

"A hungry beast of a book, rippling with slaughter and sex, powerhouse action, surreal post-human horrors and bigger-than-life heroes. Amidst the carnage, Rob Ziegler's devastated future earth is sowed with the surprising promise of redemption and rebirth. *SEED* pulses with life."
—Paolo Bacigalupi, Hugo Award-winning author of *The Windup Girl*

It's the dawn of the 22nd century, and the world has fallen apart. Decades of war and resource depletion have toppled governments. The ecosystem has collapsed. A new dust bowl sweeps the American West. The United States has become a nation of migrants—starving masses of nomads roaming across wastelands and encamped outside government seed distribution warehouses.

In this new world, there is a new power: *Satori*. More than just a corporation, Satori is an intelligent, living city risen from the ruins of the heartland. She manufactures climate-resistant seed to feed humanity, and bio-engineers her own perfected castes of post-humans Designers, Advocates and Laborers. What remains of the United States government now exists solely to distribute Satori product; a defeated American military doles out bar-coded, single-use seed to the nation's hungry citizens.

Secret Service Agent Sienna Doss has watched her world collapse. Once an Army Ranger fighting wars across the globe, she now spends her days protecting glorified warlords and gangsters. As her country slides further into chaos, Doss feels her own life slipping into ruin.

When a Satori Designer goes rogue, Doss is tasked with hunting down the scientist-savant—a chance to break Satori's stranglehold on seed production and undo its dominance. In a race against Satori's genetically honed assassins, Doss's best chance at success lies in an unlikely alliance with Brood—orphan, scavenger and small-time thief—scraping by on the fringes of the wasteland, whose young brother may possess the key to unlocking Satori's power.

As events spin out of control, Sienna Doss and Brood find themselves at the heart of Satori, where an explosive finale promises to reshape the future of the world.

Night Shade Books is an Independent Publisher of Quality Science-Fiction, Fantasy and Horror

ISBN: 978-1-59780-213-0 ❦ $14.99 ❦ Look for it in e-Book!

Fallen angels and the Fey clash against the backdrop of Irish/English conflicts of the 1970s in this stunning debut novel by Stina Leicht.

Liam never knew who his father was. The town of Derry had always assumed that he was the bastard of a protestant—His mother never spoke of him, and Liam assumed he was dead.

But when the war between the fallen and the fey begins to heat up, Liam and his family are pulled into a conflict that they didn't know existed. A centuries old conflict between supernatural forces seems to mirror the political divisions in 1970s era Ireland, and Liam is thrown headlong into both conflicts.

Only the direct intervention of Liam's real father, and a secret catholic order dedicated to fighting "The Fallen" can save Liam... from the mundane and supernatural forces around him, and from the darkness that lurks within him.

NIGHT SHADE BOOKS IS AN INDEPENDENT PUBLISHER OF QUALITY SCIENCE-FICTION, FANTASY AND HORROR

ISBN: 978-1-59780-335-9 ❧ $24.99 ❧ Look for it in e-Book!

Two years ago, on the same day but miles apart, Finn Darby lost two of the most important people in his life: his wife Lorena, struck by lightning on the banks of the Chattahoochee River, and his abusive, alcoholic grandfather, Tom Darby, creator of the long-running newspaper comic strip *Toy Shop*.

Against his grandfather's dying wish, Finn has resurrected *Toy Shop*, adding new characters, and the strip is more popular than ever, bringing in fan letters, merchandising deals, and talk of TV specials. Finn has even started dating again.

When a terrorist attack decimates Atlanta, killing half a million souls, Finn begins blurting things in a strange voice beyond his control. The voice says things only his grandfather could know. Countless other residents of Atlanta are suffering a similar bizarre affliction. Is it mass hysteria, or have the dead returned to possess the living?

Finn soon realizes he has a hitcher within his skin... his grandfather. And Grandpa isn't terribly happy about the changes Finn has been making to *Toy Shop*. Together with a pair of possessed friends, an aging rock star and a waitress, Finn races against time to find a way to send the dead back to Deadland... or die trying.

ABOUT THE AUTHOR

Thomas Morrissey has been writing since he was ten, and amused himself with a Sears portable typewriter for a toy. His first short story, "Can't Catch Me," appeared in the 2005 anthology *Brooklyn Noir*, and won the Robert L. Fish Award for Best First Published Short Story from the Mystery Writers of America. His work has also appeared in *Alfred Hitchcock's Mystery Magazine*. *Faustus Resurrectus* is his first novel, but it sure as hell won't be his last.